A BOLD ATTACK

She lowered her gaze to his mouth. Her heart fluttered at the prospect of what she was about to do. But surely it was no different than the way her pulse raced when she entered the free-for-all fighting in a tournament melee. In the melee, she'd found it was best not to dally, but to go on the offense and charge in with confidence.

The corner of Colban's lip drifted up as he taunted her. "Ye've ne'er felt the sweet surrender of a man's—"

She pitched forward and, before caution could make a coward of her, seized the back of his head and shut him up with a hard kiss.

Glynnis Campbell – Publisher
P.O. Box 341144
Arleta, California 91331
Contact: glynnis@glynnis.net

Cover design by Richard Campbell
Formatting by Author E.M.S.

ISBN-13: 978-1-63480-096-9

Published in the United States of America

BRIDE OF ICE

The Warrior Daughters of Rivenloch, Book 2

DEDICATION

For my dear readers,
who have been so patient
while we've all endured
the hardships and heartbreak
of this pandemic.
May this book take you on an adventure
long ago and far away!

OTHER BOOKS BY
GLYNNIS CAMPBELL

THE WARRIOR MAIDS OF RIVENLOCH
The Shipwreck (novella)
A Yuletide Kiss (short story)
Lady Danger
Captive Heart
Knight's Prize

THE WARRIOR DAUGHTER OF RIVENLOCH
The Storming (novella)
A Rivenloch Christmas (short story)
Bride of Fire
Bride of Ice
Bride of Mist

THE KNIGHTS OF DE WARE
The Handfasting (novella)
My Champion
My Warrior
My Hero

MEDIEVAL OUTLAWS
The Reiver (novella)
Danger's Kiss
Passion's Exile
Desire's Ransom

THE SCOTTISH LASSES
The Outcast (novella)
MacFarland's Lass
MacAdam's Lass
MacKenzie's Lass

THE CALIFORNIA LEGENDS
Native Gold
Native Wolf
Native Hawk

ACKNOWLEDGMENTS

A heartfelt shout-out to my team...

Amy, Kirby, and Abby
who take the ball and run with it

Jill
who adds enthusiasm to every task

Mel, David, Nicholas, Alessandra, Erica, and Skye
for their marketing brilliance

The Jewels of Historical Romance
who are always full of advice and support

My family
who respects my writing time, even in lockdown

Jeri Ryan and Justin Hartley
for their inspiration

CHAPTER 1

Rivenloch, The Borders, Scotland
Autumn, 1155

hallidis Cameliard and her cousin Feiyan stared at the gaping hole in the storeroom wall, peering into the long, dark tunnel that led from Rivenloch castle to the woods. For a moment, neither of them could speak.

Then a single word fell from Hallie's lips like a cold curse. "Jenefer."

Feiyan crossed her arms and sighed in disappointed agreement. "Jenefer."

Hallie knew Jenefer was impulsive and impatient. But the three cousins had made a pact. They'd vowed that whatever action the Warrior Daughters took against the invader, it would be together.

Jenefer had broken that pact. Using Rivenloch's secret passageway, she'd stolen off into the night to face the enemy alone.

Now she'd ruined everything.

Hallie had hoped they wouldn't need to face the enemy at all. By her reckoning, their parents would return on the morrow with good news. Everything would be decided without resorting to underhanded tactics.

"Maybe 'tisn't too late to stop her," Feiyan offered. "I'll get my weapons."

"No weapons," Hallie said, catching Feiyan's arm. "No one's starting a war on my watch."

Feiyan's eyes simmered with rebellion. But while their parents were away, Hallie had been left in command. Feiyan had to obey her.

As the firstborn, Hallie would one day take her mother Deirdre's place as Laird of Rivenloch. And she took those responsibilities seriously. Unlike Jenefer, who acted first and sorted things out later.

"But we'll go after her, aye?" Feiyan asked. "We won't let her face a savage Highlander alone."

"Aye, we'll go." Hallie drew her brows together. Jenefer hadn't given her much choice. The three cousins had been sworn allies since they were young lasses. "But 'twill be a mission of peace."

"I'll fetch my cloak," Feiyan said, whirling away like mist.

Hallie recognized the need for haste. Kin was kin.

But she refused to rush blindly into peril. If Jenefer was in trouble, it was trouble of her own making. The impetuous lass probably deserved whatever she'd started.

Still, Hallie understood why she'd taken action.

The three lasses had been left powerless, reduced to pacing the halls of Rivenloch while their parents were off petitioning the king for ownership of Creagor, the castle and land adjoining theirs.

Since the previous laird of Creagor had died childless, Jenefer had been led to understand the holding would one day be hers.

Unfortunately, Scotland's thirteen-year-old king didn't see things that way. The newly crowned King Malcolm had offered the border keep as a prize to a Highlander.

A Highlander.

Which was, of course, insufferable.

For generations—from the time their first Viking ancestor had wedded a Pictish warrior lass—the Rivenloch clan had protected the border lands. A long line of Rivenloch warriors had served the rulers of Scotland with loyalty and honor.

To think that a beardless lad sitting upon the throne would snap his fingers and award precious Creagor to a barbarian from the Highlands was unfathomable.

Still, war was not the answer. Their parents recognized that. It was vital to choose one's battles.

Her mother had taught Hallie about swordsmanship and conflict strategy. But it was the skills of diplomacy and compromise—maintaining the fine balance between what one deserved and what one was willing to sacrifice—that would make Hallidis Cameliard a great leader.

And now, it was incumbent upon her to decide which weapon in her arsenal would best achieve those ends.

She'd have to be swift. Impetuous Jenefer might already be neck-deep in trouble. But Hallie wouldn't go unprepared.

Tossing back her long blonde braid, she gathered her skirts and hurried toward the armory to speak with someone she could trust.

"I don't trust the lass," Rauve d'Honore admitted, shaking his shaggy head as he sharpened his sword on the spinning whetstone. "Your hotheaded cousin acts ere she thinks."

Hallie scanned the armory. Three knights chatted in one corner. Two more were occupied, polishing their chain mail. They were safely out of hearing.

"Aye, I know," she murmured, "which is why I must leave at once."

"Now?"

"Aye, ere my parents return."

Rauve let the wheel slowly grind to a halt.

He scowled in disapproval.

That scowl could make grown warriors quake. Especially since Rauve towered over nearly everyone. Even Hallie, who possessed the height of her Viking forefathers. Like a grizzled black bear, Rauve could send foes scrambling for their lives with a snarl and a roar.

But Hallie remembered being bounced upon Sir Rauve's knee as a lass. He'd taught her to fight and picked her up when she'd bloodied her knee. There was no warrior more fierce, no defender more loyal than Rauve d'Honore.

"You're not going alone." He wasn't asking her. He was telling her.

She arched a fine brow. "You're not coming with me."

"The hell I'm not."

"I need you here," she said. "I need you to take command of Rivenloch in my absence. Besides, I'll have Feiyan with me."

He scoffed. "That wee mouse?"

"That wee mouse flipped you onto your back yesterday," Hallie reminded him.

Feiyan might be a bit of a thing. But her unique fighting skills—learned from her mother's servant from the Orient—served her well. She'd quickly humbled Rauve on the practice field.

Rauve grumbled and rubbed at his graying black beard with his battle-scarred paw. He sheathed his sword. Then he plucked Hallie's blade from where it hung on the wall and pressed it into her hands.

She shook her head, refusing it. "'Twill be a battle of words, not weapons."

His black eyes widened. "You cannot know that. Besides, in the woods? At night? Dangers lurk in the forest. Thieves. Miscreants. Wolves."

A snort of a laugh escaped her.

Everyone knew the story of Hallie and the wolf. As a lass, Hallie had befriended an orphaned wolf pup, which she still spotted on occasion in the forest. Legend said that as long as the beast roamed the wood surrounding Rivenloch, no wolf dared harm Hallie.

Thieves and miscreants Hallie could handle. Wolves she didn't fear in the least.

"I'll be fine," she assured him.

Rauve frowned, biting back a curse.

"You won't delay," he threatened.

"We should be back by morn."

"See that you are," he groused, "unless you'd *like* for your father to string me up by my beard and feed me to the crows."

That made Hallie smile. Her father would do no such thing. Sir Rauve was his most faithful knight. Only once had Rauve dared to disobey Pagan Cameliard, and that disobedience had saved her father's life.

If all went well, she'd return by sunrise, well before her parents.

If it didn't...

"I need you to promise me one thing," she told Rauve. "No matter what happens, you are not to march on Creagor. I cannot start a war with the neighbors."

Rauve looked deeply unhappy about that. "So you're going alone and unarmed. In the dead of night. To try to rein in your hot-tempered cousin. Who may have riled up a savage Highlander. And you'd like me to sit on my hands?"

"Exactly."

"I don't like this."

"I know. But you'll give me your word, aye?"

He muttered under his breath. Giving the sharpening wheel a kick, he laid the edge of Hallie's sword against the spinning stone. Sparks flew. The harsh whine of the blade sounded like an angry wildcat.

"Rauve?" she prodded. "Your word?"

"Aye, m'lady," he said tightly, making his disapproval clear.

He might not like it. But she could trust him with her life.

Now that Rauve's cooperation was secured, Hallie wasted no time.

She and Feiyan departed Rivenloch by the underground passageway, the same passageway Hallie's mother had used years ago to save her father. They emerged deep in the wood and set out for Creagor.

The full moon filtering through the branches lit their way. The silence was broken only by the breeze soughing through the pines and an occasional mouse skittering through fallen leaves.

Hallie's mind, however, was anything but silent. She raced through various scenarios and courses of action with duty and determination.

As they neared Creagor, she drew her cloak about her. The air was colder and windier than she'd expected. If Jenefer had stuck to their original scheme—frightening the superstitious Highlander away by feigning to be an evil spirit—she must be half-frozen by now in her sheer and ghostly disguise.

It was just as likely that forthright Jenefer had simply marched up to the keep with her bare blade, demanding the castle be surrendered to her.

Whatever she'd done, it was up to Hallie to make things right. Effective leadership required that she consider all possible outcomes. That she be ready for anything.

Still, nothing could have prepared her for what she found when they finally reached Creagor.

Beyond the copse of trees at the edge of the wood, down a long, gradual slope, surrounded by a wooden palisade, the castle gleamed like a pale gem in the moonlight.

The grass of the vast clearing was bedewed by shimmering crystals, frozen by the chill night air and stirred by the wild wind that blew through the glen.

But the magical peace of the landscape was broken by the scuffle taking place on the sward below.

Hallie narrowed her eyes.

Feiyan gasped.

Their cousin Jenefer was grappling with a giant.

He was armed with a claymore.

And she was as naked and defenseless as the day she was born.

CHAPTER 2

Colban an Curaidh jerked his head upright and blinked back sleep. He should never have offered to take the night watch at the palisade gates of Creagor.

Despite his best efforts, he kept dozing off in the dark. After an exhausting fortnight of travel from the Highlands and a full day of settling the clan into their new home, he could hardly keep his eyes open.

But Colban was a man of duty. He'd made a promise. As Laird Morgan Mor mac Giric's oldest and most loyal friend, Colban had vowed to keep the laird safe. He wasn't about to break that promise.

Morgan needed him. He hadn't been himself lately. Not since he'd lost his wife in childbirth.

Colban had done his best on the long journey to their new home to be Morgan's right hand man, covering for him, acting as a leader in the laird's stead. He'd spent all day making decisions on Morgan's behalf. Organizing the household. Directing the servants. Sorting out the livestock. Stocking the armory.

Finally, Colban's patience had worn thin. Frustrated over Morgan's lingering grief and numb disinterest, Colban had tried to knock some sense into the laird. His good intentions had culminated in a juvenile battle of fists between the two. A fight that had ultimately jarred the laird back to life.

Now, however, Colban wondered if reviving him had been so wise after all.

It was Laird Morgan himself who'd just startled Colban awake. Bursting out of the palisade gates past him. Spitting curses. And brandishing his claymore.

Colban shook off the cobwebs of sleep, watching Morgan storm across the field and wondering where the devil he was headed. When he spied the target of Morgan's wrath, his heart seized.

In the moonlit mist of the frozen sward stood a single lass. Pale. Naked. Shivering.

By all rights, she should have been screaming in terror, running away as Morgan Mor charged toward her.

Instead, the intrepid lass held her ground, standing up to her attacker as if she had the power of all the angels on her side.

Colban's jaw tensed as he clenched his fist atop the palisade fence.

What the devil was Morgan doing?

Surely he wouldn't harm a defenseless lass.

Morgan was a good man, a fair man. Aye, he hadn't been himself lately. But that didn't mean he'd abandon his honor.

Still, Colban didn't dare leave anything to chance.

What if Morgan hurt the woman in his ire? What if he killed her?

There would be no warm welcome for the mac Giric clan at Creagor if its laird murdered one of the local lasses.

When he saw Morgan begin to confront the young woman, Colban knew he had no choice but to intervene. Someone had to reason with the laird and balance the odds for the helpless lass.

Startling them would be dangerous and might cause a

tragic accident. Carefully closing the gate behind him, Colban quickly and quietly headed toward the trees.

He was only halfway to his goal, approaching with stealth, when he glimpsed two more figures emerging from the shadowy edge of the wood.

The arrival of more possible assailants changed Colban's purpose. With Morgan outnumbered, now he had to make sure it was a fair fight for the *laird.*

Unfortunately, he'd left his claymore behind.

But armed with his wits and his courage, Colban was never completely defenseless. And once he heard female voices coming from the new arrivals, he breathed a sigh of relief. A pair of lasses? Those he could handle with his bare hands.

Morgan had one lass engaged. All Colban had to do was steal up and intercept the nearest arrival, the smaller, dark-haired lass. Surely, once two of them were caught, the third would surrender.

If he and Morgan couldn't manage three wee maids on their own, they didn't deserve their claymores.

Or so he thought. Until, just as he came within range of his target, she attacked without warning. Something—her fist? her elbow? her foot?—came out of nowhere to strike Colban's jaw with punishing force, rocking his head back and making his vision swim.

An instant later, she somehow tossed Laird Morgan, still clutching the naked maid, flat on his back.

Then, while Colban staggered, struggling to make sense of what had just happened, from three yards away she pitched her arm violently forward. He felt the hard impact of a weapon striking his chest.

Several thoughts flashed through his mind in an instant.

He was dead. She'd thrown a dagger at him and killed him.

There was no pain yet. But there would be.

He couldn't die. Who would protect the laird?

How could he have been killed by a lass? *A lass?*

After a moment, he realized the curious sharp star protruding from his padded cotun hadn't actually penetrated his chest. But relief mixed with rage when he realized the wee dark-haired lass had probably *meant* the weapon to pierce his heart.

He plucked the strange steel piece from his cotun and dropped it on the sod. Then, with a growl of ire, he lunged forward, upending the malicious maid like a sack of barley over his shoulder.

It was only then that he turned and got a good look at the *third* lass.

What he saw took his breath away, stopped his heart, and nearly made him drop his burden.

A beautiful Valkyrie appeared to have fallen from Valhalla. The maid was tall and slim. Not willowy, but strong. Despite her plain dress—a simple, woad-blue kirtle with a girdle of leather wrapped in silver chain, and a small silver pendant—she had a regal bearing.

If her two companions were as savage and scrappy as wildcats, she appeared to be their calm mistress. Courageous. Cool. Collected.

Her long braided hair, several shades blonder than his, shone like white samite in the moonlight. She lifted her chin high with pride and held her gently angled jaw steady. Her bright eyes gleamed with intelligence. But it was on her soft, full, kissable mouth that Colban's eyes focused.

When she began to speak, he was so distracted by the lovely movement of her lips and the even tone of her voice—in light of the violence surrounding her—that he hardly heard her words. Until she casually suggested that he and Morgan release her friends.

Release them? The vicious, spitting lasses who were still struggling in their grasp? She had to be jesting.

His heart was still pounding from his brush with death. There was no way in heaven—or Valhalla—that they were going to let the bloodthirsty wenches loose to do more mischief. Especially when they discovered the dark-haired one was harboring several more pointy and vicious weapons.

Still, it was a valiant attempt on her part to secure their freedom.

In the end, Morgan had no choice but to take the maids prisoner and hold them in the castle for the night for everyone's safety. They could sort things out on the morrow.

The laird, who trusted no one else to keep the wily wenches from escaping, stored them in his bedchamber and guarded the door himself.

And Colban, trusting no one else to serve as the secondary line of defense, returned to his post at the palisade gates.

He was secretly glad Morgan was watching over the lasses. After a final lingering look at the one they called Hallie, Colban didn't trust anyone else to keep their hands off the breathtaking Valkyrie.

CHAPTER 3

Once Hallie spied the comfortably appointed bed-chamber with the enormous, fleecy bed that would serve as their prison, her mind was made up.

Their captors might be savage Highlanders. Burly. Brutal. Bold.

But the laird obviously meant them no harm. He'd treated them with honor, graciousness, and civility. With little more than a word of warning against their escape, he'd closed the door behind him. She could therefore expect him to be reasonable on the morrow when she negotiated for their release.

If she could just keep her ungrateful cousins from interfering with those negotiations. Neither of them appreciated the careful diplomacy Hallie had employed, the diplomacy that had won them the Highlander's trust and their comfortable lodgings for the night.

At the moment, beneath her surface of icy calm, Hallie seethed with irritation and disappointment. Irritation that impulsive Jenefer had acted alone, without thought of the consequences. Disappointment that Feiyan had flouted Hallie's authority, bringing weapons and nearly killing an unarmed man.

If Hallie couldn't manage to rein in her own cousins' rebellious habits, how would she manage to get them out of this? And how was she ever going to take command of an entire clan? It was a laird's responsibility to keep her clansmen safe, and that included keeping them safe from their own foibles.

Now Feiyan and Jenefer had begun bickering so loudly they'd awakened a babe in the adjoining chamber. It was crying inconsolably.

With an exasperated sigh, Hallie made her cousins swear they wouldn't attempt a brash escape until she sorted things out. Then she burrowed under the fleece to try to get a good night's sleep.

That was not to be.

Though Hallie managed to half-doze through hours of wailing, it was the babe's abrupt silence in the middle of the night that startled her awake. She rose up on her elbows, instantly suspicious.

A chill draft was wheezing through the window. The fire had blown out. The shutter must have come ajar.

Hallie felt her way in the dark, intending to secure the loose latch. But when she got to the moonlit window, the breath froze in her throat.

The end of a bedsheet was tied to the shutter. She peered out over the edge of the window. Another bedsheet was tied to the first. The fabric swirled in the breeze, lashing the stones of the castle.

Her heart plummeted.

Had her cousins broken their word? Had they climbed out the window and escaped? Had they abandoned her to the enemy?

Damn their lies. A lairdship was based on clan loyalty. Could she not even count on the allegiance of her own cousins? If they'd only waited till morn, she could have gotten them all out of this.

Thinning her lips in aggravation, she scoured the sward below, looking for signs of the wayward lasses. A wisp of cloud moved across the face of the moon, sending a shadow across the distant field below. As it passed, a beam of light glinted off something in the grass.

The arsenal Feiyan had been forced to surrender.

All the soldiers of Rivenloch possessed valuable weapons of war. But Feiyan treated hers like jewels. Her unique blades and spears and axes were precious works of craftsmanship.

On the wet sod, they could rust or—worse—be stolen.

Maybe Feiyan had only climbed out the window to retrieve her weapons. Maybe she meant to come back.

But a snort and a snore sounded behind Hallie. Feiyan hadn't left at all. She was still in bed, asleep.

Suddenly, from the adjoining window—the chamber harboring the crying babe—Hallie heard raised voices.

She cocked her head to listen.

There was no mistaking that stubborn tone of challenge.

It was Jenefer.

She hadn't fled after all. She must have used the bedsheets to make her way to the window of the room next door.

And by the agitated sound of her voice, the foolish lass was going to get them all into trouble.

Hallie had to do something.

She dared not rely on the loyalty of her cousins.

Feiyan may not have made her move yet, but at some point, she was bound to risk life and limb to get her weapons back.

And hotheaded Jenefer was going to start a war with that sharp tongue of hers.

Hallie had to take matters into her own hands.

Locating her boots and cloak in the dark, she dressed quickly. Then she crept back to the window. She tightened the knot around the shutter. Praying she wasn't making a mistake, she slipped over the ledge.

She'd made her cousins promise they wouldn't flee.

She'd said nothing about making her *own* escape.

The bedsheets proved sturdy enough. Hand over hand, Hallie lowered herself along the castle wall. At the end of the rope, still several yards above the ground, she took a calming breath and let go, landing as softly as a cat.

She needed to reach Rivenloch before her parents returned. Hopefully, Feiyan and Jenefer could stay out of trouble till then.

Hallie didn't intend to start a war. Hers was a mission of diplomacy. But without the assurance of her cousins' cooperation, she needed leverage. She had to stack the odds in her favor. Which meant she'd have to gather a good number of Rivenloch knights and return to negotiate for the release of Feiyan and Jenefer.

She pulled the hood of her cloak close about her face. Then she crept across the dewy grass toward the palisade gate, keeping a watchful eye on the parapets.

At Rivenloch, there were always half a dozen guards patrolling the castle walls. But it appeared Creagor couldn't spare the men.

She'd taken careful inventory when she'd first been brought through the great hall. If the men gathered there were any indication, their numbers were few.

Not that they were any less of a threat.

They were a burly bunch of Highlanders, broad of back and wide of chest. Two of them—the laird and his golden-haired companion, the handsome one Feiyan had almost killed with her throwing star—towered above the rest.

No sooner did she begin to muse about the invaders than she realized she'd been spotted. Perhaps ten yards before her, standing atop the palisade gate, was one of the pair of lofty Highlanders himself. The man with the golden hair. His arms were crossed over his massive chest as he frowned down at her.

"Who goes there?" he demanded.

She froze, keeping her face concealed in the hood. Under normal circumstances, Hallie had an answer for everything. But for an instant she couldn't think.

It certainly wasn't because of the way the moonlight was shining on his fair hair. Or the impressive breadth of his shoulders. Or the ringing command of his voice.

He'd only startled her, standing there like the all-powerful Heimdall, guarding the gates of Asgard. That was all.

Colban hoped the beautiful runaway couldn't tell he'd been dozing a moment ago. Between the fog of sleep and his surprise at seeing the hooded but unmistakable Valkyrie stealing toward him in the starlight, he was having trouble gathering his thoughts.

Torn between his duty to protect the clan and his fascination with the warrior lass, he blurted out, "Halt!"

She glanced around her, probably wondering who he was addressing. "I *have* halted."

So she had. He cursed under his breath. For the love of Brighid, why couldn't he think straight?

In his embarrassment, he growled, "I asked ye, 'Who goes there'?"

He expected her to confess. Once confronted, she had two choices. She could throw back her hood and boldly claim her identity. Or she could lower her head and surrender with a sigh of defeat.

She did neither.

Instead, she scoffed at him. "For shite's sake, don't get your braies in a twist. I'm just the new servant, going to gather mushrooms in the wood."

He frowned. Did she not realize he recognized her? Did she think she was fooling him?

The new servant, indeed.

"Mushrooms?" He arched a dubious brow, wondering how far she was willing to carry this farce. "Indeed? In the middle o' the night?"

"Of course in the middle of the night," she reasoned. "The best mushrooms are gathered by the light of a full moon." She shook her head. "Did you not know that?"

Colban had never heard such a thing. Was it even true?

"Mushrooms," he repeated.

"If you must know, they're for an elixir to calm the babe," she smoothly confided. "No one can sleep with that racket."

That he could almost believe.

"So if you'll stand aside..." she said.

Almost believe.

But now that he was fully alert, he remembered his duties.

With finality, he said, "No one is to go past these gates."

She was silent for a moment. Then she shrugged. "Fine. 'Tis your head." She turned to go back to the keep.

"Wait," he said, startled that she'd surrendered so quickly. "What do ye mean?"

"I mean, the laird will be mightily vexed if I don't return with his mushrooms," she warned. "And I'd hate to be in your boots when he has to come slogging out here in the middle of the night, clenching his fists and cursing your name because he can't sleep."

Unfortunately, that sounded exactly like Morgan. The babe had been a source of anguish and frustration for him for weeks.

But Colban wasn't a fool. And neither was Morgan. He would never let a captive wander out the palisade gates, much less send a maidservant into the woods on a midnight errand.

The lass shuddered once from the cold. "I told him I'd return in a trice with the mushrooms. But if you won't let me pass, well, I won't stand out here, shivering." She moved to go.

"Wait."

She paused.

Colban knew the Valkyrie would never surrender so easily. If she didn't manage to slip out the palisade gates, sooner or later she'd look for another means of escape.

If he let her go now, he could track her, learn what she intended. That could be more valuable than confronting her with her lies.

He pretended to reconsider. "How long will ye be?"

"Not long."

"And ye swear ye'll come back straightaway?"

"What else would I be doing in the woods on a night like this?" She shivered again.

It didn't escape his notice that she hadn't answered his question directly. But he couldn't argue with her. It sounded like a plausible excuse. After all, what reasonable lass would venture alone into the woods on a frosty night unless someone had commanded her to do so?

"Very well," he said, climbing down to unlatch the gate. "I'll come with ye."

"Nay!" she blurted, then softened her answer with a laugh. "Don't be daft. I'll be fine. Besides, aren't you supposed to be guarding the gates against folk going *in?*"

He hesitated. She was a clever lass. But he was clever as well.

He rubbed thoughtfully at his chin. Then, wondering if he was doing the right thing, he opened the gate for her.

As she swept past him with her face concealed, he inhaled, stealing a breath of her essence. Wafting off of the fearless maid was the scent of wool and spice and intrigue.

"Do not tarry," he told her, watching her go and carefully noting the spot where she entered the wood.

CHAPTER 4

allie held her breath as she strode purposefully toward the trees. She could feel the Highlander's eyes on her the entire way.

Not that that was unexpected. Men were ridiculously easy to distract. Even in battle, when it came to throwing off an opponent, sometimes a cool smile and a toss of her pale tresses worked as well as a shield.

Still, she felt sorry for the guard. He seemed like a good man. Honorable. Loyal. Well-intentioned.

It wasn't his fault that he was too simpleminded to see through her ruse. To notice how she'd evaded his questions. To wonder why she'd never exactly identified herself.

She didn't expect him to follow her. She didn't even worry that he'd notice when she was gone for more than a "trice." Indeed, the poor man looked bone-weary. She half-expected him to drift off to sleep before she reached the forest.

Hopefully, he wouldn't be punished too severely in the morn when the laird discovered he'd allowed their prisoner to stroll out the palisade gates.

Meanwhile, she'd hasten to Rivenloch. Knowing Rauve, he'd be awake, worried about her. They needed to assemble a contingent of knights and return.

Fortunately, despite the dark of night, some moonlight filtered through the pines to light her way. But the breeze-blown branches made the shadows shift across the trail in eerie patterns. More than once, she was startled by a movement she perceived at the edges of her vision.

Shaking her head at her own foolish fears, she straightened her shoulders and continued along the path.

Still, she couldn't dispel the nagging sense that something was watching her. And as she progressed deeper into the forest, she kept seeing flickers among the trees. Hearing strange whispers of sound amid the sighs of the pines.

Maybe it was only the wind, making the leaves of the elms quiver and the hair stand up on the back of her neck.

Maybe it was only wee beasts hunting in the night. Wildcats chasing owls. Owls swooping down on mice. Mice scrabbling after beetles.

Disgusted by her trepidation, she frowned, gathering her cloak more tightly about her and training her eyes on the trail.

She was Hallidis Cameliard, after all, the daughter of Deirdre, Warrior Maid of Rivenloch. She'd fought alongside the sons of Vikings and faced down giants in battle. Why was she shivering like a leaf?

Though she hated to admit Rauve was right, she wished she had her trusty sword on her hip.

She continued for another half a mile. The sensation persisted. Highly alert now, she narrowed her eyes and strained her ears. Something or someone was following her. She was sure of it.

Several yards later, she heard a menacing growl from the bushes behind her. She went still.

Strangely, her first response was relief. She'd been right. It hadn't been her imagination. Something *was* stalking her.

Her second response was naturally to defend herself.

Careful not to make any sudden moves, she slowly turned to face the threat.

An enormous gray wolf emerged from the bushes. Its hackles were raised. Its head was lowered. And its teeth were bared.

But that wasn't what alarmed Hallie.

What made her breath catch and her heart pound with fear was the man beyond the wolf. The handsome guard from the palisade gates was charging up the path toward the beast, brandishing a blade.

Colban had never meant to let the lass venture so far. But she was obviously familiar with the woodland path. And she took damned long strides. By the time he'd buckled on his claymore, secured the gate behind him, and set off after her, she'd disappeared from sight.

Now that he'd finally caught up with the fleeing maid, miles later, he was glad he'd decided to pursue her.

Perhaps a dozen yards separated them now. But crouched between the two of them was an enormous wolf. A slinking, growling, snapping beast. A beast that could devour the helpless lass with one clap of its slavering jaws.

Colban had to save her.

"To me!" he bellowed at the beast, advancing with his sword, hoping to distract it.

It worked. The wolf turned toward him. Its lips curled. Its growls intensified.

"Don't move!" he hissed at Hallie. "And don't turn around!"

The wolf wasn't alone. Beyond the lass, he could see the glow of several more pairs of eyes in the trees surrounding her. If she saw them, she'd panic and run. If she ran, the pack would surely chase after her.

"Nay!" she screamed.

He'd forgotten to tell her not to scream. The wolf's head swung back around in her direction.

"Nay, to *me!*" he yelled again.

The wolf turned again to snarl at him. Behind the great beast, he saw the other wolves creeping steadily forward. He might be able to hold them off for a bit. But eventually they'd attack the prey they perceived to be the weakest. Hallie.

The lass was unarmed and unarmored. She had no defense against a pack of hungry wolves. They'd easily run her down.

He had to do something.

She cried out, "Lower your blade!"

He scowled. That was the *last* thing he should do.

"Listen to me," he growled. "See that tree beside ye? When I give ye the word, I want ye to scramble up as fast as ye can. Can ye do that?"

"What?"

"Don't look down. Just climb up. And close your eyes. No matter what ye hear, keep your eyes shut tight. Stay there. Once the morn comes—"

"What are *you* going to do?" she demanded.

"Whate'er I have to."

Colban didn't know if he'd survive a whole pack of wolves, even armed with his claymore. But he could at least survive long enough to get the Valkyrie to safety.

Being mauled by wolves might not be a glorious way to die. But he'd never been destined for glory. Honor wasn't his birthright. He'd earned every ounce of it he possessed. And he wasn't about to abandon that hard-won honor now.

Hallie stood transfixed. The man clearly didn't realize the danger he was in or he wouldn't have made such a suggestion.

"There's a whole pack of them," she explained.

"I know."

She blinked in surprise. "You can't fight off a whole pack."

His jaw tightened. "I can fight them off until ye're safe."

Her heart melted a little. He'd risk his life for her? Faith, he didn't even know her.

She couldn't let him do that. She was fairly sure she could get the wolves to back down, once they perceived he wasn't a threat.

"Nay," she said. "You've got to put down your sword."

The wolf growled at him in agreement.

Unfortunately, that made the man clutch even tighter to his claymore. "Nay."

"Listen. Do you trust me?"

He frowned. "Nay. Why would I trust ye?"

His reply took her aback. But she supposed she'd done little to earn his trust. After all, she'd tricked him into letting her escape.

"I know these wolves," she said. "I can save your life. Lower your weapon, and they won't attack."

"The hell they won't. I pray ye, for the love o' God, lass, shimmy up that tree ere I—"

"What if I promise to return to Creagor?" she blurted out.

"What?"

By his determined scowl and the stubborn set of his jaw, she knew he meant to fight off the wolves. And mere words from her weren't going to convince him to do anything else.

As long as he believed she was in danger, chivalry prevented him from laying down his sword.

And as long as the wolves believed she was in danger, they'd defend her from the stranger with the blade.

But if she bargained with him, if she offered him what he wanted most, perhaps he'd comply.

"Surrender your sword," she repeated, "and I'll go back with ye to Creagor."

The wolf growled in impatience.

"Climb the tree," he countered, "and I'll surrender my sword."

She frowned. God's eyes, he was a willful knave. But what other choice did she have? If she did nothing, blood would be spilled. And that was the last thing she wanted.

"You swear it? You'll drop the blade?" she asked. "On your honor as a warrior?"

She wondered if Highlanders even *had* honor. But she prayed the man would comply. If he didn't lower his weapon, the wolves would surely attack him.

"Don't ye trust *me?*" he said, tossing her words back at her.

Oddly enough, she *did* trust him. Still, it was with a good deal of reluctance that she eased toward a sturdy oak, grasped the lowest branch, and pulled herself carefully up the trunk, finally settling on a thick limb out of their reach.

The wolves abandoned her then and crept toward the man with the sword.

She could see the Highlander's inner battle as his knuckles whitened around the hilt of his claymore. She understood. A warrior's sword was his natural defense. Surrendering it in the face of danger was completely at odds with his instincts.

"Lay it down!" she hissed. "Hurry!"

His mouth twisted with misgiving as he cautiously lowered the blade to the forest floor.

Surely the wolves would retreat now. The man was no longer a threat.

But they didn't.

Apparently, they weren't convinced the Highlander meant her no harm.

Thankfully, the Highlander wasn't so naïve. He had expected as much and was prepared.

As soon as one of the wolves lunged forward, he grabbed hold of the broad limb of a sycamore overhanging the path and swung himself up to safety. The wolf missed his ankle by an inch.

The beasts continued to range beneath the tree, growling and snapping in frustration at the prey they couldn't reach.

Hallie was mortified. She couldn't look the man in the eye. She'd been so sure her wolf—the one she'd hand-raised—would back down once the threat was gone.

Now both of them were helpless and weaponless, treed, at the mercy of the circling beasts. And it was Hallie's fault.

She expected the Highlander to rail at her. To accuse her of trying to get him killed. To curse in frustration at their predicament. To bellow in rage.

But he didn't. And his silence was almost worse.

Eventually the wolves stopped pacing. Hallie hoped they'd given up the hunt and would return to their den. That was not to be. Instead, they bedded down at the foot of the Highlander's tree in patient wait.

Hallie perched atop the oak limb, waiting for them to leave.

An hour passed. And then another. And another.

It was almost dawn when the wolves finally rose on silent haunches and slunk away into the woods. Hallie glanced over at the Highlander to see if he'd noticed.

He was slumped against the trunk, fast asleep. His mouth was half open. His long legs dangled over the thick branch.

Her lips curved up in a rare smile. He looked less like a fierce Highlander and more like a helpless lad now.

Then she sobered as she realized she had the advantage. While her pursuer slumbered, she could clamber down the tree. Seize his sword. And steal away to Rivenloch. Right under his nose.

It was what cunning Feiyan or impulsive Jenefer would have done. Hallie could be halfway home before the dozing Highlander woke.

Then she sighed. Hallie wasn't like her cousins. She'd made the man a promise. She'd sworn she'd return to Creagor with him.

He might be her enemy. But she couldn't leave him to the wolves. He'd held up his end of the bargain. Against his instincts—and common sense, it turned out—he'd willingly surrendered his blade.

She had to keep her word. She owed him as much.

But she had another weapon left in her arsenal. Her wits. With a hostage in tow, she could change her strategy. She'd never specified exactly *when* she'd return with him to Creagor.

CHAPTER 5

Something poked Colban, waking him with a start that nearly toppled him to the ground.

"Bloody...!"

He'd forgotten he was in a tree. He made a quick grab for the limb to keep from falling into the jaws of...

The wolves were gone.

In their place stood a smug Valkyrie with a sword—*his* sword. She must have poked him with it.

He wondered how long she'd been standing there.

Then he wondered if she woke up every morn, looking as fresh and beautiful and magnificent as a newly blossomed rose.

"We should go now," she said, interrupting his wayward thoughts, "ere they return."

He was exhausted. His bones ached, thanks to a night spent huddled in a tree. He was in no shape for a long journey. But he knew she was right.

The sun had just lifted its yellow head above the horizon. It wasn't too late for the wolves to return for one last kill before they retired to their den for the day.

He nodded, raking his tangled hair back from his brow.

Then he realized their situation. He'd been snoring away in a deep sleep. Oblivious to the world. The wolves had gone. The warrior lass had confiscated his claymore.

She could have easily escaped.

But she hadn't. She'd kept her promise. The lass appeared to be a woman of her word.

Still, he wasn't sure he trusted her to keep it. Not while she was the one holding the claymore.

He swung down from the branch and dropped onto the path. Facing her, he was astonished again by her impressive height. He had to lower his gaze only an inch to stare into eyes as calm and blue as the summer sea.

A sunbeam shot through the trees, gilding her ice-blonde tresses. Warming her cheek with a rosy blush. Brushing her lips with a gentle kiss of light.

For an instant, he couldn't speak. Couldn't move. Couldn't breathe.

Then she spoke, startling him from his reverie.

"Let's go," she said, nodding to indicate the path ahead.

He frowned, confused for a moment. The Valkyrie might be fierce and beautiful. But she apparently had no sense of direction. It was a good thing he'd followed her into the woods.

"Creagor is back *this* way," he said. He cocked his head in the direction they'd come and held his hand out for his claymore.

"We're not going to Creagor."

Her chilling assertion sent a shiver along his spine. His eyes flattened. His lips thinned.

"Ye made a vow," he reminded her.

"And I'll keep it." She lowered her eyes. "Just not yet."

"Not yet? What is that supposed to—"

Her hand tightened on the claymore.

He muttered a curse. She'd seemed so honorable, so upstanding. But he should have known better than to take her at her word. To a lass like her, words were tools to be bent to her will.

He shook his head. A wise man never relied upon a

woman. They were about as trustworthy as wolves.

It was a shame. He'd half-hoped to have a pleasant stroll back to Creagor with the lovely lass on his arm.

That was obviously not to be.

But he had no intention of going with her to Rivenloch, if that's what she planned.

He gave the sword a fleeting glance. The blade might be lowered. But her grip at on it was firm and at the ready.

Still, she was only a maid. And the claymore was heavy. He could wrench the blade from her hands before she found the strength to lift it.

As if she read his thoughts, she said, "Don't try anything foolish. I'd hate to have to disfigure that handsome face."

She was clearly mocking him. Handsome? He was a mess from his fight with Morgan. His brow was cut. His eye was bruised. His lip was swollen.

And though she appeared cool and fearless, he wasn't threatened by her.

She might be tall. But he was far stronger.

She might be disarmingly attractive. But he could ignore her looks.

She might be trained as a warrior. But he'd spent a childhood fighting for his life.

Confidence compelled him to disregard her warning. To take a risk.

He cast up his left arm in front of his face as a diversion. Then he lunged forward with his right to seize the hand holding his sword.

The two things he didn't count on were her speed and cunning.

Anticipating his attack, she stepped backward. When he reached to grab her wrist, his fist closed on empty air.

Once he was thrown off-balance, it took only a hard shove at his right shoulder to send him sprawling to the ground.

Shocked and angered at his quick demise, he scrambled to right himself. But by the time he flipped over onto his elbows to face her, the point of the sword was already against his throat.

He grimaced as she applied pressure. Not enough to pierce the skin. Just enough to make her point.

"I warned you," she told him.

Every fiber of his being rebelled against the fact that a woman was threatening him—with his own blade.

Surely he could gain the upper hand.

He sighed, feigning surrender. "Aye, lass, I suppose ye—"

Mid-sentence, he ducked his head back from the sword. Batted the blade aside with the flat of his palm. And rolled away in the opposite direction.

Yet again, before he could get his knees under him to spring upward, she stomped her boot on his backside, forcing him down.

In the next instant, the claymore pricked at the back of his neck with deadly intent.

"Well, now you've given me no choice," she said. To his astonishment, her voice was still calm and collected.

He gulped. Was she the kind of coldblooded killer who would slay him while he lay helpless on his belly?

Being torn apart by wolves in the service of chivalry was one thing.

Having a woman sever his spine with his own blade was another.

He growled over his shoulder. "Ye'd slay an unarmed man?"

"Slay you? Nay."

For one fleeting moment, hope flared in his chest. Maybe she had a shred of decency after all.

Then she added, "But if you don't yield, I won't hesitate to maim you. Slice off an ear. Collect a finger. Carve a roast from your—"

"Fine. I yield." He shuddered.

"Cross your hands behind your back," she commanded.

He hesitated. What was she planning?

"Now," she bit out.

She jabbed his neck hard enough to show she was serious. Hard enough to draw a sharp breath of pain through his teeth.

He complied with her demand then. But his face flamed with anger and humiliation. How had things come to this?

The merciless maid shifted the claymore until the entire length of the blade's keen edge rested against the back of his neck. She held it in place with her foot while she bound his wrists together. It was a precarious position. One movement of his head, and the blade would sink into his flesh. One slip of her boot, and he'd be decapitated.

He held his breath as she used the silver chain from her leather girdle to bind his wrists. Like the wench herself, it turned out the belt was less a thing of delicate beauty, more a deadly weapon. The chain was not silver as he'd imagined, but forged of interlocking links of strong steel. She must wear it expressly for occasions like this, he thought bitterly, when she decided on a whim to take a man captive.

Once his hands were bound, she removed the blade from his neck.

He exhaled in relief. It seemed he'd keep his head another day.

Then she hunkered down beside him, speaking in a soft, low, throaty voice. A voice at odds with her harsh words.

"Make no trouble, and I won't have to mutilate you. But cry out, and I'll gag you with your own leine. Attack me, and I'll relieve you of an ear. Try to run, and I'll bind your ankles and *drag* you to Rivenloch. Do you understand?"

He glared at her boots. Aye, he understood. But he was too full of frustration and shame to meet her eyes. His mouth worked as he resisted the urge to defy her.

"Do you *understand?*" she repeated.

"Aye," he growled.

How could his noble intentions have gone so wrong? How could he have let her make him a hostage? He should have left her to the wolves. Hell, she might have singlehandedly slaughtered the whole pack.

In the end, he had no choice but to admit he'd been bested by a lass. Much to his chagrin and disgrace and fury.

Of course, he had no intention of letting her take him all the way to Rivenloch. He'd be vigilant. Sooner or later there would be a moment of weakness. Complacency. Misplaced trust.

Whether she *helped* or *hauled* him to his feet was a matter of opinion. Somehow he managed to stand. Then, at the prodding of the claymore, he started down the trail.

His fate might be bleak. But the morn was no reflection of that. As if mocking his misery, the sun danced merrily among the branches. Squirrels made chase across the mulch as they foraged for fallen acorns. Birds seized the rare moment of autumn sunlight to twitter madly from the trees.

He expected the warrior maid to be cocky. Full of swagger and bragging. Proud and gleeful, like the morn.

Instead, she traversed the bright woods as quietly as winter, silencing the autumn cheer like solemn frost.

He supposed she had good reason to be sober. No doubt the weight of what she was doing lay heavy upon her shoulders. Absconding with him to Rivenloch, she was playing a dangerous game of chess.

Laird Morgan held her queens. And she meant to get them back, using—for leverage—one of his valuable knights.

But she didn't realize the truth.

Colban an Curaidh might be Morgan's right hand man. But he was hardly valuable. He wasn't even a proper member of the clan. He was baseborn. A foundling. An outcast. The mac Girics might have taken him in. But he was an outsider.

Even as a lad, he'd recognized that.

And as an adult, he knew his place.

Colban was a pawn. And pawns were meant to be sacrificed.

Still, he'd prefer not to lose any body parts in defense of his laird.

The lass had claimed his claymore. But he still had a formidable weapon at his disposal. The persuasive power of his words.

CHAPTER 6

This wasn't the first time Hallie had taken a captive. She knew all their tricks. Charging like an ox. Yelling for help. Fleeing on foot. Feigning illness.

She hoped he wouldn't try anything foolish. The thought of marring his handsome face bothered her.

Of course, she'd do what she had to do. But she wasn't so blinded by purpose that she couldn't see how magnificent a man he was. Nor what a shame it would be to ruin such magnificence.

Not only did he exceed her in height. He possessed a fine figure as well. His shoulders were broad. His legs were long. His arms were capable.

But aside from his warrior attributes, there was something in his face—as damaged as it was—that quickened her heart.

Behind the bruises, his dark brown eyes shone with wisdom and experience, like ancient polished gems. Beneath the cut on his forehead, his brow creased with earnest honor. His nose was straight, and his cheekbones were unbroken, signs of expert fighting skills. His square jaw was covered with stubble a shade darker than the streaked blond hair he'd earned from a life spent laboring under the sun.

His lips, though swollen on one side, looked capable of

expressing both grim determination and gentle mercy. Of bellowing curses. Or whispering persuasions.

As he seemed about to do.

"Ye should know ye need not fret about your cousins," he assured her. "They will be safe."

"Jenefer and Feiyan?" She smirked. "I'm more concerned for your laird. My cousins can be...wily and unpredictable."

She creased her brows. Why had she told him that? Why was she even engaging in conversation with him?

It was far more difficult to inflict necessary harm upon a captive once she befriended him. Furthermore, the Highland cadence of his voice—the playful lilt crossed with a gruff manliness—was fascinating her ears in a troubling manner.

"Still," he said, "I assure ye Laird Morgan is a man of honor."

She couldn't resist reminding him, "You mean the man who charged at a lass—an unarmed, *naked* lass—brandishing his claymore?"

The man sighed. "God's truth, he hasn't been himself o' late."

She pressed her lips together. That piqued her curiosity. But of course he *knew* that. He was trying to provoke her into conversation.

She refused to be drawn in. Prying further would be a mistake.

He added, "Not since he lost his wife."

Shite.

Lost his wife?

Now the rogue was trying to play on her sympathies. Having failed to reason his way to freedom, he was attempting to thaw her heart.

She wouldn't allow that. She refused to ply him for details. It didn't matter. Whatever tragedy the new laird of

Creagor had endured didn't change the fact that he was holding her cousins against their will in his bedchamber.

Knowing the laird had had a wife, however, made her wonder if the woman had given him an heir ere she died. Being in line for a lairdship herself, Hallie thought often of such things. And thinking of heirs made her remember the babe next to the laird's bedchamber.

"That babe wailing all night..." she murmured.

"'Tis Morgan's," the man volunteered. "The poor wee thing has no ma. She died givin' birth to the lad." He let out a breath full of sorrow. "The bairn doesn't even have a name. The laird is too heartbroken to give him one."

Hallie cursed under her breath. Against her will and to her aggravation, the shield of ice surrounding her heart cracked just a wee bit.

"Morgan came to Creagor, hopin' to make a new beginnin'," he told her. "Alas, he's been met by foes."

For an instant, Hallie felt a splinter of guilt. Losing his wife was bad enough. But to face the prospect of losing his holding...

Then she furrowed her brow. "Wait. He attacked those foes while they were unarmed."

The man shook his head. "'Tis true. Melancholy has made him reckless. But I assure ye he's a decent man. No harm will come to your cousins."

He wasn't telling her anything she hadn't already guessed. From her interactions with the laird so far, she'd learned he was—on the whole—fair and reasonable. To be honest, in his place, even *she* might have gone after Jenefer with a blade. The wench had a way of drawing an attack with a sneer and a few choice words.

Still, Hallie could see the value in allowing the man to rattle on about his master's qualities. Knowing one's enemy—and their weaknesses—was the best way to prepare for battle, should it come to that.

So she encouraged him.

"You sound certain of that. Tell me more about this 'decent' laird of yours."

A smile lurked at the corners of Colban's mouth.

The lass had fallen neatly into his trap. By inviting her curiosity, he'd opened the door to reason with her.

Now, with the right words, he could placate her fears. Soothe her distress. And hopefully prevent a war.

"Laird Morgan? He's a man of honor and truth. Brave. Forthright. Loyal."

"Loyal enough to abide by the wishes of the king?"

"Aye."

"Even if the king decrees that Creagor belongs to my cousin?"

Colban knew that wasn't true. He'd been there when the messenger arrived, announcing the death of Morgan's uncle. Morgan had always been in line to inherit the keep.

"Impossible," he told her. "Creagor has belonged to the mac Giric clan for centuries."

"Young Malcolm is a new king. He may have his own ideas about who can best protect the keep."

"He made his decision. He awarded Creagor to Morgan, who is blood kin." He hoped she wouldn't press him on that. Though Morgan had the king's word, the written document had not yet been received.

"He may regret decisions made in haste," she said adding pointedly, "like awarding a Lowland keep to a Highland laird."

He drew his brows together. Was that what the lass and her cousins were so peeved about? The fact that the clansmen squatting on the precious land adjoining theirs were Highlanders?

He bristled at that. As an orphan with no real clan or claim,

Colban had always been grateful for the home the mac Girics had given him. They were good folk. Kind. Compassionate. Welcoming.

To think a Border clan would torment Morgan, arguing against his claim due to the place of his birth touched a raw nerve in Colban.

His ire was magnified by the fact that the lass had introduced doubt now and made him wonder. Was King Malcolm trustworthy? Would the new king honor the pledges of the old?

Malcolm was inexperienced, perhaps malleable. Was it possible the king would award castles on a whim, with no regard for tradition or clan bloodlines?

Colban shuddered at the thought. But he refused to betray Morgan by casting any suspicion on his tenuous ownership of the holding. Negotiations had to be made from a position of strength, not doubt.

So he spoke with a confidence he didn't feel.

"Creagor has been tended by Morgan's uncle for the last fifty years."

"That may be. But 'tis Rivenloch knights who defended Creagor while the rest of the mac Girics were...what? Tending coos in the faraway north?"

"Tendin' coos?" Colban felt the blood start to throb in his temples. "I'll have ye know the mac Girics have the finest fightin' forces in the Highlands."

"Indeed?" she said. "Why?"

He stopped in his tracks, turning to scowl at her. "What do ye mean—why?"

"'Tisn't as if you *need* a fighting force. You only quibble among yourselves, aye?" She shrugged. "Who stole whose coo? Who's been swiving the sheepherder's wife o'er the hill? Which lad has the biggest—"

"Hold on now!" Now he was truly riled. "Are ye insultin' my clan?"

She arched a slender brow at him. "'Tisn't as if you've ever faced a *real* foe."

His eyes widened in shock.

Her voice was full of cool pride as she proclaimed, "For hundreds of years, the warriors of Rivenloch have engaged in full-scale battle against the English for control of the Border lands. We're the progeny of Vikings, and we've guarded Scotland for generations of kings. There is no better force to defend Creagor."

"Is that so?" He glared at her in challenge. "Then why has Rivenloch sent *three maids* to steal her from her rightful owner?"

For an instant, the Valkyrie was rattled. She blinked, lost for words.

He pressed his point. "If Rivenloch's forces are so formidable, why were ye sneakin' about in the dead o' night?"

While she was flummoxed, he delivered the killing blow. "And if ye're so keen on defendin' Creagor, why have ye absconded with the man who was guardin' the gate?"

She gave a quick gasp. But her retort was like a slim dagger slipped between his ribs. "You mean the man *dozing* at the gate?"

He colored. Somehow she'd found a chink in his armor. But before he could bite out a word in his defense, she poked his hip with the sword, prodding him down the path again.

"Go."

His face burning with humiliation and rage, he stalked down the path with new determination. Now he was *eager* to get to Rivenloch.

This lass might be lovely and desirable. But she was as cold and cunning as a serpent, twisting his words and biting him where he was most vulnerable with her deadly fangs.

Surely the *men* of Rivenloch would be more reasonable.

Hallie hated to admit it, but this Highlander wielded a weapon far more pointed and powerful than his claymore. He was gifted with a sharp tongue and a sharper wit.

Even she, who prided herself on her way with words, had trouble defending against his logic.

She dreaded to think whose soft minds he might bend to his will once they arrived at Rivenloch.

Nonetheless, it was a risk she had to take. She couldn't hold him captive in the forest forever. Not with wolves ranging the woods.

Besides, the man now seemed hell-bent on getting there as quickly as possible, swallowing up the trail with his long strides. He probably hoped to outdistance her or at least make her struggle to keep up with him. But she matched him, stride for stride, and it wasn't long before she glimpsed the gray stones of Rivenloch through the thinning branches of pine.

Of course, they were noticed as soon as they emerged from the trees. The guards atop the battlements were already awake and alert.

By the time they reached the castle wall, Sir Rauve himself had arrived to open the palisade gate. By the look of him, he hadn't slept a wink. And he minced no words as he ushered them in.

"Where are the others?" he growled.

"Captive," she replied.

He bit out a curse. "And this one?" He glowered at the Highlander.

"Leverage," she said.

Rauve grunted. "Who is he?"

"No one," the Highlander answered before she could reply.

She shook her head. "He's the usurper's right hand man."

"I tell ye, I'm nobody," he insisted. "Ye're goin' to a lot o' trouble for naught."

She and Rauve exchanged a knowing look. They'd heard that line of reasoning before from captives.

Rauve gave him a threatening smile. "'Tis no trouble, I assure you."

To her surprise, the Highlander didn't cower in the least.

"I may owe my allegiance to Morgan Mor mac Giric," he told Rauve, "but I'm not valuable to him. He won't hesitate to sacrifice me, should it come to that."

He sounded quite reasonable. He sounded like he was telling the truth. But she wasn't fooled.

"Don't be ridiculous," she said smoothly. "I saw how distraught your laird was, thinking Feiyan had killed you."

"What? Feiyan tried to kill you?" Rauve blinked at the man. "And failed?" He regarded the captive with new respect.

"'Tisn't the point, Rauve," she said. "Besides, if she'd meant to kill him, he'd be dead."

Rauve narrowed his eyes pointedly at the man's face, riddled with cuts and bruises. "Bloody hell, Hallie. I thought 'twas a mission of peace."

Before Hallie could explain, the prisoner hastened to say, "No *lass* gave me these injuries, I assure ye."

It must chafe at his pride to be taken captive by a mere lass. Men always expected women to be frail and powerless.

But his next words surprised her.

"These were given to me by the man from whom ye seek ransom." He cast his eyes down in shame. "So ye see how…valuable…I am to him."

Hallie's throat caught. Was it true? Had Morgan Mor mac Giric inflicted this damage?

She glanced at Rauve. His brow had darkened. Such abuse from one's laird was unconscionable.

Against her will, she began to feel sorry for the man.

Was he telling the truth? Was he as invaluable and dispensable as he believed? Had she made a mistake in taking a hostage who was worthless?

She studied his face. Surely he wasn't worthless. Not only was he a formidable warrior. He was bright. Honorable. Dedicated. Of *course* he was valuable. How could he *not* be?

He must be lying to her. Yet she'd never she seen a man look so guileless. Beneath brows creased in an earnest frown, his eyes shone with sincerity.

She challenged him with her stare. Waiting for him to blink. Waiting for his mask of honesty to crack. For his gaze to slip away and reveal his lie.

It never did.

Indeed, she began to feel discomfited by the steady gaze he returned. Her cheeks grew hot. Her heart beat rapidly. She felt as if she were slipping into the deep, dark sea of his eyes.

Then, before she could either break him or drown in his gaze from the attempt, the unthinkable happened.

From the distant slope behind her came a sweet, musical squeal of delight. "Hallie!"

CHAPTER 7

It required all of Colban's willpower not to look away. Staring into the Valkyrie's eyes was more demanding than he imagined.

But he dared not waver, lest she doubt his words and think him a liar.

So he fixed his forthright gaze on her, while her eyes of crystal blue ice pierced his soul and probed the darkest recesses of his heart.

Who would have surrendered first, he'd never know. Their contest of wills was cut short by a feminine cry in the distance.

The Valkyrie flinched at the sound.

Behind him, the newcomer tripped merrily down the rise, crying, "Is it him, Hallie? Is it The One?"

Colban saw Hallie's jaw tighten.

The new arrival appeared to be a younger version of Hallie. A lass on the verge of womanhood, she was lanky, too tall for her kirtle. She had a snow-blonde braid and large blue eyes.

The hulking bear of a guard moved to block Colban's view of the lass, snarling, "Isabel! Go back to the keep."

Undaunted by his growls, Isabel replied, "Pah! You're not my laird."

"What do you want?" Hallie said with cold warning.

"I was watching you from the parapets," she said, trying to peer around Rauve's massive bulk. Then she gushed, "'Tis him, isn't it? You've finally found The One. I knew it. He's tall and handsome and... Oh, Hallie, I'm so happy for you."

What did she mean? *The One.*

"Cease, Isabel," Hallie bit out. To Colban's amazement, the unflappable Valkyrie was blushing. "'Tisn't what you—"

Isabel gasped, then blurted out, "I'll plan the wedding! We can have it after Martinmas, when the snow's on the ground, and—"

"Weddin'!" The word burst out of Colban, unbidden. Was that what the lass meant, calling him The One?

"Enough, brat," Rauve said, planting himself squarely in Isabel's path. Then he addressed Hallie, nodding toward Colban. "Where would you like me to stow him?"

"Oh!" Isabel exclaimed. "Our bedchamber! He can have my side of the bed, Hallie, and I'll sleep with Swannoc," she eagerly offered. "That way, the two of you can be together."

The horrified look on Hallie's face would have been amusing, had it not mirrored Colban's own shock.

The young lass, impatient with Rauve's interference, gave his black beard a hard sideways yank. He staggered out of her way. Then she glided forward, flashing Colban a kind smile.

"I'm Isabel, Hallie's sister. Who are you?"

"He's nobody," Rauve growled, rubbing his offended chin.

"He's not a guest," Hallie told her. "He's a hostage."

The smile froze on Isabel's face as she glimpsed Colban's chained hands. Then, perusing his injured face, her brow crumpled in dismay. "Did you do this, Hallie? Did you hurt him?"

"'Tisn't your concern," Hallie snapped, clearly upset by the accusation.

Isabel pouted. "How could you be so coldhearted, Hallie? That's why it's taken you so long to find The One. Everyone's afraid of you."

Hallie's gasp of hurt was so slight it was almost imperceptible. But Colban heard it. Her sister had touched a nerve.

In the next instant, Hallie's eyes frosted over. "Go back to bed, Isabel."

"Bed?" Isabel scoffed. "I've been up for hours. So why are you holding him hostage?"

"I warned you," Hallie bit out, "this is not your affair."

"'Tis, if I'm giving him my side of the bed."

"You'll do no such thing. He'll stay in...in..."

She struggled to come up with a proper cell. Apparently, none of the Border castles had been built with accommodations for prisoners.

"The laird's chamber is empty at present," Rauve suggested, "I can keep watch over him there."

"Aye. Good." Hallie straightened. Then she faced Isabel. "As for you, say a word to anyone about this, and I'll throttle you with your braid. Do you understand?"

Isabel scowled. "See?" She picked up her skirts, and stomped off, snarling back over her shoulder, "A heart of ice."

Hallie wanted to smack her meddling sister.

The One indeed.

She compressed her lips.

There was no such thing as The One.

There never would be.

Not for Hallie.

Hallie was destined to be a powerful laird. She had no use for a husband, except to forge a favorable alliance and create heirs. And for that, a suitable match would be chosen for her by the king.

Her wee sister was a foolish lass. A hopeless romantic.

She believed in true love. In couples destined to be together. In happily ever after.

Maybe that would be true for Isabel. As the fourth in line, she was a lass with no responsibilities. No expectations.

For Hallie, however, love was not in the stars.

But a heart of ice?

Hallie only did what she had to do. What was required of a woman in her position. She'd had to harden her heart in order to survive.

Nonetheless, as she nudged the captive forward, she took care not to jab him too forcefully with the point of the sword. There was no need to be unnecessarily rough. After all, a damaged hostage was of little value.

The moment they breached the castle walls, Hallie knew Isabel had disobeyed her. What had the wag-tongue told the clan? That her captive was The One? That Hallie had beaten a defenseless man to a bloody pulp? That she meant to keep him in her bedchamber?

Whatever it was, the news of an exciting arrival had spread like wildfire. It seemed the entire clan had rushed to the courtyard—some fresh from their beds—eager to feast their eyes on the captive. They stared at him as if they'd never seen a hostage before.

"Shite," she muttered.

Brand, Hallie's middle brother, loped up to meet her. At fifteen, he was half-lad, half-man. His upper lip was downy, but he still moved like an awkward pup.

"Is it true?" he asked, his face alight as he perused the captive. "Did he put up a fight?" Then he spied her sword. "Sard a bard! Look at that sword. You seized it from him, didn't you, Hallie? Is that a claymore?"

"Aye," she said with a scowl. She didn't need her little brother admiring the weapons of the enemy.

"Is he a Highlander?" Brand's eyes went wide with

amazement as he neared the hostage. "Are you a Highlander?"

Hallie's oldest brother, named after their grandfather Gellir, arrived next. A year older than Brand and as grim as the grave, he caught his brother's sleeve.

"Get back, Brand," he warned. "You should ne'er approach a prisoner."

Brand frowned in annoyance and pulled free of Gellir's grasp. But he heeded his brother's advice, taking a judicious step away.

Meanwhile, in the midst of the courtyard, Isabel was conspiring with three of her friends. She whispered something to them, and all four began staring at the Highlander with dreamy eyes.

"Enough!" Hallie announced, holding up a hand for quiet. It was time to set things straight.

She handed the claymore and the prisoner off to Rauve and waited for silence.

When the crowd hushed, she made the announcement. "You should know, Jenefer and Feiyan have been taken prisoner at Creagor."

There was a loud collective gasp.

"What!" Gellir snarled. His brows collided. His fists clenched. "By whom?" He looked ready to kill whoever had captured his cousins. And anyone else who got in his way.

"*We'll* get them back," Brand bravely chimed in. "Won't we, Gellir?" Then his gaze dropped to the sword in worry. "Wait. Do they *all* have claymores?"

"I can put the hostage in irons," Rauve offered, "and have the men ready to attack ere breakfast."

Grumblings of vengeance began to circle the crowd.

"Nay." Hallie held her hand up again to silence the plots that were hatching throughout the clan. "There's no cause for war. Not yet. Feiyan and Jenefer are being kept by the Highland laird, mac Giric. And they're safe for now."

She hoped that was true. She glanced briefly at the Highlander's battered face, wondering again about the man who'd inflicted those injuries.

"I've stolen his right hand man as leverage," she told them.

"His right hand man," Brand repeated in awe, eyeing the prisoner with new respect. "Brilliant."

"What's his name?" one of Isabel's friends called out, eliciting giggles from the group of lasses.

Hallie ignored her. She didn't know his name. She didn't *want* to know his name. Becoming too familiar with one's foe—like getting too close to a prisoner—was a sure way to give him the upper hand. Even Brand knew that.

But before she could stop him, the Highlander answered. "Colban," he called out to the crowd. "I'm Colban an Curaidh."

Bloody hell. Now he'd done it. Every lass at Rivenloch would be whispering the handsome captive's name, as if he were some kind of tragic hero. Even now, she could hear the murmurs from Isabel's swooning friends.

She had to put a quick halt to this.

"There will be absolutely no fraternizing with the prisoner. No one is to look at him. No one is to speak to him. And no one is to exact vengeance upon him." She gave stone-faced Gellir a pointed glance. "He's here for leverage only, as a means to get Jenefer and Feiyan back."

"Wherever will you *hold* him?" cheeky Isabel asked.

Her suggestive choice of words was no mistake. *Hold* him? Hallie clenched her teeth at the insinuation. She was tempted to *hold* her little sister by the scruff of her neck.

Rauve replied to Isabel with a glare of warning. "He'll be under my watch, lass. That's all you need to know."

Hallie narrowed her eyes at Isabel. She wondered if there was anywhere Colban would be safe from the attentions of a pack of lusty and determined lasses.

Gellir was still eager for battle. "When do we storm the gates?"

"We won't be storming the gates."

His shoulders fell in disappointment.

She didn't need to explain herself. Until her parents returned, Hallie was laird. The clan was obliged to obey her without question.

But she believed, as did her mother, in leading by reason and inspiration, not by brute force.

So she told them, "We should receive news from the king very soon, establishing once and for all our ownership of Creagor. I plan to hold the mac Giric's man hostage until then. 'Twould be foolish to attack. After all," she said, giving the clan folk a cool smile, "we wouldn't want to damage the castle that will soon be ours, would we?"

The clan cheered.

She hoped she was right about that. Creagor had indeed been awarded to the Highlander. Only by the grace of her mother's influence over the king would that decision be altered.

Hallie couldn't help but feel a shiver of doubt as the crowd parted to let Rauve through with the prisoner.

Colban an Curaidh.

She wished she'd never heard his name.

And now she wished she could forget it.

She spoke just enough of the Highland tongue to translate his title.

Colban the Champion.

Not mac Giric. Not mac anything. How valuable could the Highlander be if he didn't have his clan's surname?

CHAPTER 8

Colban had to admire the Valkyrie. For a lass of tender years, she had her clan well in hand. She was levelheaded, brilliant, and in command.

Now that he'd taken the measure of the warriors in the courtyard, he was relieved they didn't intend to attack Creagor. Not only were mac Giric's forces outnumbered. Aside from Morgan and himself, their men would have been dwarfed by the towering Rivenloch knights, half of whom looked like Vikings straight off a longboat.

He didn't fool himself. Things could still go badly.

When Hallie discovered that Creagor did indeed belong to the mac Giric clan by right of the king, her air of calm could very well turn to frost. She might—with calculating malice and a cold heart—use him as a pawn in a deadly game of revenge.

But he'd glimpsed something in the courtyard that gave him hope.

He'd seen how much Hallie loved her clan.

From her infuriating, dreamy-eyed romantic of a sister. To the fierce young man eager to defend her. From the gape-jawed lad with the curious mind. To the grizzled black bear of a guard who had her back.

Hallie wouldn't do anything to bring harm to them. He was sure of it.

All Colban had to do was keep the peace and make no trouble.

As Rauve steered him past the bevy of young lasses, who were fluttering their lashes and sharing secrets behind their hands, he thought that might be easier said than done.

He was glad when Rauve ushered him to safety in the great hall, securing the door behind him.

Then Colban stopped in his tracks. He'd already been amazed at first sight of the castle, which was easily twice the size of Creagor and far more imposing than anything in the Highlands. The outer wall, with its gate offset from the inner wall, was ingenious. The enormous courtyard, which enclosed numerous stalls and gardens, was impressive. The keep at its center was well-fortified and well-guarded.

But the great hall was a thing of majesty. Its ceiling soared high above the rush-covered floor. Morning light streamed in through the arched windows, illuminating dozens of colorful shields and pennons hung on the walls.

They were trophies, he realized. The trophies of defeated enemies. And there were at least a score of them. His let out a breath. He hoped he could keep the targe of mac Giric from hanging among them.

Rauve guided him up a set of spiraling stairs at one corner of the hall, then along a passage to a wide oak door.

"A word of warning," Rauve grumbled. "Hallie may be a wisp of a thing. But don't underestimate her."

Colban nodded, though he wouldn't call Hallie "a wisp of a thing."

"You'll be imprisoned here," Rauve continued. "But as long as you act honorably, you'll be treated with fairness. You'll also be safe. Her brother might issue threats, but he'll do you no harm."

Colban appreciated Rauve's reassurances. Her brother's smoldering, youthful rage couldn't be easy to contain.

"To be honest," Colban confided, "I'm more worried about Hallie's schemin' sister."

To his surprise, the growling guard actually barked out a laugh at that. "Isabel's a lovesick lass, to be sure. But she's not grown enough to get past my sword. At least not yet."

Rauve opened the door to a beautifully appointed bedchamber.

Colban thought there must be some mistake. This was hardly a prison cell. It was, however, proof of Hallie's evenhandedness. After all, her cousins were being held in similarly luxurious quarters at Creagor.

"Hell," Rauve groused. "Someone left the shutters open. I'll get a fire going. You're no good to us, frozen to death."

Colban murmured, "I'm a Highlander. 'Twould take more than this kiss o' frost to freeze my bones, I assure ye."

He perused the chamber. A large bed draped at the corners in dark blue velvet took up most of the room. A carved oak chest stood at its foot. The hearth was flanked by a chair with cushions and a small table, which held a wash basin, a ewer, a stack of linens, and a small assortment of combs and bottles. Three empty cloak pegs and a sconce with a beeswax candle graced one wall. And a small curtained opening indicated an adjoining garderobe. It was the grandest bedchamber he'd ever seen.

"Sit," Rauve commanded, guiding him to the chair while he gathered up anything he deemed of value or possible harm from the room, bundling them into a linen square. Then he opened the door and yelled out, "Bart!"

A few moments later, a freckled youth scrambled into the room.

"Light the fire, lad," Rauve told him, placing the bundle near the door. "Then lock this in the storeroom."

While Bart started a fire on the hearth, Rauve removed the steel chain binding Colban's wrists and outlined the terms of his captivity.

"I'll be standing guard at the door. Another guard will be posted outside, below the window. Only a child could fit down the garderobe hole. And setting the room on fire will just mean a painful death for you."

Apparently, Rauve had already thought of every means of escape.

"You'll be brought meals," he continued, "and water for washing." Then he narrowed his eyes. "But make no trouble or—"

"I'll make no trouble," Colban assured him, rubbing his freed wrists, "nor abuse your generosity."

Rauve sniffed at that. But Colban could tell the guard was pleased by his praise. In that way, they were kindred spirits. Colban knew all too well that a man's loyalty and kindness too often went unrecognized.

"Ye're lucky to have a merciful mistress," Colban said, casually pressing his fingertips to the tender flesh of his swollen eye. It wouldn't hurt to perpetuate the myth that *his* laird had mistreated him. The less value Rivenloch believed Colban had, the less leverage they could exert over Morgan.

Rauve, discomfited by the compliment, mumbled, "I'll get someone to tend to your injuries."

"My thanks." Then, realizing it would serve him well to be thought a hero, Colban let out a sigh of relief. "I'm just glad I was fit enough to save Hallie from the wolves."

From the hearth, Bart coughed.

"What?" Rauve asked.

"There was a pack o' them in the woods. We were lucky to escape with our lives. I told Hallie to climb a tree while I fended them—"

"A pack of wolves?" Rauve's bushy brows lifted.

Bart snickered.

Colban frowned at him. What was wrong with the lad?

Rauve crossed beefy arms over his chest. "You saved Hallie from a pack of wolves?"

The lad was grinning now. What was so amusing, Colban didn't know. But before he could scold the lad for finding humor at Hallie's peril, Hallie herself opened the door and breezed into the room.

The power of her presence was undeniable. Bold and beautiful, she inspired awe and commanded admiration. Maybe Bart was right to laugh. Maybe the Valkyrie *could* handle a pack of wolves on her own.

But beneath her air of cool competence, Colban glimpsed a hint of distraction in Hallie's eyes. He'd seen a similar overwhelmed look from Morgan many a time over the last weeks. Leadership was a burden not easily borne by one person alone.

"Is the chamber secure?" she asked Rauve, glancing around the room.

Rauve ignored her question. "Is it true, lass?" he demanded. "Did you clash with wolves in the wood?"

"What?" Caught off her guard, she colored. "'Clash' is a strong word. We weren't in any real danger."

"No danger?" Colban's brows shot up. "We were treed all night."

"They wouldn't have harmed us," she muttered, though her blush gave her away. She turned to Rauve. "You know he'd never hurt me."

"I warned you, lass," Rauve said. "Wolves are not to be trusted. You may have raised him from a pup, but he's grown now. To him, you're prey."

She turned to Colban, swiftly changing the subject. "You must be hungry."

Colban probably *was* hungry, but he hadn't noticed. He was still digesting the notion that Hallie was friends with a wolf.

She didn't wait for a reply. "I'll send someone up with breakfast." Then she addressed Rauve. "Have you seen Ian?"

"Not this morn," Rauve replied.

Bart rose from the merrily crackling fire he'd laid. "I heard him talking to Gellir at breakfast, m'lady," he volunteered, "saying he needed a bit of peace and quiet."

"If you're done here, Bart, go look for him," Hallie said. "Maybe he's in the garden. Or the dovecot. Or hiding in a garderobe somewhere."

Bart gave her a bob, snatched up the linen bundle by the door, and left.

"As for you," she said, finally turning her full attention on him, "I expect you'll try to escape."

He took a breath, intending to assure her he would do no such thing.

But she smoothly continued, "You won't succeed. My men are loyal. Clever. *And,*" she added pointedly, "well-rested."

Rauve straightened with pride.

"But I *will* have your solemn oath," she added, "that you won't harm my clansmen."

"You have it," Colban replied.

Rauve grunted, puzzled by Colban's ready agreement.

So Colban explained to him, "Like ye, I want this matter settled as quickly as possible. Without bloodshed." He'd seen the might of the Rivenloch knights. To challenge them before reinforcements arrived at Creagor would be suicide. "A negotiation is always preferable to a skirmish." He glanced again at Hallie. "Right?"

For one precious instant, Hallie's eyes softened in surprise. For one precious instant, he felt the warmth of her approval and wondered what it would be like to feel the heat of her love.

Then she lowered her gaze. And when she lifted it again, her eyes were glazed over with ice. She'd returned to being his captor.

Eyeing his claymore, propped against the wall, she told

Rauve, "Hang that thing in the armory. Out of Brand's reach."

And then, as brisk as the winter wind, she swept from the room.

"She's a fine one," Rauve remarked when Hallie had gone.

"Aye," Colban agreed. It was a shame they were foes. She would make a good ally. And he could think of things he'd rather do with the lovely lass than fight her.

"Sharp," Rauve said. "Beautiful. Powerful enough to cleave a man's arm clean off, aye?"

Colban blinked, startled. Then he saw Rauve was examining his claymore. "Oh. Aye."

"Do all your men carry these?" Rauve asked casually.

The guard wasn't fooling him. Like any clever warrior, Rauve was attempting to discover the strength of his enemy.

"All o' them," Colban said with a glitter of humor in his eyes. "E'en the bairns."

Rauve smirked at Colban's jest.

"But ye needn't fret," he told Rauve. "My laird won't attack Rivenloch. Not to ransom a bastard. Hell, I doubt he'll notice I'm missin'."

That was a lie. But he hoped, once Morgan discovered that both his right hand man and the Valkyrie were gone, he'd assume that Colban had gone after the lass and would ultimately capture her. Not the other way round.

Under that assumption, Morgan had no reason to come to Rivenloch. The laird's best course of action was to hold onto the two remaining lasses until the messengers from the king arrived with the documents that would prove his ownership of Creagor.

If all went well, the prisoner exchange would be bloodless.

"You may be a bastard," Rauve said, rubbing doubtfully

at his jaw. "But I doubt you're worthless. Not carrying a blade like that."

A tapping at the door saved him from having to defend his worthlessness.

It was an apple-cheeked old woman.

"Hallie said I'm to treat his injuries," she explained to Rauve, showing him her things.

"Burunild," the guard grunted, motioning her in.

As she crouched beside Colban to dab at his cuts and bruises, she shook her head and clucked her tongue in sympathy.

He wondered if she'd feel the same, knowing he'd earned the injuries in a fair fight and that he'd done just as much damage to Morgan.

While she was finishing, another rap came at the door. A young lass—one he'd seen in the courtyard, giggling with Isabel—had brought him breakfast. She turned pink at once, shoving the tray of frumenty and oatcakes at him, and then wheeling with a delighted squeak as she hurried out the door.

"Witless wench," the old woman muttered.

The enticing scent of apples and warm oats made his belly rumble.

"Poor lad. Did your laird starve you as well?" the old woman asked with a frown as she gathered her things. As she rose to go, she leaned down and confided in a loud whisper, "You might be better off staying here at Rivenloch. You'd be treated fairly. No one beats a servant here. Faith, half the clan maidens are already twitter-pated o'er you. You'd probably find a wife in no time."

"That will be enough, Burunild," Rauve said, ushering her out the door and closing it behind them.

Colban found the woman's words amusing and thought-provoking. He was being treated more like an honored guest than a hostage. He shook his head, wondering what would happen if a hostage refused to be returned.

After the tender care of his injuries and enjoying a hearty and delicious meal, he sat on the edge of the bed, intending to rest a moment before determining his next course of action.

Hours later, he awoke with a snort. He found himself sprawled in the middle of the plush velvet coverlet with his long legs hanging off the bed. He rose up on his elbows, blinking to clear his vision.

Then he rasped in a startled gasp.

From within the folds of the bedhangings, studying him with the intensity of a hawk on the hunt was a young lad with ice-blond hair.

CHAPTER 9

"**W**hat do you think causes snoring?" the lad asked.

Colban froze, as baffled by the question as he was by the lad, who'd seemed to appear out of nowhere.

"Is it the lungs, collapsed in sleep, gasping for air?" the lad continued. "Or is it the voice producing the sound, as a means of assuring others that one is still alive?" The lad held a quill over an open ledger, as if he intended to record Colban's reply.

"What?" He prayed the lad wasn't some fae being—that Colban's life didn't depend on his answer—because he could think of none.

The lad set aside the quill and ledger and emerged then, crawling across the bed to sit cross-legged in front of him. Once out of the shadows, he looked to be an ordinary young man of perhaps ten years, with the same fair hair and blue eyes as Hallie.

"Sometimes the hounds snore," he said. "But I've ne'er heard a snoring mouse. Have you?"

Colban blinked. "Who *are* you? How did you get in here?"

"I've been here since you arrived."

"That's impossible."

The lad was taken aback. "You don't believe me?" Then he furrowed his pale brows. "I suppose there's little proof for you, since you've been only partially conscious most of the day. But I assure you I've been here. I've been watching you sleep."

The lad said that as if it were a *good* thing.

"Who *are* ye?" Colban asked again.

"Oh. I'm Ian."

"Ian. Ye're the one Hallie was lookin' for. She sent Bart to—"

"I know. I was here. Remember?"

Nay, he didn't remember.

Ian shrugged and whispered, "I stayed quiet, because I didn't *want* to be found." He leaned closer. "But who are *you?* Besides some sort of Highland hostage who fights off wolves and lasses with a claymore."

Colban had to smile at Ian's appraisal of him.

"My name is Colban. Colban an Curaidh."

"That means 'the Champion.'"

"Aye, it does."

Slowly, so as not to startle the lad, Colban dragged himself upright until he was sitting cross-legged as well. He could see the sun had moved across the sky. It must be late afternoon.

"You don't have your sire's name," Ian remarked.

"Nay. I don't have a sire. I'm a bastard."

"You *must* have a sire," Ian informed him. "It takes both male and female to produce offspring."

A grin tugged at Colban's lips. He wondered if the lad knew all the details about procreation as well.

"Aye, I *do* have a da. Somewhere. But I don't know who he is."

Ian's eyes widened at that. Then he said thoughtfully, "'Tis a pity. A da is a good thing to have. My da taught me how to read and fish and play chess. Do you know how to play chess?"

"Aye."

Ian sprang abruptly from the bed and rushed to the wooden chest at the foot of it. Lifting the lid, he retrieved a board and a velvet satchel. Then he climbed back onto the bed, setting the board between them and shaking the pieces out of the satchel.

"White or black?" he inquired.

The lad obviously hadn't received the warning about not fraternizing with the prisoner. And now Colban supposed they were going to play chess, whether he wanted to or not.

"Black."

What he really wanted to do was eat. He hadn't supped since morn. Neither had the lad, if he'd been watching him sleep the entire day.

Ian began distributing the pieces. "My ma taught me how to play hnefatafl as well. Do you know it?"

He shook his head.

"'Tis a Viking game, similar to chess," Ian said.

"Is your ma a Viking then?" Colban asked, lining up his pieces.

"My mother was born in Scotland. But her ancestors were Vikings. Where was your mother born?"

A dozen replies flitted through Colban's head. In a brothel. Out of wedlock. On the wrong side of fate. Into the arms of despair.

In the end, he decided on, "In the Highlands."

"And is she a good ma?" Ian put his last pawn into place.

"She's gone."

"Gone?"

"She died when I was a lad."

Ian's brow crumpled in distress. "You have no parents at all then."

"I have a clan." It was true. Spending his youth with Morgan, he'd grown to think of Laird Giric and Lady Hilaire as his mother and father.

"My mother is the laird of our clan," Ian volunteered, "though my sister Hallie is watching o'er us while she's away."

At that revelation, dangerous thoughts began to swirl through Colban's brain.

He edged one pawn forward.

He could use this chance meeting with the laird's son to his advantage. It would be the work of an instant to seize the wee lad and take him hostage. Even without a weapon.

Anyone could see how easily he could break the lad's scrawny neck. In the blink of an eye. With his bare hands.

Using the son of the laird as a shield, he could get past Rauve. Once all of Rivenloch understood the threat Colban posed, he'd be granted free passage back to Creagor.

Once at Creagor, he would not only provide Morgan with a third hostage, but he could give the laird useful information about Rivenloch's defenses if war came to pass.

Colban wouldn't even be breaking his word. He'd made no specific promises about taking hostages.

"Well?" Ian had made his move. Now he looked up at Colban with wide blue eyes.

But Colban couldn't do it. It was a matter of chivalry. No matter how desperate the situation was, threatening to harm a helpless lad went against his sense of honor. Honor he'd cultivated all his life.

In a few days, he told himself, things would work themselves out, and he'd be returned to Creagor. There was no need for bloodshed. Or violence. Or carrying off wee Viking lads.

He slid another pawn forward.

"Have you e'er watched a lightning storm?" Ian asked.

Colban grinned. The lad was an endless font of questions. "Aye."

"'Tis curious, isn't it, how the branches of lightning form like the branches of a tree."

"I suppose so."

"I was almost struck by lightning once." He lowered his voice to confide, "I was watching a storm atop the tower. My grandfather told me not to go up there. But 'twas too exciting to resist."

"What happened?"

"My skin started to tingle. And my hair stood on end. All at once, with a loud crack, the lightning struck the tower wall right next to me." His eyes widened with the memory, then lowered to the chessboard. "Your move."

To Colban, the lad's mind moved like lightning, darting about in seemingly random patterns.

While Colban was choosing which piece to move, Ian volunteered, "I've built a siege engine."

"Is that so?"

"Well. A model of a siege engine. Da won't let me have the timbers to build an actual engine. At least not until the model proves its worth. Would you like to see it?"

"Is it in here?"

"Nay. I keep it in the stable. But I can show it to you from the window later."

"I'd like that."

As strange as it was, Colban was enjoying Ian's company. The lad was bright and fearless and full of curiosity. For someone who'd claimed to need peace and quiet, he chattered endlessly. And he played chess with a skill far beyond his years. Indeed, Colban might well lose this match.

But there was something Colban could *win* from his encounter with Ian. Something that would serve him well in the critical days ahead. He could win the lad's trust.

"What are ye writin' there?" Colban asked, nodding at the ledger the lad had set aside.

"Everything."

"Everythin'?"

"Would you like to see?"

He nodded. What Colban saw in the ledger left him speechless. Crowded onto each page were dozens of drawings and hundreds of words, written in tiny letters. On one page was a sketch of a mill, a v-shaped flock of birds, and what looked like a design for a knight's helm. Another was filled with lines of text. A third featured a detailed cart and several depictions of flowers. A branching tree took up one entire page. Squeezed between the branches were hundreds of words, written in tiny letters. Colban wished he could read them.

"Ye made these?"

"Aye."

"They're wondrous indeed." He turned the page and narrowed his eyes. "And this?"

"'Tis Rivenloch. I'm working on the defenses." He pointed out the various features. "Here's the courtyard. And the great hall. And the armory. Here's where we are right now."

Colban had to temper his excitement as he scanned the illustration. It was a detailed map of the castle. Nothing could be more valuable to the mac Girics, should they need to lay siege to Rivenloch.

"I think 'tis your play," Ian reminded him.

Colban returned the ledger to him with a wink. "And I think ye're eager to pummel me."

Ian grinned.

Colban studied the board and finally slid a bishop forward.

"Are you sure you want to do that?" Ian asked.

Colban wasn't sure. But he'd already made his move. "Aye. Once a man makes up his mind, I believe he should commit to that choice and follow through with—"

"Checkmate."

How the imp had infiltrated his ranks so quickly, he couldn't fathom.

But before he could recover from the shock, there was a sound at the door. Ian gasped, upsetting the chessboard and scattering pieces across the coverlet. As the door swung open, Colban instinctively leaped from the bed to defend the lad.

In the doorway stood the Valkyrie. She was breathless and beautiful. Her blue eyes were cold and fierce.

Hallie had been scouring the castle for her missing youngest sibling all day long. He hadn't shown up for supper, and now the clan was gathering for the last meal of the day.

There was still no sign of her parents. Ian was her responsibility. She needed to locate him before the inquisitive lad heard about the hostage and made it his mission to question him.

She'd checked the storeroom to be sure Rauve had concealed the tunnel entrance and that Ian hadn't escaped through the passage.

She'd searched the dovecot where he sometimes liked to observe the birds.

She'd looked in the armory, where he spent hours designing armor plate and war machines.

Finally, she'd been forced to give up. She'd told herself Ian would probably turn up before nightfall. After all, he'd have to eat eventually.

So would Rauve.

When she came upstairs to relieve him, Rauve was slowly pacing along the hallway, bored with the task of guarding the door.

"Go on to dinner," she told him. "And take your time."

"But the prisoner..."

"He won't know you've gone. I'll watch the door." As Rauve left, she had a second thought. "Bring a platter up when you return. I don't want to starve the hostage."

Rauve was long gone when Hallie, leaning back against the opposite wall, began staring at the door, transfixed by a sickening thought.

Ian had wanted peace and quiet. What was more peaceful and quiet than her parents' abandoned bedchamber?

"Shite," she breathed.

Dreading the worst, she braced herself and pushed away from the wall, hesitating as she reached for the door handle.

When she finally shoved open the door, her greatest fears were realized.

"Ian." The word came out of her on a rush of air.

Ian sat cross-legged on the bed, no more than four yards away. But between Hallie and her innocent little brother loomed the scowling Highlander, menacing and deadly.

"Don't be angry, Hallie," Ian called out. "We were only playing chess."

His sweet voice caught at her heart. He had no idea what peril he was in.

Curse the Fates. She'd brought no sword. And she'd just sent Rauve downstairs to dine.

The tension was palpable as Hallie and her captive stared at each other in silence, at a horrifying impasse.

Her throat closed with alarm, but she held her breath, maintaining an icy glare. She might fear for Ian's welfare, but she dared not reveal that fear. Nor that she was at a disadvantage.

By the calculating glint in his eyes, the Highlander knew he had the upper hand. The lad was in arm's reach. And by now loose-tongued Ian had probably revealed he was the laird's son, therefore a valuable hostage.

"I promise I wasn't boring him," Ian added, as if that were her greatest concern.

Her little brother was a genius when it came to facts and figures, brilliant beyond his years. But he had the trust and naivete of his age, which was a tender ten years old.

Her throat thickened as she continued to stare at the Highlander. If anything happened to Ian...

And then a curious thing occurred. Colban an Curaidh's hard brown gaze softened with kindness. His shoulders dropped. His fists relaxed. And he stepped out of the way.

"He didn't bore me," he said. "But he did beat me soundly at chess."

Hallie was stunned. There was no reason for the Highlander to surrender. As a captive, he should do everything in his power to escape. She expected no less. She had fully expected him to seize Ian and hold him as a counter hostage.

But he hadn't.

He'd done the gallant and chivalrous thing.

She'd always believed the tales about rough-hewn Highlanders. That they were savages. Undisciplined. Incapable of honor. Even *he* had tried to convince her he was worthless.

But his actions proved the stories wrong. Only a keen sense of virtue could prevent him from taking what would have been an easy means of escape.

Hallie released an awe-filled breath. She wondered if the Highlander could see the flood of relief in her eyes. Relief and respect.

She wouldn't thank him aloud. But she conveyed her gratitude with a subtle nod of her head.

He nodded back. The hint of a smile graced his lips.

"'Tis time for dinner, Ian," she choked out. "Come now."

"But what about Colban?"

She winced. Colban. Apparently, they'd exchanged first names. What other information had they exchanged?

"I'm having food brought up for him," she said, summoning Ian with a wave of her hand.

"Then I'll dine here as well," Ian decided.

"What? Nay."

Ian raised his stubborn chin. "We can't just leave him alone, Hallie. His mother is dead. And he doesn't even know who his father *is*. He told me so."

The Highlander's mouth opened in surprise. He was obviously unaccustomed to wee lads who blurted out truths.

"Did he?" she asked.

This was an interesting coil. Perhaps it wasn't so bad that Ian had had time to interrogate the captive, after all. Colban an Curaidh had confessed he was a bastard and an orphan. Perhaps she could glean more useful information from her little brother.

On the other hand, it made her wonder... What had Ian revealed to the prisoner about Rivenloch, about *her?* The possibilities were unsettling.

"I've been alone before, lad," Colban said. "Go on now and do what your sister says."

He was making a point. Letting her know Ian had indeed revealed he was her brother. It was Colban's way of telling her he was well aware of the leverage he was giving up by not seizing the lad.

"Will *you* at least keep him company, Hallie?" Ian asked as he climbed down from the bed.

"Of course." She gave the Highlander a grim smile. "I'll be watching his every move."

"Fine," Ian conceded with a sigh. "But I have to put away the chess pieces first."

"I'll put them away," Colban offered. "Ye go on now. Go eat."

Ian looked crestfallen, but he grabbed his notebook and quill and climbed off the bed.

"I'll be fine," Colban assured him. "Besides, I obviously need to practice my game if I can be trounced by a scrap of a lad."

Ian grinned.

As Hallie ushered her brother to safety out the door, her mind whirled like a tempest.

On one hand, she was grateful for the Highlander's mercy.

On the other, she knew it gave him an advantage.

Because he had shown restraint, the scales were tipped in his favor. She owed him a debt of honor.

And because she now *knew* things about him, because he'd shown his true colors, she could no longer consider him a nameless, featureless foe.

He was Colban an Curaidh, poor orphan, unfortunate bastard, worthy champion.

She lifted a brow. She was beginning to understand why he was called The Champion. He really *did* look heroic, standing with proud confidence in the glow of the fire, his arms crossed in challenge.

He was chivalrous enough to confront wolves in her defense. Honorable enough not to harm an innocent child, even when it would be to his advantage.

He deserved her gratitude.

With one hand on the door, she murmured, "My thanks."

He shrugged. "I vowed I'd hurt none o' your clansmen."

"So you did. But you wouldn't be the first man to break a vow."

"Fair enough. But may I give ye a piece of advice?"

She bristled. What possible advice could he have?

His eyes smoldered with humor. "The next time ye want to rescue a wee lad from a brawny foe, ye might want to bring a blade."

Heat flushed her cheeks. Being unarmed *had* been a tactical mistake on her part. But she wasn't about to admit it.

She gave him a grim smile. "I assure you I'm just as deadly with my bare hands."

Then she ducked out the door before he could test that lie.

CHAPTER 10

allie was glad the Highlander couldn't see her as she paced outside the door, fuming. It was completely unlike her to charge into a possible conflict without her sword. Hell, it was completely unlike her to be fuming.

What was wrong with her? What was it about the Highlander that made her feel off-guard? Off-balance? And out of sorts?

Hallie prided herself on ruling with an even temper. While others panicked around her, she cultivated an air of composure. It was the key to good judgment.

As a leader, she was efficient. Fair. Diplomatic. She never let emotions interfere with her decisions.

She had experience beyond her years. It was part of her training to be laird. She'd solved disputes. Issued orders. Taken prisoners. Fought in battle. All with an uncluttered mind and a steady hand.

But this hostage was ruffling her unruffled calm.

What was it about Colban an Curaidh? His courteous manner? His trickster's tongue? Those deep brown eyes that danced when he spoke? His inexplicable kindness? The charming lilt of his words? His tragic past that tugged at her heart? Or the impressive cut of his figure that disrupted her senses?

She whirled and sent her skirts swirling like a violent squall around her. And then she stopped, closing her eyes, willing the storm to quiet.

Surely it was none of those things.

One man could not affect her so profoundly.

She was only concerned for the welfare of the clan. Aware of the danger and the high stakes of her choices. Wary of making an incorrect decision when the entire responsibility rested on her shoulders.

Calmer now, she was still relieved when she heard footsteps coming up the stairs. Rauve was returning to take up his post. And he would have had the foresight to bring a weapon.

When she turned, however, it wasn't Rauve who appeared, but her conniving sister with a platter of food.

"What are you doing here?" Hallie demanded.

"I've brought dinner for Colban….unless…" Her wide and innocent eyes filmed over with ridicule. "You don't mean to starve him until he bends to your will, do you?"

"Isabel," Hallie bit out in warning.

"'Tis rather cruel. But 'tis no worse than your beating him, I suppose."

"Once and for all, I didn't beat him, Isabel." She took a step forward, wagging her finger in Isabel's face. "And I gave you direct orders not to fraternize with the prisoner."

"I don't know what that means." Isabel shrugged. "Besides, I'm not going to…frat-whatever with him. I'm only bringing him food. Ian told me you were going to dine with him."

"What?"

"His words were you 'didn't want Colban to be lonely'."

Hallie would have to have a talk with Ian about the definition of a hostage. And she didn't care for the hopeful gleam in her sister's eyes.

Isabel continued, waxing romantic. "'Tis such a merciful

gesture on your part. An offering of peace to a tortured soul. Sharing a meal and conversation. Gazing—"

"Nay," Hallie said, refusing to be maneuvered by her little sister. "You go in. Leave the platter on the table. And come straight back."

Isabel was visibly disappointed, but she nodded. "Fine."

She carefully opened the door for Isabel, aware Colban could be crouched behind it, ready to spring.

He wasn't. He was standing at the window. When he turned, the setting sun made a halo around his blond head, making him look like an angel. A powerfully handsome angel with broad shoulders, a massive chest, and sparkling brown eyes.

"Sir Colban!" Isabel cried, dashing into the room past her.

Hallie, choking, made a grab for her and missed.

"I've brought you dinner," the willful maid gushed.

Ignoring Hallie's instructions, Isabel rushed directly up to the Highlander and pressed the platter into his hands.

He gave her an uneasy smile. "My thanks."

"Isabel," Hallie hissed. Her silly sister had practically cornered the poor man against the window.

"Oh!" Isabel exclaimed in feigned surprise. "I've brought enough for both of you. Hallie thought you'd like company."

Hallie gave her a chilling glare.

"Did she?" he asked.

"Oh aye," Isabel insisted. Then she added in a loud whisper, "She might look fierce, but she has a tender heart."

"That will be enough, Isabel," Hallie said. "Leave the food and go."

"Aye, m'laird," Isabel said on a sigh, giving Colban a brief curtsy.

As she headed back toward the door, she winked broadly at Hallie. When she turned to flutter her fingers in farewell to the Highlander, Hallie smacked the mischievous maid on the bottom. Isabel yelped and hastened out the door.

When Hallie's gaze returned to the prisoner, he was still standing by the window, resembling an angel. A *fallen* angel, she amended. From his bruised face, it looked as if he'd taken quite a tumble out of heaven.

"Ye don't have to keep me company," he said, guessing Isabel had fabricated her offer. "Though, as ye can see, 'tis too much for one man."

She lowered her eyes to the platter. A large trencher of fresh-baked bread sat in the middle. By the mouthwatering smell wafting through the chamber, it was filled with beef pottage. Beside it was a salat made of winter greens. Atop a linen napkin were a pair of apple coffyns, still steaming and fragrant. And two empty silver goblets stood beside an open bottle of red wine. Expensive French wine that should have been reserved for honored guests.

She licked her lips. She hadn't had time for breakfast, and she'd only picked at supper. It seemed like a shame to let all that food go to waste.

"Ye may as well join me," he urged.

Despite the hunger pangs in her belly, she told him, "I don't fraternize with prisoners."

"Fine. I won't fraternize with ye. We'll just sup together, and I won't say a word."

She smirked. His eyes were dancing. He clearly had about as much respect for her boundaries as Isabel did.

Then again, what could it hurt? Was she so weak-willed that she couldn't sup with the man without losing her power over him?

He was her prisoner. She was laird here. This was her castle. Her servants. Her food. Her domain.

"I'll sup with you," she agreed, closing the door behind her. "But only so I can keep an eye on you."

Colban suppressed a smile. For a prisoner with whom no one was supposed to fraternize, he certainly had a lot of people keeping an eye on him.

But he didn't mind having the Valkyrie as his guard. She was beautiful and fascinating. Even if they said nothing, she was a lovely sight to look upon, with her fair tresses, her crystal eyes, and lips that rivaled rose petals in their velvety perfection.

He cast about the chamber, looking for a place where they could share the dinner. Only the bed afforded enough room. So, ignoring the disconcerting detail that they'd be sharing a bed, he set the platter in its midst.

As wary as a wildcat, she took a seat across from him. Then she offered him the spoon while she poured the wine.

His hunger heightened the flavor of the pottage. The beef was tender. The herb-filled broth was thick and rich with cabbage, neeps, and onions. It was difficult not to eat the whole meal himself.

But when he'd finished half, he handed the spoon to Hallie and started on the salat. By this time in the Highlands, the greens were gone, grazed by beasts or buried under snow, so it was a rare treat to enjoy fresh fennel and parsley.

Only the wine was a disappointment. It was cloyingly sweet. But he was thirsty, so he gulped it down with a wince and a slight shudder.

When he put down the empty goblet, Hallie was regarding him with horror.

"You're supposed to sip it," she scolded, "not guzzle it down. Have you never had wine before?"

"I've had it once before. At Morgan's weddin'. But it didn't taste like this."

She arched an indignant brow. "You probably can't get good French wine in the Highlands."

"Maybe that's a good thing. To be honest, this is a wee bit hard to swallow."

Hallie frowned and took a sip of her own wine. Then she made a face of such pure disgust that Colban couldn't help but chuckle.

"What *is* this?" she asked, peering into her goblet as if the answer lay there. "Something's wrong with it."

Colban's grin faded quickly as a terrible thought came to mind. "It hasn't been poisoned, has it?" Bloody hell. He'd gulped down the whole goblet.

"Nay." But he could see by her expression that she wasn't certain of that. "Surely not."

Colban suddenly felt sick, as if poison were already infiltrating his veins. "Your older brother—"

"Gellir? If he wanted you dead, he'd use a blade, not poison." Her reassurances were less than reassuring. "Besides," she reasoned, "there were two goblets. Who would want to poison *both* of us?"

She sniffed at the bottle, then filled his goblet with the rest of the wine. A sprig of something fell out.

"What's that?" he asked.

She pinched it between her thumb and finger to examine it closely.

"Rosemary." She took a sip from the goblet. "And honey." Her sigh was like a breath of frost. "Isabel."

Why sweet Isabel would want them dead, Colban couldn't fathom. And as far as he knew, rosemary and honey couldn't kill a person. "'Tisn't poison."

"Nay."

"Then what is it?"

"'Tis a potion."

"A potion?" His brows shot up. "What kind o' potion?"

She muttered under her breath, "A love potion."

Colban coughed. Or laughed. He wasn't sure which. While he was deciding whether that was amusing or mortifying, a young voice floated up from outside the window.

"Colban!"

He and Hallie exchanged frowns.

"Colban!" the cry came again. It sounded like Ian. The lad must have gulped down his dinner. "Come quick!"

Hallie rounded on Colban with a chilling glare. "Did you put him up to something?"

"What?"

"Did you tell Ian to help you flee out the window?"

The idea was absurd. "Why would I—"

"Because if you endangered my brother in an attempt to flee..."

"I don't intend to flee."

"Don't be ridiculous. Of course you intend to flee. Why wouldn't you?"

"Colban!" Ian called insistently. "Come to the window!"

"If I wanted to flee," he told her, "I certainly wouldn't do it in the broad light o' day. And not with a wee lad yellin' loud enough to alert the whole keep."

She bit the corner of her lip. Surely she could see he was right. But then her eyes narrowed to dubious slits. "Still, you don't deny you'll try to flee."

"I *do* deny it," he said. "If I wanted to flee, I'd have done so by now."

She scoffed at him. Clearly she didn't believe him capable. And that chafed at his pride.

Nonetheless, he told her calmly, "Hear me well, m'lady. I want peace as much as ye do." He had no wish to see how Morgan's diminished forces would fare against the knights of Rivenloch.

"Why should I believe you?"

Bloody hell. There had been several times he could have seized the advantage. As secure as she thought this bedchamber was, he'd already glimpsed numerous avenues of escape.

He could have taken a hostage—Ian or that woman who'd seen to his hurts.

He could have tricked Rauve out of his weapon.

He could have convinced lovesick Isabel to help him flee.

It was only honor and reason that kept him prisoner here. Did she not know that?

"Ye still don't trust me?" he asked.

"Give me one good reason to trust you."

His mouth fell open. He'd saved the ungrateful lass from a pack of wolves. Yet she had the audacity to question him?

The cool, superior, irritating shimmer of doubt in her eyes pushed him over the edge. Trust him? He'd give her reason to trust him.

Without warning, he used his left hand to upend the platter, spilling its contents off the end of the bed with a crash.

While she gasped in surprise, he snatched the wine bottle from her with his right hand.

Wrapping the fingers of his left hand around her neck, he shoved her down onto the bed. Then he broke the bottle against the bedpost, holding the jagged edge against her throat.

"Now do ye trust me? Ye see, if I actually wished to escape, I could do it in the wink of an—" He strangled on the last word as he suddenly felt her fist clench like an iron vise around his ballocks.

CHAPTER 11

hallie had acted on instinct. He'd moved so fast, she'd had no time to think. But she'd been trained in defense from the time she was a wee lass. Even without a weapon, she was never defenseless.

Her action had its intended effect.

His eyes were no longer drilling into hers with triumph and dark threat.

He stiffened. His gaze widened. He gulped.

"Checkmate," she whispered.

At an impasse, neither of them dared move for fear of inflicting damage. Their breathing was shallow as their eyes locked, each waiting for the other to flinch.

But they were evenly matched. Equally vulnerable. And while they engaged in that close and silent battle, something began to change.

Hallie grew painfully aware of just where her hand was nestled. And as the taut moment dragged on, her intimate assault began doing curious things to his eyes...and her senses.

Smoldering within his tense stare was a glimmer of desire. A spark of lust. A flame of longing.

Her nostrils flared. No one had ever looked at her with such fire. For a lingering moment, she felt his heated gaze penetrate her icy shell, thawing her bones. Melting her heart. Touching her in her most secret places.

It was foreign and frightening.

And for one terrible instant, she feared she might succumb to the flames. Sink into the dangerous depths of his eyes. Maybe even surrender to the powerful urge to press her lips to his warm and tempting mouth.

And then Ian cried out again, breaking the fragile thread of desire.

"Colban!"

Slowly, carefully, Colban removed the shard from her throat and tossed it aside. Just as cautiously, she released his ballocks.

When they had both retreated to their respective sides, he mumbled, "I don't think that love potion is workin'."

Hallie wasn't so sure. She had the pounding heart and trembling limbs to prove it. And she blushed to think where she'd just been touching him.

But Colban *had* made his point. Though thus far he'd been polite and obliging, there was a serious and deadly side to him. He could be ruthless, clever, and capable when he had to be.

If he was civil, it was because he'd *chosen* to be civil.

She could trust him.

"Col! Ban!" Ian's voice was thin with frustration.

Still shaken from their encounter, Hallie crossed her arms defensively and nodded toward the window. "Go on. See what he wants ere he summons the whole clan."

Colban nodded. But he seemed likewise uneasy as he picked his way around remnants of spilled food to the window.

He peered down. "What is it, lad?"

"Watch!" Ian called up.

Her little brother was always hungry for an audience. Whether it was to see his inventions or listen to his theories, to examine his drawings or hear his verse, Ian loved nothing better than a new set of eyes and ears with whom to share his work. Particularly since he'd exhausted nearly everyone in the clan.

She supposed there was no way to prevent Ian from fraternizing with the prisoner. But she'd at least make sure it was only at a distance, where Colban could do him no harm.

She didn't worry the Highlander would hurt the lad now. He'd proved he was a man of his word. She believed his vow that he'd bring no harm to her clan.

But there were other ways to manipulate one's enemy.

Without even trying, he'd already found his way into Isabel's heart and the hearts of several young swooning lasses. He'd befriended Ian with a game of chess. He'd convinced old Burunild, who'd treated his hurts, that he was in need of motherly affection. Brand and Gellir spoke with awe about the man's claymore.

The prisoner wasn't going to insinuate himself into the Rivenloch clan. Not on her watch. Not while her parents were away. And her cousins were in danger.

Hallie set about collecting the shards of the wine bottle. She might trust Colban now. But fate, like the wolves in the wood, had a way of turning on a person, biting at the most unexpected times.

Colban called down to Ian, "That's very...impressive. Did ye build it yourself?"

Ian was probably showing off his latest project. A waterwheel propelled by buckets that filled and emptied with water.

"Are ye certain 'tis safe?" Colban asked.

Safe? Of course it was safe, Hallie thought. What could be unsafe about a wee toy waterwheel?

She picked up a shard shaped like a tiny dagger and placed it on the platter.

"Aye," Ian replied. "I've taken precautions this time."

Hallie froze. Precautions? *This* time? What was Ian showing him?

"I'm using a leather ball," Ian called out.

"I see."

"Last time I used a rock," Ian said proudly, "and it made a dent in Rauve's helm."

Hallie gasped.

Not the trebuchet.

She dropped the platter and rushed to the window, pushing Colban aside.

"Ian Cameliard of Rivenloch!" she bellowed. "Don't you dare—"

She was an instant too late. The lad had already loaded the sling of the wooden siege engine with a missile and raised the counterweight. As Hallie reached the window, the cord twanged, dropping the weight and releasing the arm.

Colban had heard of trebuchets. But he'd never seen one in action. Though the device was only about the size of a wheelbarrow instead of the building-high behemoths used in warfare, its force was undeniable.

Flung from the jointed arm, the apple-sized leather ball shot forward at great speed. It scattered a flock of hens in its wake, ruffled the skirts of a passing maidservant, and hit Ian's older brother, who just happened to be crossing the courtyard, catching him hard in the belly and bowling him over.

Hallie gasped as Brand fell to the ground, laid low by the leather ball.

"Sorry, Brand!" Ian cried out.

Brand groaned, clutching his belly. Gellir, the oldest, ran to his brother, dropping to one knee to make sure he was unharmed.

"Ian," Hallie ground out, "what did our da say?"

Ian lowered his head and dug his toe into the soil. "Not to fire the trebuchet in the courtyard."

"And what did he say would happen if you did?"

"Nay, Hallie," the lad protested, "Please don't destroy it. I was only showing it to Colban."

"The *hostage*," she corrected, "has no interest in such playthings."

Colban would beg to differ. A siege engine that could fire missiles with such speed and force was of great interest.

"Besides," Gellir called out, casting a dark glance at Colban, "you're revealing a secret weapon to the enemy."

"Nay, I'm not," Ian argued. "'Tis a...a show of force. Now that he's seen our might," he reasoned, "his army won't dare to attack Rivenloch."

It was brilliant—and somewhat true. Colban stifled a smile of admiration. The lad was apparently as inventive with his excuses as he was with his devices.

"Put it away, Ian," Hallie commanded. "Brand, will you live?"

Brand sat up with the aid of his brother. He was clearly in pain. But seeing Colban watching him, he snorted once, and labored to his feet.

"I'm fine," he insisted, demonstrating his own show of force despite the strain in his voice. "No toy siege engine will lay me low."

Gellir tried to loop his brother's arm over his shoulder. But Brand batted away his help, limping bravely across the courtyard under his own power.

Meanwhile, it was a brooding and disappointed Ian who rolled the trebuchet back to the armory.

Colban stole a sidelong glance at Hallie. For an instant, he glimpsed the weight of duty reflected in her face.

"They must be a handful," he murmured in sympathy.

Then her mask of icy indifference returned. "I can handle them."

He had no doubt of that. His ballocks still throbbed from her handling of *him*.

"Ye won't destroy his toy, though?" he prodded. "'Tis impressive." He let the shine of humor creep into his eyes. "If ye can reload it fast enough, ye could lay low an entire army. One by one. In a day or so."

There was a subtle, reluctant twitch of amusement in Hallie's lips. But it vanished when a knock sounded at the door.

Before Hallie could give her permission to enter, Isabel rushed in.

"Did you finish dinner?" the lass eagerly asked.

Then her gaze lowered to the floor, littered with greens, overturned trenchers, and smashed apple coffyns.

She gasped, and her brow furrowed. "What happened?"

"You," Hallie accused, starting toward the lass. Isabel inched backward in retreat. She might have fled. But Hallie closed the door behind her, sealing her escape and cornering her. "What did you put in the wine?"

"N-nothing."

"Isabel?"

She bit her lip and glanced nervously at Colban. "I only...flavored it a wee bit."

"Flavored it. With rosemary and honey?"

"Fine," Isabel admitted. "'Twas a love potion. But 'twas perfectly harmless. Besides, you needed something to smooth o'er your...hostilities."

"Smooth o'er..." Hallie said in disbelief. "There's a reason to be hostile. The Highlander is a hostage. A foe. A usurper."

Colban took issue with the last term. Creagor rightfully belonged to the mac Girics. "Now just a moment. I'm not a usur—"

"You have no right to stick your nose into my affairs, Isabel," Hallie scolded.

Isabel thrust out her chin. "I do when you're too blind to see what's right in front of you, Hallie."

"And what's that?"

They stood nose-to-nose now, and Isabel gave Colban one quick glance before she whispered, "He *is* The One."

"Oh, for the love of—"

"I know you don't want to hear it, but 'tis the truth."

"Go, Isabel," Hallie said, opening the door.

"You'll see," she promised. Then she turned to Colban with a sympathetic smile, fluttering her fingers and her eyelashes. "Farewell."

Hallie closed the door on her conniving sister. Then she busied herself, cleaning up the mess on the floor.

She'd never been so humiliated.

Keeping a hostage required a firm hand. A show of strength. The capacity for violence and the willingness to use it.

In the space of half a day, her unruly siblings had completely undermined her authority.

How would she maintain the Highlander's respect when she couldn't even control her own clan?

"Let me help," he offered, hunkering down beside her. "I made the mess. I should clean it up."

She sighed in spite of herself. Now he was offering to do her a kindness? For a savage from the Highlands, he was certainly well-mannered, more so than her own family.

She nodded. Together they made quick work of the scattered dinner.

All was going well until they reached for the same overturned goblet.

Their contact was brief. But in that instant, with his hand enveloping hers, she felt the gentle warmth of his flesh. The potent strength of his grip. The calluses of a man seasoned in battle. A determined man who'd battled his way up through the ranks.

In that fleeting moment, she realized he was the most dangerous foe she'd ever met.

Not because of his size. He was no bigger than some of the clansmen she'd handily tossed to the ground.

Not because of his strength. Strength was a double-edged weapon she could turn on a man in the blink of an eye.

Not because he was clever. Hallie was clever. Growing up in a warrior clan, she'd learned, while men could not always be overpowered, they could usually be outwitted.

Nay, he was dangerous because he was persistent.

The bruises marring his face? The pain in the depth of his eyes? The rough calluses lining his palms?

They were proof of unflagging determination. This foundling Highlander was seasoned by struggle. He'd had to fight for everything he possessed.

She could see that now.

Born a bastard, abandoned as an orphan, he must have fought to earn his place with a respected clan. He must have battled long and hard to become the laird's trusted right hand man. Worthiness couldn't have come easy for him.

Colban an Curaidh wasn't dangerous because he'd been given the title of The Champion.

He was dangerous because he'd earned it.

CHAPTER 12

Colban was beginning to wonder if there was something to that love potion.

With their fingers tangling awkwardly on the goblet, an invisible current coursed between them. Powerful as lightning, it stirred his skin and heightened his senses, as if it might strike at any moment to fill him with sparks and lay him low.

And the expression on Hallie's face—her look of breathless wonder—quickened his heartbeat and heated his blood.

Besotted by an intoxicating blend of desire and awe, he was reluctant to let go of her.

Only when their gazes collided over the goblet, when the soft melt of her eyes frosted over, did he finally release her.

It was probably his imagination anyway. A beautiful Valkyrie of noble bloodlines couldn't possibly be attracted to a baseborn Highland soldier.

And he couldn't possibly be the least bit interested in a maid who'd taken him captive, threatened to maim him, and was more than willing to sacrifice him as a pawn. Could he?

Before he could think about it too deeply, Hallie finished cleaning up the mess, muttered a hasty farewell, and left.

One thing he knew for certain. Contrary to what her little sister believed, Hallie of Rivenloch did not have a heart of ice. Within a thin and frosty shell beat a vibrant pulse of deep passion and great tenderness. One need only crack the shell to reveal the warmhearted woman within.

Armed with this new knowledge about his captor's vulnerability, Colban was left with an uncomfortable choice. A decision that troubled his heart and nagged at his conscience.

Should he continue to bide his time, remain civil, and wait to hear from Morgan, trusting the king's promise was reliable?

Or should he exploit Hallie's weakness and worm his way into her heart, knowing he might need to turn on her to protect Morgan's claim?

His instincts were for compassion.

But the sense of duty to his clan was strong in him.

Did he have the fortitude to do what must be done, in spite of the emotional damage it might inflict?

He ambled to the window, gazing to the courtyard below.

At one end stood the quartet of young lasses with Isabel. As he appeared, they gasped and giggled, shyly waving his way.

Against the opposite wall leaned Gellir, sharpening his sword with a whetstone and glaring up at him.

It was exactly how Colban felt, imprisoned by honor and caught between love and war.

After a short while, he tired of both the admiring glances and the stare full of hate. Restless, he backed away from the window.

In the rugged Highlands, Colban always had something to do. Cattle to herd. Fish to catch. Walls to repair. Sheep to shear. Game to hunt. Cloaks to mend. The line between subsistence and death was narrow. Survival required vigilance and hard work.

Of course, no matter how hard he worked, Colban would always owe the Giric clan a great debt. They had taken Colban into their fold, despite the shameful and unfortunate circumstances of his birth. Laird Giric and Lady Hilaire had allowed him to be raised alongside their own son. He owed them a debt he could never repay. He owed his life to Morgan and his clan. He never forgot that.

Living with that knowledge, however, meant he'd never experienced a time of leisure. A time when debt and duty weren't foremost in his mind.

Every decision he came to hinged upon its effect on the clan.

Every choice he made was weighed by whether it would be good or bad for Morgan.

And lately, while Morgan languished over the loss of his wife, Colban had had to step into the role of the laird himself in order to protect Morgan from his own grief.

With such responsibility came great rewards. But sometimes it was exhausting to devote oneself to the service of others. He'd seen that in Morgan, and he felt it in his own life as well.

Sometimes, especially considering his humble beginnings, Colban felt overwhelmed by the sheer magnitude of his duties.

And sometimes he wondered if he'd lost his own identity somewhere along the way.

Was it thus for Hallie as well? Did the burden of responsibility sit heavy upon her shoulders? Had she given away so much of herself to the clan that she didn't remember who she was?

That would explain the targe of ice around her heart. The protective layer that kept her from acknowledging her own emotions when the clan needed her to be strong.

But he knew her icy heart was penetrable. He'd glimpsed an undeniable tenderness in her. In her affection for Ian.

In her sisterly frustration with Isabel. In her concern for Brand. And her understanding of Gellir.

It seemed all virtuous people in a position of power, whether it was the king, a laird, or the laird's right hand man, must deny their own desires for the good of the whole. Whether it was right. Or fair.

He scraped a chair across the floor to sit near the fire.

As he gazed into the flames, he realized a curious irony.

Being held prisoner here was the first time he'd experienced freedom. It was the first time he'd been separated from the Girics. The first time he'd actually considered his own circumstances, needs, and comforts—if even for one brief moment—apart from Morgan.

He took a deep breath, stretched his legs out toward the hearth, and let it out in a long, relieved sigh.

The moment wouldn't last, he knew. Soon he'd learn whose side the king had taken. Soon he'd have to choose whether to undertake careful negotiations or prepare for battle. Soon he'd have to decide whether to betray the Rivenloch clan who'd shown him mercy or the mac Giric clan to whom he owed allegiance.

Soon he'd be called upon to use the shrewd and seasoned workings of his mind. But for now, he would listen to his heart.

Colban woke with the sun. He'd slept atop the bed, wrapping himself in the coverlet. But the Lowland weather was so mild compared to the snowy Highlands that he didn't realize he'd left the shutters open all night nor that the fire had dwindled.

He arose with a stretch, raked back his hair, poked the fire to life, and then stumbled toward the garderobe. On his return, he glanced out to the yard below.

Poor Gellir was still leaning against the courtyard wall.

He must have been there all night, guarding against Colban's escape. His locked legs were holding him upright. But he was fast asleep. His sword hung limp in his hand. His head lolled upon his shoulder. And his mouth was open wide enough to accommodate a sparrow's nest.

Colban wasn't the only one to spy Gellir, asleep on the watch. Brand, recovered from the trebuchet mishap, was stealing up on his slumbering sibling. Crouching before him, he slipped his hands around Gellir's heels. Then, with a mischievous jerk, he pulled the lad's legs out from under him.

Gellir landed with a yelp and a thud on his hindquarters, dropping his sword, which sent Brand into maniacal fits of laughter.

Infuriated, Gellir scrambled onto his feet. He lunged toward Brand, wrapping vengeful hands around his brother's neck, choking him off mid-laugh.

But Brand wasn't as helpless as he appeared. He plowed a fist into Gellir's belly. When Gellir folded forward with a grunt, Brand snatched the dagger from his brother's belt.

Gellir clapped his empty sheath. Then, aware of his disadvantage, he released his brother and made a swift retreat. Bending down, he swept up his sword in rage.

Colban stiffened. It looked as if Gellir would lop off Brand's head in the next moment.

"Enough!" came a cry from across the courtyard.

Hallie came striding across the green. But this was a Hallie he hadn't seen before. Clad in chain mail, bearing a blade and shield, she looked like a warrior queen on a mission of vengeance.

As she charged forward, her blue tabard whipped around her like angry ocean currents. She tossed her shield and helm aside, and the sun glinted off her bright hair and her silver blade.

The brothers lowered their weapons.

Colban crossed his arms, leaning a shoulder against the window to watch.

"Gellir was asleep at his post," Brand accused.

Gellir scowled. "I was only...resting my eyes."

"You were snoring," Brand insisted.

Hallie turned on Brand. "So you attacked your brother while he was helpless?"

"What? Nay." Brand straightened defensively. "'Tis like Ma says. In battle, you have to take every advantage that's given you."

Hallie suddenly seized the dagger from him with her free left hand. A quick flick of her wrist sent it point-first into the sod. "Like that?" she asked.

Colban snickered. She was certainly a cocky lass.

His pride bruised, Brand folded his arms and thrust out his stubborn chin.

"And you," she accused, facing Gellir. "You should have summoned a man to relieve you."

"I'm fine," he lied.

"Is that so?" she asked. "Your reflexes are fine?"

He scowled. "They're bloody perfect."

Brand, sensing what was about to happen, scrambled in retreat.

"Come on then," Hallie invited, raising her sword. "Let's see those perfect reflexes of yours."

Colban narrowed his eyes. Gellir wasn't actually going to fight his sister, was he?

The lad might be younger and shorter than Hallie. But he was packed with burgeoning muscle and full of youthful rage. One slip of the lad's impetuous blade could do her serious harm. And she'd cast aside her helm and shield.

Colban clenched his fists on the ledge of the window as they warily circled each other.

Graceful Hallie looked impossibly defenseless against her aggressive brother.

Of course, that hadn't stopped her from subduing Colban last night in the woods. And it wasn't stopping her from challenging Gellir now.

Like a wildcat, she suddenly sprang, taunting him with attacks from all angles. Again and again she thrust and slashed, driving him back as he struggled to keep up his defenses.

Gellir staggered and floundered, barely able to knock her sword aside before the next attack came. After two dozen blows, she'd backed him against the wall.

"Now," she said, "go get some sleep."

Then she made the mistake of lowering her blade and turning away. While her back was turned, enraged Gellir raised his sword to lash out at her.

The breath caught in Colban's throat as he waited for tragedy to unfold.

But Hallie whirled, anticipating his move and intercepting his blade in a grating slide of steel and sparks.

She shoved him away. "Are you sure you want to do this?"

He nodded, and she shook her head, preparing to engage again.

He lunged at her.

She batted away his blade.

Gellir, gripping his hilt in both hands, took a swing at her throat.

She ducked beneath the sword, and it whistled through the air with such force it spun Gellir backwards.

Before he could turn round, she prodded the lad's backside with the point of her sword, hard enough to make him yelp.

Colban could almost feel the waves of rage and humiliation roiling off of Gellir as he stumbled forward.

Brand, who'd been watching them from what he thought a safe distance, chortled with glee.

But the lad's mirth was cut short when Hallie lunged toward him, jabbing his shoulder and proving he wasn't quite out of range.

"What are *you* laughing at?" she asked Brand.

While Brand blinked in surprise and pain, Gellir crowed at his brother in smug approval, "Ha!"

Then, while Hallie was still engaging Brand, Gellir pried the dagger from the ground.

Colban's eyes widened. His heart dropped. His mouth went dry.

Gellir was going to stab his sister in the back.

"Nay!" The word exploded from Colban's lips, drawing all eyes to him.

But the dagger was already in motion.

Time stood still as Colban watched the blade, winking in the dawn's light as it lunged toward Hallie's defenseless body.

His heart stood still as well.

CHAPTER 13

hallie's ability to outguess opponents was her secret weapon. She was always one step ahead in any skirmish. It was how she knew Gellir would come after her while she was entangled with Brand. And how she managed to anticipate the dagger's path toward her back.

If she hadn't, that cursed Highlander's sudden outburst might have thrown off her timing and caused considerable damage.

But she was already in motion. Wheeling reflexively, she swept her sword down to block the dagger, colliding with the blade at exactly the right spot.

Gellir dropped the weapon, shaking his hand from the impact, and glared at the Highlander.

Brand, still clutching his shoulder where Hallie had poked him, gaped up at Colban.

And Hallie turned a frosty glower on the man at the window. "What do you think you're doing?"

Colban seemed taken aback. "What am *I* doin'? What are *ye* doin'? Tryin' to get yourself killed?"

Even her brothers scoffed at that. The notion was ridiculous. Hallie had defeated half the knights of Rivenloch. She could certainly handle Brand and Gellir.

She narrowed her eyes. "Maybe *you're* trying to get me killed."

"What?"

"By distracting me."

"Distractin'?"

"I don't know how they spar in the Highlands," she said. "But at Rivenloch, coming between two fighters is a sure way to get someone killed."

"I wasn't tryin' to get ye killed. Bloody hell, I was tryin' to save ye."

Save her? For an instant, Hallie hesitated, struck by the impossible possibility that Colban the Champion was trying to be *her* champion.

Unfortunately, it was enough of a hesitation to allow her meddlesome sister to burst onto the scene, trailed by her retinue of young lasses, at the worst possible moment. Where Isabel had come from, Hallie couldn't guess. The maid seemed to have a nose for intrigue and ears everywhere.

"Oh, Hallie!" Isabel gushed as she rushed into the courtyard. "Did you hear that?" She turned aside to explain excitedly to her companions, "Sir Colban was trying to save Hallie." At her prompting, the lasses waved shyly up at Colban. "What a noble gesture," she added dreamily, clasping her hands beneath her chin. "So chivalrous and romantic."

"Stay out of this, Isabel," Hallie warned.

"But Hallie, he just admitted he was acting to save your life." She smiled at her companions. "No wonder they call him The Champion." They sighed in agreement.

That was nonsense, wasn't it? After all, he was a bloody Highlander. A usurper. Her enemy.

Yet what other reason could there be?

"You addlepates," Gellir growled at the lasses. "Of *course* he wants to save Hallie's life. He knows if something should happen to *her,* he'd have to deal with *me!*"

"And me!" Brand chimed in.

"You two?" Isabel laughed. "Don't be tomfools."

Gellir sneered, "Who are you calling a tomfool?"

"You, if you think a Highlander is afraid of two half-grown—"

"Half-grown? I'm not half-grown, you fluff-headed flea-brain!"

"How dare you call me that, you...you pinheaded churl!"

"You're nothing but a pack of blathering ronyons!"

"And you're a pair of oafish cumbergrounds!"

"Dimwitted damsels!"

"Loggerheaded lads!"

The two factions continued hurling insults at each other like missiles from a trebuchet. Hallie sighed, knowing she was going to have to end this skirmish ere it turned into full-scale war.

Isabel had just called Gellir a skelpie simpleton when Hallie heard a curious sound intruding upon their battle.

Mirth.

She stole a glance at the Highlander at the window.

He was laughing.

While the fierce campaign raged below, he chuckled at each new insult.

Hallie arched a brow of disapproval. She was trying to rein in the youths' misbehavior, not encourage it. Was he laughing at her expense? Or did he only find their bickering entertaining?

Of course, it *was* entertaining. No one was more creative with insults than her siblings. The education of the children of Rivenloch had been rich and ribald. She supposed to a stranger's ear that wealth of words must be a source of great hilarity.

When Brand called Isabel a fustilugs fopdoodle, Colban burst out with laughter that was so full of delight, Hallie couldn't help but feel the tug of a smile at her own lips.

His laugh was as warm and delicious as honey, pouring out to soften and sweeten the bitter conflict.

It was also contagious. A giggle bubbled up in her own throat as she realized how ridiculous their name-calling had become.

When one of the vexed but less clever maids of Isabel's retinue branded Brand a pricky pudding prick, the ensuing gasps of shock caused an immediate ceasefire.

But when Colban's howls filled the silence, Hallie could no longer hold back. Her peals of laughter joined his, rolling out like church bells.

This naturally earned them the scorn of both factions. Now united in their fury, the lads and lasses turned on them.

"You're in charge, Hallie," Isabel pouted. "You're supposed to be defending us."

"You seem to have matters well in hand," Hallie said, fighting back a giggle as she thought again of that pudding prick remark.

"As for you, hostage," Gellir snarled at Colban. "'Tisn't your affair."

"'Tisn't?" Colban replied with an innocent grin. "Wasn't it me ye were fightin' o'er?"

As her siblings frowned in consternation, Hallie shook her head. "You don't actually remember what you're fighting about, do you?"

No one could answer, which made Colban snicker.

Hallie straightened. "Sheathe your weapons, all of you. Gellir, off to bed. Send Erik to stand guard."

"But I'm not—"

"Isabel, you and your lasses will spend the day mending the lads' stockings."

The lasses erupted in gasps of disgust while Brand grinned.

But Isabel's lips and eyes narrowed with scheming. "Of course. We'd be glad to."

"And don't even think of sewing them shut," Hallie said.

Isabel frowned and sighed. "Fine."

"Brand, you'll write a letter of apology to the lasses."

"What? Ach!" He rolled his eyes. "Sod a cod."

"One *without* profanity. And all of you—"

"M'lady, come quick!" came a cry from across the courtyard.

She whirled. The young lass who tended the doocot, was wringing her hands. "What is it?"

"Ian. He's bothering the doves."

"Again?"

Only a few days before, Ian had absconded with one of the doves, trapping it in the buttery to study its wings. The startled bird had left feathers all over the room and laid an egg under the shelf.

Hallie's shoulders fell. She'd donned her armor, hoping to get started early on the practice field. Now it seemed she'd be delayed.

"Send the lad up here," Colban suddenly suggested. "I'll keep him out o' trouble."

Surely he wasn't serious. Colban may have earned her trust. But no matter how tempting his offer, it was irresponsible to let her brother fraternize with a hostage. Wasn't it?

"We can play chess," he added. "I owe the lad for the drubbin' he gave me yesterday."

Nay, she didn't want the Highlander to think she couldn't handle her own siblings, let alone her own clan. And she absolutely didn't want to give him the chance to pry any more secrets from loose-lipped Ian.

"I have chores for him," she lied.

Colban breathed an invisible sigh of disappointment. He liked the lad. And he'd hoped to glean more information from him.

Following the lively entertainment of the morn, most of the day was deadly dull. After a breakfast of frumenty with raisins, he spent the next hours staring at the rafters, stirring the fire, and standing at the window in the hopes of getting a glimpse of the beautiful Valkyrie. She crossed the courtyard several times, but always in a tabard-flapping hurry.

Gellir's replacement, Erik, standing guard at the courtyard wall, seemed more interested in mining his nose than conversing with a hostage.

Everyone who passed by was on a mission. Herding geese. Transporting goods. Chasing after stray children.

Rivenloch had a busy household. How a single lass managed it all, he didn't know. Even Morgan, with his much smaller clan, relied upon Colban to be his eyes and ears. To serve as an advisor. A protector. A confidant. And a friend in dark times.

Someone like Colban could have helped Hallie. He'd spent his life at the right hand of a laird. He could spot trouble about to happen and was quick to quell it. He was a worthy diplomat who could broker peace before the rumblings of dissidence ever reached the laird's ears. He could sense when the laird was stretched too thin, and he was skilled at taking up the slack.

If only they were allies instead of foes, Colban could have lent a hand to the overworked lass.

Instead, he was reduced to pacing the chamber in frustration and boredom.

Thankfully, Ian's chores didn't keep the lad busy for the entire day. Just after noon, he arrived, rolling a wheelbarrow full of stones across the sod and dumping them into a pile below Colban's window.

"Hist, Ian, what's that?" Colban teased in a loud whisper. "Are ye stackin' stones to help me escape?" He grinned.

Ian took his question seriously. "Nay, we don't have

enough stones. 'Twould probably take three or four days anyway. And Hallie would notice straightaway."

"I see. What do ye have planned then?"

"I'm going to teach you to read."

"Read?" He lifted his brows. "Me? With stones?"

"Hallie won't let me come to your chamber anymore, so 'tis the best I can do. You should be able to see well enough from there."

A smile pulled at the corners of Colban's mouth. Ian might well be the most determined lad he'd ever met.

No one had ever thought to teach Colban to read. The skills required of a laird's right hand man were a strong arm, a loyal heart, and a keen nose for the scent of danger. Reading was a luxury. At least in the Highlands.

Nonetheless, he was bored. He might as well humor the lad.

So he watched as Ian meticulously arranged some of the rocks into a large curve.

"This is a C," Ian said. "You can make it with your hand, like so." He held up his left hand, mimicking the shape by curving his fingers and thumb. "You do it."

Colban obliged him. "Like the wanin' sliver o' the moon."

"Aye! Now watch," Ian said, arranging more rocks beside the curve, into a circle. "This is an O." With a finger, he traced the shape his mouth made as he said the letter.

Colban grinned. "O," he repeated.

"And next..." Ian placed two rows of rocks in angled lines. "L. 'Tis like a leg with a wee foot."

"L."

"C, O, L," Ian told him, making a sweeping motion with his hand. "COL."

A shiver tightened the back of Colban's neck. The same kind of shiver he got when he sensed an impending threat. But this was a frisson of excitement.

"Ye're writin' my name," he said in wonder. He'd never seen it before. "Do the rest," he urged.

He suddenly realized the value of knowing how to write his name. With such knowledge came power. Men wrote their name at the bottom of documents that imparted land and goods and rights. Betrothals could be forged. Cattle could be purchased. Hell, even Morgan's claim to Creagor relied upon the king writing his name on a document.

The wee lad was bestowing upon him a gift of great magnitude, whether he knew it or not.

"B," Ian said, adding in a loud whisper, "which looks like buttocks, aye?"

Colban was going to say breasts. "Aye."

"And this...is an A." Ian cocked his head. "I suppose it resembles a wee cottage."

Colban nodded.

"Lastly..." Ian said, arranging the rocks in a zigzagging line. He scratched at his head. "'Tis an N, but I'm not sure what—"

"'Tis the path o' my claymore when I knock a blade aside." He smiled, mimicking the motion with his sword arm.

"That's it then. C. O. L. B. A. N. COL-BAN. COLBAN."

It seemed simple enough. Moon, mouth, leg, breasts, cottage, claymore. He could remember that.

"I can't bring you a notebook," Ian confided, "but you can practice writing on the hearthstones with ashes from the fire."

"I can." He would. Indeed, it would give him a certain satisfaction to inscribe his name on the hearth of his captors.

"Would you like to see *my* name?" Ian asked.

"Aye."

"'Tis much shorter. Watch."

He picked up the stones of the first four letters of

Colban's name. In the empty spot, he made the shape of a single line, like a man standing alone.

"Ian," the lad said.

Man, cottage, claymore. "Ian," he repeated.

"Oh! And I can show you Brand," he offered.

He took away the first letter. In its place he laid out the pair of breasts again, followed by a shape that looked like a knight holding a targe. After the cottage and the claymore, he placed a final letter.

"That looks like an apple coffyn, doesn't it?" Ian said.

"Aye." It did resemble the round pastry filled with fruit and folded in half. His belly grumbled with hunger at the suggestion.

"B. R. A. N. D. BRAND."

Breasts, targe, cottage, claymore, coffyn.

There was just one other word he wanted to see. A word that might serve him well one day.

"Can you write Hallie?"

"Oh, aye!"

Enthused by Colban's interest, Ian quickly scraped away all of the stones except for the cottage. In front of the cottage, he made a shape like a gate. After the cottage, he placed letters he'd used before—two legs and a man—and added something that resembled the head of a pitchfork.

"H. A. L. L. I. E. HALLIE."

"Hallie," Colban breathed. Gate, cottage, leg, leg, man, pitchfork.

"That's all for now," Ian decided. "I'll show you more later. I've got to take these rocks to the garden."

"My thanks, lad."

"Be sure to practice."

"I will."

His own name he'd scrawl on the Rivenloch's hearth.

Hallie's name he'd sear into his memory.

CHAPTER 14

allie became so busy, she never made it to the practice field.

First there was a squabble in the kitchens when Tommy the turnbrochie fell asleep at his post and burned the roast.

Then she had to assist when one of the hounds began delivering a litter of four pups.

No sooner did she finish with the birth than the maidservant Gillian tripped over a cat on her way to the kitchens, cracking the entire basket of eggs meant to replace the burned roast. The cat lapped up the remains, further enraging the cook.

Next, a sheep slipped into a bog and needed rescuing.

Then she had to scribble out a hasty order for Abygail so the maid could purchase cloth for winter garments before the market closed.

Three coos went missing, likely reived by the neighboring Lachland lads. Hallie sent the Gordon twins off to reive them back.

After shooing Ian out of the doocot, she'd tasked him with transporting stones from the orchard to the herb garden, mostly just to keep him occupied and out of trouble.

But now that it was nearing time for supper, she figured

the lad had come inside. After searching every inch of the keep, from the storerooms to the garderobes, the unthinkable occurred to her.

Against her orders, Ian might have returned to their parents' bedchamber to play chess with the hostage.

She took the stairs two at a time.

Rauve pushed off the door when she arrived. "What is it?"

Her heart in her throat, she asked, "Ian. Did he go in?" She nodded at the door.

"Nay. No one's come in or out since breakfast."

She wasn't convinced. After all, Ian had hidden in the room all day yesterday, unbeknownst to any of them. The lad had a knack for finding his way into all sorts of places he wasn't supposed to be.

"Let me in," she said.

"Are you sure?" Rauve asked. He clearly disapproved of any contact between the hostage and the laird he was assigned to protect.

"Aye."

With a disgruntled scowl, he stepped aside.

When she pushed open the door, the Highlander was hunkered down before the fire with a chunk of coal, looking as guilty as hell. He glanced up, biting his lip, like a lad caught with his hand in the honey jar. When she saw what he'd done, she understood why.

"What do you think you're doing?" she demanded with cold accusation. "Defacing the laird's bedchamber?"

Even as he flushed with guilt, he managed to shrug in defiance. "There's naught else to do."

Behind her, Rauve growled. "I could find him something to—"

"That won't be necessary," she said, closing the door and shutting Rauve out of the conversation before she glided forward. "So what filth have you drawn there?"

She expected a lewd illustration of fornicators or a bawdy depiction of a cock and ballocks. It was the sort of scribbling her brothers loved to leave in the garderobes.

Instead, he'd written his name.

"Colban?" she read.

He blinked in surprise. "Ye can read that?"

"Of course."

The Rivenloch children had all been taught to read. Reading empowered a person. And since Hallie was to inherit the lairdship, it was vital that she be able to understand contracts and documents.

But she realized it was a rare talent for a woman to possess. And the fact that he was staring at her with wonder and admiration secretly pleased her.

"I did it right then?" he asked.

"What?"

"I wrote the letters right?"

She realized his eyes were sparkling, not with amazement over her ability to read, but with pride over his ability to write. Indeed, he seemed so pleased, she decided she wouldn't tell him the L was backwards. But before she could marvel at how a Highland warrior—an orphan and a bastard—could come by such knowledge, he gave her the answer.

"Ian was showin' me a few words."

She lowered her brows and scanned the room. "Ian is here?"

"Nay, just outside."

She brushed past him and went to the window. Sure enough, the lad was in the courtyard, tossing rocks from the grass into the wheelbarrow. But she could clearly see the pattern of the remaining stones on the sod. They made an incriminating H.

"Ian!" she barked. "What are you doing?"

The lad jumped. "What you asked. Taking the stones to the herb garden. I just spilled a few."

"Oh aye? Then what's that?" She nodded to the letter.

"How did that happen?" he marveled. "'Tis a perfect H."

"Ian," she warned, "were you teaching the hostage to read?"

He kicked at the wheel of the wheelbarrow. "Maybe." In his defense, he added, "'Tis so boring to cart stones back and forth, Hallie. Besides, Da says the gift of knowledge is the best gift of all."

Hallie sighed. Ian was bright and well-intentioned, but sometimes his affections were misplaced. "I don't think he meant for you to give gifts to hostages."

"Sorry."

"So what is the H for?"

He hesitated, and then gave her a wide-eyed smile. "Hostage."

Colban coughed.

Ian was a quick thinker. That was certain. But Colban didn't suppose Hallie was going to allow him to continue his lessons.

Sensing she might punish the lad for his efforts, he told her, "'Tis my fault. I was restless. I asked the lad to entertain me."

She arched a fine brow. "You're lucky he didn't entertain you with the trebuchet again. He might have knocked out your teeth."

He chuckled.

Her eyes glimmered in response.

Hallie of Rivenloch was not coldhearted at all. Though why Isabel thought so was understandable. Like a rampaging Valkyrie, Hallie could steel herself to look fierce and full of icy threat.

But behind that shield was a woman of subtle wit and warm humor. A woman who certainly commanded his respect. But also a woman he could grow to like.

He hoped he wouldn't need to betray her.

"You must be hungry," she said. "Supper is on its way. I've no idea what the cook has made. The turnbrochie burned the roast, and the maidservant cracked the basket of eggs meant to replace it. But—"

She was interrupted by a knock on the door.

Rauve called out from the other side. "Supper for the hostage?"

"Come in," she said.

It was Isabel who brought supper, though Colban was more interested in what was on the platter than who was carrying it. He hadn't realized how hungry he'd become. But he did notice the array had been made up for two again.

"I've come to apologize," she told him with a meek bow of her head, "for our shameful behavior this morn. The words you heard were spoken in the heat of battle. I assure you 'tis not our normal manner of speech and—"

Hallie choked over that obvious falsehood, but let her continue.

"And I assure you, 'twill not happen again."

Colban gave her a nod of acceptance. "We'll speak no more of it, aye?" He reached eagerly for the platter.

Hallie grasped his forearm to stop him and narrowed her eyes at her sister. "You didn't *flavor* the wine again, did you?"

Isabel shook her head.

"And are you finished with the lads' stockings?"

"Aye."

"Good," she said, adding pointedly, "You're free to go now."

A twinkle emerged in Isabel's eyes as she whispered to him. "'Twas so brave of you to come to Hallie's rescue."

"Isabel," Hallie warned.

"He did, Hallie. You're just too stubborn to see it."

"Off with you," Hallie ordered, "ere I find more stockings for you to mend."

The lass scurried out the door, sidling past a gray-haired man with his cap in his hands and a worried frown on his face.

"Sorry to trouble you, Hallie," he said, "but the stallion's loose in the lists again."

Hallie gave a last longing look at the platter of food. "Enjoy your supper." Then she followed the man out the door.

Despite his hunger, Colban was sorry to see her go.

Meanwhile, Rauve still stood in the doorway, scratching at his beard and glancing at the supper. The man must be hungry as well. Like Colban, he'd had no relief all day. He supposed it would be rude not to share.

"Come join me," he said. "There's enough for two." To be honest, Colban was hungry enough to finish off both coffyns, the entire trencher of pottage, the two tankards of ale, and the pair of berry-topped custards winking at him from the tray.

Rauve tried and failed to look reluctant. "Perhaps I will," he grumbled. "I'd go down to the great hall to sup, but no one's here to relieve me. And Hallie's got her hands full today."

"So it seems. Come in."

The coffyns were flaky, stuffed with smoky bacon and onions. Thick vegetable pottage filled a pair of trenchers. The tankards brimmed with cool, foamy ale. And the cream-colored custard was drizzled generously with honey and chopped rosemary.

Honey and rosemary. Colban shook his head. It seemed the scheming Isabel had done it again. He wondered if Rauve would fall prey to the lass's love potion.

He didn't. After wolfing down his portion, Rauve smacked his lips, wiped his beard, gave Colban a nod, and returned to his post.

And Colban returned to practicing letters, drawing

them on the hearth with a piece of coal, then wiping them away with the sleeve of his shirt.

The shadows had grown long and his saffron sleeve was black with ash when he heard the sound of swordplay outside his window.

In the courtyard below, by the afternoon light, a well-rested Gellir battled with Brand. This time it was no wild and angry fight, but a controlled practice. The brothers moved slowly, studying each angle of attack, working out new defenses.

He watched them for several moments as they repeated the same movement over and over. Gellir slashed at Brand's head. Brand deflected the blow with his shield. Then Gellir wheeled away, returning to lunge forward with a thrust to Brand's heart.

Each time, Brand had difficulty crossing his shield quickly enough from high on one side to counter the strike on the opposite side.

"Brand," Colban finally called down. "Instead o' blockin' his second thrust head-on with your shield, turn sideways. That way ye can dodge the blow and divert it with your blade."

"What?" Brand asked, squinting up toward the window.

"No one asked you, hostage," Gellir sneered.

Colban shrugged. "Just tryin' to help the lad."

"He doesn't need the help of a Highlander."

"Wait," Brand said. "What did you say?"

"Don't listen to him, Brand," Gellir growled.

"After ye toss away his first blow," Colban said, "turn sideways to him. Use your blade to deflect the second thrust."

"Like this?" Brand lifted his shield high on his left, then turned to his left side, leaving his sword arm behind him.

"Nay, turn the other way, to the *right* side."

"What would you know of real fighting anyway?" Gellir

argued. "You've probably never even *seen* an Englishman."

"True. But unless they're twelve feet tall with horns and claws, I suppose they fight the same as any other men."

"So like this?" Brand asked. After raising his shield, he turned to the right, sweeping his blade before him.

"Aye, exactly. Ye make a smaller target that way, and your blade does the work o' defense."

"Come at me, Gellir," Brand said, facing his brother.

"'Tisn't going to work," Gellir warned.

"Come."

Of course, it *did* work.

Brand was delighted.

Gellir was peeved.

"What else can you show me?" Brand asked.

"Traitor," Gellir accused.

"'Tisn't treason to steal the weapons of the enemy," Brand countered.

Gellir fumed in silence.

Colban took that as a challenge.

"I have another maneuver," he said. "But I doubt ye can do it."

"What is it? I can do it," Brand said. "Let me try."

"I don't know," he said with a dubious grimace, rubbing his chin. "It requires a steady hand and a long reach. Maybe when ye're older..."

"Show me."

Gellir scowled. "Brand, he already said you can't do it."

"I want to try."

Colban shook his head. "Very well. But I'm warnin' ye, take care. Don't hurt yourself."

"I won't."

While Gellir crossed his arms and glowered, Colban talked Brand through the motions.

"First, ye sweep your sword just inches above your foe's head, like so." He demonstrated a leftward slice.

"'Twill make him duck, aye? Then, while ye're spinnin' away with the force o' your sword, ye toss your shield o'er his right shoulder."

"Toss away your shield?" Gellir's voice was thick with sarcasm. "Oh, that's brilliant."

"Aye, and here's the key," Colban said. "While he's distracted by the shield, ye come full circle with your blade, dropping it low to knock his feet out from under him."

Gellir scoffed. "Oh, aye."

"'Tis tricky. Not many can do it," Colban said with a shrug. "But ye can try."

"Come on, Gellir," Brand said. "Come at me."

"This is stupid," Gellir muttered. Still, he unfolded his arms, picked up his shield, and swept up his blade.

Brand extended his weapon as far as he could to graze Gellir's head. But no matter how many times he made the attempt, the angle was too steep. He wasn't tall enough for the maneuver.

"I told you it wouldn't work," Gellir said.

Colban sighed. "Aye, ye're a wee bit too short. Maybe when ye're full-grown..."

"*I'm* full-grown," Gellir snapped. "Come on, Brand. Let me try it."

Colban stifled a smile as Gellir performed the move with carefully measured grace. He swept his blade easily over Brand's head. Cast his shield over the lad's shoulder. And spun round to ostensibly finish him at the ankles.

The defeated Brand was the one to cheer. "Swive a swan! That was brilliant, Gellir. I was fully waylaid by your shield, even when I knew 'twas coming! Do it again!"

Gellir wore an expression of reluctant pride. "Fine."

He repeated the maneuver a dozen times. Each time, his speed increased and his accuracy improved.

"I didn't think ye could do it, Gellir," Colban said. "But ye've got the grace of an assassin. Fluid and deadly."

His praise clearly pleased Gellir, though the lad was determined not to show it.

"So now I have to work out a defense," Brand decided.

"Against that?" Gellir scoffed. "There is no defense."

"I'll find one," Brand said. "Go again. Slowly."

Colban was fascinated by their process. It made sense. Working out a defense should be the natural extension of any new offense developed within the ranks of one's own army. It would better *all* the warriors' skills.

Eventually, Brand *did* find a good defense.

The seventh time Gellir swung around low with his sword, Brand simply jumped over it. The momentum of his unobstructed blade threw Gellir off-balance. Brand gave him a shove with his shield that sent Gellir stumbling backward.

Colban was impressed.

So was Hallie, who arrived in the courtyard just in time to witness the exchange.

"Clever, lads," she decreed. "Did you come up with that yourselves?"

Gellir glanced up at the window. Colban quickly withdrew into the shadows. He'd let the lad take credit.

But before Gellir could reply, Brand boasted, "I came up with the defense."

"Let me try," Hallie said.

Colban arched a brow as he peered out from the darkness. Borrowing Brand's sword and shield, Hallie mimicked Gellir's attack.

Colban had thought Gellir an agile fighter. But Hallie moved with an elegance and economy of motion that was breathtaking to behold. Her arc with the blade was seamless. She tossed off her shield with the ease of a falconer releasing a bird of prey. And when she swept her sword low, it was with such speed that Gellir barely had time to jump up to avoid being cut off at the ankles.

The lad managed to evade injury. But when he looked up toward Colban again, seeking his approval, Colban withdrew entirely from the window.

He told himself he wanted to let the lads bask in their own glory.

But the truth was, watching Hallie was doing something strange to him.

His heart thrummed.

His blood warmed to a simmer.

And there was a definite tightening in his trews that hinted at something more than a thirst for battle.

CHAPTER 15

hallie followed Gellir's gaze to the window. It was empty. Perhaps the lads hoped to impress the Highlander with their fighting skills.

But Colban was probably busy, defacing the plaster walls with the letters Ian had taught him.

She sighed and returned to sparring with her brothers, distracted by troubling thoughts. Though she hated to admit it, *she'd* hoped to impress the Highlander with her fighting skills.

She told herself it was to earn his respect.

No matter the outcome of the siege ahead—whether Rivenloch or mac Giric won Creagor—it would be useful for Colban to witness firsthand the fighting strength of her clan.

If he saw it for himself, he would pass the information along to his laird. Rivenloch's reputation as a force to be reckoned with would stand. And if the king ultimately decreed they should be neighbors, that knowledge would ensure they'd live in peace.

But there was more to it than that.

A part of her wanted to show him who she was. To let him see her—not struggling to run a household or squabbling with her siblings or dragging sheep out of the muck—but at her best, with a sword in her hand and a cold gleam in her eye.

Why she should care what he thought, she didn't know.

After all, if things went well for Rivenloch, he'd hie to the Highlands within a sennight, and she'd never see him again.

And even if they went badly, if mac Giric won Creagor, the silent grudge between the clans would make it unlikely their paths would cross.

So what was this curious connection she felt with Colban an Curaidh? Was it because he was *her* hostage? Was it because they shared a sense of unflinching loyalty? Or the fact they found humor in the same things? Was it admiration for his warrior's body? Appreciation for his honor? Respect for his fighting spirit?

Was he The One?

That sudden thought popping into her head so disturbed her she almost missed the slash Gellir leveled at her thigh. She managed to block it with her shield. But the impact made her stagger in retreat. She landed with a humiliating plop on her hindquarters.

Reflexively, she cast a glance toward the window to see if Colban had seen her. And that filled her with even more self-disgust.

Why should she care what he thought? He was nobody. He was a Highland foe. A hostage. An orphan. A bastard. He certainly wasn't The One. No matter what Isabel said.

Gellir held out a hand to her. But even before he pulled her to her feet, a new responsibility reared its head. The laundress came scurrying across the courtyard toward Hallie with a dispute that needed settling.

It was hours before Hallie finally found time to address the platter of supper left in her bedchamber.

Isabel was already asleep in their bed.

The bacon coffyn was cold. The pottage had hardened into a paste. But the ale was drinkable. And the sweet custard was delicious. She'd slurped up the last of it when she realized it was drenched in rosemary-studded honey.

"Isabel," she said under her breath.

Her little sister was incorrigible.

She was also awake.

She smiled sleepily. "You'll thank me later, Hallie. You'll see."

Hallie didn't believe in love potions. She kept telling herself that, all the way to the armory.

Yet this morn, she was troubled by her unsettling fascination with the Highlander. Thoughts of Colban an Curaidh had consumed her all night. She'd gone to bed, imagining his twinkling eyes. She'd dreamt of his broad shoulders and impressive stature. Her first waking thought had been of his snow-melting smile.

The best way to purge distractions, she'd found, was to engage in swordplay. Nothing required such undivided attention. When one's welfare was at risk—when a stray thought could mean a painful slash, or the loss of a finger, or worse—it was easy to set aside everything but the immediate threat.

Still, as she prepared for combat in the hour before dawn, something was definitely wreaking havoc with her. And she wasn't sure battle was the answer.

Donning her padded cotun, her fingers fumbled with the buckles.

When she snatched her shield from the wall, it slipped out of her grasp and almost rolled away.

As she reached to claim her sword, her gaze was drawn to the Highlander's claymore hanging above it. Distracted, she paused.

The claymore, like the Highlander himself, was formidable. Long and powerful and heavy, its design and heft were magnificent. Like the man, it also had obvious flaws. But it had been well-loved, well cared for.

Nicks marred the steel. But the blade was sharpened to a keen edge.

The maker's marks on the crossguard were long worn away. But the metal was polished to a high sheen.

Pressed into the weathered leather hilt were the impressions of Colban's hands, each finger delineated by a dark indentation.

Blood surged to Hallie's face. She remembered all too well the touch of those warm fingers on hers.

Her thoughts were abruptly scattered as she heard the Rivenloch knights coming to the armory, their raucous laughter echoing along the passage.

As they arrived, she snatched the sword from the wall and made a grab for her helm, intending to shove it down over her head to hide her blush. But in her haste, she knocked the helm to the floor. It clanged loudly enough to turn all their heads.

"Hallie. You all right?" one of them asked. "You're up early."

Mortified, she swept up her shield and tossed her braid over her shoulder with a cool confidence she didn't feel. "Just restless. Eager to leave one of you idle sluggards in the dust."

They laughed at that.

One of the knights nodded toward her weapon. "Are you going to try the claymore then?"

The claymore? In that instant, she suddenly noted the weight of the sword in her grip. The width of the crossguard. The indentations in the hilt from fingers larger than hers.

Shite. Somehow she'd whipped the wrong sword off the wall.

Another knight elbowed the first. "Don't be ridiculous. 'Tis nigh as tall as she is."

"Aye," a third agreed, "and far too heavy for a lass."

She wasn't fooled by their taunts for an instant. They knew she couldn't resist proving them wrong. She might have made a mistake, seizing the Highlander's sword. But she wasn't about to back down now. She gave them a grim smile.

"If that wee mouse of a Highlander can handle it," she boasted, "then 'twill be like a child's dagger in my hands."

The knights guffawed at her cocky claim.

"I'll take that challenge," one of them called out as he thrust his arms into his cotun.

"Me as well," another added, plucking his sword from the wall.

"I wager we'd *all* like to take a crack against a Highland claymore," a third said.

The rest cheered in agreement.

"Fine," she said, wondering if her arm would hold out. Even carrying the thing to march Colban through the woods had tired her shoulder. A claymore was a two-handed weapon, heavy and slow. Hallie was accustomed to fighting with speed, not force.

"I'll meet you on the field," she said, intending to take a few practice swings before she engaged with an opponent.

"The field?" one of the knights scoffed. "I say we show our Highland hostage what Rivenloch knights are made of, right, lads? Let's spar beneath the prisoner's window."

Hallie's brows collided. She'd come to the armory to forget about Colban an Curaidh, not to taunt him.

But already the men were urging her on, their eyes full of eager fire.

She could hardly deny them. Having an enemy to intimidate fueled the knights, spurring them on to fiercer battle. Besides, what would she say? That she didn't want to spar in front of Colban because the idea made her heart flutter?

"Very well," she conceded drily, arching her brow to add,

"but afterward, you'll pick up your own lopped-off limbs from the courtyard."

The men roared with laughter at that.

Despite her levity, Hallie had serious reservations about her decision. After all, what message would that send to Colban?

If she fought well with his weapon, defeating her own men, it would prove the superiority of the Highland claymore over the Lowland longsword.

If she fought poorly, it would mean she didn't deserve her reputation as a fearsome warrior lass, a dangerous foe, an enemy to be feared.

Under the circumstances, Hallie couldn't help but think she was making a tactical error.

Something had stirred Colban from sleep.

He groaned. His head was still foggy with dreams. Rubbing at one eye and stumbling from the bed in naught but his braies, he made his groggy way toward the garderobe.

As he passed the window, the sound of steel on steel made him frown.

Who was crossing swords at this ungodly hour?

Blinking his eyes to try to clear the cobwebs, he opened the shutters and peered out into the dim light before dawn.

On the ground below, he saw the swirl of Hallie's tabard.

His eyes widened.

The lass was confronting a pair of giants. Defending herself with *his* claymore—a two-handed blade that was far too heavy for her. She fell back as the bloody savages attacked her on two fronts.

Then his heart dropped to the pit of his stomach.

Beyond the two brutes, out of the thick morning mist, emerged an entire army of huge, blade-wielding knights.

The castle was under siege.

And Hallie was out there alone.

Colban didn't think. Or blink. Or hesitate.

He stepped up onto the ledge and leaped from the window into the fray with a bellow of fierce challenge.

The drop was longer than he expected. The landing made his bones shudder. But he barely felt the impact. His sole focus was getting Hallie out of danger. He could deal with his own injuries later.

The two giants stood frozen with shock. In that instant, he tore his claymore from Hallie's hands and set her behind him.

"Go!" he commanded.

There was no time to see if she'd obeyed.

Colban clenched his fists around the familiar weapon.

He'd never survive. He knew that. He had no targe, no cotun, no chain mail. Hell, he wasn't even wearing his boots. But maybe he could buy Hallie time to escape.

He blew out a bracing breath. Set his jaw. Then turned to face the pair of towering foes and the massive army behind them.

CHAPTER 16

hallie was too stunned to move.

In one moment she'd been playfully sparring with two of her knights.

In the next, like a dark, avenging angel, wearing naught but his braies, the reckless Highlander had swooped down out of nowhere. He'd reclaimed his weapon from her. Shoved her away like a bothersome pup. And was now taking over her fight.

How dared he?

How *had* he?

The drop from the window had to be ten yards. Only a fool would attempt it.

Yet here he was. He'd landed on his feet. By some miracle, he seemed uninjured. But judging by the fierce look in his eye, he intended to inflict some injuries of his own.

"Come on!" he shouted in invitation, brandishing his claymore.

The two knights accepted his challenge. They charged at him with their swords flashing.

Twisting his shoulders with violent force, Colban blocked the first blade with his own. The second he caught at the hilt, sending it sailing across the courtyard. Then, returning with a hard downward chop at the first sword, he broke the blade in half.

Hallie's mouth dropped open.

Having effectively disarmed both knights in the blink of an eye, the Highlander cast a quick glance over his shoulder.

"Go, Hallie! Run! I'll hold them off!"

Still reeling at how quickly he'd dispatched her knights, she whipped the helm off her head.

Hold them off? What the bloody hell did *that* mean?

The Rivenloch knights seemed just as mystified.

But when Colban charged forward—his brows lowered in grim determination and his claymore raised in challenge—there was naught they could do but respond.

The Rivenloch knights took up their weapons. And Hallie watched, slack-jawed, as the half-naked Highlander swiftly disarmed three more of them.

One sword he wrenched away by brute force with his left hand.

One he destroyed with a powerful hack of his claymore.

And one he removed with a sweep of his blade that stripped the man's gauntlet off as well, sending the sword flying in its grip.

After that, all chaos broke loose.

Like a roiling sea, the Rivenloch knights surged forward in waves. Their chain mail shivered. Their sabatons pounded the sod. Their swords glinted with the cold dawn's light. Sparks and curses and fists flew.

Hallie's heart pounded as awe and dread flooded her veins in equal measure.

Did the brazen hostage think he could take on the whole fighting force of Rivenloch? Surely he realized a company of armored knights could cut his unprotected body into minced meat.

Yet he battled like a raging beast. Lunging and slashing at them with the ferocity of a cornered boar. Desperate. Powerful. Fearless.

Was he mad? Was this some reckless and misguided attempt to escape? Did he honestly believe he could defeat her entire army?

Or was it a mission of suicide? Did he intend to sacrifice himself as a pawn to destroy her leverage against his laird?

Whatever the truth, there was one rule of warfare Hallie knew she dared not break.

Never kill a hostage.

Over the cacophony of scraping steel, clanking armor, grunts of pain, and roars of challenge, she cried in command, "Take him alive!"

The Rivenloch knights instantly tempered their attack. Chivalry and fighting fairly were ingrained in the disciplined warriors. They knew the hostage's worth. They would take him alive.

Colban raged against the surging sea of knights until they completely surrounded him. Until he was able to stay on his feet only by force of will.

It took a dozen men to subdue him. Half of them stole up behind him while the rest pressed him back with a wall of shields. But they finally seized him by the arms. Pried the claymore from his steely fists. And wrestled him to the ground.

Outnumbered, overpowered, and pinned by a dozen sword points, Colban at last had to admit defeat.

His breath came in burning gasps. Hot fear and fury pulsed through his veins. And now he began to feel the throbbing in his ankle where he'd twisted it in his wild leap from the window.

He supposed they'd slay him now. But at least he'd die knowing he'd done his best to give the Valkyrie a fighting chance against the invaders.

He prayed Hallie had listened to him. Fled fast and far.

Hidden in a place they'd never find her.

Squinting against the blinding light of dawn, he spat out one final defiant curse. "Rot in hell, ye sheep-swivin' cowards!"

The rising sun was suddenly eclipsed by a figure towering over him. The leader of the army, no doubt. The one who would deal the killing blow.

In a brazen act of courage, Colban glared boldly at the faceless warrior.

The last thing he expected to hear was a woman's voice. "Are you hurt?"

He frowned.

Hallie. Why was she here?

He'd told her to flee.

If she didn't escape, the knights would...

He narrowed his eyes.

The knights weren't attacking her.

"Are you injured?" she repeated.

Confused, he gave a small shake of his head.

"What the devil are you doing?" she demanded. "Attempting escape? Or trying to get yourself killed?"

Before he could answer, one of the knights replied. "I think he was trying to save *you*, Hallie. From *us*."

The rest of the knights laughed low.

"What?" she said. "Why would he..."

Colban blinked as he slowly realized the truth. These weren't invaders. They were Hallie's own forces. He'd been protecting her against her own men.

But why had they attacked her?

Or had they? Was it possible his blurry eyes and sleep-addled brain had misinterpreted what he'd seen?

If so, they must think him a fool.

"God's wounds, did you see him leap from the window?" one of the knights said in awe.

Another marveled, "'Tis a wonder he can walk."

A third gave a low whistle. "And the way he wielded that claymore..."

"Like a bloody berserker..."

"Broke my blade, he did."

"Mine as well."

"Tore my gauntlet clean off."

"Lucky he didn't tear your *hand* clean off."

"Stop," Hallie said, holding up a hand to silence them before they could dizzy him with their praises. Then she hunkered down beside him, close enough that he could see the sky blue accusation in her eyes. "That isn't true, is it? You weren't trying to come to my...?"

The way she said it—in disbelief—chafed at him. He scowled in silence. Of *course* he'd been trying to come to her rescue. What man with any ballocks would not?

From the back of the company, Brand pushed his way forward. "Why would he come to her rescue? Hallie can handle herself. Besides," he sneered, "when a lass is in trouble, 'tis usually trouble of her own making."

One of the knights gave the lad a chiding smack on the back of his head. "Half-baked whelp."

Another added, "You've got a lot to learn, lad."

A thin cry from a window above interrupted their discourse. It was Isabel.

"Oh Hallie, what have you done?" she lamented, clutching the neck of her night shift and wailing in despair. "You killed him, didn't you? How could you? You've ruined everything!"

"He's not dead, Isabel!" Brand yelled back. "Don't be a chit!" Which earned him another smack.

But Hallie was paying no heed to her siblings. Her frosty gaze thawed as she looked at Colban in wonder.

"You could have been killed," she murmured.

"Aye."

"Why would you risk your life...for a foe?"

He knitted his brows. How could he explain what he didn't understand himself? He hadn't made a decision. It had just happened. He hadn't thought. He'd acted on instinct. He'd seen the beautiful Valkyrie in danger and done what had to be done.

In the end, he shrugged. "They don't call me 'an Curaidh' for naught, I guess."

The knights chuckled.

But Hallie was too lost in thought to find humor in his remark. She stared at him as if he were a knot she needed to untangle.

Normally Colban appreciated the attentions of a beautiful woman. Hallie's gaze was sweeping over him like a caress, touching his snarled hair, his stubbled jaw, his heaving chest.

But her intense scrutiny was unsettling. Particularly now. His blood was still hot from battle. They were surrounded by her clan. And he suddenly realized he was clad in naught but his linen braies.

Finally she showed him mercy.

"Let him up."

The knights withdrew their swords. She held out a hand to help him to his feet.

Manly pride made him turn down her gesture. He wasn't about to be coddled by a woman he outweighed by half. He might be vanquished by her knights. But he could damn well rise and stand on his own two feet.

He rocked forward and made the attempt. But as he stood, a searing bolt of pain shot up his left leg. He hissed, shifting his weight to favor his right leg.

Hallie seized his elbow to give him balance. "You *are* hurt."

One of the knights remarked, "He's lucky he didn't break his neck in the fall."

Gellir, who'd apparently just arrived in the courtyard, said, "What? What fall? What happened?"

"'Twas no fall," Isabel called down, adding in a sigh, "The Highlander leaped from the window to save Hallie."

"The window? *That* window?" Gellir asked, nodding toward the laird's bedchamber. "Impossible. 'Tis nigh thirty feet."

"Thirty-two feet, eight inches," said young Ian, trailing behind him.

Isabel sighed again. "A mere trifle for a hero."

Brand gushed, "He took on the whole of the Rivenloch army, Gellir. You should have seen him."

As the knights recounted the details, speaking in glowing terms, Colban became more and more discomfited by all the attention.

He was no hero. He was a fool. A misguided fool who had leaped before he looked. Humiliated himself in front of all of Rivenloch. And gained naught for his efforts but a twisted ankle.

"Is it broken?" Hallie murmured.

"Nay," he said with a grimace, "just wrenched, I think."

"'Twas a mad thing to do," she muttered. But there was a curious tenderness in her gaze. As if she was moved by his gesture.

And then he said something undeniably mad. "Maybe. But I'd do it again."

She glanced up in touched surprise.

Before he could regret his reckless words, Gellir came forward and ducked under his arm. "I'll take him upstairs."

Hallie nodded.

Ian said, "And I'll fetch Burunild to see to his injuries." He screwed up his young forehead. "'Tis likely just a sprain. 'Twill need a cool compress and wrapping to hold it in place."

An hour later, Burunild crouched before Colban as he sat in the bedchamber chair, carefully tying off the cloth brace around his ankle. He still wasn't dressed. As soon as she was finished, he intended to remedy that.

But before he could even throw on his leine, Hallie breezed into the room. Her gaze lowered to his bare chest. A faint, becoming blush rose in her cheeks. She averted her eyes and addressed the healer.

"How bad is it?"

"Not bad," Burunild proclaimed. "A wee bit of rest, and he should be fine." The maid winked at Colban. "No playing champion for a few days, aye?"

He gave her a sheepish smile.

"Good." Hallie awkwardly cleared her throat. Then she ambled past, absentmindedly picking up his leine from the bed. She creased it between her fingers as she crossed to the window.

Meanwhile, Burunild gathered her things and bid them both farewell.

Once they were alone, Colban turned his attention toward Hallie, who gazed out through the shutters, biting her lip in restless silence. With the sun gilding her hair and illuminating her face, she looked more like an angel than a Valkyrie. She was beautiful. Breathtaking. Arousing.

How could he regret leaping from a window to save such a prize?

Of course, she wasn't *his* prize. But it was hard to convince the beast betwixt his thighs that she wasn't here for his pleasure. And that was becoming more painfully apparent with each passing moment.

Still avoiding his gaze, Hallie peered down over the window ledge. She shook her head, murmuring, "That fall could have killed you, you know."

"'Twasn't a fall," Colban reflexively corrected. He'd made a reckless choice in leaping from such a great height. But he hadn't fallen. He wasn't clumsy.

"Right."

Meanwhile, his eyes were on his leine, which he was beginning to need with a quiet sort of desperation. At the moment, her fists were clenched in it, twisting wrinkles into the linen.

When she finally faced him, she seemed to have forgotten his state of undress. Her eyes flared with a quick intake of breath.

"You should get dressed," she muttered in distress.

"I would, but..." He gestured toward his leine.

She looked at the garment in her hands as if she had no idea how it had come to be there. "Oh!"

She thrust it toward him. When he reached for it, their fingers met. She recoiled as if she'd been burned.

He slipped the leine over his head and tugged it down over his lap, grateful to cover the rapid appearance of desire.

She cleared her throat. Then she picked up a poker and jabbed at the fire, which was already crackling with cheery flames. A curious conflict warred in her eyes. Something between worry and irritation.

Finally she replaced the poker. Faced him. Crossed her arms. Raised her chin.

"Listen," she said with uneasy authority. "You must cease leaping from windows and...and fighting off wolves on my behalf. I command it."

He almost laughed at that. She might as well command him to cease breathing.

But she was serious.

He lowered his brows and fought back a grin. "Is that so?"

"Aye."

He mused over that, rubbing his chin. "And why exactly?"

Hallie blinked.

Why. She'd been asking herself that ever since he'd faced off against the beasts in the woods.

Why would he want to help his enemy? Why should he care what happened to her? And why should he so cheaply value his own life?

The conclusion niggling at the back of her mind was—as Isabel kept insisting—the Highlander had affections toward her.

The idea was ludicrous. Preposterous. Inconceivable.

Yet her heart fluttered at the thought.

What other reason could there be?

No one defended Hallidis of Rivenloch. Her little brother was right. She wasn't the sort of woman who needed defending. Trained as a warrior, destined to be laird, she'd been taught to be self-sufficient.

She had to be as strong as any man. Thus no man had ever tried to be her champion.

Now, for the first time in her life, a stranger sought to protect her, not because it was his duty as a member of the clan, but purely because he didn't want her to get hurt.

She was touched. Flattered.

She was also troubled.

First, because it was a dangerous mistake to trust a captive, whose prime objective was always to escape.

And second, because this foolhardy hostage with his misplaced heroics was beginning to tunnel his way into her heart. Even now she could feel him sapping her supports and undermining her resistance.

Her eyes melted when she looked at him. Her breath softened when they spoke. Her pulse quickened when he was near. And if they happened to touch, the brush of his skin awakened her senses in a curious and enticing way.

Clearly, allowing anyone that kind of power over her mind and body could prove deadly. No matter how pleasant and intriguing and welcome his attentions felt.

Besides, Hallie had no right to feel affection for a man. Any man. She was well aware of that. She was the heir to the title of Rivenloch, with all the responsibility that came with that. Her heart was not her own to give. Her hand was a matter of strategic alliance. Her clan and her inheritance were a royal gift to be bestowed upon whomever the king chose.

So how could she answer him?

Why should Colban the Champion refrain from being *her* champion? Why should he stop risking his life for her?

In the end, she gave him an answer that was technically true. A brusque, honest, chilling answer. Even if it wasn't the answer in her heart.

"Because you're no use to me dead."

CHAPTER 17

The Valkyrie's words felt like a blunt knife shoved between Colban's ribs.

For a stunned instant, all he could say was, "I see."

A stony silence fell as his hurt slowly coiled into anger.

Damn it, twice now he'd been willing to forfeit his life for the lass. Even her men were impressed by his deeds.

True, this time his judgment had been faulty and his rescue misguided. But his sacrifice had been genuine.

Was this how she repaid him? With cool indifference and callous rejection?

Maybe Isabel was right. Maybe Hallie was too cold and unfeeling for her own good.

Bitterness compelled him to remind her of the cost of his actions. Indicating his injury, he said with heavy sarcasm, "Then I must apologize for damagin' your goods and decreasin' my value."

It gave him some satisfaction to see her color at his remark. Then she breezed past, muttering, "Breakfast will be up soon."

When she closed the door behind her, he was left with an ache in his gut. An empty place that no amount of frumenty was going to fill.

For a brief moment, he'd felt *something* burning between them. A spark of life. An ember of affection. A flame of lust.

For an instant, he'd forgotten they were foes. He'd seen her as a capable warrior. A brilliant commander. A clever lass. An alluring woman.

Just as he'd let his instincts guide him in defending her, he'd allowed his heart to lead him in desiring her.

But his instincts had been wrong. It appeared his heart was as well. And he was paying the price of his miscalculation with a throbbing ankle and a hollow chest.

With a sniff of self-disgust, he pushed up from the chair to test his bandaged limb. Putting weight on it sent a twinge up his leg that made him grimace and sit back down. He supposed he'd limp for a few days. But the pain would remind him never to come to Hallie's rescue again. At least not without a formal invitation.

Her indifference did serve one useful purpose. It made the prospect of betraying her much more palatable.

Battling her knights had already taught Colban a valuable lesson. While his claymore had proved a powerful weapon against Lowland longswords, the pace of fighting was quicker with a lighter blade. The Rivenloch soldiers had been able to spin and dodge, maneuver and infiltrate his defenses while he was still hefting his heavy weapon.

Morgan's forces were unaccustomed to that kind of warfare. Pitted against such an army, they would find their legs cut from beneath them before they could even raise their swords.

Colban had to warn them. He had to train them. He had to study the Lowlanders' fighting style and their weapons and pass that information along to Morgan.

He'd seen Rivenloch's numbers now and witnessed their impressive unity. They were formidable and awe-inspiring.

Not that the men of the mac Giric clan weren't intimidating in their own way. Wild and fierce, they brandished their blades and gnashed their teeth, charging like a herd of galloping beasts. Morgan's warriors could make the enemy soil their braies ere they could engage their weapons, if they dared to stand their ground.

But these Lowlanders fought shoulder to shoulder, battling as a single force. They operated as smoothly as the gears of a gristmill. When one man fell back, another would take his place. Without a word, they sensed when and where to fill gaps in the line, maintaining an unrelenting and impenetrable advance.

If that army attacked Creagor now, the castle would fall. Good mac Giric men would die. And what was left of the clan would be sent hobbling back to the Highlands in disgrace.

Colban couldn't let that happen. He had to learn all he could about Rivenloch. Her defenses. Her weaponry. Her strengths and weaknesses. Which ramparts were unassailable. And where the chinks in her armor were.

He knew just where he could unearth that kind of information.

Hallie's siblings.

Hallie might have turned a cold shoulder to him. But Brand admired him. And Gellir was growing to respect him. They could teach him all about Rivenloch's fighting style and tactics.

Young Ian hungered for Colban's company. Studying that detailed notebook of his would tell Colban all he needed to know about the castle defenses.

As for Isabel, she'd hand him her heart if he asked. It would be child's play, coaxing her to reveal Hallie's vulnerabilities.

Indeed, he'd just begun to consider who he would question first when the lovesick lass knocked at his door.

"Sir Colban? Are you dressed? May I come in?"

"Aye, come in."

She pushed through the door with a platter of food. "I've brought you brea—"

He figured his leine was long enough for decency. Until the lass's eyes dropped immediately to his bare legs—and her platter almost followed.

Perhaps he should have put on his trews before he let her in. These Lowlanders didn't seem to run about bare-legged the way they did in the north.

To close her jaw and break the awkward silence, he donned his trews and nodded toward the platter. "Did Hallie send ye?"

"Nay. I mean, aye!" She closed the door behind her. "She insisted you have a hero's breakfast, since you saved her life and all."

Colban smirked. He didn't believe that for an instant.

The platter was piled high with oatcakes, butter, bacon, bread, frumenty, cheese, sweetmeats, and ale. It appeared the lass had raided the pantry and brought him a feast fit for an army.

He took the tray from her, setting it on his lap. "Hallie agreed to this?"

Isabel nodded, insisting, "She said 'twas the least she could do."

He doubted that. He suspected Hallie would just as soon feed him gruel.

Isabel clasped her hands meekly before her, almost as if in prayer. "I know my sister seems hard and heartless. But I beseech you, don't judge her in haste. You'll see. She's not as unfeeling as she seems."

"Hmm." He buttered half an oatcake and offered it to the lass.

She shook her head. "I've already eaten."

He popped the oatcake into his mouth.

She began to pace, wringing her hands. "'Tis only that Hallie is going to be Laird of Rivenloch one day. She'll have to manage the lands and command the army. So she has to prove her worth. And sometimes that means she has to black an eye. Or break a nose. Or lop off a finger."

Colban nearly choked on the oatcake.

"But I'll tell you a secret," she confided in a murmur, stopping before him. "She's never actually killed a man before."

"That's...comfortin'." Of course, Hallie had already assured him he was no use to her dead. He took a sip of ale.

"And..." She glanced left and right as if she feared someone might be listening. Then she lifted her brows to impart the grave significance of what she whispered. "I don't think she's ever kissed a man either."

Somehow he managed to swallow the ale and keep up a pensive frown.

Isabel seemed to sense his doubt. "I know 'tis hard to believe. But you don't know her like I do."

Here was his opportunity. "So tell me, since ye know her so well. What is this 'not as unfeelin' as she seems' sister o' yours really like?"

Isabel's eyes lit up. She hopped up onto the bed, dangling her legs over the edge and kicking her slippered feet back and forth as she warmed to the subject.

"Hallie is fierce but fair. Above all else, she cares for the clan. She loves and protects all of us. Faithful Sir Rauve who's guarding you. Burunild who dressed your wounds. Bart who laid your fire. Wee Tim who mucks out the stalls every day. John and James, who tend the sheep. The Rivenloch children just learning to crawl. Even the wrinkled white-haired wenches who bicker all day."

Colban chewed thoughtfully at a bite of bacon. Hallie's loyalty to her kin was likely her fatal flaw. It was the reason she'd taken such drastic action—absconding with him—in order to protect her foolish cousins.

"She's generous," Isabel continued. "She's always buying us gifts from the fair. New weapons for Brand and Gellir. Something scholarly for Ian. A trinket for me. Oh!"

Hopping down from the bed, she came close. She reached for the sheath at her hips and whipped out a dagger. For an instant, Colban wondered if she meant to stab him. But she turned the blade in her hand to show him the haft. It was a small eating dagger, and the delicate handle was inlaid with pearl.

"She brought me this last spring. Isn't it beautiful?"

Colban swallowed the bacon as he nodded.

Two thoughts popped into his head as he studied the jeweled crossguard.

One, the lass was entirely too careless. He could easily snatch that dagger from her, leaving her at his mercy.

Two, Hallie must be a woman of wealth to afford such a lavish gift. Was her wealth inherited? Or won off of unfortunate foes?

"And what does she purchase for herself?" he asked.

Isabel furrowed her brows as she put away her dagger. "Not much. Maybe new stockings. Or tallow candles. Once she bought an orange. I don't think she liked it."

He'd heard of oranges, though he'd never tasted one. They came from far away. And foreign merchants seldom traveled to the remote Highlands.

Isabel gave a sharp, startling gasp. "Are you thinking of getting her a gift?" Her eyes brightened. "That's brilliant! She can hardly refuse a gift. And it would surely soften her heart toward you."

Colban's jaw hung open. Was she mad? He had no intention—and little hope—of softening Hallie's heart. But before he could tell her so, Isabel began pacing again, twirling the dagger in her fingers and chattering all the while.

"She has little use for ribbons or jewels. And she's got

plenty of daggers. Ink? Too practical. A bottle of French wine or beeswax candles? Nay, gone too soon. Something lasting, like an ivory comb or a silver chalice..."

Colban's head was spinning. A silver chalice? The lass must think he was made of coin. He had absolutely no intention of buying a gift for his captor. Not only was he certain it would do naught to soften her heart. But he knew the only "gift" she was interested in was the return of her cousins.

"I know!" she suddenly cried. "I know the perfect gift for my sister!"

Before she could reveal her perfect gift, there was another knock on the door, accompanied by an announcement of, "Breakfast!"

Apparently, Rauve was no longer overseeing who came in and out of Colban's room.

Brand didn't wait for an answer, but shouldered his way in. Carrying a platter piled high with fruit tarts, he grinned and kicked the door shut behind him.

His face fell when he saw the tray already on Colban's lap. His brow furrowed when he saw who had brought it.

"Isabel! How did you get in here?"

"I knocked," she said, adding pointedly, "and waited for permission. You can take that food away. I've already brought him breakfast. Shoo."

"Don't shoo me."

Before they could begin bickering, Colban said, "'Tis fine. He can stay. I'll have the tarts for supper." Salvaging Brand's pride would serve Colban well when he wanted information out of the lad.

"Fine," Isabel agreed. Anger smoldered deep in her eyes, but she kept a civil tongue for Colban's sake.

Brand set the platter on the bed. "I brought cherry and apple. I wasn't sure which you preferred."

"I like both," Colban said.

"Aye, right?" Brand enthused. "'Tis like choosing a weapon. Sometimes you like the reach and power of a full blade. And other times you want the speed and flexibility of a dagger."

"What are you jabbering about, Brand?" Isabel said. "'Tis pastry filled with fruit."

"Oh, Dizzy Izzy, you wouldn't understand." Brand smirked knowingly at Colban.

Isabel bristled. "You'd better guard your tongue, Braying Brand."

When her fingers tightened on the dagger, Colban decided to intervene before a full-out battle could ensue.

"I wouldn't mind tryin' one o' those cherry tarts right now."

Brand brushed past Isabel, dangerously close to her bare blade. But he passed unharmed and offered the platter to Colban.

Colban took one of the jewel-red tarts.

"Did ye break your fast yet?" he asked Brand, who was eyeing his bountiful feast. "I have far more than I can eat. Here, have a bit o' bacon and an oatcake."

Colban could feel Isabel's frosty glare from a yard away. She'd brought the food for *him*, not for her pesky brother.

Colban took a bite of the cherry tart and then cooed to her, "Oh, lass, ye must try one o' these. They're like a wee bite o' heaven."

Her feelings somewhat mollified, she put away her dagger and came forward to take a bite of the tart.

She closed her eyes, savoring the sweetness. "Cherry is my favorite," she divulged, licking her lips.

"Which does your sister prefer?" he murmured. "Cherry or apple?"

Brand barked out a laugh. "Hallie? She wolfs down food so fast, I doubt she tastes it."

Isabel jabbed the sharp point of her elbow into Brand's

belly, hard enough to make him cough out crumbs of oatcake.

"Don't be an oaf," she scolded. "'Tis only that she has no time to dawdle over dinner. She's too busy training, protecting your worthless arse."

"Trainin'. Indeed?" Colban interjected, heading off another skirmish. "What weapon does she prefer then?"

Brand straightened proudly. This was something he knew. "Oh, Hallie's weapon of choice is definitely the longsword. She's deft and strong. And none can match her for speed."

"Aye," Isabel admitted, adding carefully, "though she's clever enough to avoid a fight when she can. She's not a violent person by nature."

Brand scoffed at her. "You didn't see her lay the friar out flat when he dared to put a hand on her—"

They were startled by a sudden single pound on the door, as if someone had struck it with a battering ram.

"Stand back from the door!"

"Gellir?" Brand murmured.

Isabel nodded.

"Did you hear me?" Gellir added.

Colban realized the lad must be addressing him. "Aye. I'm well away."

The door opened an inch, and Gellir spoke through the crack. "I've got a dagger at the ready. So don't try anything."

The three of them exchanged puzzled glances.

Colban replied, "I won't. Ye have my word."

Gellir must have used his boot to swing the door open. One hand gripped a small dagger. The other held aloft a platter draped with a napkin. He stopped with a scowl. "What the devil?"

"Don't be an arse, Gellir," Isabel scolded. "Poor Colban can hardly walk. He's not going to wrestle you for that plate of...whatever you've brought."

Gellir closed the door and lowered the dagger. "Why are you here?"

Isabel raised her chin. "Why are *you* here?"

"Even a hostage needs a proper breakfa-..." He glanced at the two trays. "What's that you're feeding him? Tarts?"

Brand took offense. "What's wrong with tarts?"

"He's a man of war. He needs something of more substance than tarts."

Brand countered, "He likes tarts."

"Besides," Isabel chimed in, "he has all this as well." She swept her arm toward the feast she'd brought. "So he doesn't really need more of your..." She narrowed her eyes at his platter. "What *is* that?"

Gellir whipped off the napkin. An enormous slab of glistening meat sat on a flat trencher of bread. "A roast."

"A roast?" Isabel snickered. "A whole roast?"

Gellir's face clouded. "I'll have you know it came at a great price. I had to promise the cook a new cleaver."

To keep the peace, Colban said, "Thank ye for your generosity. Let me sample that roast then, since it came at such a cost."

Gellir wasn't about to let Colban have the dagger. So he cut several slices from the roast himself. Then he offered the platter to Colban.

The siblings all waited with bated breath as he took a bite. The beef was savory and succulent, fattier than the meat of the wild cattle grazed on Highland grasses. He nodded his approval.

"That's a meal for a champion," Gellir boasted.

In truth, it was more like *a dozen* meals for a champion. He hoped the lad didn't expect him to finish off the roast.

"Ye've been very kind," Colban said with gentle diplomacy, adding a wee lie. "In truth, I feared your sister might wish to starve me for my foolishness this morn."

As predicted, all three rushed to her defense.

"Hallie wouldn't do that!" Isabel assured him.

"I wouldn't let her," Brand said.

"Our sister can be firm," Gellir said, "but she's not cruel."

It appeared her siblings were as loyal to her as she was to them. Still, they'd gone behind her back to bring him food.

"There's far too much here for me to eat alone," he said. "I hope ye'll join me and indulge yourselves. Gellir, can ye carve up the rest o' this roast while Brand gives everyone a tart?"

They seated themselves on the edge of the bed, filling their bellies. Before long, their chins were shiny with beef fat and their fingers were sticky with fruit.

"What's going on?" came a wee voice from the open doorway.

Ian had entered so quietly, no one had noticed. In one hand was his ubiquitous notebook. In the other was a long wooden staff.

"Come on in, Ian," Brand called out. "Shut the door."

Mildly annoyed, Isabel asked, "You didn't bring food too, did you?"

"Wait," Gellir scowled. "Did you come here alone?"

"Aye." Ian closed the door. "But I didn't bring food. No one told me to bring food. Were we supposed to?"

"What *did* you bring?" Gellir nodded toward the wooden staff.

Ian hurried forward. "A crutch. 'Tis oak. It should be strong enough to support your weight," he told Colban. "About half a sack, aye?"

Colban had no idea how much he weighed.

Ian handed him the wooden crutch. "Here. Try it. The length is three-quarters of your total height, which I estimate is seventy-four inches. So I set the crossbar at fifty-five and a half inches."

"Ye made this?"

"Aye."

Colban couldn't imagine how the lad could have garnered so much information about him, things he didn't even know himself. Nor how he could have fashioned the crutch so quickly. But his siblings seemed unimpressed. They must be used to Ian's genius.

"I haven't used a crutch before," Colban said.

"Here," Ian offered, setting his notebook on the table. "I'll show you."

He helped Colban to rise.

"Tuck it here, on the opposite side of the injured limb," he instructed, slipping the crutch under Colban's arm. It fit perfectly. "When you walk, instead of stepping on your foot, let the crutch take the weight."

"Like this?" He took a stumbling step forward.

Ian caught his forearm so he wouldn't fall. "Aye, that's it."

With Ian by his side, he made slow progress. When he reached the window, Isabel cheered as if he'd completed a pilgrimage.

"Now you try it alone," Ian encouraged.

Colban limped back with the aid of the crutch, faltering only once and leaning on the table for balance. Ian rushed forward to help, but Colban warned him away with a quick, "I can do it." He took two more steps, then collapsed back into his chair.

Brand and Isabel clapped in congratulations.

Colban grinned. "'Tis amazin'," he told Ian. "This will be o' great aid. Thank ye, Ian."

The lad glowed with pride.

"I'll need more practice," Colban said. "In the meantime, who's hungry?"

A few moments later, Ian was squeezing in between Brand and Isabel, consuming an apple tart. It seemed food was an effective way to silence the lad's ongoing commentary. For a long while, the only sounds in the room were chewing and slurping while Colban practiced limping past the hearth on the crutch.

He wondered how long it would be before he wouldn't require the thing. Before he'd be back in fighting form. Before he'd be well enough to escape to warn Morgan, should the need arise.

He hoped it wouldn't come to that. Glancing up at the four siblings seated in a row on the bed as they licked their fingers and smacked their lips, he couldn't help but smile. They might be on the verge of adulthood, but in some ways they were still as innocent, honest, and trusting as children.

Getting to know them was a double-edged sword, because he was growing to like them. Betraying them would break his heart.

CHAPTER 18

Why the kitchens were so bereft of food this morn, Hallie couldn't understand. The cauldron of frumenty had been scraped clean. There was no bacon. And not a crumb of a fruit tart remained.

Battling Sir Colban must have worked up the knights' appetites, because they'd all but cleaned out the pantry as well. And now she didn't know what to give the Highlander for breakfast.

She supposed she shouldn't be disappointed. After all, most captors forced hostages to subsist on bread and water. Hell, some let them starve. If she wanted to be feared as a fierce Border laird, she had to harden her heart against showing too much mercy.

On the other hand, she had to admit Colban the Champion *had* committed a noble gesture this morn, even if it was misguided. His kindness should be rewarded. And she felt she owed him an apology of sorts for her callous remark about being of no use to her dead. While that was technically true, it had naught to do with her feelings about his worth.

As she headed for the larder to see what she could scrape together, her thoughts were a snarl of confusion.

All her life, Hallie had been drilled on the various

situations that might arise when she was laird of Rivenloch.

She knew the castle protocols for an English attack.

She knew how to settle clan disputes over personal property.

She knew how to hire and dismiss maidservants and turnbrochies.

She knew how to purchase goods. How to rally the knights for battle. How to plan banquets.

She knew what to do about lazy crofters, sickly sheep, and unfaithful wives.

She could handle thieves, beggars, nuns, cattle reivers, harlots, murderers, unexpected guests, and—until very recently—wolves.

But this hostage had broken a link in the perfectly meshed chain mail of her command.

His actions were nothing like she'd been taught to expect.

He had no birthright, yet he possessed the qualities of a noble.

He had no education, yet he had a quick and clever mind.

And he had more honor than common sense.

His unpredictability made him a threat, especially when the first rule of warfare was to know one's enemy.

She sighed. She'd hoped her parents would be home by now. But seeing she was going to have to maintain the role of laird a while longer and possibly deal with the matter of Creagor herself, she needed more information. As unsettling as the task was, she had to find out exactly who Colban an Curaidh was. And how valuable he was to his laird.

Deciding on a stack of oatcakes, a dish of butter, and a cup of ale, she made up a modest platter for the prisoner.

Once his belly was full, she could start her interrogation.

Standing outside the bedchamber, she steeled herself for the encounter, determined not to let the Highlander's kind eyes and silver tongue distract her from the fact he was a hostage and a foe.

She wasn't prepared for what she found when she opened the door.

Seated at the foot of the bed like four hens crowded together on a perch were her siblings. They'd been clucking away like hens as well, until she came in.

"Hallie!" Isabel exclaimed, choking on the apple tart she was holding aloft.

They froze like figures sitting for a painting, all eyes on her. Hallie saw instantly why the pantry was bare. Platters piled high with food were balanced on their laps. Brand was guzzling from a cup. Ian was chewing on a piece of hard cheese. Gellir's cheek bulged with whatever he was eating. They looked as guilty as hell.

Before she could ask them what the devil they were doing and remind them of the definition of fraternizing with the enemy, Colban, standing at the window, came to their defense.

"'Tisn't their fault. They only brought me a bite to eat. They feared ye might decide to starve me." His eyes flattened, and his next words were as jarring as a well-aimed slap in the face. "O' course, I told them ye'd ne'er do such a thing. After all, I'm no use to ye dead, aye?"

Isabel swallowed her bite of tart and let out a nervous giggle, as if he'd made a clever jest. "Would you like to join us? There's enough for everyone."

"I knew you wouldn't starve him, Hallie," Brand assured her. "I just thought you might be too busy to remember to feed him."

"Don't be ridiculous," Isabel chided. "Can't you see she brought him food? 'Tis a whole platter of..." Her face fell in disappointment. "Oatcakes."

Gellir spoke around the food in his mouth. "I'm mostly here to look after the others. And to make sure the hostage doesn't try anything treacherous." He tried to maintain a grim tone. His overstuffed mouth ruined the effect.

"I made him a crutch," Ian proclaimed.

Colban held the wooden staff aloft for her to see.

"Leave. All of you," Hallie said. She'd deal with their insubordination later. Right now she needed to interrogate the prisoner. And she couldn't very well do that with her chatty siblings inserting their opinions every few moments. "And take your feast with you."

They reluctantly slid down from the bed and filed past her to the door.

"Sorry," Brand mumbled.

Gellir frowned. "Sure you don't need extra muscle?"

Hallie shook her head.

"You won't hurt him, will you?" Isabel whispered.

"Only if I have to."

She couldn't bear to look into Isabel's dismayed eyes. She had no intention of hurting Colban. But it would be foolish to admit that.

Ian called back over his shoulder, "If you need any adjustments to the crutch, let me know. I can whittle it down. Or make a pad for the top. Or—"

"Go," Hallie swatted him on the hindquarters as he passed.

After they had filed out, she made a mental note to post Rauve at the door again. Not to keep the hostage in. But to keep everyone else out.

When she'd closed the door on them, Colban told her, "Don't punish them. They meant no harm. They just wanted to keep me company."

But Hallie was no fool. She could guess what he'd been up to. "What did they tell you?"

"What do ye mean?"

She leaned against the table, her arms crossed over her chest. "While they were lavishing you with a feast fit for royalty, what secrets did you pry from their innocent minds?"

Colban blinked in feigned astonishment.

"I don't know what ye're talkin' about."

Damn her cunning. The wily wench had seen right through him. He hadn't pried nearly enough secrets from her siblings in their short time together.

At least Ian had conveniently left his notebook behind. It sat on the table behind her. He hoped she wouldn't notice it.

He shrugged. "We were only woolgatherin'. Ian was explainin' how he made the crutch. Brand and Gellir wanted to hear about the fight, blow by blow. And Isabel was showin' off the pearl-handled dagger ye bought for her." He took a sip of ale from his cup and lifted his brows. "Must have cost a bonnie penny, a dagger like that." Maybe he could pry from her the source of Rivenloch's wealth.

But she ignored his unspoken question. "She knows how to use that dagger. Don't be gulled by my little sister's sweet smile. Cross her, and she'll strike you faster than a snake."

He doubted that. Isabel might have a sharp tongue. But the squeamish lass probably didn't have the stomach to cut the head off a landed trout.

"Brand can be a braggart," she warned him. "So anything he said to you was likely an exaggeration."

Colban smirked. "Ye mean ye don't have an army o' wolves and twelve siege towers?"

Her eyes glittered at his unexpected jest, and she responded in kind. "Oh, aye, those we have," she said drily. "But his accounts of warrior falcons in chain mail are largely exaggerated."

Colban chuckled in surprise. The lass had an unpre-dictable sense of humor. And she wasn't afraid to use it.

"What about Gellir?" he asked.

"Gellir." She narrowed her gaze. "Do you have any brothers, Highlander?"

He narrowed his eyes in return. Why would she ask that? "None that I know about."

"Then you don't know how fierce a brother's love is." She uncrossed her arms to run a finger idly along the edge of the table. "Gellir would die before he'd divulge anything that might endanger his siblings."

Perhaps. But Gellir was young. The youth's misplaced admiration for Colban and his pride in Rivenloch would lead him to reveal useful information without even realizing it.

Colban had already learned much about the Lowlanders' fighting techniques, watching the two lads battle beneath his window.

"But perhaps you do understand," Hallie allowed. "'Tis possible you protect your laird with the same sort of brotherly devotion. You grew up together, aye?"

"Aye." He supposed there was no harm in telling her the truth about that.

"Of course, it would have been clear that he was heir to the title, while you…"

He chafed at the uncomfortable reminder that he was of lesser status and not born into the clan.

Hallie's fingers drifted toward one of the tiny bottles on the table, and she casually picked it up.

Colban stiffened. Her fingers were only inches from Ian's notebook. If she happened to notice it…

She uncorked the vessel, taking a sniff. "You were more like his guardian, protecting him from injury, risking your life for him while you had to fend for yourself."

He bristled at that. "Nay, 'twasn't like that at all.

There was many a time Morgan saved me from harm."

"Indeed?" She corked the bottle again and raised a dubious brow. "He didn't protect you from my cousin."

Her cousin? The one who had come out of nowhere like a bolt of lightning and hurled the wicked steel star into his chest?

Before he could tell her that *nobody* could have protected him from that, she set the bottle down and added, "You could have been killed."

That was true. But it wasn't Morgan's fault.

"And leaving you alone to guard the gate." She clucked her tongue and picked up a second bottle, this one of amber glass. "Why not simply station a pair of fresh men-at-arms there?"

He frowned, wishing he could get her away from the table.

She was right about the gate, of course. The task should have been left to fitter men. Colban had had very little sleep. But guarding the keep had been *his* idea.

"Leaving you to battle the entire Rivenloch army by yourself..." Hallie shook her head in wonder, lifting the bottle to squint at its contents. "And why hasn't he sent anyone to find you?" she mused. "'Tis almost as if he considers you...expendable."

Expendable?

The word jarred him from his self-doubt. Suddenly he saw her ploy. Colban himself had insisted he was a worthless hostage. The clever Valkyrie was trying to trick him into admitting he *was* valuable after all.

Now that he was on to her game, he could make a move of his own.

He straightened and gave her a smoky smile. "I am expendable. And I warned ye about that before. He won't pay a farthing to see me returned, let alone surrender the castle that is his birthright."

Disappointment made a tiny crack in her mask of confidence.

Nonetheless, she continued. "That remains to be seen. How well is your laird connected to the new king? Has he even met him?"

"There have been...correspondences."

"Correspondences. That's all?" She flashed him a cool smile. "Even now my kin are seeking an audience with the king. They're petitioning him and his court for ownership of Creagor."

Bloody hell. Was that true? Had her clan gone to the king in person to usurp Morgan's legacy?

Colban didn't want to think about it. Morgan might not have the status of the Rivenloch clan. But he'd already lost his wife. He didn't deserve to lose his holding as well.

If the outcome turned out to be unfavorable to Morgan, it was up to Colban to find a way to seize the advantage.

His glance fell on the notebook. The castle plans sketched there might help. If he could hide it somewhere until he had a few hours to study them...

"The Rivenloch warriors have guarded the border for centuries," she told him, "conquered many a rival army. The shields of the fallen line the great hall." She set the bottle back down. "I saw no such shields on the walls of Creagor."

In the Highlands, resources were scarce. If you were lucky enough to obtain a shield from your foe, you didn't hang it on the wall. You repainted it and put it to good use. But he wasn't going to brag about thriftiness. Instead, he gave her a cocky grin.

"They wouldn't all fit."

She smirked at his boast. Then she began drumming her fingers on the table, an inch from Ian's notebook.

He had to find a way to lure her away from the precious thing before she discovered and confiscated it.

"Why would a Highlander want to live at Creagor anyway?" she mused. "Wouldn't you rather be among your own kind?"

"My own..."

He tamped down rage at her obvious slight. His own kind indeed. She was poking him. He refused to be goaded into anger. Besides, he could give as well as he got.

"We're not so different, Highlanders and Lowlanders," he said. "We serve the same king, do we not? Ye and I have a sworn duty to protect the innocent. Defend the weak." He shrugged. "Why else do ye think I leaped from the window?"

It took an instant for her to realize he'd just insulted her, calling her weak. Her eyes frosted over like ice crystals. But she too refused to be prodded to anger.

"'Twas a wild and reckless move," she claimed.

"Ye say that as if 'tis a bad thing."

"'Tis bad when one is responsible for keeping the peace at the border." She leaned back against the table, blocking his view of the notebook. "Oh, I'm sure you'd frighten the English with your undisciplined brawling. At first. But they'd return again and again. For that, you need a trained army. A killing machine that operates smoothly and efficiently."

"And Rivenloch has that army?"

"We do."

He hated to admit she was right about their smooth operation. He'd witnessed that himself, battling against them. But there was something she'd overlooked. "So ye're predictable."

"What?"

He limped closer with the aid of the crutch. If he could reach the table, he could tuck the notebook out of sight behind the basin before she noticed it.

"Ye say ye've fought the English for centuries, aye?" he asked.

"Aye."

He sidled up to the table and set his crutch against the wall, resting his fingers on the lip of the basin.

"Then they know your every move," he said. "How ye form your lines for battle. When ye'll advance. When ye'll retreat. They know how ye deploy your archers and at what point ye send in the men-at-arms. They likely even know who your best swordsmen are." He leaned forward to confide, "Rivenloch is...predictable."

While she was reeling from that insight, he pretended to lose his balance. Flinging his arm out for the crutch, he missed and sent it clattering to the floor.

In the moment while her eyes were drawn to the fallen crutch, he slid the basin in front of the notebook, concealing it from view.

It was a matter of reflex for Hallie to lunge for the falling crutch. But even as her fingers closed around the freshly smoothed wood, she realized she'd made a tactical mistake.

Colban had dropped it on purpose. As a distraction.

Like her, he must have spotted Ian's notebook.

Ian never went anywhere without it. It contained all of his notes, sketches, plans. It also contained something that might be of use to a hostage. A detailed map of Rivenloch and an accounting of its defenses.

Had Ian left it behind by accident? Or had Colban had taken it?

Whatever the truth, it was clear Colban meant to keep it.

That was going to be a problem. Colban might not be able to read. But he could find someone who did. And he could study drawings. She couldn't give him access to anything that might compromise the security of Rivenloch.

She'd hoped to surreptitiously slip Ian's notebook into her satchel. If Colban didn't know its value, she wasn't about to alert him to it.

But when she rose to return the crutch, he'd neatly slipped into the space between her and the table, blocking her access.

She could see by the flicker in his dark eyes he knew exactly what he was doing. Which meant the time for mincing words was over.

"Give it to me."

He reached for the crutch. "Give what to ye?"

She pulled the crutch out of his reach. "Hand it over."

"What are ye talkin' about?"

"You know."

He reached out again. She pulled the crutch back again. "I don't know."

"Give it to me," she said, "and I'll give you the crutch."

He lowered his hand and frowned in disbelief. "Ye'd keep a crutch from a lame man?"

She narrowed her eyes. "Only a lame man who's a thief."

"A thief? Me?" His surprise and dismay seemed almost genuine. Almost.

"Stand aside."

"Give me the crutch, and I will."

She cautiously handed him the crutch.

He tucked it under his arm. With a glare of hurt meant to invoke pity, he limped aside.

Her smug victory was cut short when she slid the basin over and found nothing. She scoured the table, beside the basin, among the bottles, behind the ewer, under the table. It was gone.

"What did you do with it?"

"With what?"

"Is it on your person?" She quickly perused him, letting her eyes trace the curve of his shoulders, the expanse of his chest, his cocked hips, his bare calves. Where could he have stashed it?

His eyes narrowed to smoky slits as he opened his arms in invitation. "Would ye like to search me?"

Aye, in fact, she would. But she wasn't about to say so. She'd be a fool to give him that advantage.

She'd never admit it, but she felt a strange, inexplicable current when the Highlander drew near. A curious force that threw her off-kilter and made her feel dangerously vulnerable. Standing this close, she could feel the heat shimmering off his skin and sense the harnessed power of his muscles. His musky, masculine scent dizzied her. And when he gazed at her like that—his warm brown eyes smoldering like coals and dancing like sparks...

Aye, she'd like to search him. She'd like to tear his clothing from him and explore every inch.

But she had to ignore that urge.

Before all else, she was a warrior.

He had something of hers. And she needed it. Now. Before she fell prey to his lusty distractions.

CHAPTER 19

Colban figured he had Hallie at a disadvantage now. He'd slipped the notebook into the back of his trews. It was lodged against the small of his back. As long as he didn't turn his back on her, she'd never find it.

He could see the frustration in her eyes. She knew he had the book. She *did* want to search him.

Of course, she'd never admit that. Nor would she do it. His proximity was having an effect on her. He saw it in the trembling of her lips. The flush of her cheek. The softening of her gaze.

At first he thought she might be afraid of him. Impressed by his size. Intimidated by his dominance.

Now he recognized the signs of desire.

He should know. He felt it as well. A yearning to draw closer. To haul her into his arms. To bury his face in her silky blonde tresses.

For one brief instant, as their gazes connected, he felt a surge of something even more irresistible than desire.

Fascination.

He wanted to know more about the Valkyrie. Wanted to thaw her icy layers and expose the unique woman beneath. Wanted to know her thoughts, her hopes, her dreams.

Then he felt the sudden prick of sharp steel against his belly.

He stiffened as his fascination curdled into disappointment.

Her glare was hard now. "Give it to me."

He wasn't going to surrender the precious notebook without a fight. Not now. Not when she'd had the audacity to draw a blade on him. A blade he was almost certain she didn't have the nerve to use.

Deciding it was a wager he was willing to make, he straightened to his full height and dared her, "If ye're so certain I have somethin' o' yours, why don't ye take it from me?"

"You realize I'm holding a dagger?"

"I know ye don't want to damage me. Ye've said as much. And ye won't kill me. Isabel said ye'd ne'er killed a man."

The subtle twitch of the dagger was the only indication that his words had rattled her.

But her gaze was steady as she replied, "Do you think I'd tell Isabel if I had?"

She had a point. One he hadn't considered. Perhaps it was best to get her mind off of violence. Perhaps he should try to confiscate that dagger.

"She also said ye'd ne'er kissed a man."

The second accusation seemed to rattle her far more than the first. She drew in a sharp breath and found herself at a loss for words.

"'Tis true then, isn't it?" he pressed, lowering his gaze purposefully to her mouth.

If he could distract her with a kiss—nothing seductive, just a sweet, simple brush of his lips—maybe it would be enough to tease the dagger from her grip. Maybe he could even make her forget about the notebook.

He continued to gaze at her pink, ripe, inviting mouth and let his tongue slip out to wet his lower lip.

Every bell in Hallie's head was ringing in alarm. The hostage was too close to her, literally and figuratively.

Thanks to her conniving sister, Colban knew two of her most closely held secrets. And that put her at a disadvantage.

Even now, she could feel the melting heat of his lusty gaze.

What he didn't know was, while she'd never been kissed, it wasn't for lack of opportunity. In the past few years, several lads—most on a dare from their fellows—had tried to kiss Hallie. Most of them had been discouraged by an icy glare. A few had earned scars from the attempt.

For Hallie, hostility was the swiftest natural defense against aggression.

But that was when she wanted to *eliminate* the aggressor. In this instance, when she needed something in return, different tactics were required. She had to keep Colban off-balance to claim with stealth what she couldn't seize by force.

She lowered her gaze to his mouth. Her heart fluttered at the prospect of what she was about to do. But surely it was no different than the way her pulse raced when she entered the free-for-all fighting in a tournament melee. In the melee, she'd found it was best not to dally, but to go on the offense and charge in with confidence.

The corner of Colban's lip drifted up as he taunted her. "Ye've ne'er felt the sweet surrender of a man's—"

She pitched forward and, before caution could make a coward of her, seized the back of his head and shut him up with a hard kiss.

At least that was her intent.

What actually happened was her lips contacted his. He twitched in surprise. Their teeth clacked together. And she recoiled.

It was as jarring as two swords clanging.

In a clash of blades, she would have retreated and tried again.

But when she tried to pull back, he caught her jaw. Sweeping his hand over her cheek, he slipped his fingers into her hair to hold her steady.

"Like this," he murmured against her mouth.

His lips were incredibly soft upon hers. For a rough-hewn Highlander, his touch was unexpectedly gentle. His breath, warm and scented of apples, stirred her senses.

Though he'd fallen neatly into her trap, she suddenly felt more like prey than predator. His kiss was doing strange things to her. Making her head sing. Weakening her knees. Sending white-hot current through her veins. Burning like banked coal between her legs.

Waves of pleasure threatened to rock her off her feet. Instant by instant, her control slipped away. She had the vague, distant thought that she must seize the advantage. Take the upper hand. Leave *him* incapacitated by longing.

Then he clasped her head in both hands, tilted her jaw, and teased her mouth open with his own. His tongue flicked out, making her gasp and searing her senses like lightning.

At that moment, she knew she'd met her match.

Drawn into an abyss of desire, she let the dagger slip from her fingers. As it clattered on the floor, she moaned against his mouth. Collapsed into his arms. And fell into the kiss.

Time dissolved as she gave in to lust and curiosity. She answered his mouth's sweet assault with kisses of her own. Her fingers tangled in his hair, bunched his leine, grazed his throat, swept over the vast expanse of his chest with feverish need.

When he wrapped his arm around her back to pull her closer, she didn't even think to resist. Emboldened by longing, she surged forward, grasping his arse and hauling him up against her.

The bulge pressing against her abdomen inflamed her desire. His groan of pleasure took her breath away.

Colban was in over his head. He knew that now.

He had intended the kiss to be a light distraction. After all, a lass's first kiss was usually an awkward peck full of flustered blushing.

He meant to set her off-balance, at which point she'd rush from the room and forget all about the notebook.

Never had he imagined Hallie would kiss him back. Never had he dreamed she'd return his advances with such passion and heat.

Her lips were insistent and demanding. Her ragged breath seared his cheek. Wherever her hands touched him, they sparked fire.

Now he was engulfed in a dizzying blaze of desire. His head spun as if he'd taken a blow to the helm. His hands grasped in desperation at her tresses, as if they could keep him from being consumed by the flames. His mouth fed on her with greedy abandon. Within his trews, he was throbbing with need.

All thought, all reason, all purpose fled his mind. He wanted only this. Only her.

He longed to roar out his claim upon her, toss her on the bed, and sink his aching lance into her welcome warmth.

She wanted it too. He could tell from the wild smoldering in her eyes. The breathless begging of her gasps. The mad clawing of her fingers. The pressure of her hungering body against him.

He yearned to get past the torment. Purge this inconvenient attraction between them. He'd not had a woman in weeks. It would be over in a moment.

Yet in some deeply buried place in the back of his mind, he knew he'd do no such thing. Seducing maids was dishonorable. Taking a virgin was not the conduct of a champion. Even if the virgin was his foe.

He might be a low-born Highlander. But his reputation as a gentleman was untarnished. And he wanted to keep it that way.

Hallie was an innocent victim.

He'd gotten them into this predicament. It was up to him to get them out. As painful as it was, he decided he'd just have to live with the discomfort of unrequited lust.

Then Hallie did the unthinkable.

She reached between them and slid her hand into his trews, closing it around that part of him that most wanted her caress. He sucked in a shocked breath as his unruly body roused to her touch. Squeezing his eyes shut at the divine sensation, he growled in his throat—half in approval, half in anguish.

Like snow in the sun, his control melted away, leaving him in a puddle of his noble intentions.

She obviously wanted this as much as he did. Or perhaps Lowland lasses were just more forward about their needs than Highlanders. This lass certainly was. And she seemed to know exactly what she was doing.

It was possible she'd lied to Isabel about never killing a man. He was certain now she'd lied about never kissing a man. By the way she was caressing him, she'd done far more than kissing.

He leaned his brow upon hers, closing his eyes to relish the perfection of the moment before kissing her again. Her breath was like the warm breeze of summer. Her lips were as soft and sweet as peaches.

At her gentle urging, he grew more and more rigid by the moment in her hand. Then, inspired by her brazen gesture, he let his hands slide down from her face, past her throat, where her heart pulsed against his thumbs. His fingers brushed her delicate collarbone and then plunged farther, delving beneath the edge of her kirtle to claim the silken treasure of her ripe breasts.

One sharp gasp, and she snatched out of his grasp. Dropping him from her hand like a blade hot off the forge, she stepped away.

He reeled in disappointment, but not surprise. *This* was the reaction he'd predicted, after all. It had only been delayed. And now he half expected her to slap him for his insolence.

She didn't. She blushed, lowered her eyes, muttered under her breath—a stammer of disbelief or apology, he wasn't sure which—and stumbled toward the door.

He should have been pleased. He'd succeeded. He'd distracted her so thoroughly, she'd completely forgotten about the notebook.

Yet that wasn't what he felt as she fled, closing the door behind her with hollow finality. His loins ached. His hands felt empty. His heart sank.

What had started as a ploy had become real for him. He *did* desire the Valkyrie. He *did* want to kiss her. Hold her. Make love to her. And for one shining moment, he'd felt his affections returned.

But such dreams were foolish. She was his captor. He was her foe.

Clearing his throat, he shook off the dregs of desire. Raked his hair back. Adjusted his trews. And reached behind his back to retrieve the notebook.

It wasn't there.

CHAPTER 20

hallie fled down the corridor with breathless haste.

She should have been grinning in triumph. The notebook was snug in her satchel, bouncing against her hip as she took the stairs.

Yet all she felt were the pangs of guilt.

Why was she running?

She wasn't fleeing Colban, though she felt compelled to get as far away from him as she could.

She was instead pursued by her own misplaced desires, from which there was no escape. She'd barely left with her dignity. Hell, she'd barely left with her virginity.

She hadn't realized how hot the flame of lust would burn between them. Like an entranced moth, she'd strayed too close. Now her wings were singed, and she wasn't sure she had the strength to fly from him again.

When she emerged onto the great hall, Isabel was there, chatting excitedly with her friends. They silenced at her appearance.

"Hallie, what's wrong?" Isabel asked.

"Wrong? Nothing's wrong." Holy hell, could they tell? Was it obvious? Did the glow of seduction linger on her face?

"You look...troubled," Isabel said. Then her slim brows rose together in a wrinkle of dismay. She lowered her voice to a whisper. "Oh nay. You hurt him, didn't you?"

Irritation flared in her at Isabel's assumption.

"I didn't touch him." She flushed at her own outright lie. She had indeed touched him. In a very inappropriate manner.

Isabel squinted her eyes in suspicion. "Then why are you upset?"

"I'm not upset," she said, adding pointedly, "At least I *wasn't*."

That was another lie. Hallie was absolutely upset. Why? She wasn't sure. After all, she'd won, hadn't she? She'd outwitted Colban and taken the notebook straight off of his person.

Thankfully, Isabel abandoned her line of questioning. She brightened and announced, "Never mind. I have just the thing to cheer you up."

Her group of maidens giggled and nodded.

"We're assembling an entertainment."

Hallie knew better than to be pleased by that news. Isabel's schemes oft went awry. "What sort of entertainment?"

Isabel shrugged. "Some music. Some dancing. A play."

It seemed harmless. And it would keep Isabel occupied and away from the hostage. "Fine."

Isabel turned to the maids. "Your brothers can be the noble knights. Brand can play the wizard. And I'm sure Ian can find a way to make the dragon breathe fire and smoke and—"

"Wait," Hallie interrupted at the mention of Ian's name. She dug in her satchel for the notebook. "Give this to Ian when you see him. And warn him if he's careless with it again, I'll have to hold onto it for safekeeping."

She supposed it was a blessing that Isabel had decided to enlist her siblings for this entertainment of hers. That would make four less problems to deal with in the busy day ahead.

In a way, she was grateful for the myriad challenges that cropped up all day long. They kept her mind off an uncomfortable reality, a reality she didn't want to face.

She was attracted to the Highlander. Not only was he a tempting feast for the eyes. He was brave. Loyal. Strong. Clever. All the things a champion should be.

Colban an Curaidh wielded some mysterious power over her senses. He took her breath away. Hastened her pulse. Sapped her strength. Weakened her resolve.

Indeed, she'd come dangerously close to yielding to that power.

And part of her didn't find that abhorrent. Part of her felt a thrill of adventure at the prospect of surrendering in his arms.

It was a terrifying truth. One she dared not dwell on. So before she could allow herself to think too deeply, she threw back her shoulders and set out to face the responsibilities of the afternoon.

First, she helped to round up a trio of stray sheep. Then she settled a quibble between the blacksmith and the stable lad. A sickly old hound required her care after that. By mid-afternoon, she oversaw the repair of the quintain that had been splintered in the last practice. Afterwards, she took stock of the castle stores in preparation for winter, writing out orders for those who would need to procure goods. Then she had to punish wee Robbie, who'd stuck his thumb in all the pies, by making him serve as the baker's apprentice for a week.

When she finally finished lending a hand in repairing the thatch of the dovecot and mulching the strawberries against frost, it was time for supper.

For several peaceful hours, she'd successfully forgotten about her handsome hostage.

Until Isabel plopped down beside her for supper in the great hall.

"Sorry we're late."

Her little sister was decked in her finest gown of rose velvet. Her hair was woven into a fantastic tangle of braids. And her face was powdered and painted in a way that made her look more like a woman than a lass.

Before Hallie could ask what the devil she was up to, Isabel drew her finely penciled brows together. "Did you send supper up to Sir Colban?"

To be honest, it had slipped her mind. "I was about to," she said, summoning one of the maidservants to make up a platter. "Why are you dressed like that?"

"'Tis for the entertainment. Remember? After supper, we're going to perform in the courtyard."

Hallie frowned. "In the courtyard?"

"Aye," she replied, stabbing a parsnip with her pearl-handled dagger and popping it into her mouth. "You don't want a fire-breathing dragon in the great hall, do you?"

"Fire-breathing dragon?"

Brand slid onto the bench next to Isabel. "Aye, Hallie, wait till you see it! Leap a sheep! 'Tis brilliant."

Hallie pointed her dagger in threat at the two of them. "If you burn the keep to the ground while our parents are away..."

"'Tis perfectly safe," Ian told her as he seated himself beside her. "I wanted to use Greek fire, but Gellir thought 'twas too risky. So I've settled on peat fire in a great helm, with a bellows to—"

"Greek fire?" Hallie choked on a turnip.

Greek fire was a concoction so savage and dangerous that most civilized armies still refused to use it.

Gellir ruffled Ian's hair as he joined them at the table. "I'll get lads with full buckets of sand to stand by."

At least Gellir had a cool head on his shoulders. He was taking the proper precautions.

Still, it was with a certain amount of trepidation that,

an hour later, Hallie sat in her assigned spot in the courtyard to watch the spectacle.

Seated on a faldstool cushioned with sheepskins, she was surrounded by the entire clan. Some crowded together on benches dragged from the great hall. Some sat on plaids spread on the ground.

It didn't escape her notice that Isabel had arranged the entertainment to take place directly below Colban's bedchamber.

And when Hallie glimpsed up to see Colban's face at the window, her heart skipped a beat. Her face warmed. Her breath grew shallow. Sparks of lust ignited her senses.

When it came to the Highlander, it seemed, as with Greek fire, there was no way to extinguish the persistent flames of desire.

What the devil was going on? Colban had just polished off his pea and parsnip pottage when the castle folk began to assemble below his window. A square area was roped off in the middle of the courtyard. To one side was a folded screen. A small raised platform was located in the midst of the square, with an upright wooden beam lodged in its center.

He hoped they weren't setting up a whipping or an execution. He had little taste for that sort of bloodthirsty display. It was one thing to kill a man in fair combat. And it was fair and just to execute a man for his sins. But he didn't approve of making a spectacle of punishment, of seeking enjoyment from the suffering of others.

Besides, he'd had enough suffering for one day, considering his humiliating defeat at the hands of that crafty Valkyrie.

There she was now, being seated at the center of the crowd. Despite his irritation at being outwitted, his heart leaped at the sight of her. Whatever mischief she'd perpetrated upon him, she remained as lovely as winter snow, as alluring as a summer loch.

Still, it stung to realize how gullible he'd been. How easily she'd deceived him. He'd actually believed that she too was overcome with lust. That she was drowning in the depths of desire beside him. That the same force of attraction pulling at his heart and shattering his thoughts affected them both.

He supposed he had to admire her skills. That level of deception was probably useful in combat. And it did amuse him to try to determine exactly when she'd lifted the notebook from him. While they were kissing? Or while she had her hand wrapped around his...

"Sir Colban an Curaidh!"

Startled from his musings, Colban looked down to see Isabel, gowned like a princess, gesturing up at him with one graceful arm.

"'Tis in your honor we present this entertainment!"

God's blood. His honor? Oh aye. He'd all but forgotten about his heroics of the morn. They seemed to pale in comparison to the humiliation he'd endured since. Nonetheless, with all eyes on him, he waved back. At least the clan wasn't planning to torture anyone.

Isabel turned to address the crowd in dramatic tones. "I bring you a tale of true love and loyalty. Of unmatched chivalry and noble sacrifice. A tale with fierce warriors, lovely maidens, magical enchantment, and a fire-breathing dragon."

All the children gasped in awe at that.

"But first we shall hear a stirring ballade from Boniface," she finished as a man armed with a lute came forward.

What followed was an excruciating and highly romanticized account of Colban's leap from the window and his ensuing battle. By the end of the performance, Colban decided they *had* decided to torture someone. His ears burned, and his smile of gratitude strained the corners of his mouth.

Isabel then announced Agile Giles, a lad in tattered clothing who could juggle four hen's eggs in various manners without breaking a single one.

A white-haired blind woman swathed in colorful scarves was introduced as Sofia the Seer. She waved her hands about wildly, summoning various people in the crowd to come forward so she could touch their sleeve and tell them what their future held.

She foretold wealth for a bright-eyed lad, two dead sheep for an old man, another babe for Rauve in the summer, and victory for a knight in the spring tournament.

Finally she lifted her finger to Colban. "You. Champion."

Colban scowled. He didn't want to have his destiny foretold. He didn't believe in such drivel.

"Throw down an article of your clothing."

One of Isabel's bolder friends squealed, "Throw down *all* of them!" A spate of girlish giggles followed.

Colban wanted to withdraw from the window. But everyone was staring expectantly at him now. Gellir. Brand. Isabel. Hallie. He supposed it would be easier to comply and dispense with this nonsense.

He didn't have any spare clothing. And he wasn't about to tear a sleeve off his only leine. But since his foot was bandaged at the moment, he supposed he didn't need his boot.

"Ye'll return this, aye?" he called down, garnering laughter from the clan.

He tossed it onto the green, not far from where he'd landed this morn. A man picked it up and handed it to the seer.

"What do you see?" Isabel eagerly asked, clasping her

hands hopefully beneath her chin. "What's in the stars for our champion?"

Colban smirked and folded his arms. He expected Isabel had paid the woman to predict a romantic match between her sister and The One. A quick glance at Hallie's tensed jaw told him she suspected the same.

But the old woman's face clouded. She clutched the boot to her bosom as if it were an injured kitten.

"A dark time is ahead for you, I fear," she intoned.

Despite his disbelief in her sight, her words felt like a cold dagger sunk in his chest.

"Nay, nay, nay," Isabel complained. "That can't be right. Try again."

The woman shook her white head. "I see loneliness and heartbreak."

Isabel's face fell, and the crowd silenced.

The old woman's predictions were nonsense. Of course they were.

Determined to make light of her comments, Colban shouted, "There will be heartbreak if I don't get my boot back."

His words relieved the tension as the crowd chuckled. But they didn't erase the furrow from between Hallie's brows. And they didn't banish the chill from his soul.

Nor could they remove the disappointment in Isabel's eyes, disappointment she quickly hid with a quavering smile. Ushering the seer aside, she introduced a consort to play while her friends danced and frolicked about with garlands of ivy and hawthorn berries.

The main play featured two youths in armor, one lad wrapped in a plaid like a Highlander, Isabel and two of her friends dressed in finery, a fur-robed lad introduced as the Laird of Rivenloch, and a cloaked wizard with a beard made of moss who looked and sounded suspiciously like Brand.

The story was fairly simple.

According to the wizard, centuries ago, Rivenloch had been besieged by a terrible fire-breathing dragon. Each year, the dragon visited for three days. And on each of those three nights he demanded the sacrifice of a virgin for his supper.

Every year for centuries, the knights of the castle had tried their best to defend the virgins. Every year, they had failed, the wizard said, gesturing to a folded screen in front of the curtain wall. Two lads moved the screen aside to reveal a great pile of armor and what Colban hoped were beef bones.

While the lad playing the laird despaired over their hopeless predicament, night fell. At last, the dragon made its appearance at the top of the wall.

Colban grinned at the sight. The spectacle inspired oohs and ahhs from the clan, as well as frightened whimpers from several of the younger children.

Ian had definitely had a hand in creating the impressive beast. Two giant reptilian legs, sporting daggers for claws, perched atop the wall. A great mail-covered head with eyes of amber glass peered down at the crowd as the beast puffed smoke from between its jaws.

In Gellir's disguised but unmistakable deep and surly voice, the dragon demanded a virgin for his supper.

The laird reluctantly offered a maiden as sacrifice. The brave and noble virgin was led up the stairs of the platform and tied to the post.

But before the dragon could claim its feast, a young knight leaped in front of the platform with a sword to save the maiden from her horrible fate.

"Fear not!" he declared. "My steel will defeat the beast!"

There was much hacking and roaring back and forth. But eventually, the knight was flung onto the pile of armor with a mighty crash. In a haze of smoke, the virgin disappeared, apparently consumed by the dragon.

Even Colban had to blink in amazement at the effect. He supposed it was done with a secret door in the platform. But it had been executed so quickly while all eyes were fixed on the dragon that no one saw the lass vanish.

The castle grieved all the next day, lamenting when the dragon returned at nightfall and a second virgin volunteered to save her clan. This time, the knight who stepped in to rescue her was armed with a bow and arrows.

"Fear not!" he announced. "My fire will defeat the beast!"

He lit a pitch-dipped arrow and fired it from the bow. The arrow trailed flame across the sky, landing with a thunk between the dragon's eyes.

There was a tense moment when Hallie shot to her feet, no doubt fearing her siblings' antics would either kill someone, set the castle on fire, or both.

But the fire sputtered out. Hallie sank back onto the faldstool.

Once again, the dragon triumphed. The hapless knight was tossed onto the pile. The second maiden was consumed in a cloud of smoke.

On the third and final night, the maiden who allowed herself to be tied to the post was Isabel. She smiled with calm confidence as the youth dressed like a Highlander stepped forward on her behalf, completely unarmed.

"Fear not!" he cried. "My heart will defeat the beast!"

The dragon chortled. "Your heart? That soft and tender thing that tastes so lovely going down my gullet? I shall dine on yours after I eat this virgin."

With that, the dragon turned toward Isabel, blowing out a thick, smoky cloud.

But when the air cleared, Isabel was still there, grinning in victory.

The dragon snarled in rage, sending out another billow of roiling smoke.

Again, Isabel emerged triumphant.

"Nay!" the dragon howled. Exhaling with the last of his strength, he expelled a pathetic gray puff. "How can this be?" he despaired. "How can I be defeated by a weak human heart?"

"Because you don't understand the power of love," the youth declared, rushing to untie Isabel. "This day, while your belly was craving virgin flesh, my heart stole it from you." He turned to the crowd to announce, "We were wed this morn. She is no longer a maiden."

Colban almost choked on surprise. He had not foreseen that twist in the tale.

As for the crowd, their reaction was mixed. Some crowed at the clever ruse. Some gasped in outrage. Some silenced. Some erupted with laughter.

Hallie slowly rose, stone-faced and pale, as if she feared the young lad's claim upon Isabel might be more than just a part of their performance.

But Colban sensed there was more behind Isabel's story. There was a reason Isabel had dressed the hero like a Highlander. She was sending a message to her sister about the man she persisted in calling The One. It was a clumsy attempt at making a love match between the two of them, made clumsier by the fact that Isabel had performed the play for all the clan to see.

Hallie's frown made it clear she saw the parallel too and did not approve.

Before Hallie could order a halt to the play, Isabel sent a panicked glare toward Brand the wizard. He raised his arms and hastily intervened.

"Because the champion was true of heart," he cried by way of explanation, "the castle was saved! The dragon returned no more! And thus were born the immortal words, the rallying cry of Rivenloch—*Amor vincit omnia! Love conquers all!*"

The clan cheered, and the performers immediately launched into a celebratory dance. In the aftermath of the revelry, the details of the play were forgotten.

But not by Colban.

Love conquers all?

Surely the Lowlanders didn't really believe that. Aye, civility was useful in negotiations. And diplomacy was helpful when seeking peace. But when it came to war, a sturdy claymore served a man better than Cupid's arrows.

Still, as he watched Hallie rise and turn to leave the courtyard, he felt a bolt of longing pierce his heart. Remembering the silken threads of her hair between his fingers. The sparkling crystal of her melting eyes. The spicy-sweet taste of her warm mouth.

"Did you like the play, Sir Colban?" Isabel called up to him.

"What? Oh, aye."

"I'll bring up your boot when I'm finished here."

He gave her a preoccupied nod.

"Did you know 'twas me?" Brand yelled out, removing his hat. "'Tis a good disguise, aye?"

"Brilliant," Colban replied, distracted as he sought Hallie, who had disappeared into the crowd.

"What did you think of the dragon?" Ian called out from atop the curtain wall. His arm was wrapped companionably around one of the dragon's legs. "I used a bellows to make the smoke. I wanted to use Greek fire, but—"

"I told him 'twas too dangerous," Gellir chimed in beside Ian.

"Impressive," Colban said vaguely, unable to locate the Valkyrie.

Gellir spoke to his brother. "I don't think he knows about Greek fire, Ian. I don't think they have it in the Highlands."

Suddenly their words sank in, and Colban gave the lads his full attention. "Hold on. Greek fire? Ye know how to make Greek fire?"

"'Twas a bit tricky figuring it out," Ian said, "since the formula is a secret."

Gellir was right. They'd never encountered it in the Highlands. Foreign armies had never invaded that far north. But the horrors of Greek fire were legendary. Unable to be extinguished, the vile substance clung to whatever it contacted—stone walls, armored men, even the surface of water—and burned for hours. If Rivenloch truly held the secret to Greek fire, they were a formidable foe indeed.

"Anyway," Ian continued, "I think the peat worked to good effect, though Sir Rauve may need a new helm." He knocked on the dragon's steel head. "This one's gone all smoky inside."

Colban was only half-listening.

Part of him was worrying about the possibility of Rivenloch using Greek fire to kill his clansmen at Creagor. He was calculating the chances of confiscating Ian's notebook again, where the formula for the destructive substance was probably recorded.

And part of him was distracted once more by the beautiful Viking princess he'd finally spotted in the crowd, making her way to the great hall.

Love conquers all?

Then what bloody use could Hallie possibly have for Greek fire?

CHAPTER 21

As she walked stiffly across the courtyard, Hallie wished she'd let Ian use his mix of Greek fire for the dragon. The conflagration might have been a useful distraction from the heavy-handed message Isabel had delivered in her play.

Love conquers all.

Bloody hell.

Now that she thought about it, it was hardly a fit rallying cry for a clan of warriors in charge of defending the Scottish border. And it was a weak warning indeed to someone bent on claiming the neighboring castle.

Rivenloch's byword should be Loyal and Invincible.

Or Always Up for Battle.

Or Foes Beware—We Have Greek Fire.

While Hallie agreed war was not the answer here—at least not while her cousins were held captive at Creagor—neither was undermining all the leverage Rivenloch had by befriending her enemy.

She would not be cruel to her captive. But neither should she be too familiar.

Isabel had gone too far this eve with her play. Wrapping the champion in a plaid. Casting herself as the heroine when she knew very well people remarked on Isabel's resemblance to Hallie. And then suggesting that they'd outwitted a dragon by swiving...

Her cheeks grew hot as she neared the door of the great hall. But she couldn't stop herself from casting one last curious glance toward the bedchamber window.

Colban was there in all his handsome glory. His hands rested with quiet strength on the sill as he leaned out over the ledge. His golden hair shone in the moonlight. And where his leine gapped away, she glimpsed the sculpted contour of one broad shoulder.

Engaged with her chattering siblings, he didn't notice her, which was fortunate, because Hallie tripped at the sight of him. Her breath caught. Her heart bounded against her ribs. And she couldn't get inside the castle fast enough.

When Isabel came to bed hours later, Hallie pretended to be asleep. She didn't want a loud confrontation with the lass while the hostage was in the adjoining chamber. But on the morrow, she'd corner her scheming little sister and let her know in no uncertain terms how she felt about the prisoner.

"He's a hostage. No more," Hallie insisted, spooning frumenty from the steaming cauldron into a bowl for Colban's breakfast.

Isabel lifted a brow in doubt and reached into a jar on the kitchen shelf to add a far too generous handful of dried apples to Colban's frumenty.

"Our *cousins* are hostages," Isabel reminded her. She affected a sigh and creased her brow in worry. "I can only hope their captor isn't cruel and coldhearted."

"I'm not col-..." Hallie began, then tempered her tone. "I'm doing what I must do, Isabel." To assuage her sister, she added, "And I'm sure Feiyan and Jenefer are fine."

"Are you?" Isabel added a fat stack of oatcakes to the platter. "Did you see the bruises on poor Sir Colban's face?

What if Colban's laird raises a hand to our cousins? What if he tries to starve them?"

Hallie removed half of the oatcakes from the platter and steered Isabel out of the kitchens.

She had her own concerns about Morgan Mor mac Giric's patience, especially when it came to Jenefer's inflammatory nature. But fretting over it served no purpose.

Isabel tried to take the platter from her. "I'm going to question Colban," she decided, "and find out what kind of a man his master is."

"Oh, nay you won't," Hallie countered, holding fast to the platter. "You've caused enough damage as it is."

"Damage? Me?" Isabel's eyes grew dewy with hurt. "I've done naught but try to make peace—"

"I'll take him his breakfast," Hallie insisted. "You gather your lasses and go down to the loch. Maybe you can bring in one last catch of salmon ere winter."

Isabel's hurt vanished as quickly as it had appeared. She couldn't resist a day of fishing. "You're sure?"

"I'll see the *prisoner* doesn't go hungry. You see the *clan* doesn't."

Isabel skipped away, all but forgetting the captive.

Hallie nodded in satisfaction. That should keep the lass busy for a good part of the day.

Meanwhile, perhaps it was a good idea to get further reassurances from Colban. She was getting a bad feeling about her parents petitioning the new king. They should have returned by now. Every day without word from them was a day the ownership of Creagor remained in question. Every day that decision was prolonged, the odds of harm to her cousins increased.

She took the tray upstairs, opening Colban's door with her free hand. She expected to find the occupant pacing across the chamber or tending to the fire or staring wistfully out the window.

But he was still asleep. And he didn't awaken when she entered.

He might be an impressive warrior. But he didn't make a very good guard. Three times now she'd been able to slip past his drowsy watch.

She closed the door softly behind her and observed him in silence.

No longer fierce and challenging, he appeared as innocent as a bairn. His brow was untroubled. His hair was unkempt. His jaw was relaxed, and his lips parted just enough to emit the soft, growling breath of slumber.

He was helpless. At her mercy. Thoroughly subdued. Exactly where she should want a foe to be.

Yet dominance was not what she felt when she looked at him. As she continued to stare—at the stray lock of golden hair dangling over one eye, at the slow rise and fall of his chest as he breathed, at his bare toes peeping out from the bandage—her heart melted.

Not often, but more of late, Hallie had been thinking about the man she would eventually wed. Wondered what he would be like. Whether she would grow fond of him. How it would feel to wake up to the same face every day for the rest of her life.

She would have no choice in the selection of a husband, of course. The position of laird of Rivenloch was too valuable to king and country to be left to chance. Her marriage would be a carefully arranged alliance.

But once in a great while—when she was lying in bed at night or bathing in the loch on a lazy summer day or watching her parents gaze longingly into each other's eyes—she indulged in a selfish dream that she would one day find a love match.

Looking at Colban now, she felt closer to that tantalizing dream than she'd ever felt before. She could easily imagine awakening with the Highlander beside her each morn, savoring the simple beauty of his face. The idle power of his body. The soothing sound of his breathing. She could even imagine growing to care for him.

She bit her lip, indulging in the fantasy.

The champion had much to recommend him as a husband.

He was a fine warrior. His skills with the claymore, his strength, and his spirit inspired admiration among her men.

His loyalty and chivalry were undeniable. Not only did he place his laird's life above his own. He'd risked death to come to *Hallie's* rescue, unwilling to leave her in the hands of attackers. Her parents would doubtless consider him a valuable addition to the Rivenloch army.

He would make an excellent father. He had a way with children. He knew how to listen to Ian. How to charm Isabel. How to make Brand worship him like a hero. Even how to impress dour Gellir.

Her husband's most important duty, of course, would be giving her heirs. Whether Colban was capable of siring offspring she didn't know. But she remembered the lust in his eyes. The heat of his kiss. The quickening in his braies.

The memory of touching him triggered a wave of molten desire. If Colban an Curaidh was unable to plant his seed, it wouldn't be for lack of trying. Not only was he well-equipped for the task. He also seemed to have no qualms about a woman overstepping the bounds of propriety. Looking into his eyes. Kissing him. Caressing him.

Nor did he hesitate to return her affections. Claiming her lips with his enticing mouth. Grazing her bosom with his rough fingertips.

She was still adrift in a sea of sensual musings when Colban wakened with a gasp.

She gasped in response, almost spilling the frumenty.

"Hallie."

Her name spilled out on a sigh, disrupting her thoughts the way a sudden breeze stirred the leaves. He rose on his elbows, and his leine slipped off one magnificent shoulder.

Her heart leaped. Her nostrils flared. She thrust the platter forward, as if it had the power to shield her from temptation. "I brought you breakfast. I thought you'd be up by now."

Up? Colban *was* up, though not in the way Hallie imagined. He was still savoring the dregs of a delicious dream about silky blonde hair and crystal blue eyes, of tender lips and a velvety hand wrapped around...

"I hope you like apples," she said.

Apples. That seemed somehow fitting. Hallie looked as tempting as Eve, radiant and breathless, offering him a feast for his eyes, as well as his belly.

"Love them," he rasped out.

He wanted to fetch the platter from her. But not in his present condition. Clad only in his thin leine, he feared he'd look like he was coming at her with a lance. He bunched the coverlet over his lap.

She awkwardly cleared her throat and averted her gaze. Setting the platter on the edge of the bed, she walked stiffly toward the window, then threw open the shutters.

He grimaced as blinding light streamed in.

"Oh. Sorry."

"Nay, 'tis late," he said, shaking the sleep from his head and pulling the platter onto his lap. He took a bite of frumenty. It was warm and delicious, spiced with cinnamon and apples. "I hardly slept a wink, fightin' for virgins half the night."

Her eyes widened. "What?"

"In my dreams," he clarified. "Isabel's play? I must have battled a dozen fiery dragons." He didn't add that his defeat of the last dragon had won him the devoted affections of a certain beautiful Valkyrie.

"My sister is quite the storyteller," Hallie said in mild irritation. She faced the window, frowning into the distance. "Her head is full of improbable tales. Magic. Miracles. Impossible creatures." Her voice grew wistful. "Unlikely endings."

Was that regret he heard in her voice? Did she not believe in happy endings? In his dream, at least, the ending had been happy. It had been more than happy. It had been fulfilling. Inspiring. Satisfying.

But it had only been a dream. Just as Isabel's play was only a story.

Hallie probably didn't believe in dreams. She seemed to be a lass firmly rooted in reality, who had no time for sentiment or romance. If he'd realized that yesterday, he might have been able to see through the ruse of her lusty advances.

Still stinging from her deception, he wanted to forget how easily he'd been gulled. In fact, considering how thoroughly she'd deceived him, he figured he owed her a bit of revenge.

"An unlikely ending, to be sure," he agreed. But then he let a wicked gleam enter his eye. "After all, everyone knows dragons aren't that choosy."

Hallie, rising to the bait, whirled to face him in disbelief. "What?"

"Dragons," he said, shaking his head. "They're pesky, to be sure. And they eat once a week, not once a year. But they're not at all picky about their fare."

"You're jesting, aye?"

"Nay, 'tis true," he assured her. Then he whispered as if in confidence, "They can't actually tell the difference between the flesh of a virgin and that of a harlot."

She stared at him for a moment, as if questioning his sanity. "There's no such thing as dragons."

He shrugged. "Maybe not in the *Lowlands*."

There was a tiny instant of doubt in her eyes before she noticed the twinkle in his.

"Bloody knave," she chided, clucking her tongue.

He lifted one corner of his mouth in a sly grin.

Then, as smoothly as she'd slipped the notebook from his belt, she added, "Everyone knows the only strange beasts in the north are those that come from Highlanders swiving sheep."

Her insult was so unexpected and comical that he almost snorted frumenty out of his nose. "Swivin' sheep? Ach, ye're a wicked lass." The hint of amusement in her gaze only encouraged him. "The rumors are completely unfounded. After all, why would we swive sheep when we've got so many bonnie coos?"

The laugh that burst out of her was broken and rusty, as if it hadn't been used in a while. But it was open. And honest. And it rocked him to the core.

He wanted more of it. More of her musical laughter. More of her brilliant smile. More of her humor-softened gaze.

"Ian's dragon, though..." He whistled. "*That* was a thing o' beauty."

"For shite's sake," she teased, her eyes dancing, "have you no lasses in the Highlands?"

None as beautiful as ye.

That was his first thought. But it would have been foolish to blurt that out, no matter how true it was. So instead he asked, "Have ye ne'er been to the Highlands?"

She shook her head.

He suddenly longed to whisk her away to the home he loved. To take her by the hand and run laughing with her across the moors, through the woods, past the lochs, into the mountains.

"Och, lass, ye'd love the mac Giric land." For the moment,

his lust was at bay and his breakfast forgotten. "There's not a bonnier spot in all o' Scotland." He set the platter aside and rose with the aid of his crutch.

"Despite the dragons?" she quipped.

"Despite the dragons." He grinned.

She smirked. "It can't be as beautiful as Rivenloch."

"'Tis...different." He hobbled toward the window to join her. "The mac Giric property is bordered by majestic peaks o' stark stone," he said, waxing poetic. "In winter, they're covered in snow, whiter than sheep's fleece. But in spring, they weep waterfalls as tall as a castle." He gazed out toward the rolling hills and thick forest, painting a different landscape in his imagination. "Under the summer sun, the lochs gleam like a fierce blue blade. And at this time o' year, the hills are cloaked in brilliant purple heather. Burns flow through the glens, silvery and bright, like..." He hesitated and let his gaze roam down her fair tresses. "Like your hair."

Only then did he realize how close he was standing to her. Close enough he could have twined a lock of her bright hair around his finger. Close enough to feel her warm breath upon his face. To smell the womanly fragrance of her skin. To gaze into her eyes and glimpse the sparkle of reflected enthusiasm. Shared joy. And the tiniest glimmer of hope.

"Ye should come sometime," he whispered.

His gaze fell to her tempting lips, which parted in longing.

In another moment, he would kiss those lips. He was sure of it. He felt drawn by an irresistible force. Compelled to her like steel to a lodestone.

She felt it too. He was sure of it. He could see desire misting her eyes as they dipped to his mouth.

But he hesitated an instant too long. And in that instant, something shifted.

Her gaze faded into dismay, then sorrow, and finally frosted over with solemn duty.

She turned away, fixing her eyes on the horizon.

"I can't just dash off any time I like," she told him, though her voice cracked with regret. She cleared her throat to regain her composure. When she spoke again, it was with the cool authority of a leader. "And if your clan remains here, you won't be able to either. Defending the border requires constant vigilance. 'Tis a position of great responsibility. There's no time for jaunts off to the Highlands. You'll have to forget all about your idyllic home."

He frowned. The tempting lass he'd nearly kissed was gone. In her place was a woman who issued orders and commanded armies. A woman who was used to putting country before clan. And clan before self.

Morgan Mor mac Giric had been like that...before his wife died and his world went awry. Colban had always been there for him when the demands of being a laird's son became too great and Morgan needed to get away. Whether that meant taking a bracing hike up to the snowy brae. Or casting a line into the trout-choked river. Hazarding a refreshing dip in the loch. Or a relieving plunge into one of the willing wenches of the neighboring clan. Colban covered for him.

"Surely someone can give ye a reprieve?" he said.

She straightened defensively. "The enemy never sleeps. So I can't afford to."

"The enemy?"

"Those who threaten Scotland."

"So ye *are* defendin' the keep against dragons?" he asked, hoping to return the smile to her face.

He failed.

She narrowed her eyes. "I'm defending it against something more insidious than dragons."

"Ah. So ye mean the English."

"The English. Turncoat clans." Her gaze sharpened like a pointed dagger. "Anyone who threatens our claim to the land."

Her unspoken warning was clear. Highlanders were on her list of enemies.

"I would think ye'd be glad of allies in your fight," he countered.

"Allies?" she scoffed. "Is that what you are?"

"Why not? We're both Scots, aye?"

By her furrowed brows, she didn't quite believe that.

"We share a common foe, at least," he said. "I don't like the English any more than ye do."

"I doubt you've ever *seen* an Englishman."

"True," he admitted. "But I can tell ye this." He sobered, pinning her with eyes as grim as the grave. "I too will fight anyone who tries to take away what's mine."

CHAPTER 22

hallie's breath caught.

The intensity of Colban's stare magnified the gravity of his threat. But she sensed he was talking about more than just battling the English. More than defending Creagor and challenging Rivenloch.

There was a solemn vow in his eyes that said he protected everything that he deemed belonged to him. Whether that was a country. A castle. Or a wife.

That kind of chivalry was rare. Her father possessed it. So did her uncles. Most of the men of Rivenloch had had to learn that kind of loyalty.

But unless the woman was their laird, perhaps one in a dozen men had the kind of the honor to risk their life for a lass. And no one risked their life for a lass they hardly knew. No one but Colban an Curaidh, who had leaped from a window to save the woman who'd taken him prisoner.

Once again, admiration and adoration washed over her like a warm wave, softening her sharp edges, lapping gently at her soul.

"Besides," he murmured, "if we end up neighbors, we'll have to be allies. With the English at our door, we can't afford to be wagin' war upon each other all the time."

She bristled at the suggestion Creagor might indeed fall into the hands of Morgan Mor mac Giric. Nonetheless, she nodded.

"So for the moment, until we get word from the king, why not make a pact o' peace between us? An alliance between Rivenloch and Creagor?"

A pact of peace sounded dangerously close to fraternizing with the enemy. And yet it made sense. There was no point in engaging in aggression before it was absolutely necessary. Unless harm was done to her cousins, hostilities could wait until the king's decision was announced.

And as she looked into Colban's earnest, inviting eyes—eyes that sought her trust and melted her heart—the prospect of a pact of peace seemed pleasing indeed.

He offered her his hand, palm up.

Hallie hesitated. She gazed down at his battle-callused hand, extended to her in welcome. Should she trust him? Was that wise? Did Colban actually have the authority to speak on behalf of his laird? Would a pact secure a guarantee against attack? Or would she be letting down her guard and inviting invasion? And how did she know she was making the decision based on logic and not her emotions?

"'Tis the Rivenloch creed, after all, isn't it?" he asked. "Love conquers all?"

That was true.

But it was a fool who made peace with the enemy without negotiating first for some gain.

"I'll make a pact with you on one condition."

"Aye?"

"I'll have your word that if your laird has harmed my cousins in any way, the pact is deemed broken. Whatever damage he has inflicted will be upon your head. *You* will be punished for his deeds."

"Done."

He answered so quickly and with such confidence that she was taken aback. "You're sure of that?"

He gave her a curt nod. "I know Morgan Mor mac Giric like I know my own claymore. I know the damage he can do. But I also know his limits. My laird won't harm a hair on their heads."

She stared at his hand, still extended, waiting for hers.

The fate of Rivenloch rested in her decision about whether to trust him. A pact between them would ensure neither army would attack before her parents could return. That was what she'd always intended.

There was no doubt in her mind that Rivenloch would triumph in any battle between them. But she didn't want to needlessly sacrifice even one Rivenloch soldier. She didn't want to endanger the lives of her cousins. And if, by some travesty of justice, the king *did* award Creagor to mac Giric, she didn't want to make foes of her new neighbors.

Making peace official was perhaps for the best.

But when she finally reached out to accept his offered hand, he pulled it back.

"I too have a condition," he said.

She blinked. Surely he wasn't serious. "I'll remind you, you're my hostage. You have no leverage. I'm only agreeing to your pact to ensure the safety of my cousins and to avoid all-out war. You know you're outnumbered at Creagor. I need not agree to your demands."

"True," he admitted with a shrug. "'Tis only a matter o' courtesy, as one champion to another."

Champion? Her? He was clearly trying to flatter her. And the flattery didn't bother her as much as it should have.

"'Tis a negotiation between equals, aye?" he continued. "Then think of it as a noble gesture on your part. A sign o' chivalry. And respect."

His words prickled. Was he daring to challenge her honor?

She was laird of the most powerful Scots clan guarding the border.

He was a Highland soldier who fell asleep on his watch.

Nonetheless, there was wisdom in what he suggested. If she wished to negotiate peace, she would do well to tamp down her outrage and treat him with deference.

"Fine," she decided. "What is your condition?"

He took a deep breath and exhaled it. "I'd like a bath."

"What?"

"I've been here for half a week. Before that, I was travelin' on the road for a fortnight. I stink to high heaven. I'd like a bath."

She hadn't noticed. To her, he smelled like the outdoors. Of pine forests and wood smoke. For a moment, she was stunned by his curious request.

At her silence, he prompted, "Ye do take baths in the Lowlands?"

"Of course."

A bath? Why would he request a bath? Could he intend some trickery? Some ingenious scheme for escape requiring a tub full of water?

Her hesitation amused him. "'Tisn't too much to ask, is it? A hot bath to ensure peace between our clans?"

He'd forced her hand. But she had to conclude there was no mischief afoot. "Fine. I'll have Bart bring up a tub this even."

"Peace 'tis then." He extended his right hand again.

She stared down at it a moment longer before accepting his offer. As she slipped her hand into his, she felt curious warmth, as if a coal was enclosed between their palms.

His clasp tightened. His eyes smoldered into hers. And she had a sudden misgiving about the peace they were brokering.

She no longer felt in control. Unable to resist his dark, compelling, heart-melting eyes, she was also in no hurry to withdraw from the reassuring grip of his hand. Her command was slipping away from her, moment by moment. And yet that felt deliciously dangerous.

"Aye," she managed to murmur. "Peace."

Yet as they continued gazing into each other's eyes, sharing desire through the conduit of their joined hands, she felt anything but peaceful.

Colban suddenly realized the solution. It was in the rallying cry of Rivenloch. Love conquers all. The way to dispel hate was through love.

He'd told Hallie he'd fight anyone who tried to take away what was his. All the mac Giric men felt that way. The answer to peace between their clans was obvious. They needed to bind the two clans together by marriage. Find one Rivenloch lass willing to serve her clan by sacrificing herself to a mac Giric.

Colban was fairly confident the king was going to rule in Morgan's favor. By blood and by rights, Creagor belonged to the mac Giric clan. The Laird of Rivenloch may have petitioned the king for ownership of the keep. But Rivenloch already possessed a generous holding. Indeed, too much control of the border by a single powerful clan could be seen as posing a threat to the king's authority.

According to Ian, his parents had been expected to return three days ago. Their delay indicated trouble with the negotiations. Colban suspected they were having difficulty convincing the king to award Creagor to them.

It was tempting to think of that as a victory for the mac Girics. But Colban wasn't so sure.

What would happen when the king failed to yield to Rivenloch's demands? When he instead awarded the keep to Morgan?

Creagor was miles away from the throne. A vengeful Rivenloch could wreak havoc upon Morgan and make minced meat out of the mac Girics ere the king could intervene to enforce his will. Hell, they might even blame the casualties on the English.

Colban needed a way to ensure Morgan's continuing safety at Creagor. A way to guarantee there would be no heated battle for the castle. No question of ownership. And no animosity between the clans.

The two clans needed to forge a lasting alliance. One that couldn't be broken. One that would ensure ongoing peace for generations.

For that, the king had to be convinced that a marriage between the clans would strengthen the border alliance and keep the English at bay.

But first, he had to persuade Hallie it would be good for Rivenloch.

At the moment, she looked highly persuadable. There was a soft glow in her eyes and a yielding pressure in her hand.

But she had a streak of loyalty and willfulness in her that would always make her place the clan's needs above her own. Her warmth would vanish in an instant if she perceived Colban as a threat to Rivenloch, if she saw him, not as a gallant diplomat, but as a coarse Highland barbarian.

Convincing her of his worth and his wisdom required him to be at his best. Responsible. Capable. Devoted. And smelling a good deal better than he did at the moment. Which was why he'd requested a bath as part of their negotiations.

Nonetheless, it was with reluctance that he extricated his hand from hers and stepped back to allow her to leave.

Just before he lowered his gaze, he thought he glimpsed a hint of regret in her eyes. And though she addressed him with dignity, there was a flustered note in her voice. "About your bath... I'll have... I'll have..."

"Bart?"

"Aye, Bart. I'll send him up after supper."

"My thanks." As she gave him a curt nod and swept toward the door, he added, "Ye won't be sorry."

As she hurried out the door, he grimaced.

Ye won't be sorry?

Those weren't exactly the words of a gallant diplomat.

He sighed. Battle strategy he knew. But he was unpracticed at peace negotiations. They were going to be a challenge. He would have to take his time. Temper his thoughts. Tame his tongue. All while in the presence of a formidable Valkyrie.

"Oh, nay, you won't," Hallie commanded.

Isabel scurried around their bedchamber with a wicker basket full of linen cloths and sponges. She pilfered several tallow candles and vials of herbs and oils from the table, tucking them into the basket.

"But someone has to scrub his back," Isabel replied with a shrug.

"Scrub his..." Hallie grabbed her arm and spun her around. "Not you, Isabel. We have maidservants for that."

Isabel glared pointedly at her arm, still in Hallie's grip, until Hallie was shamed into releasing her.

"Burunild is assisting the midwife," Isabel informed her. "Abygail has gone to visit her sister. Hilda is caring for her new babe. Gillian is ill with a fever. And the rest have gone to bed."

"Gone to bed?"

Isabel shrugged. "You kept them quite busy today."

That was true. Hallie believed that idle hands caused misbehavior, especially when it came to Isabel's companions. She sighed, then grumbled, "Bloody hell, he's a grown man. I'm sure he can scrub his own back."

Isabel's jaw dropped. "'Tis a matter of common courtesy, Hallie. You know that. Rivenloch has a reputation to uphold. If word got out that we'd left a guest unattended at his bath..." She shuddered.

"Rivenloch's reputation isn't built on our bathing services."

"But such rudeness is a... What's the word you taught me? A travesty." Isabel shrugged. "Besides, I don't mind doing the task."

"That's my point, Isabel."

"What?"

"I'm sure you don't mind at all," Hallie said, inexplicably irritated. "Your friends are doubtless awaiting your salacious gossip."

"Salacious?" She blinked. "What does that mean?"

Hallie cooed in imitation of Isabel's friends, "Oh, Isabel, tell us all about the Highlander. How tall is he? Are those muscles real? Just how broad *is* his back?" There was more, but she wouldn't go down that path with her little sister.

"What if I promise to keep my eyes closed?" Isabel offered.

Hallie let out an all-suffering sigh. This was ridiculous. There was no way she was going to allow her virtuous little sister to bathe a naked, healthy, warm-blooded Highlander.

"Give me that," she muttered, grabbing for the basket.

Isabel pulled it out of her reach. "But Hallie—"

"I'll be damned if I'm going to leave you alone with a hostile hostage."

She made another grab for the basket, catching one side of the handle.

But Isabel wouldn't let go of it. "Didn't you say you agreed to a pact of peace? So he's not hostile."

"Give me that basket," Hallie warned, tugging harder.

"Be reasonable, Hallie," Isabel argued, tugging back. "I know what I'm doing."

"Nay." She refused to put her little sister in harm's way. It was too risky.

"But Hallie..."

"Nay. And that's final."

Isabel stamped her foot, but she still clung to the basket. "No one else is available for the task. And his bath is growin' cold."

Surely *someone* was available. Hallie racked her brains.

At waging war, she was an expert. At managing the household, she was highly efficient. But mastering the fine details of hospitality had always seemed a pointless pursuit.

Nonetheless, as laird, it was up to her to solve the problem. And in the end, she resorted to what always happened when she was unable to get cooperation from others. She took matters into her own hands.

Seeing no other course of action and cursing herself for a fool, Hallie muttered, "I'll do it."

"What?"

"*I'll* do it."

Isabel stifled a laugh. "You?"

Her scorn seared Hallie like the kiss of a hot coal. She pinned Isabel with an icy glare. "Aye. Why not?"

"Oh Hallie," Isabel argued, her patronizing voice full of pity, "you don't have a woman's touch. You might as well send Sir Rauve to do the task."

That did it. That settled Hallie's resolve. She would take no more ridicule from her meddling sister. She snatched the basket out of Isabel's grip and nodded toward the door. "Go."

Isabel pressed her lips into a pout. "You're making a mistake."

Hallie couldn't agree more. But it would be a bigger mistake to cede to Isabel's whims. "Out."

"'Twill jeopardize the peace if you hurt him, you know."

"I'm not going to hurt him."

"Maybe not on purpose, but..."

"Go, Isabel."

Isabel picked up her skirts and stomped out the door, angry that all her best laid plans had gone awry.

But now that Hallie was left holding the basket, she began to wonder if perhaps Isabel's plans hadn't gone awry after all.

She got the sinking feeling that this was exactly what her conniving little sister had intended.

CHAPTER 23

Seated on the bed with the leg of his trews bunched above his knee, Colban had the bandage around his ankle halfway unwrapped when there was a knock at the door.

"Come!" he called out.

Bart had come and gone after filling the large wooden tub with buckets of steaming water. Colban expected that was the old maidservant, Burunild, arriving to help him at his bath.

As the door opened, he said, "I think the swellin's down alrea—"

He looked up.

It wasn't Burunild.

"Hallie." He didn't know whether to be pleased or horrified.

Hallie, carrying a basket brimming with linens, sponges, candles, and bottles, looked as uneasy as he felt.

"What's all this?" he asked, though it was clear they were items meant for his bath.

"I've come to assist you." By her grim expression, one would think she'd come to torture him.

Perhaps she *had* come to torture him. Just the thought of Hallie attending him at his bath—peeling his clothes from his body, drizzling warm water over his skin, running her fingers over every inch of him—seemed like delicious torment.

He wasn't sure any of that was wise. Not in his present state. Though the swelling in his ankle had gone down, he couldn't say the same about other parts of him, not with an enticing Valkyrie in the room.

"Bart told me that Burunild—"

"Burunild was called away. And no one else was available." She sounded rather defensive. "I tried to find someone else. Abygail. Gillian. Hilda. They were all occupied or asleep."

"I see." He averted his eyes, returning his attention to unwrapping his ankle. If she'd tried to enlist so many others, it was clearly a task she was loath to do. Which was fine. He didn't want her to do it anyway. Did he? "Well, I'm sure I can manage alone. Just leave the basket beside the tub and—"

"Nay, I can do it. I said I would. And I will." She seemed resigned, as if she'd been commanded to do something repulsive. Like emptying his chamber pot.

The tone of her voice ruffled his feathers. She didn't have to sound quite so unhappy.

"Look, ye clearly don't *wish* to," he muttered. "I understand. Ye're the laird. Ye shouldn't have to perform the work of a maidservant."

His words seemed to annoy her. "You doubt I'm capable?"

He furrowed his brows. "I didn't say that."

"I won't hurt you," she blurted out, "if that's what you think."

He blinked in surprise. That wasn't at all what he thought.

She seemed flustered by her own admission. She lowered the basket onto the floor beside the tub and removed two candles. Gripping them like a pair of daggers, she cast around the chamber, uncertain where to put them.

Colban might have found her awkward determination amusing if he weren't growing harder by the moment, imagining her candle-gripping fists wrapped around...

He nodded at the candles and managed to mumble, "Just leave them on the table." Then, deciding it really would be best if she left, he said, "I'll be fine. Really. I'm sure ye have more pressin' duties. Like ye said, the enemy ne'er sleeps."

Again, she seemed irritated by his words. "Just because I'm in command of the knights doesn't mean I can't do more...womanly...tasks."

"O' course not."

"I know how to give a man a bath."

"No doubt." His voice cracked on the words as he imagined her sliding her palms over his chest, his stomach, and lower. "I just meant ye needn't trouble yourself."

"'Tis no trouble."

She planted the candles on the table and plucked a bottle from the basket. Removing the stopper, she poured a generous dollop of clove oil into the bath water, swishing it in with her fingers. Her eyes skimmed the surface of the water with cool indifference. But her hand stirred an agitated current beneath, and when she lifted her hand to shake the water from her fingers, it was with an abrupt flick of her wrist.

"Unless you'd *prefer* someone else," she said. Her casual shrug was unconvincing. "I suppose I could call Bart back if—"

"Bart?" he squeaked. Bloody hell, did she honestly think he wanted to have his back scoured by a scrawny youth with grimy knuckles? "Nay, thank ye."

On the other hand, the way the lass was stirring his blood, perhaps a good rough sponging was just what he needed to scrub the lust from his body.

From the moment she'd entered the bedchamber, Hallie had been determined to foil Isabel's efforts at fomenting romance. She'd intended to remain aloof yet civil.

Thorough yet perfunctory. To perform the task with the same efficiency she used to polish a suit of armor.

But Colban an Curaidh was not a suit of armor. He was a living, breathing man. He had thoughts and feelings, opinions and desires.

He also had eyes that could drown her in their depths. And a body that could make her forget she was a warrior lass.

The way she felt right now—off-kilter and distracted—he could easily bend her to his will. And that would be perilous indeed.

So, like a nervous novice in her first skirmish, she found herself sizing up her foe. Measuring his mettle. Delaying engagement for as long as possible.

"The water's growin' cold," Colban said.

She exhaled her worry on a sharp breath. She could do this.

"Climb in. I'll lay out the linens."

She rummaged in the basket, dropping a sponge into the bath. Lifting the linens one by one, she arranged them painstakingly atop the coverlet of the bed. She lit the candles from the flames on the hearth and replaced them with trembling fingers.

Meanwhile, from the corner of her eye, she watched Colban strip off his leine.

She saw men in all states of undress every day. It was inevitable when one spent as much time as she did in the armory. Colban was no different than most of the fit Rivenloch knights with his powerful shoulders. Broad chest. Well-defined arms. Flat stomach.

But the way his shoulders flexed and his muscles rippled took her breath away. And when he removed his trews, baring his firm hindquarters, her heart began thumping like a fulling mill. As he climbed into the water, he looked like some magnificent god returning to the sea.

Her fascinated gaze was drawn again and again to his enticing contours. And the sight of him—so close, so real—muddled her brain and tied her tongue in knots.

But it was too late to withdraw now. She'd committed to giving him a bath. With a shaky sigh of resolve, she knelt beside the tub.

Colban was staring hard at the water between his knees, as if he might boil it with his focused glare. As she neared, he moved his hands casually to his naked lap, cheating her curious eyes.

She told herself Colban an Curaidh was only a man, not a god.

As if further proof of that, when she lifted her wet sponge to his brow, she noticed a faint scar at his hairline. That was good. Perhaps if she could focus on his imperfections, she wouldn't be distracted by his perfections.

She nodded to the thin white line. "How did you get that?"

His fingers traced the mark. "Glancing blow of a dagger."

She nodded and rubbed across it with the wet sponge.

He closed his eyes. She continued laving his face, trying to employ what Isabel called "a woman's touch."

She dabbed lightly at the mottled flesh beneath his eye. "Your bruise is healing."

He nodded.

Perhaps this wouldn't be so hard, after all. If she just imagined the Highlander was one of her own knights or her brother...

She moved the sponge along the square edge of his jaw. His face was swarthy, weathered by the elements and shadowed by dark stubble. She remembered the sensation of his beard-roughened skin against her cheek.

Shivering at the memory, she pressed the sponge carefully against his split lip. His mouth opened at her touch, and she could see the white tips of his teeth.

Teeth that gleamed when he laughed. Flashed when he snarled. Teeth that might nibble a path of delight along her neck.

Frowning at that wayward thought, she wet the sponge again and gently tucked his hair behind his left ear. There was a healed nick at the top of his ear.

"What happened here?" she asked, tracing the place with a fingertip.

"Fell and hit a rock, reivin' a coo," he said, smiling at the memory. Before she could ask him if he was in the habit of stealing cattle, he added, "I was a wee lad, provin' my mettle to the clan."

His other ear was flawless. But as she squeezed the sponge to drizzle water down his neck, she found another scar just above his collar bone. This one was clean, angled, and oddly familiar.

"Sword?" she guessed.

"Aye."

With a warrior's camaraderie, she pulled aside her leine to show him a similar scar on the side of her neck. "I was twelve. Fighting Jenefer. Didn't raise my shield fast enough."

He lifted his brows, impressed. "Twelve? Well, *I* was old enough to know better," he admitted, his eyes dancing with humor beneath languorous lids. "I was showin' off for the lasses."

She smirked. This was not so bad. They were conversing now. Everything would be fine. As long as she could forget he was her enemy. And a hostage. And the most handsome warrior she'd ever...

Distracted, she dropped the sponge. Her gaze followed its path. It sank betwixt his knees.

Though he quickly intercepted it, retrieving the sponge for her, it wasn't before she glimpsed what lay beneath the surface of the water, below his hands.

Blood rushed to her cheeks.

Why? She didn't know. Such a thing shouldn't disturb her. She'd seen plenty of men with their blades unsheathed. Some of them hung like lifeless eels. Others resembled stiff daggers about to strike. That Colban fell into the second group made her blush with pleasure. At least she knew she wasn't the only one afflicted by lust.

Clearing her throat, she resumed her task, cupping water over his shoulders and circling the sponge across his chest, trying to be as economical as possible in her movements. He tipped his head back to give her access, and she could feel his gaze burning through the narrow slits of his eyes.

To her consternation, she kept letting her glance slip to his hands, half hoping he'd accidentally reveal himself again. He did not.

Thwarted, she moved behind him. He dutifully leaned forward so she could scrub his back.

"I should warn ye..." he began.

She gasped. A bundle of scars crossed his back diagonally from his right shoulder blade to his left hip. They were long, shallow, and raggedly healed. Only one thing made those kinds of slashes.

He'd been whipped.

Ice flooded her veins as she asked, "Who did this? Morgan?"

"Morgan? Nay!" he was quick to answer. "Indeed, Morgan was the one who *saved* me."

"Saved you from whom? His father? A foe?" She clenched the sponge with killing force.

"Neither," he said with a shrug. "A pair o' mac Giric men who didn't want a harlot's son in the clan. They were hopin' to whip me to the Devil's door, I'm certain." He added, "If it troubles ye to look upon—"

"Nay." Astonished by her own volatile reaction and how quickly she'd rushed to his defense, she took a calming breath. "Not at all. Our scars are part of who we are, after all."

Still, she had to wonder what kind of monsters took a whip to a person because of the circumstances of his birth, circumstances over which he had no control?

As she began to bathe his back with care, she asked, "How old were you when this happened?"

"Ten."

"Ten?" Her heart sank. "'Tis Ian's age."

"I suppose so."

"And Morgan defended you?"

"As best he could. We were both wee lads. But o' course, him bein' the son o' the laird..."

"They had to do his bidding."

"Aye."

For him, the scars might be old and long healed. But to Hallie, the wrongness—and her outrage over it—was fresh.

She didn't know what they did in the Highlands to lads who perpetrated such diabolical deeds. But if she were his laird...

She squeezed all the water from the sponge in one cold fist. Revenge began to crystallize in her veins as she dreamed up fitting punishments for the kind of brutes who would dare raise a lash to a helpless lad.

Narrowing icy eyes, she asked, "Where are these men now? Did they come with you? Are they staying at Creagor?"

CHAPTER 24

Amazed at the serious tone of Hallie's question, Colban craned his neck to look up at her. Retribution rang in her voice. And the cold fire of justice burned in her eyes.

"Who?" he asked. "The ones who did this?"

"Aye."

"Why do ye ask?" he ventured.

"They should be brought to justice," she said, scowling. "Stripped of their lands and armor and made to...to herd sheep in the hills."

He nodded, biting his lip to keep from smiling at a Lowlander's idea of punishment. The fact that she was up in arms over what had been done to him, that she wished to right that wrong, even after all these years, melted his heart. He was pleased beyond measure that the warrior lass wanted vengeance on his behalf. But he didn't want her to think the mac Girics let crimes—even those against a harlot's son—go unanswered.

"They were banished from the clan the next day. Sent away."

"Sent away where?" she persisted.

"Why do ye want to know?" he said with a lift of his brow. "Do ye intend to chase them to the ends o' the earth?"

"Maybe."

He grinned. "Well, I'm sorry to disappoint ye, my fierce avengin' angel, but no one knows where they went. They were ne'er seen again."

She nodded, but he couldn't miss the hint of regret in her eyes. The lass *wanted* to punish his abusers. Even though he'd recovered from the incident—even though the unwanted foundling had emerged a champion—Hallie wanted to heal the scars of injustice.

That touched him deeply.

It also reaffirmed the wisdom of forming an alliance with Rivenloch.

The lass who would one day rule the warrior clan was devoted to justice, protective of honor, loyal to what was right and fair. She would not let good deeds go unrewarded. Nor would she let wrongs go unpunished.

She was the last person he would want as an enemy.

Indeed, the more time he spent with her, the more he realized she would make a good friend. Despite their thorny beginnings, the willful lass was beginning to grow on him.

Hallie was hardly cold and unfeeling, as Isabel maintained. After all, she didn't mind his scars. She didn't blame him for the circumstances of his birth. And now that she'd managed to get him into the tub, she didn't even seem to be that bothered by having to scrub his back.

While she was feeling so amenable, he thought he could tell her about his idea.

As she held his elbow to swab his upper arm, he said, "Ye know, I've been mullin' it o'er—this matter o' the ownership o' Creagor."

She gave him a guarded, "Aye?"

"I think there may be a way to forge an alliance, no matter what the king decides."

"An alliance? Why?" She lowered her eyes, and a slight crease appeared between them. "Once he decides in

Rivenloch's favor, you'll return to the Highlands. Won't you?" Was that hope or regret he heard?

"Ah, but what if he rules in the mac Giric's favor?"

"He won't do that," Hallie was quick to say, though there was a scintilla of doubt in the wavering of her voice. "It makes no sense. Strategically. Logistically. Practically."

She began scrubbing a bit too fiercely at his forearm. He stayed her hand before she could scrub the skin away.

"Just bear with me a moment."

She dropped the sponge in the water and sat back on her heels. "Fine."

He picked up the sponge, rolling it idly between his palms. "'Twouldn't be the first time a king made an impractical decision. To curry favor. Or gain land. Or just on a whim."

He could see by the grim set of her mouth that Hallie knew the truth of that all too well. In the Highlands, king and country were a vague concept. Laws were made by and for those who lived far away. But for Hallie, dwelling closer to the seat of Scotland's power, royal edicts were real. They had immediate consequences.

"Go on," she said.

"What if neither of us has to lose?" he suggested. "What if we *both* claim Creagor?"

"Both?" She blinked.

He continued, gesturing with the sponge to emphasize his point. "What if we forge a different kind of alliance? One more bindin' than that o' the king. One made in the presence o' God."

She looked at him with skepticism. "A holy alliance?"

"Of a sort." He racked his brain for a good example. "Consider Isabel. What if Isabel were betrothed to a mac Giric lad?"

"What mac Giric lad?" she demanded with a fierce scowl.

"I'm not sayin' she is," he clarified. "But what if she were?"

"Not Isabel. When my sister marries, 'twill be for love."

"O' course." He smiled. The hardhearted warrior lass had a soft spot for her little sister. "Perhaps Abygail then or..."

"So you're suggesting a marriage between our clans."

He took a tenuous breath, hoping she wouldn't reject the idea out of hand. "Aye."

"To keep the peace."

"Aye."

She furrowed her brows and tapped thoughtfully at her lip.

She was silent so long, Colban began to fret she might reconsider.

"'Twouldn't have to be Abygail," he offered. "Maybe Gillian or—"

"My cousin."

"What?"

"My cousin is of marriageable age now."

Colban gulped. He hoped she wasn't talking about one of the two hellions he'd tangled with on the field at Creagor. The hostages Morgan was holding even now in his bedchamber. Colban wouldn't wish either of those wild wenches on any of his clansmen.

Hallie was beginning to think the Highlander might be on to something.

If by some chance Rivenloch didn't win Creagor, if her cousin didn't get the castle she'd been promised, Jenefer wasn't the kind of lass to surrender with grace. In fact, she'd probably harass and harangue the mac Girics for the rest of her life.

But if she wed a mac Giric, it wouldn't matter which

clan the king favored to claim Creagor. Rivenloch would maintain a controlling piece of the land.

Naturally, as soon as that thought formed, several obstacles popped into her head.

First, her cousin Jenefer refused to be commanded by anyone. The fiery lass could hardly follow *Hallie's* orders. There was no way she'd agree to an arranged marriage. Especially to a Highlander, whom she considered savage and inferior.

Second, Jenefer believed Creagor was hers by rights. She didn't think a marriage was required to grant her dominion over the land. No matter what the king decreed.

Third, Jenefer was impossibly hotheaded. Even if she did agree to wed a mac Giric, the marriage probably wouldn't last a sennight. The bride or the groom would be killed ere the honeymoon was over.

"Not Jenefer," she decided.

"Ye mean the other one?" Colban asked. "The one who tried to kill me?"

She grimaced. Feiyan wasn't always so bloodthirsty. But she was unpredictable, which made her seem untrustworthy. Whoever married her would spend half the time watching his back and the other half wondering where she was hiding.

Still, Feiyan would be more amenable to a political alliance. Her heart, as capricious and elusive as the lass herself, belonged to no one. If she ended up unhappy with the arrangement, she'd simply slip away with none the wiser.

Colban stared down at the water. His face was unexpectedly grim.

"Very well," he said. "If ye give me your word she won't try to murder me with one o' those pointy toys o' hers, then I suppose 'tis worth the sacrifice."

"Sacrifice? What sacrifice?"

"I'll take the lass to wife."

The bottom dropped out of her heart. "What?"

He exhaled a long breath. "If it means peace between our clans, 'tis a sacrifice I'm willin' to make."

Suddenly, Hallie couldn't draw air into her lungs. Just the thought of lithe and lovely Feiyan with her arms wrapped around Colban's neck and her legs entwined with his made her feel ill.

She couldn't allow it.

She *wouldn't* allow it.

"Don't be ridiculous. You can't wed Feiyan."

"Why not?"

"She's...she's...I can't promise she *won't* try to kill you." In a panic, she stooped to an outright lie. "You wouldn't be the first man she killed in cold blood."

He gulped. "Is that so?"

Even as the words left her lips, Hallie regretted them. Why the devil had she said that? Feiyan had done no such thing. She might be sneaky and vicious and underhanded. But she'd never even seriously injured a man who didn't deserve it.

"Well," Colban mumbled, "I suppose murderin' the bridegroom might damage the alliance a bit."

"Aye. So you see? 'Twould be an empty sacrifice." Only half-relieved, she twisted her fingers in her lap. "On the other hand, why should it have to be *your* sacrifice?"

He shook his head. "Och, when it comes down to it, I couldn't ask anyone else to do it. To marry a foe? To wed out o' duty and not fondness? 'Twould be cruel."

Before this week, Hallie had given it little thought. After all, *she* was expected to wed out of duty and not fondness. It had never seemed cruel to her.

Until now.

Over the last few days, she'd sampled something more delicious than duty. More savory than responsibility. More nourishing than power.

She'd had a taste of affection. A wee taste, to be sure. But it had been sweet and warm and filling. And now the thought of marrying a man for whom she didn't have those feelings left a bitter taste in her mouth.

And if Hallie—whose prize for sacrificing marital happiness would be the lairdship of all Rivenloch—felt the unfairness of that, she couldn't imagine how it must feel to be Colban. He had naught to gain from a loveless union but the satisfaction that he'd done his master a noble service.

If only the union binding their clans weren't loveless... If the bride and groom actually *cared* for each other...

She tucked the corner of her lip under her teeth as an idea began to form in her brain that was intrepid. Impulsive. Irresponsible. A reckless scheme with as many loose ends as a frayed rope. But one that was more satisfying than she cared to admit.

She could marry Colban.

The future Laird of Rivenloch could seal the alliance with the Champion of mac Giric.

The idea made her heart flutter. But she was certain her excitement was from finding the perfect solution to a problem. Nothing more.

After all, it was the sensible thing to do. They were already reasonably compatible. And they were both aligned as to their purpose, willing to sacrifice their own happiness for the good of their clan.

Their union could forge an unbreakable bond, enriching the power of Rivenloch, and creating a formidable force along the border.

The more she considered it, the more brilliant a solution it seemed. And the more right it felt.

All she had to do was convince the king of the wisdom of such a union.

Persuade her parents of the Highlander's worth.

And make Colban agree to the terms.

As he sat stewing in the bath, Colban mentally ticked off the possibilities for a Rivenloch wife out of the limited choices he'd seen.

If not one of Hallie's cousins, then who?

One of Isabel's friends?

They were too young. No matter how long the betrothal, he'd never be able to bed one of them without feeling like he was bedding a child.

What about the blind seer?

Her infirmity didn't bother him, though she was several years his senior. But what was it she'd predicted for Colban? Loneliness and heartbreak? Surely she'd not wed a man for whom she'd foretold such a bleak future.

He was reduced to Burunild, whom he supposed would be a godsend when it came to looking after his injuries. If he could overlook the fact she was ancient enough to be his grandmother.

Hallie would probably find excuses for all of them anyway. Her fierce cousins notwithstanding, she clearly didn't wish to sacrifice any of her clanswomen to a baseborn Highlander whom she thought swived sheep.

He sighed, wondering what other eligible Rivenloch maidens might look past his humble beginnings and find him palatable.

He'd be far more palatable once he finished this bath, he supposed. He returned to scrubbing his ribs, working his way down his abdomen and lower.

Hallie offered him her hand. "*I'll* do it."

He raised his brows. *Now* she wished to help him with his bath? *Now?* When he was about to wash his ballocks? He didn't think so.

"Nay, thank ye." he said with a chuckle.

She blinked. "What do you mean, nay?"

"I can manage it from here." The last thing he needed during these sensitive negotiations was to lose control and embarrass himself like a randy oaf.

She looked flummoxed. "You won't consider it?"

He gave her a baffled frown. She seemed overly offended. "I'd...rather ye didn't."

"You feel naught for me then?" she said stiffly, dropping her offered hand in her lap.

"What?" He creased his brow in confusion. Had the naughty lass not stolen a glimpse of his nether regions? Did she not realize it was his feelings for her that had *caused* his agitated state?

She muttered, "Maybe, if you gave things time to grow..."

"Grow?" He was already full to bursting. "I hate to disappoint ye, but—"

"Then don't," she insisted. "Say you'll agree."

His mouth worked as he battled indecision. Till now, she'd treated him with civility and generosity. He didn't wish to jeopardize their arrangement and ruin the truce between them. So rather than risking offending her further, he shook his head and handed her the dripping sponge.

"Och, fine," he said in exasperation. "Do your worst. Just don't blame me for what ensues. A man doesn't always have reign o'er such things, ye know."

When he glanced up, she was staring at the sponge as if in confusion. Her gaze flitted to the beast between his legs.

"Best hurry," he said. "I don't want the water to get cold." If she thought he wasn't "grown" now, he couldn't imagine what she'd think when the chill shrunk him.

"Aye. Fine. If that's what it takes..."

The look in her eyes was dazed yet determined as she studied his anatomy. She swallowed hard, as if she were planning an attack on a wild boar. When she rose up on her knees, lifting the sponge like a weapon, he realized she'd never done this before in her life.

"Hold on," he said, catching her wrist before she could plunge it into the water. "Why do ye want to be doin' this?"

"Like you said, 'twill bring peace to our clans."

"Washin' my cock will bring peace to our clans?" he blurted out.

"What? Nay! Who said anything about washing your bloody...?" she exclaimed, casting the sponge into the bath. "God's eyes, Highlander! Will you take me as your wife or not?"

CHAPTER 25

Colban was rendered speechless. He tried to replay their conversation, unable to fathom where it had gone astray. But none of that mattered.

"My wife?" he finally choked out.

"Aye. What did you think I was offering?"

"It doesn't matter."

What mattered was Hallie was offering herself in marriage. The beautiful warrior lass wanted to wed him. *Him.* An orphan. A bastard. A Highlander with no coin or name.

And by her eyes, she was dead serious.

"Me?" he ventured. "Ye wish to wed *me*?"

"Aye, though I can see you're not enthused about the idea."

Not enthused? His heart was pounding like a swordsmith's mallet. And beneath the water, he stood as proud as a claymore.

She continued. "You said you were willing to make a sacrifice for your clan. So am I. 'Twas never my lot to marry for love. But you and I, I think we have at least... an understanding. I think we could make a...a compatible marriage that would benefit both our clans."

Colban couldn't breathe. An understanding? Compatible? God's blood! She was the most desirable woman he'd ever met. This was an offer beyond his wildest dreams. Never had he imagined himself worthy of her affections. Never had he expected she would settle for anything less than a laird.

She mistook his speechlessness for reluctance. "There will be time later to become better acquainted and..." She lowered her eyes and mumbled, "Nurture our affections."

Hell, his body wanted to nurture their affections at once. Wedding the magnificent Valkyrie? Waking up to her each morn? Making love and bairns and memories with such a woman?

It seemed too good to be true. His heart soared at the prospect.

Yet it would be a blunder of negotiation to let her believe he could be so easily won. So instead of shouting out in triumph to the sky, he pensively rubbed his chin.

"I think perhaps I could grow to care for ye, as long as..." He slipped her a sideways glance. "Ye don't intend to slay me in my sleep like Feiyan, do ye?"

She smirked. "Nay."

"Or kill me in a fiery rage like Jenefer?"

"If you like," she quipped with dry humor, "we can write that into the marriage vows."

Keeping a grim face, he nodded, pretending to consider her terms. "I'd also like apple coffyns every day."

She wasn't fooled for an instant by his ridiculous demand. "Every *other* day."

He gave her a sly grin. "What about daily baths?"

She gave him a wry smile. "Don't press your luck."

He feigned a loud sigh of disappointment.

"So what say you?" she asked. "Are you willing to take me to wife? For the good of our clans?"

His smile faded as the import of what he was promising sank in. For him, it meant more than the good of the clan.

Once he gave his word, he would be her husband, not only in name, but in deed. He'd be required to honor his vows.

To be faithful to Hallie. To protect her with his sword. To defend her with his life. To be her champion forevermore.

It was a weighty decision. One he was compelled to make after knowing his bride for less than a sennight.

But one he was confident he would not regret.

"Aye, m'lady," he told her. "I would be honored to be your husband."

"Good. 'Tis done then." She offered her hand once again to seal the vow.

There was just one problem with Hallie's very sensible, practical alliance between two "compatible" people who had "an understanding."

He had no intention of letting her marry him for political gain.

He intended to ensure she married him for love.

He meant to prove he was The One. Convince her he was a suitable suitor. A devoted champion. A worthy husband. By the time they recited their vows, he would have Hallie of Rivenloch solidly embedded in his heart and eating out of his hand.

As if proving his point, he took the hand she offered, turned it over, and placed a tender kiss in her palm.

When he looked up, a gentle wonder lit her gaze.

Suddenly, he didn't wish to let go of her. He wanted to clasp Hallie's hand forever. Drawn into the crystal depths of her eyes, enclosing her fingers in his own, he felt a rightness, a belonging he'd never felt before.

From the time he'd laid eyes on the beautiful Valkyrie, he'd been dreaming of holding her in his arms. Of kissing her mouthwatering lips. Of running his hands through her silvery tresses and over her glorious skin.

Now he had a lifetime ahead of him to do just that.

Yet he felt like he didn't want to lose a moment.

Hallie didn't want to waste another instant. Now that she'd come to a decision, she saw no reason to hold back.

From their first touch, she'd felt something special between them. A spark of life. A whisper of something far greater and more powerful.

Now that they'd made a commitment, there was no excuse not to further explore that feeling.

She slipped her hand through his, locking their fingers together.

He lowered his head again over their joined hands, brushing her knuckles with his lips. When he lifted his head, his gaze focused on her mouth.

She could read his intent at once.

"Shall we seal our vow with a..." he began.

She didn't let him finish. Rising on her knees, she caught the back of his head with her free hand and pulled him forward for a kiss.

Startled for only an instant, he began to answer with tentative kisses of his own. They were soft at first, as if he were tasting blancmange, relishing the smooth, silky sweetness.

But soon the pressure of his lips coaxed hers open, and he deepened the kiss. Their breath mingled as she sighed in awe and discovery. Her eyelids grew heavy. Her limbs melted. Their mouths met and fed and battled and soothed while a warm vibration of longing swirled around her head.

He loosed his hand from her limp fingers and lifted it to capture her cheek. Nudging her jaw open with his thumb, he slanted his head and gently swept his tongue inside.

While fragrant steam rose from the bath, molten desire radiated through her body. Filling her veins. Igniting her senses. Thawing her heart.

The playful splash of water slurping at the side of the tub contrasted with the rough and hungry growl rising in her throat.

She wanted more.

No longer tenuous, his kisses became insistent, demanding. She welcomed his aggression, answering him with a passion of her own, exploring his mouth with her tongue and letting her hands range over his tempting flesh.

Her fingers glided across his smooth, wet skin. She tracked the insistent throb of his pulse in his corded throat. Sighed over the supple muscle of his magnificent chest. Gasped at the hard pucker of his nipple as she brushed it with a fingertip.

A low groan escaped him. She responded as if the primitive sound were the call of a wolf to its mate. Every nerve awoke. Every sense was heightened. She felt an almost irresistible imperative to join with him.

And then he made things worse.

He began to return her explorations in kind. He traced the contours of her jaw and neck with his thumbs. Tugged open her kirtle until it rasped from her shoulders. Slid the backs of his scarred knuckles slowly across her bosom, then lower, over her breasts, making her breath catch as he brazenly brushed across her nipples.

At his touch, a bolt of current, as lethal as lightning, shot through her body, wringing a gasp from her. Need licked at her skin and coursed through her veins.

Breaking free just long enough to wrench the pesky kirtle and leine from her arms, letting them drop to the floor at her knees, she faced him with raw lust and bold challenge.

His gaze raced over her with a brazen thirst that filled her with heady triumph and sent her desire spiraling to new heights.

"Och, lass," he despaired, "ye tempt me sorely."

Her thrill of victory didn't last long. Once she lowered her gaze beneath the water and spied the beast rising from its nest of dark curls, passion quickly wiped the satisfied smile from her face, leaving her mouth open in awe.

Several thoughts raced through her mind in the span of an instant.

He was beautiful.

He was attracted to her.

He was ready for her.

One day soon, she would become his wife.

At which time he would consummate their marriage.

With *that*.

And suddenly it seemed so...impossible.

But before she could dwell too long on the physical logistics of mating, he seemed to sense her hesitation and released her.

"I'll go no further, lass," he said on a sigh, withdrawing and using his hands to shield his erection from her view. "I don't wish to frighten ye."

He meant to do the gentlemanly thing. He meant to protect her from his raging appetite. To guard her from harm at his hands.

His mistake was using the word, "frighten."

Hallidis of Rivenloch wasn't afraid of anything. Least of all the sort of blunted dagger that every milkmaid's mother in Scotland had been impaled with at one time or another.

It was only doubt and misgiving that made her hesitate.

In battle, such doubt came from not knowing one's foe, being unable to predict behavior or anticipate attacks.

The answer then was not to withdraw, but to lean in. To learn everything she could about Colban an Curaidh.

Though Colban had retreated, his chest still heaved with lusty breaths, and there was a shimmering spark in his eyes where desire smoldered. It would take but a small nudge, a whisper of encouragement to make that spark flicker back to life.

"I'm not afraid," she told him.

With confidence born of willpower, she reached into the water and moved his hands aside. Then she slipped her hand carefully around him, grasping him as she would a sword.

He sucked a hard breath between his teeth. For one shameful instant, she feared she'd hurt him. But a quick glance at the pleasure in his eyes disabused her of that notion.

It was not unpleasant, holding him like this. His velvety smoothness would not injure her, she was sure.

He'd closed his eyes. She took the opportunity to lean forward and steal a kiss.

He responded at once, cradling her head in his hands and delving deeply into her mouth, letting their tongues mate in liquid ecstasy.

Beneath the water, her fingers skimmed along his length. He pulsed within her hand, which she slid all the way up to the hilt.

He groaned as if in torment, and Isabel's warning haunted her.

"Is that too rough?" she murmured. "Have I hurt you?"

He answered with a sultry chuckle. "'Tisn't pain, lass."

His hand made a swift but sensual trek down her body, past her breasts, across her abdomen, and lower. He slipped his fingers into her nest of curls, stroking her there like a kitten.

Then he eased a finger between her nether lips, trespassing into the very place where all her desire centered.

At his touch, a surge of need blew through her soul like a hot wind. Her entire body felt suddenly aflame.

He was right. It wasn't pain. It was like a sweet torment. A pleasurable, unquenchable longing for more.

She writhed against him, delighting in the pressure and friction of his fingertips grazing her flesh.

Below the water, he moved in a similar fashion against her palm, like a dagger seeking the sheath of her hand.

Soon their exploration took a serious turn. A turn from which there was little hope of return. Temptation would not be denied. Longing became need.

Caught up in a growing firestorm of sensations, billowing quickly out of control, Hallie gasped for breath.

Colban answered with a groan, resting his brow on her shoulder as if he battled some inner demon of his own making.

And in that moment of torturous restraint, hovering on the edge of desire and sin, of what they longed for and what was forbidden, a dangerous notion flickered to life in Hallie's fevered brain.

Why should they hold back?

Why shouldn't they simply follow their instincts? Let nature guide them? Strike while the iron was hot?

She wanted him.

He wanted her.

What would seal their union better than consummating it?

And then an even darker thought intruded upon her reasoning.

If she surrendered her virginity to him, it would be difficult, if not impossible, to undo their betrothal and deny their marriage. No one could foil her plans. Not her parents. Not even the king.

Coupling with the handsome Highlander was not only a desirable option. It was a damned clever strategy.

Colban was going to shame himself. He could feel it.

It had been a while since he'd unleashed the beast. And it was roaring for release.

He had to stop the lovely lass before it was too late to stop. The last thing he wanted was for his bride to see him gushing in the bath like a beardless lad. She might have second thoughts about marrying a man with so little control.

So he reluctantly withdrew his fingers from her warm and lovely nest, ignoring her sigh of dismay.

Grasping her shoulder, he lifted his head and, with a wordless look of apology, pushed her gently away. He pulled out of her grip, shivering in spite of himself at the divine sensation.

At the interruption, her eyes narrowed with impatience. But impatience rapidly turned to confusion and then disappointment. She assumed he was rejecting her.

Moved by the bleak hurt in her eyes, he knew he couldn't simply abandon her. There was but one thing to do to convince her of his devotion. He had to finish what he'd started, one way or the other.

He had to act swiftly, before her desire could wane. He emerged from the bath like Lir, the sea god, dripping as he caught her under the arms and lifted her to her feet. Stepping from the tub, he swept her onto the bed.

She made no protest. Indeed, her gaze burned even brighter with craving as he laid her on her back atop the linens. For a moment, he could only stare down at her in wonder.

How had this happened? How had he won the hand of the beautiful Valkyrie? Did he even deserve such an amazing reward?

Now was not the time for second thoughts. She was aching. And he knew how to ease her.

"Close your eyes," he murmured.

"I'm not afraid," she protested.

He smiled. "Nor should ye be."

He eased himself onto the bed beside her. Lying on his side, he used the tip of his finger to trace a line down her center, from the top of her brow, between her closed eyes, down her nose, over her lips, which parted at his touch.

Before he was through, those lips would sigh with delight, beg him for mercy, and cry out in ecstasy. Soon they would recite wedding vows. And he hoped one day they would utter words of love from her heart.

He continued on his journey, tracing her chin and her throat, where her heart throbbed in anticipation, sinking into the hollow of her collar bone, smoothing the silky flesh between her breasts.

The pounding need in his groin was only growing worse. And he would find no ease from her today. But it was a small price to pay to earn her trust.

His fingertip grazed her abdomen, circling her navel, and slipped into the golden curls guarding her womanhood.

She arched up to meet him, and he pressed the heel of his hand down, eliciting a soft moan of pleasure from her.

She stiffened when he threw his leg over her thighs, anchoring her to the bed. But once he began ministering to the throbbing ache betwixt her legs, she relaxed back on the feather-filled pallet.

Watching her face as he tenderly stroked her delicate flesh was almost more than he could bear. Her eyes squeezed shut with fierce need. Her mouth opened in breathless awe. She rocked her head as she floated in a world where suffering was a hair's breadth away from satisfaction.

Furrowing his brow with his own torment, he swooped down upon her, capturing her rough gasps and lovely sighs in his mouth.

He knew the moment she began her ascent into the heavenly realm of surrender, when she'd reached the point of no return.

Her focus became so centered, she was no longer able to return his kisses. Her fists clenched the linens. Her breath caught in shallow gasps. Her body went rigid.

He watched her with awe as she finally yielded to her passions. He felt her release almost as if it were his own as, with a ragged cry of ecstasy, she arced in a blissful seizure and finally shuddered back to earth.

For a brief moment afterward, he held her in his arms, soothing her with soft murmurs, despite the white hot lust yet raging in his loins.

And then, just when he was convinced she was a beautiful angel, fallen out of the sky and left for him as a gift from God, she perpetrated a most devilish deed.

CHAPTER 26

Once, in a tournament melee long ago, in the midst of triumphant battle, Hallie had taken an unexpected blow to the helm. A blow that left her sitting on her arse, groggy and disoriented.

That was how she felt now. After a thrilling moment of unbridled joy and glowing satisfaction, now, in the dazed aftermath of her earthshaking release, she felt weak. Spent. Useless.

Colban had guided her on a remarkable journey—climbing up and cresting a great mountain, soaring blissfully across the sky, and finally plunging off a cliff of ecstasy.

Yet even in her dizzy state, she could sense the dramatic trek had changed her. It had forged her into a new weapon. A weapon that was stronger. More determined. And more willful.

Once she was rejuvenated and empowered, she felt it was only right to return his lusty overtures. To prove to him she could give as good as she got. But also to seek sweet revenge for the devastating blow he'd dealt her. To claim victory over the Champion. And to truly seal their bond.

Before he could brace for her swift attack, Hallie rose up and rolled him onto his back. While he lay pinned there in surprise, she boldly reached between their bodies, finding the still swollen evidence of his desire.

He groaned at her touch.

But when she guided him toward the aching hollow of her womanhood, he choked out a warning. "Easy, lass."

"I want it," she assured him. "I want this."

"Ye say that now," he said on a rueful chuckle, "but later ye may regret—"

Quickly, before he could change her mind and she could lose her nerve, she thrust him inside her, sheathing him like a blade.

He grunted in surprise and pleasure.

But like a blade, despite his velvety warmth, he wounded her. She winced as pain seared her loins.

Seeing her recoil, he sucked in a sharp breath of empathy between his teeth. "Och nay," he despaired, his brow crumpling in dismay. "Are ye hurt? I'm so sorry, lass."

It stung, but not nearly as bad as the cut of a knife. Sorry? What was he sorry for? She'd known to expect pain. And it wasn't like she'd given him much choice in the matter.

"I'm not sorry," she rasped out.

She reeled at the recklessness of what she'd done. It was the kind of impulsive action Jenefer might have taken. The kind of stealthy maneuver Feiyan might have planned.

But she'd accomplished what she'd intended. The consummation was complete. And in fact, the discomfort was already receding, replaced by a curious fullness.

"It shouldn't have been like this," he insisted. "It can be so much better."

She swallowed as the burning subsided, then said, "Show me."

He gazed up at her then with smoky eyes, raw with need, yet full of compassion. "Ye're certain?"

"What's done is done," she said. "If we're to be married, what difference does a few days make?"

Her words convinced him. He nodded. "If ye'll allow me," he ventured, "I can help ease the pain."

She nodded. Now that she'd accomplished what she intended, perhaps it was best to let him take the reins.

Staying within her, he rolled her gently onto her back. Holding his weight on one hand, he used the other to carefully massage the place where they were united.

Gradually, her discomfort abated, and another sensation surfaced. Hunger for more.

"Better?" he asked tightly.

She opened her eyes a fraction. Only then did she glimpse the excruciating restraint in his firmly clamped mouth. The tension in his jaw. The naked avarice of his gaze. The longing he denied himself for want of giving her comfort.

That expression infused her with renewed yearning. The fact he would suffer his own pain for the desire to please her moved her beyond words. She felt a tightness in her throat. A surge of affection. An impulse to reward him for his kindness.

"Aye," she breathed. "Much better."

To her surprise, when he carefully withdrew, she missed him at once. When his fingers danced upon her most sensitive spot, she thrust her hips upward, enveloping him once more.

He tensed, but this time she knew it was in pleasure, not pain.

Again he retreated, arousing her with deft movements of his fingeritps.

Again she surged forward, making him grimace with lust.

Their motion became a whirlwind of sensation, as he teased and tempted her flesh to higher arousal. And Hallie, encouraged by his reaction, drove him to greater heights of passion with her thrusts.

Again and again they collided. She clung to him for purchase, wrapping her arms around his neck and her legs around his hips, finally digging her heels into his buttocks to coax him deeper, harder, faster.

This time, they scaled the slope of revelry together. Their breath made a swirling mist of desire. Where they joined, sweat glossed their skin. Their gasps and groans made sensuous music on the air while their hearts beat in tandem.

Soon she found herself standing again at the precipice of surrender as warm ardor bubbled up inside her, filling her veins and melting the ice around her heart.

But this time she wasn't alone. This time, he suffered along with her, writhing in delicious torment and gasping in exhilarating anguish. With a last bellow of conquest, he clung to her as they pierced through the clouds in a glorious victory. Then together they dove earthward, shattering on the ground into a thousand pieces.

For a long while, neither could speak. The air was filled with their labored breathing. The soft crackle of the fire. The feathery rustle of the mattress.

Finally, in the wreckage of their passion, Colban broke the silence.

Lifting himself on one arm, he brushed the hair from her brow with the back of his fingers. When she opened her eyes, he was staring down at her with such fondness that she felt her throat close.

"Och, Hallie," he sighed in regret, "I have a confession. I hate to tell ye, lass. But I fear I cannot marry ye for convenience."

His words, at odds with his expression, instantly chilled her heart. She froze in shock as a dozen wretched thoughts drifted like snow into her tormented mind.

Was Colban breaking his word? Had he never intended to keep it? Did he not care about peace between their clans?

Or was it something else? Had he found her lacking? God's blood! Did he already have a wife?

Panic squeezed her lungs. God's eyes, she'd given him her maidenhood.

"What do you mean?" she croaked.

He deflected her worry with a tender look. "I mean what I feel for ye is much more than an 'understandin'."

Suddenly she couldn't breathe. Or speak. The curses of hurt and betrayal died on her lips.

He smiled sheepishly. "I fear I'm in love with ye, lass."

She blinked. He could have knocked her over with a feather.

But in love with her? How could he be in love with her? He hardly knew her.

The idea was preposterous. Wasn't it?

Of course, she had to admit she felt a certain fondness for him as well. She admired his courage. Respected his loyalty. Appreciated his kindness.

Just the sight of him—standing at the window, hunkering by the fire, brandishing his claymore in battle, reclining in naked splendor in the bath—made her heart pound.

Even now she felt desire and affection for him filling her veins, like one of Isabel's elixirs of love.

The words gushed out of her before she could stop them. "I fear I love you as well."

Almost immediately she regretted her carelessness. Confessing her feelings was an irresponsible and unwise thing to do. With those words, the protective icy shell around her heart splintered, leaving her completely vulnerable.

Damn it. She owed her strength to that armor. It was what had always kept her calm. And safe. And separate.

It was also what had kept her alone.

The stark truth of that paralyzed her.

Until this moment, she didn't realize just how alone she'd felt. And now, as Colban's soft brown eyes melted her with adoration, she couldn't imagine life without him.

She *was* in love with him. For better or worse, their hearts were forever entwined. And soon they would take the vows to prove it.

But for now she would rest, content for the moment to lie in his comforting arms, feeling his breath upon her brow, his chest rising and falling, his flesh melding with hers.

There would be time later to sort out her feelings.

She needed to close her eyes. Just for a wee bit. Just until she could recover from the remarkable adventure she'd just had.

Colban thought he was the luckiest man alive.

The most beautiful woman in all of Scotland had promised her hand in marriage, gifted him with her virginity, and declared her love for him.

The fact that she had fallen into a deep sleep almost instantly afterward wasn't a reflection on his charm. Rather it was a testament to her comfort, her trust in him.

She *could* trust him. He was nothing if not loyal. He might not have the trappings of nobility. But he was a champion at heart. She could be confident of his love. Always.

It was with that promise that he too drifted off to slumber.

So at ease was he, dozing with the Valkyrie in his arms, he didn't rouse again until the room was dark, the fire was cold, and the chill of midnight intruded upon their warm embrace.

His first thought upon waking was for her honor.

He had to get her back to her chamber.

Hallie could divulge the news of their betrothal to her clan in her own time. She didn't need the help of mischievous wagging tongues.

Careful not to wake her, he rose and dressed quickly. He managed to slip her leine over her head, and she drowsily poked her arms into the sleeves.

Then he grabbed her kirtle and slippers and whisked her up into his arms to carry her. Avoiding the slick patches on the floor, he limped to the door and peered out.

No one was guarding the corridor. So he crept to the door of her chamber and gently pushed inward.

By the dim glow of firelight, he saw Isabel was already asleep in the bed. He prayed she wouldn't wake up and do something drastic. Like scream.

She didn't.

Colban slipped Hallie carefully beneath the coverlet and tucked the linens in around her shoulders.

As he caressed her hair, watching her sleep in well-earned peace, he felt more than just affection for his lovely prize of a bride.

He felt a primitive drive to protect her. To keep her secure. To make the world safe for her.

He wanted to provide for her. To make her a home. To keep food on her table. To be her shelter in every storm.

And he longed to give her bairns. A whole army of wee warriors with her ice-bright hair, her brilliant blue eyes, and her skill with a blade.

With a smile of delight, he crept back to the door. Before he sneaked back into his quarters, he turned to take one last glance at his precious bride-to-be.

Most of all, he yearned to prove his love to her. To make theirs a marriage of mutual respect and empathy.

A marriage that would stand the test of time.

No matter what temptations arose to discourage them. Or what challenges arose to thwart them.

"Pssssst."

Hallie started.

"Hallie," Isabel whispered.

Hallie frowned. Why was Isabel disturbing her sleep?

"Hallie," Isabel hissed, louder this time.

"What?" she grunted.

"I told you so."

Hallie drifted off again.

Isabel nudged her awake.

"Stop it," Hallie groused.

"I said, I told you so."

"Told me so, what?"

"I told you he was The One."

"What are you talking about?"

"Colban. I told you he was The One."

That woke Hallie up, instantly orienting her. She blinked rapidly, trying to recall how she'd arrived back in her bedchamber.

"How was the bath?" Isabel pried.

Hallie blushed as the details of what she'd done came into clear focus.

"'Twas a bath," she snapped. "How do you think 'twas?"

"It took a rather long time, don't you think?"

Knowing the best defense was a good offense, Hallie retorted, "He's a rather large man."

"Ooh."

"What's that supposed to mean?"

"Nothing."

"Go back to sleep." Hallie flounced over with her back to her pesky sister.

"Did he enjoy the bath?"

"I didn't ask him," Hallie muttered over her shoulder.

"Because it *sounded* like he enjoyed it."

"What?"

"It sounded like *you* enjoyed it as well."

Hallie flipped back over so fast it made Isabel gasp. "What are you talking about?"

Isabel feigned an unconvincing yawn. "I'm just relieved no one was hurt." She rolled away, snuggling into her pillow. "Considering all the gasping and groaning that was—"

Hallie grabbed Isabel by the shoulder and whipped her onto her back. "You pesky imp! Were you spying on me?"

Isabel frowned and batted Hallie's hands away. "Don't be ridiculous. I didn't *have* to. The way you two were carrying on..."

Hallie's eyes widened, and her mouth made an O of outrage. She couldn't even think of words harsh enough to chastise her prying sister.

But chastising Isabel was the least of her worries. "Isabel Cameliard, don't you dare breathe a word about this to anyone. Not Ian or Gellir or—"

"Why would I do that?" Isabel seemed hurt by the insinuation. "Colban *does* mean to marry you now, aye? He's a gentleman, after all. He wouldn't just swive you and—"

"Shhh!" It was bad enough that Isabel knew what she'd done. Hallie didn't need to hear it described. "Aye. We're going to be married."

Isabel ducked under the coverlet to stifle a squeal of joy.

Hallie bit back a smile. It *was* good news, even if she'd hoped to break it to her siblings herself.

Isabel popped her head back out. "I'm so happy for you, Hallie. I knew he was The One. Didn't I tell you he was The One?"

"You did," she admitted, feeling rather magnanimous.

If Isabel wanted to take credit for the match, she supposed there was no harm in it.

"And now you're going to live happily ever after," Isabel said on a sigh.

"Well, I don't know about that."

A lifetime of happiness was seldom guaranteed when a marriage was made for convenience. But it secretly thrilled Hallie to think about the possibility of having the kind of lasting union her parents had.

"You will," Isabel insisted. "I can feel it." Then she yawned and gave Hallie a patronizing pat on the arm. "In the meantime, you should get some sleep. We have to start planning the wedding feast on the morrow."

Hallie smirked. A wedding feast was the least of her concerns. She had to secure permission for the marriage from her parents and the king first.

With great leadership came great responsibility. Certainly they'd see Hallie had done the responsible thing. She'd done what she was born to do—secured a husband who would bring a peaceful and prosperous future to the clan and strong offspring to carry on the Rivenloch line. Surely they would recognize that.

As if she'd read Hallie's mind, Isabel sleepily murmured, "Ma and Da are going to love him. You'll see."

She hoped so. She hoped that once she introduced Colban an Curaidh to her parents, they would agree she'd made a wise and strategic choice.

She fell asleep, dreaming of an army of sons and daughters, children with her pale hair and his dark eyes, warriors with Highland spirit and Lowland ingenuity.

Indeed, she slept so soundly that she only half stirred when she heard Isabel gasp. The lass was standing at the window by the light of midday, staring out across the hills. Suddenly her face dissolved in dismay, and she fled the room in a flurry.

Accustomed to her sister's penchant for drama, Hallie closed her eyes again, sure Isabel was panicking over something harmless. Perhaps a hound was pestering one of her kittens in the courtyard. Or maybe her friends were setting off on a fishing excursion without her.

If it turned out to be anything serious, Rauve would come knocking at the door.

CHAPTER 27

There was a frantic rapping at the door.

"Come," Colban called out from the bed before he was fully awake. He was surprised to see the day was half gone.

Thankfully, he had enough presence of mind to cover himself with a wad of bath linens when Isabel came bursting into the room.

"You have to go!" she said, her eyes as round as coins. "Now!"

"Go where?"

"Away!"

The word hit him in the gut like the butt end of a claymore. Of course he had to go away. He should have realized what had happened last night was too good to be true.

"Hurry!" she pleaded. "Get dressed!"

He sighed, then made a circling motion with his finger, indicating she should turn her back. She did.

"They'll be here any moment," she said over her shoulder. "We have to hide you."

Hide him? He was no coward. Whatever punishment a bastard was due for swiving the daughter of Rivenloch, he wasn't about to run away from it.

"I don't hide," he told her.

"Not even for Hallie?"

"'Tis naught to do with Hallie."

"'Tis everything to do with Hallie. You have to protect her."

"Protect her from what?"

"From my parents."

"Your parents?" he said, stabbing his arms into his leine. "They've returned?"

"Aye, and they mustn't find out about your marriage. Not yet. Not until Hallie can speak to them."

"How did ye know..." He frowned as he struggled into his trews. Had Hallie told Isabel about their marriage? Did that mean she wasn't sending him away after all? Did she still wish to wed him?

Like balm on a cut, hope soothed the sting of rejection.

But if Hallie had already told Isabel of their upcoming nuptials, how long would it be before the entire clan knew? Telling Isabel a secret was like touching a brand to a field of dry barley.

If Hallie's parents were here, there was no time to lose. He had to vacate the laird's bedchamber, make himself presentable, and let Hallie handle the diplomatic details of explaining the circumstances.

He picked up his boots in one hand and raked his hair into order with the other.

"Where shall I go?"

Isabel frantically straightened the bed linens. "Our bedchamber," she said. "'Twill be safe enough for the moment."

"What about the bath?" He nodded to the tub full of water that had gone cold.

There was no way to empty it quickly.

"You go on. Tell Hallie our parents have arrived. I'll take care of the bath."

He hesitated, wondering if the determined lass might

try to carry the thing to the garderobe to empty it herself.

"Go!" she urged.

As he snagged his crutch and limped to the door, he heard a splash behind him. Isabel had plopped herself into the bath, clothes and all. She sat shivering in the water with a forced flippancy, as if taking a cold bath in her leine was something she did all the time.

Shaking his head, he stole out one bedchamber door and into the next, where he was surprised to see Hallie dozing in unsuspecting bliss.

He closed the door softly behind him.

"Hallie," he whispered.

There was no reply.

He took two steps forward and tried again. "Hallie."

Still there was no answer.

He crept to the foot of the bed. Not wishing to alarm her, he gently placed his hand atop her blanketed thigh. And almost lost his head.

She sprang up as fast as a jack-in-the-box. She had a dagger in her hand—from where, he had no idea—and murder in her eyes.

Thankfully, she was half asleep, and he was wide awake. He instinctively yanked his head back and took a swipe at her wrist, dislodging the dagger and sending it flying across the room, where it skidded across on the floor.

"Colban!" she demanded, her shoulders relaxing. "What are you doing here?"

For an instant, he couldn't answer, stunned by her transformation from sleeping maid to murderous warrior and back to drowsy angel. The idea that he might actually wake up beside this lovely vision every day was hard to believe.

"Isabel sent me."

She cast a quick glance around the chamber. "Where *is* Isabel?"

"She's safe. She's in the laird's bedchamber. She told me to tell ye your parents are here."

"What? Here? Now?" Her eyes went wide. "Nay, nay, nay, nay, nay." She leaped from the bed, opened the chest at its foot, and began rifling through the contents for something to wear.

"Ye told Isabel about us?" he asked.

"She...guessed," Hallie replied, dragging out a woad blue kirtle that matched her eyes. "But she hasn't told anyone else, has she?"

"I don't think so. She told me to hide in your chamber."

"Good." She shimmied into the kirtle. "You should be safe here." She scoured the room and finally found her shoes beside the bed. "Oh! What about the bath?"

"Isabel is...in it."

"In it?"

He nodded.

Her brows creased. "I suppose 'twill have to do. She'll come up with some explanation."

She snapped up an ivory comb from the table beside the bed and hastily untangled her hair, then tied it back with a blue ribbon.

"How do I look?"

"Perfect." He wasn't exaggerating. He only hoped his appearance was half as decent when she introduced him to her parents.

Hallie had trained herself not to succumb to flattery. Still, her heart fluttered at his compliment.

Her eyes softened in a fond farewell. Then she took a calming breath, straightened, and headed toward the door. She had to concentrate on the crucial matters at hand.

Moments later, at the front gate, she greeted her parents and their small retinue with hugs and smiles all around.

"What news?" she asked eagerly. "What did the king decide?"

"God's hooks, Hallie," her father Pagan said, clapping her on the cheek. "Let us settle in first."

Her mother Deirdre confided, "We've had a long journey."

"Of course." She waved them into the courtyard. "Welcome home."

She studied their faces. But she could tell nothing from their comportment. Her parents, her aunts, her uncles all seemed carefully neutral about what had transpired.

The clan gathered in the courtyard to welcome them, and Hallie called for ale and oatcakes to be brought to the travelers.

"Where's Jenefer?" her aunt Helena asked.

"And Feiyan?" her aunt Miriel added.

Hallie's heart dropped. In her concern about what she'd arranged with Colban, she'd forgotten about her cousins being held hostage. She hoped no one in the clan would bring it up.

"They're...somewhere close by," she hedged. "But tell me, how were your travels?"

The look her aunts exchanged was maddeningly conspiratorial.

Finally, Miriel spoke. "You've been to Edinburgh, Hallie. You know how mad it can be. Bustling streets. Crowds everywhere. Nobles clamoring for the court's attention."

"But you did speak with the king?" she asked.

Helena closed her eyes to smoldering slits. "If that's what you want to call him."

Miriel cuffed her. "Helena!"

"He's a pup," Helena complained. "Bloody hell, I don't know how he's going to hold on to the crown. Your Merewen could best him in battle."

Merewen was Miriel's youngest daughter, all of eight years old.

Hallie placed a hand on her aunt Miriel's arm. "But he did give you an answer?"

Her father suddenly raised the cup of ale someone had brought him. "'Tis good to be home!" he bellowed.

The clan cheered, and Hallie was obliged to wait until they settled down to resume her line of questioning.

She turned to her uncle Colin, who would surely tell her what she needed to know. After all, it was his daughter who stood to inherit Creagor.

"What news for Jenefer, Uncle?"

He cleared his throat. Before he could answer, Helena inserted herself between them. "I think 'tis only right we tell Jenefer first, aye?"

Hallie furrowed her brows. She supposed that was fair.

Helena added, "Where did you say she was again?"

Hallie was saved from having to answer when Brand came bounding across the courtyard, followed by Gellir and Ian. "Ma! Da! Welcome home!"

Her uncle Rand ruffled Brand's hair. "I swear you've grown three inches in the last fortnight, lad."

"He's nigh as tall as my Hew," Colin agreed.

They made more infuriating chatter while Hallie stewed, worried over who might ruin everything by leaking the information that Jenefer and Feiyan were being held hostage at Creagor.

"Where's Isabel?" her mother asked suddenly.

Hallie choked on her oatcake.

Ian answered. "She's actually in your bedchamber, Ma. She's taking a cold bath."

"What?"

"She said 'twas a beauty experiment."

"Ah." Her mother raised a brow at her father. Very little Isabel did could surprise them.

After everyone had finished off their ale and oatcakes,

her mother leaned toward her to confide, "I'm proud of you, lass. Thank you for watching o'er Rivenloch in my absence." She squeezed Hallie's hand, but Hallie thought there was a touch of sadness in her eyes. "You'll make a great laird one day."

Hallie gave her a sickly smile.

The rest of the afternoon was full of frustration, with her parents giving her evasive answers about Creagor and what the king had decreed and Hallie giving her aunts evasive answers about her cousins' whereabouts.

She stole up to her bedchamber once to check on Colban. He was pacing the room, trying to walk without the crutch. Clearly he wanted to make a good impression on her parents.

"What news about Creagor?" he asked.

"None. They're closed up like clams and won't say a word until they can speak to Jenefer."

"What are ye goin' to do?"

She shook her head. "I'll have to tell them eventually."

"At least ye don't have to worry about the clan lettin' it slip."

She gave him a befuddled frown.

"Didn't Ian tell ye?" he said. "He spoke to Isabel. She told him to tell her friends that nothing was to be said about hostages. She said the word would spread like wildfire."

Hallie smiled. Of course it would. Nothing was a more effective channel for relaying information than a meddlesome young lass. In some ways, Isabel was as much a genius as Ian. Hallie would have to remember to buy her something special at the next fair.

"One way or another, I *will* have to tell them," she decided. "I'll do it tonight after supper."

"I'll be here, waitin'." Then, with charming uncertainty, he straightened his cotun. "Do I look all right?"

She grinned. She'd thought he was handsome before his bath. Now that his hair was shining and golden, and the smudges were gone from his face, he looked irresistible.

On impulse, she rushed to him, taking that irresistible face in her hands.

"Perfect," she said. Then she bestowed upon him a kiss full of gratitude. And affection. And longing. A kiss that ended too soon. "Just a few more hours," she promised.

He wound a lock of her hair around his finger. "Ye're worth the wait."

She blushed. "And then we'll have the rest of our lives together."

The more she said it, the better it sounded.

CHAPTER 28

Isabel's strategy worked. Not a single member of the clan spoke about hostages or even mentioned the names of Jenefer, Feiyan, or Colban an Curaidh all afternoon. Even forthright Ian managed to hold his tongue.

But when her cousins were still missing for dinner, Hallie knew she had to address their absence.

As it turned out, her mother wished to speak with her and her aunts in private after dinner. The four of them repaired to the solar.

Hallie closed the door, and while she had the courage, before her mother could begin, she turned to them and blurted out, "I need to tell you about Jenefer and Feiyan."

"Bloody hell. I knew it." Helena scowled, then collapsed onto a chair. "What has Jenefer done now?" Her daughter was constantly getting into trouble and dragging Feiyan into it.

"Are they all right?" Miriel's dark brows furrowed in concern as she settled onto another chair.

"Aye. They're safe and unharmed." She prayed she was right about that.

"But?" her mother prodded, crossing her arms.

Hallie paced, carefully laying out what had happened, step by step. How the three cousins had hatched up the scheme to frighten the Highlanders away. How Jenefer had stolen away on her own and Hallie and Feiyan had followed her. How they'd ended up in a midnight scrap with Morgan Mor mac Giric and ended up as the Highlander's "guests." And how Hallie had managed to escape.

Her mother listened with cool detachment.

Helena muttered curses under her breath.

Miriel narrowed her eyes, as if looking for gaps in the story.

"You should know," Hallie concluded, "when I left, I took a counter hostage."

"A hostage!" Helena shot to her feet, fire in her eyes. "Where is this hostage?"

Miriel gave Helena's skirts a chiding yank. "If you damage *Hallie's* hostage, 'twill give the Highlander reason to damage *his*."

"Exactly," Hallie explained. "'Twas only for leverage and only for a little while, to ensure the continued safety of Jenefer and Miriel until the king's official decree could be delivered."

"*This* decree?" her mother said, pulling a rolled parchment from her satchel that had the king's seal.

Hallie stared at the missive. So much depended on that small scrap of parchment. Her future. Colban's future. The future of the clan.

"Sit down, Hallie," her mother suggested.

Hallie sank into the chair behind her. But she felt no less nervous about what the document might contain.

"I have to admit," her mother continued, "your story complicates matters a bit."

"A bit?" Helena snorted, flopping back down into her chair.

Her mother silenced Helena with a dark look, then spoke to Hallie. "First, you should know the king plans to award Creagor to Jenefer."

Hallie nodded. She wasn't sure whether to be relieved or disappointed.

How would Colban feel about losing Creagor? Would he be true to his word? Would he remain here and marry her? Or would he follow his laird and his clan back to the Highlands?

"But the request was granted on certain conditions," her mother added.

"Conditions?" She supposed that wasn't unusual. That was how negotiations were made. There might be an extra forty days of service in the king's army this year or an annual rent from Creagor in the form of crops or livestock. "What conditions?"

Her mother glanced at her two sisters, who lowered their gazes to the floor. "I insisted we speak with you first before confirming anything. As a formality."

Hallie frowned. Why would they need her permission?

Deirdre's calm voice belied the impact of her words. "The king has arranged a marriage for you."

Hallie's world seemed to suddenly tilt off its axis.

A marriage?

Surely she'd heard wrong.

"A marriage?" Her voice came out on a faint wheeze.

"Aye."

She felt ill.

A silent scream built in her throat.

Now a bridegroom had been chosen for her?

Now, when she'd just met her perfect match?

It couldn't be true, she told herself. This couldn't be happening. Not now. Not when she'd only last night cast her die upon the table of fate and come up with a winning number.

Surely there was some mistake.

Her aunts were fond of mischief. Perhaps it was all a grand jest on their part, meant to rattle her.

But a quick glance at their guilty faces told her the truth. Her future had been decided. She'd been promised to another.

She swallowed back grief. Her heart ached as if mortally wounded.

Swiftly, before it could crack apart, she erected a frosty coat of armor around it. If she couldn't protect her feelings, she'd hold them together with duty and dignity.

She clenched her fists and her jaw, telling herself she had always known it would be thus. She had always known she was a pawn to be sacrificed for Rivenloch's gain.

It had been folly to imagine it would be otherwise. To imagine she'd somehow be allowed to have a husband of her own choosing.

"I see," Hallie said, strangling her tears.

She did see. It was written in their faces. Though her mother sought her approval of the match, they all desperately hoped Hallie would give them no grief. After all, Jenefer's fate relied upon Hallie's cooperation. And defying the king was a risky prospect.

Pain filled her heart. Despair drowned her soul. But she somehow managed to choke out, "Then I suppose I must make plans."

Her Aunt Helena's sigh of relief was unsubtle. "That's half the battle then."

Miriel cuffed her for her rudeness. She addressed Hallie gently. "I'm sure Jenefer will be so grateful."

Her mother smiled proudly at her sisters. "I told you Hallie would do the right thing."

Those words of praise should have made Hallie glow. Instead, her answering smile was forced and numb with cold. Mustering as much dignity as she could, she nodded her head in farewell, and moved toward the door.

Her mother asked, "Hallie? Don't you want to know who your betrothed is?"

"Nay." It wasn't Colban. That was all that mattered. "What difference does it make?"

She would let no one see her cry. She managed to leave the solar, concealing her suffering and containing her tears all the way back to her bedchamber. But by the time she reached her door, her eyes were bleary with moisture, and her throat ached with grief.

Only when she was safely behind the closed door did she bury her face in her hands. Then her tears spilled forth like the waters of a rain-swollen spring.

"Hallie?"

She gasped in a ragged sob of surprise. She'd forgotten Colban was here. And now, looking at him through tear-blurred eyes—so handsome and concerned and heroic—she felt her heart splinter into a thousand painful shards.

He'd been drinking by the fire. At her sob, he set down the cup and hurried forward, folding her in his arms.

Anguish unexpectedly poured out of her in a harsh howl of despair.

"Och, Hallie," he said, stroking her hair with trembling fingers. "What's happened? What's wrong?"

His compassion only made things worse. It would have been better if he'd been embarrassed by her tears. Or vexed with her for weeping like a child. Then she could have pretended she was better off without him.

But he was neither embarrassed nor vexed. Not even knowing why she was upset, still he was empathetic. The more she thought about that, the worse she felt about losing a treasure like him. And the more she cried, the harder it was to tell him what was wrong.

"There, lass," he crooned in her ear. "Has someone... died?"

She shook her head.

"Your parents are well?"

She nodded.

He sighed. "It can't be that dire, can it?"

She replied with a wail.

Dear God, how was she going to live without him?

How could she bear to be wed to another when her heart belonged to Colban an Curaidh?

Colban felt Hallie's despair as if it were his own. He might not know the cause of her tears. But he felt her heartache. And her soul-wrenching sobs made him feel utterly helpless.

Wolves he could face.

An army he could battle.

But this kind of sorrow was a formidable foe.

The best he could do was hold her quaking body. Murmur reassurances against her damp hair. Let her drench his cotun with her tears until she ran dry.

Then perhaps he could discover what was wrong.

He ran through several possibilities in his mind.

Perhaps the king had awarded Creagor to Morgan, and she was upset on her cousin's behalf.

That was fine. He'd half expected that outcome. There might be an initial rebellion on the part of Rivenloch, but the clan would abide by the will of the king. They would learn the mac Girics were good neighbors. And the marriage between Hallie and him would help smooth over any conflict between the clans.

Perhaps her parents were upset that Hallie had allowed her cousins to be taken hostage by Morgan.

That was fine as well. Once the ownership of Creagor was settled, the hostage situation could be untangled with no harm done. Morgan couldn't be blamed for imprisoning hostile attackers. And Hallie couldn't be blamed for taking a counter hostage. Both had acted in their clans' best interests.

Perhaps the king had unexpectedly awarded Creagor to Rivenloch.

That was a bit more upsetting. It meant that the mac Girics would be returning to the Highlands. They'd have to go without him, of course. Colban had no intention of breaking his vow to Hallie. As the future laird of her clan, she must remain at Rivenloch. And so would he.

Perhaps she was having regrets about agreeing to marry him. Perhaps, now that she'd spoken with her parents and had a whole day to consider her actions, she felt shame and remorse for what she'd surrendered.

That was not fine. That possibility made his throat close and his heart thump woodenly in his chest.

He would allow her to back out, of course, if she wished. It was a lass's prerogative to change her mind. Losing her would tear him up inside. But he didn't want a wife who didn't love him with all her being.

He continued to hold her, smoothing her hair and absorbing her sobs, until they subsided and all that remained were hitching sniffles.

She stepped away then to gather her wits and wipe away her tears. Her eyes were raw. Her nose was red. Her cheeks were flushed. And yet she was still the most beautiful woman he'd ever seen. It tore at his heart to see his magnificent warrior lass so distraught.

She looked him in the eyes and tried to speak. But even that small connecting glance made her chin start quivering again. Biting her lip, she turned away, toward the window.

"I want you to know," she said, "I...care for you."

"I care for ye as well, lass." But a shiver of doubt went up his spine at her words. Caring for him wasn't what had made her weep.

"I will *always* care for you," she said.

His heart stilled. Here it came. "But?"

"But..." She forced herself to face him. "We've both sworn to do what's best for clan and country, aye?"

"Aye." It was what they'd discussed last night. How their

marriage would unite their people and strengthen Scotland against the English.

"Creagor...Creagor has been awarded to Rivenloch."

He blinked in astonishment. He'd been so certain the king would respect tradition and the passing of property from father to son. But perhaps the new king was more malleable than the last.

"I see." He let out a sigh, but it was hard to be angry about the decision, not when it was what Hallie had wanted all along. "Well, I suppose congratulations are in order." Still, he couldn't help but feel a wee bit bitter on Morgan's behalf. "Your parents must wield great influence indeed."

Morgan would be disappointed by the decision. Not for his own sake. But for the sake of his clan, who had made the long journey to the Lowlands for naught and would now have to return in defeat.

But Colban also felt sorry for Morgan as a friend. Life had been particularly cruel to him of late. This would be yet another tragedy for him to bear.

Hallie, however, seemed to be as upset about the outcome as he was. Why should she be upset when she'd gotten what she wanted?

Was it possible she didn't understand his promise? Did she fear he might return to the Highlands with his clan?

"I gave ye my word, Hallie," he assured her. "I said I'd wed ye, and I meant it. Even if the mac Girics are no longer welcome here, I intend to do what's right by ye. I promise."

That only made tears well again in her eyes. "I know," she choked out. "But you should know that winning Creagor for Jenefer came at a cost."

"A cost?"

Her face had grown as pale and still as a chalk cliff. Her quiet manner chilled him to the bone.

"The king has arranged a marriage for me."

The world stood suddenly still.

As still as her face.

Colban felt frozen in time, unable to move. Or speak. Or breathe.

His thoughts, however, careened onward, racing through incomprehension and disbelief. He was unable to grasp the impossibility of her words. Unwilling to accept what she'd just told him.

"Nay," he decided. "'Tisn't possible."

"'Tis."

"But we've made our vows. Bloody hell, we've already—" He broke off, letting his eyes finish the sentence with a look of longing that swept from the top of her sun-kissed hair to her velvet-slippered toes.

"We mustn't speak of that," she said, panic flaring in her eyes.

Of course he wouldn't speak of it. He was hurt that she could believe he would.

"I'll find a way to fix this," he vowed.

"There *is* no way."

"Who is this betrothed?" Colban fought a sudden violent urge to slay the unnamed villain.

"I don't know."

"Ye don't know?" Colban clenched and unclenched his fists in outrage. "How can they marry ye to someone ye don't even..."

Yet even as he said the words, he knew that was the way of nobles. So it had been with Morgan. So it was with any firstborn of a powerful clan.

"It doesn't matter," she said.

But Colban saw the bleak emptiness behind her cold acceptance of her fate.

"O' course it does," he insisted. "Ye can't just trust your future to someone who doesn't appreciate your strength. Someone who doesn't respect ye. Someone who doesn't love ye."

Her eyes filled at his words.

His throat burned with frustration as he realized the futility of his argument. Part of him wanted to grab Hallie right this moment and run away with her into the night. But he knew no matter what he said or did, Colban couldn't change Hallie's destiny. He was only a lowly bastard shaking his fist at a king.

He wanted to rail against the injustice of nobility, the travesty of arranged marriages and forced alliances. But he could see that would only prolong Hallie's suffering and make things worse.

The best thing to do—the noble thing, the kind thing— was to forget what had happened between them. To tuck away his one precious, private memory of what they'd shared and forget he'd ever known Hallie.

It was the hardest thing he'd ever done to raise his targe against Hallie's broken heart. But he managed to swallow his pain, steel his features, and say what he had to say.

"I won't speak of it again," he promised. "None of it. Ye must put me someplace else for the night. In the stable or the dovecot."

"I won't let you sleep—"

He held up his hand to stop her protest. "I'm a hostage. Ye must treat me as such. On the morrow, ye'll return me to Creagor, aye?"

"Aye," she choked out.

"Then ye'll get your cousins back, none the worse for wear. And no one will ever know what passed between us."

Hallie nodded, on the verge of tears. Gathering her skirts, she began to walk stiffly toward the door. But as she drew even with him, she hesitated.

Turning toward him, the fierce Valkyrie suddenly looked as vulnerable as a child. Her wet eyes were wide and full of heartache. Her lips trembled uncertainly. "Will you...will you give me one last kiss?" she entreated him. "A kiss of farewell?"

He wanted that more than anything. He wanted to bury his face in her fragrant hair. Taste her yielding, honey-sweet lips. Press his hungering body against hers.

It seemed cruel beyond measure to leave her like this. Empty. Aching. Heartbroken.

But though it tore him up inside to disappoint her, he had no choice.

If he kissed her again, he knew he'd never let her go.

"Nay."

CHAPTER 29

allie gave a tiny gasp and then closed her lips so tightly that not even a breath could escape.

He was right. Of course he was right. It was futile to prolong their agony by indulging in a kiss.

But it didn't keep her cheeks from flushing with shame at his rebuff. It didn't keep his rejection from feeling like the slice of a blade across her soul.

"If ye'll fetch Rauve," Colban said hoarsely, "he can convey me to my new quarters."

He stepped aside so she could pass without touching him.

Her heart was breaking as, with a stiff nod, she sidled past him. She didn't trust herself to look at him. Or speak. Her eyes filled with unbearable loss. Words failed her. And then it was too late for farewells. The door closed behind her with a dull thud, like a coffin lid.

She moved soundlessly along the corridor. But in the privacy of the stairwell, she sagged against the cold stone wall. She couldn't face the clan like this. Not now. Not when her soul was laid bare and her nerves were raw.

She needed to be strong. For her clan. For her parents. For her siblings.

Her siblings.

Her throat closed as she thought about Isabel and her

matchmaking ways. How happy her little sister had been to learn that her predictions had come true. That Colban had turned out to be The One. That Hallie and Colban were going to be married. This would crush her.

She thought about Ian, who had taken such delight in teaching Colban to read and impressing him with his inventions. The lad would be crestfallen when the Highlander left.

She was certain Brand would be disappointed as well. Fascinated by Colban's techniques with the claymore, he'd been so eager to learn from the clever warrior.

Even Gellir had lost his sullen distaste for the hostage. Though he'd never admit it, he now looked up to the Highlander, regarding him with respect and admiration.

Hallie realized she was not the only one losing Colban an Curaidh.

There was nothing she could do to change that. But perhaps she could help to soften the blow.

It took several moments to don the emotional armor she required. She had to push the dreams of the last few days to the back of her mind. Put them under lock and key. She had to forget about any personal connection to Colban. As far as her parents were concerned, he was a hostage, no more.

But despite that status, she had no intention of tossing him into the dovecot or the stables. She had another idea.

The instant Hallie walked out the door, Colban's chest caved into the hollow abyss where his heart had been.

His legs buckled beneath him, and he slumped onto the bed. His eyes burned with the injustice of a cruel fate that would tempt him with Paradise one day, only to cast him into Purgatory the next.

When Rauve finally came for him, he had no strength

left for even a vague greeting. Without a word and with no prodding, he followed the burly guard along the corridor.

They'd gone but a little way when Rauve stopped in front of a door and rubbed an anxious hand across his black beard.

"Listen to me, Highlander," the man growled. "'Tis Hallie's mercy that you're staying here tonight. She refused to let you sleep in the stables, considering how you saved her and all. But I don't want you thinking you can try anything. I'll be making my bed outside this door, and if you so much as lift a finger to hurt anyone, I'll chop that finger off."

Colban didn't understand completely until Rauve swung the door open onto the bedchamber of the Rivenloch lads.

"Colban!" Ian cheered, rushing forward. "Did you hear? Our parents are home!"

Gellir rose from where he'd been poking at the fire and gave Colban a brooding glare. "I don't think he's exactly happy about that, Ian."

"Why not?" Brand asked from where he was standing on the bed. "Once Ma hears how you took on the whole Rivenloch army just to save Hallie..." He leaped from the bed to the floor and mimed slashing with a sword.

Though Colban's heart was breaking, he gave them a bleak smile.

They didn't know. They didn't realize how close he'd come to being their big brother. And how, after today, he may never see them again.

Perhaps it was best this way.

What good were hopes when they could be so easily dashed?

Yet he recognized that Hallie had placed him here in her brothers' bedchamber as a kindness. She was showing that she both cared for and trusted him.

He had turned down her final kiss. She had to understand why that had to be. Why it was folly to spend another single moment together.

Instead, she was giving him the next most precious thing she had to offer. What she knew he would treasure the most. One final pleasant memory of Rivenloch.

"So you're leaving on the morrow," Gellir said, hanging the fire iron back on its hook. There was a forced casualness to his voice that belied the disappointment in his sideways glance.

"Nay!" Brand complained. "Can you not stay a little while longer? I want to learn how to use the claymore. And I haven't shown you my hedgehog trick."

"He's a hostage, Brand," Gellir explained. "He has to be returned. That's the only way we'll get Jenefer and Feiyan back."

Brand made a sound of disgust. "Do we *have* to get them back?"

"Don't worry, Brand," Ian said. "He's going to be living at Creagor at least a few more weeks." He turned to Colban. "Isn't that right?"

Colban nodded, although he couldn't say what the future held and how long he would stay at Creagor. He didn't know if he could bear living so close to Hallie. Watching her wed another. Seeing her grow large with another man's bairns.

"Listen, lads," Rauve said, wagging a finger. "There's to be no rowdy tomfoolery this eve. Hallie is trusting you to keep quiet. If I hear a peep out of you, any sort of nonsense that will wake your parents, I'll have to move the Highlander out to the stables. And nobody wants that." He finished with a quick wink.

Colban returned the gruff old guard's generous words with a grateful nod. Despite the man's bearlike countenance, he had a kind heart.

Then Colban turned to the boys with a long-suffering sigh. "I hope none o' ye snore," he groused.

The lads laughed at that.

Then Ian lifted his brows and asked, "Do you think *lasses* snore?"

Colban gave him a wistful smile. He was going to miss Ian's odd questions. Brand's reckless enthusiasm. Isabel's gushing praise. And even Gellir's dark looks.

But most of all, he was going to miss his beautiful Valkyrie, who'd turned his head, twisted his heart, scarred his soul, and, aye, even snored a wee bit after a satisfying bout of swiving.

Hallie stared out at a night sky as black as peat. Winking between wisps of smoky cloud were cold sparks of stars. Stars she wished she could reorder to change her fate.

Her eyes stung from crying. Her throat ached from stifling her tears. But finally her heart was numb.

Then Isabel burst into the room and ruined everything.

"Where's Colban?" she asked without preamble.

Hallie clasped her hands together at her waist. How was she going to tell Isabel? How could she soften the blow?

But Isabel could already sense something was wrong.

"What's happened?" she breathed, closing the door behind her and slouching against it.

"I need to talk to you."

"You didn't change your mind?"

"Nay. Not exactly," she amended. "Why don't you sit down and—"

"I don't want to sit down." Isabel skewered her with a stare. "Did you frighten him off?"

Hallie's first response was hurt. Then she reconsidered. Wouldn't that be an easier excuse to make? That ferocious Hallidis of Rivenloch had scared off a suitor with her glacial glare and her savage tongue?

But Hallie couldn't lie to her little sister. Not just because it was wrong. But because curious Isabel would unearth the real reason sooner or later. And then she'd be hurt, not only by the truth, but by Hallie's hiding it.

"Sit down, Isabel. Please." Hallie sat on the bed herself and patted the mattress beside her.

But stubborn Isabel sank in place, sitting on the floor with her back braced against the door.

"What have you done, Hallie?" she asked with a pout.

Hallie told her as gently as possible about the situation with Creagor, about her arranged marriage.

When she finished, Isabel said nothing, but her bonnie face was full of grit and determination. "Is that it then?"

Hallie shrugged. She'd explained everything. What more did Isabel want?

She stood up. "So you still love him?"

There was no point in lying. She nodded sadly.

"And he still loves you?"

Why would he? He'd been cheated out of everything—his clan's inheritance, his freedom, his bride. There was no reason for him to trust her, let alone love her.

But he *did* love her. She'd seen that in his face. He'd donned a helm that concealed his feelings. But she knew that defense all too well.

"Aye," she admitted.

"Then all we have to do is tell everyone you've already swived him."

"Nay!" Hallie's eyes widened. "Shite, nay! Swear you won't do that."

"But why? 'Tis the truth. Besides, do you think whoever the king has picked out is going to want a sullied maiden for his wife?"

Hallie was fairly certain most brides were not virgins. But none of them confessed it. They did their best to conceal that fact on their wedding night. Still, she wasn't about to reveal any of that to impressionable Isabel.

"He must never know," Hallie said. "For my sake and for Colban's, you mustn't breathe a word. I will wed the man as I've been commanded. I won't defy the king."

"But 'tis unfair," Isabel lamented.

Isabel was allowed to think that. She was still a lass. But when that same word tried to wind its way through Hallie's brain, she fended it off like an invading army, knocking it down and crushing it underfoot.

No one had ever said life was fair.

It was far past midnight when Colban fell asleep at last. After several games of chess, stories of tournaments, contests of strength, and discussions of philosophy, the Rivenloch brothers refused to let him sleep on the floor. They insisted he crowd into the big bed with them for the few hours before his inevitable return to Creagor.

He drifted off to the soothing saw of their snores, wishing he could dream a new destiny for himself. One in which he was happily wed to Hallie. Where he gave her an army of bairns. And where these affable lads became their doting uncles.

Whatever dreams might have come were shattered in the wee hours by a thunderous pounding on the door. On his left, Brand snorted awake, clipping him with a stray fist. On his right, Ian scrabbled up in a panic and tumbled off the bed. Gellir leaped up, dagger in hand, to defend everyone.

Rauve pushed through the door. "Lads!" He glared at Gellir's dagger, as if it were no match for his tough hide. "Gellir, Brand, dress and arm yourselves. We're going to battle."

"Battle?" Brand asked, his eyes lighting up. "Where?"

"Creagor."

The word hit Colban in the chest like a warhammer.

For a moment, he couldn't breathe.

What had happened? Had diplomacy failed? Had Jenefer refused the bargain? Had she wounded Morgan? Or worse? Were the clans now at war?

"What happened?" Gellir asked.

"No time to explain," Rauve said.

"What about me?" Ian called out, popping up from behind the bed. "I want to go."

"Nay, lad," Rauve said. "You'll stay here with Brand. He'll need your help to protect Rivenloch in case of a counterattack."

"Aye, Ian," Brand said, already scrambling into his clothes. "I'll be in charge of Rivenloch now. You can set up the trebuchet atop the wall walk."

Colban set his jaw.

Counterattack? What kind of counterattack did they expect Morgan to mount? The mac Giric would be lucky to survive a siege with so few warriors in residence. The truth of that left a bitter taste of defeat in his mouth.

But what did they intend to do with *him?*

As if Rauve had read his mind, he frowned and said, "You'll come as well." Then he ducked out the door.

Colban's mouth twisted. He had hoped to be returned to Creagor today in exchange for the Rivenloch cousins. But the fact that Rivenloch was willing to charge into battle must mean that Morgan's hostages had escaped.

No doubt Rivenloch intended to use Colban as leverage on the battlefield. A pawn to wield influence over Morgan.

He stuffed his arms into the sleeves of his cotun, wondering if Rivenloch would threaten to kill him all at once or chop off bits of him at a time and fling them over the walls of Creagor as a warning.

Either way, Morgan would have to decide whether to

surrender Creagor peacefully or sacrifice his right-hand man. Once he glimpsed the might of Rivenloch's army, he'd surely realize that more than just Colban's life was at stake. Challenging Rivenloch meant risking the lives of all of his men in a contest he had no hope of winning.

How could Colban tip the scales in Morgan's favor?

The immediate battle was already lost. He knew that. But did one slim hope remain for winning the war?

Colban's gaze drifted over to the bedside table where Ian had left his notebook. Within those pages was a way to regain what was rightfully Morgan's. Mac Giric might lose the day. But with that book of secrets, they could return for vengeance.

While Ian was struggling into his trews, Colban stealthily slipped the notebook into his cotun.

It wasn't long before Ian noticed. "Has anyone seen my notebook?"

Colban occupied himself with his boots. Guilt made the book feel like a millstone pressing against his chest.

"There's no time for notebooks, Ian," Gellir said. "We've a war to wage."

"Aye, Ian," Brand said. "You can look for it later."

When everyone had finished dressing, Gellir motioned to Colban with the point of his dagger, giving Colban a look of sober shame and grim regret. "Will you come with me then?"

Colban understood what Gellir left unspoken. Ian was too young to comprehend. Brand was too enrapt with the idea of battle to notice. But Gellir and Colban both recognized that their positions had shifted.

Colban was no longer a guest of Rivenloch. He was once again a hostage. At least Gellir was offering him the courtesy and dignity of walking out of his own volition.

He nodded. He'd give the lad no trouble. As much as he wanted to do win Creagor for Morgan, he wouldn't do it by breaking his word to Hallie to keep her siblings safe. And he wasn't about to violate Gellir's trust.

The great hall teemed with clansfolk. They bustled about like hens in a crowded yard. But each person seemed to have a purpose. What appeared to be chaos was in reality a well-ordered exercise in preparation.

And heading it all up, shouting out commands from atop a trestle table, like an armored goddess directing the fates of mortals, was Hallie.

His mouth went dry. Stunned, he halted so suddenly that Gellir almost jabbed him in the back with the dagger.

"Hallie's not goin' to fight," Colban said. It wasn't quite a question. More like an audible hope.

"Aye," Gellir replied. "She's one of our best warriors."

"But what if... She could...get hurt." Even as he made the argument, he knew it was futile.

"Hallie can look after herself." This time, Gellir *did* prod him with the dagger. "Come on, no time to waste."

Brand squeezed past to clear a path in front. "The knights always gather for battle in the armory," he told Colban. "This way."

He led them through the bustling throng, past men hauling bags of grain and women gathering up children, until they arrived at the short passageway that opened onto the armory.

The armory took Colban's breath away. Not just a storage place for weapons, it was a cavernous chamber befitting a renowned warrior clan. Squires took down shields and sharpened swords. Knights donned armor, hefted helms, tightened belts. Whatever steel weapons didn't grace the walls were being buckled on and sheathed by the dozens of warriors filling the room.

The shiver of chain mail and the squeak of leather mingled with the rumble of low and somber chatter about the battle to come.

Colban imagined his companions, the few brave swordsmen of mac Giric, facing this magnificent army. His heart squeezed within the cage of his ribs, knifing painfully sideways. They would be slaughtered by these warriors.

"There they are!" a man called out from the midst of the throng. "Gellir! Brand!" The tall, tawny-haired man had a noble bearing. Creases of age and battle seasoned his face. He made his way forward to address Gellir. "Is this the Highlander?"

Before Gellir could reply, Colban straightened to his full height and looked the man in the eye. He might be a hostage. But it was a mistake to cower before one's captors. "I am."

"He has a claymore, Da!" Brand said. Then, flush with the excitement of defending Rivenloch, the lad squeezed between the rows of knights to fetch his own weapon.

Da? Colban narrowed his eyes. So this was Hallie's father, Pagan Cameliard.

His gaze slipped away to the blonde woman making her way over. She must be Hallie's mother, Deirdre, the Laird of Rivenloch.

She was tall and commanding, almost as beautiful as Hallie, with the same piercing sky blue eyes and fair hair, though her golden strands were shot through with threads of silver.

"This is him?" She swept him with a swift but thorough scrutiny, as if she were sizing up a pig for butchering.

"Aye," her husband replied.

"He'll do."

He'll do? What did that mean?

Gellir sighed and addressed his mother. "The negotiations were unsuccessful?"

"What?" she asked absently, her attention elsewhere. "Not that one! 'Tis cracked!" she shouted to a squire pulling a shield from the wall. She pointed to another. "Try that one!"

"The negotiations with the mac Giric," Gellir repeated. "They failed?"

"Failed?" she asked, mildly irritated at the interruption. "Nay."

Gellir and Colban exchanged puzzled glances. Then he asked the question they both wanted to know. "Then why are we going to war with the Highlanders?"

She frowned. "Rauve!" she called out to the burly guard. "Who's assembling the archers?"

Pagan shook his head and gave his wife a gentle nudge toward the soldiers, where she was most needed. "Go!" Then he turned to Gellir. "Now what did you want to know, son?"

Colban answered. "Why are ye attackin' Creagor?"

Pagan blinked. "We're not attacking her. We're defending her."

"Against my clan?" he asked.

"Your clan?" Pagan smirked. "Nay. Against the English."

Colban felt like Pagan had smacked him on the back of his head and rattled his brain.

Gellir sheathed his dagger. "I guess I won't be needing this after all."

"The English?" Colban echoed woodenly.

"Aye," said another nobleman who joined them, his mouth curving up into a mischievous grin. "Perhaps you've heard of them? They're a gang of troublesome folk that live just the other side of the border."

"Colin!" A woman with thick honey hair and a smoky gaze thumped the man on his chest. "Don't tease the man. 'Tis his clan they're after, and our Jenefer's in danger."

Jenefer. The fiery lass who'd been fighting naked in the moonlight with Morgan. So she was still Morgan's hostage.

And Creagor was under siege.

Colban's confused thoughts finally resolved into sharp focus.

Bloody hell. The *English* were after Creagor.

His heart turned to stone.

Morgan was no match for the English, who had armies of thousands. Not with a bare bones retinue. Few provisions. And no experience fighting foreigners.

"Take heart, Highlander," said another nobleman, giving him a friendly wink and clapping him on the back. "The warriors of Rivenloch never lose."

A small, dark-haired woman beside him said softly, "Thank goodness, our clever Feiyan escaped in time to alert us."

These were the parents of the lass who'd tried to kill him? Strange. They seemed too kind to have raised such a bloodthirsty daughter.

"You!" Laird Deirdre barked, tossing a coat of chain mail at Colban and almost knocking him down. "This should fit."

He frowned down at it.

Rauve pushed his way forward, thrusting a shield at Colban. "Well, what are you waiting for, lad? Are you coming or not?"

This wasn't a skirmish between clans.

It was a war between countries.

They would be fighting on the same side.

"Fetch me my claymore," he ground out.

CHAPTER 30

A battle was just what Hallie needed. It gave her something to focus on. Something other than the loss of the Highlander she'd begun to love. Something besides her bleak future with a stranger. There was nothing like clashing with the enemy to exorcise the frustration from one's soul.

Though she knew there was little chance the skirmish with the English would come to Rivenloch, her responsibility in times of war had always been to prepare the castle for attack.

Brand was old enough now to take command of the keep. But she needed to leave it in the best possible shape for siege when the army left and he was in charge.

So she surveyed the great hall from atop a trestle table, directing the castle folk as they brought the livestock within the castle gates and the foodstuffs into the keep.

The clan executed the defenses with expert care, weaving between one another as smoothly as warp and weft on a loom.

Only one anomaly—Isabel skulking about the great hall—caused Hallie concern. The lass had never exactly promised to keep the indiscretion between Hallie and Colban secret. And she seemed to be seeking an audience with anyone who would listen.

Of course, that was the least of Hallie's concerns at the moment. It had been a long while since anyone had dared cross the Rivenloch clan. She hoped her combat skills hadn't grown rusty.

As for Colban, he must feel completely out of his element. He had never even seen an Englishman, let alone fought one. And now he'd be thrown into battle in the midst of an army of unfamiliar warriors.

A frisson of worry rattled her. What if something happened to him? What if he was wounded? Or worse?

She couldn't live with herself if he was hurt because of her.

She was the one who had forced him to come to Rivenloch.

She was the reason he hadn't been at Creagor to defend his laird when the English first attacked.

Perhaps it would have been better if she'd never met Colban an Curaidh.

She swallowed down a thick lump in her throat. There was no time for guilty musing and melancholy regret. The sooner the keep was prepared, the sooner she could arm herself, march to Creagor, and right her wrongs.

Isabel arrived then with brusque impatience, planted her hands on her hips, and announced, apropos of nothing, "'Tis Archibald Scott." She stuck out her bottom lip in displeasure. "I thought you should know."

"Isabel, I'm busy," Hallie said, distracted. She called out to a servant, "Mind the hounds! See you don't trample the pups."

"That's who you're going to be stuck with," Isabel said.

"What are you talking about?" Hallie frowned at a maid balancing too many loaves of bread in her arms. "Someone help her! Aye, Abygail, good!"

"I got his name from Feiyan," Isabel said. "She said to ask Aunt Miriel, who said to ask Aunt Helena, who said to ask Ma."

What Isabel was blathering on about, Hallie didn't know. But when it came to making siege preparations, the lass had responsibilities as well. "Aren't you supposed to be gathering the children in the chapel?"

"Fine," Isabel said, but she spat out her parting words again with a shudder of disgust. "Archibald Scott, Hallie! Ugh."

Isabel's words echoed meaninglessly in her brain. But a few moments later, a tremor of recognition shivered up Hallie's spine. Archibald Scott. She knew that name. What was it Isabel had said? That he was the one she'd be *stuck* with?

Her betrothed. Isabel must have been talking about the man she was to marry.

Her heart dropped.

She remembered Archibald Scott. He'd come to Rivenloch years ago, when Hallie was a child and Archie was a young man a decade older.

She and her cousins had secretly mused that he had a willow branch in place of a spine, for it seemed he was afraid of everything. Swords. Spiders. The dark. He'd never learned to ride a horse or wield a blade or fish in the loch. To the cousins, he seemed utterly useless.

It appeared that now, however, the king had found a use for him.

Hallie swallowed down bitter resignation.

She'd hoped to be saddled with a man she could—if not love—at least respect. Now a happy marriage seemed even further from her grasp.

Still, Jenefer's inheritance depended upon Hallie obeying the king's will. So she would marry the coward.

She supposed there were good things about wedding a timid man. Archie would never beat her. And it would be useful to have a husband who was afraid to question her commands.

While she stewed in discontent, her cousin Feiyan swept across the great hall toward her in a purposeful swirl of black, looking none the worse for her captivity.

"'Tis time," Feiyan said. "Are you ready?"

Hallie gave the hall a final perusal. Preparations were well underway. She was no longer needed here.

She hopped down from the table, and they proceeded together to the armory. Even if Feiyan had disobeyed Hallie's orders by fleeing Creagor, Hallie was grateful to have her skillful cousin fighting beside her.

"How many English are there?" she asked.

"'Tis Firthgate. Nothing we can't handle."

"Good."

"But the English are the least of our troubles."

Hallie frowned. "What do you mean?"

From out of nowhere, Isabel suddenly intruded upon their conversation. "She means the marriage arrangements. There's a problem."

"Don't say another word, Isabel," Feiyan scolded. "But aye," she admitted, "if what my mother says about the king's decree is true, there are going to be...complications."

"What complications?" It was bad enough to be cursed with wedding a man who was whey-faced and faint of heart. Was there worse news?

Isabel edged in close and whispered, "Yours is not the only marriage that's been arranged."

"What?"

Feiyan scowled. "Damn it, Isabel, 'tis meant to be a secret. Where did you hear that?"

Isabel shrugged. "I pried it out o' my ma."

"And who else have you told?"

"No one." At Feiyan's darkening glare, she repeated, "No. One."

"Who is it?" Hallie asked. "Who else is to be wed?"

Feiyan murmured, "I'm not at liberty to s—"

"Jenefer," Isabel answered, earning her a chiding cuff on the shoulder from Feiyan.

Hallie gaped. "Jenefer?"

"But you didn't hear it from us," Feiyan warned.

Hallie shook her head in disbelief. "She won't do it," she whispered. "Jenefer won't be forced to do anything. Least of all marry a man she doesn't know."

"That's not the problem," Feiyan said. "She knows him."

"'Tis Morgan mac Giric," Isabel volunteered.

"Morgan?" Hallie blurted. Feiyan winced, and Hallie lowered her voice to a murmur. "Jenefer would sooner kill him," she predicted. She'd seen her attack the Highlander. Her hotheaded cousin loathed Morgan mac Giric with a passion.

Feiyan grimaced. "A week ago, I would have agreed. But much has happened in the last few days."

"Exactly," Isabel said, "which is why *everything* must be brought to light." She gave Hallie a pointed, pressuring glare. "Everything."

Hallie returned an icy look of warning. If her little sister mentioned her tryst with Colban, she would string the lass up by her braids.

Turning the conversation back to Jenefer, Hallie asked, "Do you honestly believe Jenefer will wed Morgan?" She couldn't imagine her cousin bedding a Highlander, much less mothering his squalling infant.

"Honestly? I think she would. But I don't think 'tis possible. Not now."

Hallie glowered at her cousin. Sometimes Feiyan's elusive answers were worse than not knowing anything.

"Because there's a third party involved?" Isabel said, giving Hallie a smug smirk.

"How did you know about that?" Feiyan said with a puzzled scowl. "I've told no one."

"No one had to tell me. I know the king can't force

someone to wed *one* person," Isabel said proudly, as if she'd deciphered a coded missive, "if they've already slept with *another*."

"Shouldn't you be going to the chapel with the others?" Hallie cut off Isabel before she could spill the family secrets to everyone within hearing. Whatever Jenefer had or hadn't done, it was her own body and her own affair. Just as Hallie's indiscretions were her own business.

But Isabel persisted. "Isn't that right, Feiyan? If a person is sharing a bed with someone, the king can't just—"

"You!" Hallie blurted out quickly, motioning to a squire in the armory. "Fetch my helm!" Then she flashed Isabel a glare that would melt steel.

"Aye," Feiyan replied to Isabel. "One cannot have two wives."

"Or two husbands." Isabel turned to Hallie in triumph. "See?"

Isabel was spouting nonsense. Hallie didn't know exactly what *complications* Feiyan was talking about concerning Jenefer. But when it came to Hallie, no vows had been spoken. No matter how much Isabel wanted to believe the Highlander was The One, what had happened between them was not a marriage. It was a tryst.

She turned toward Feiyan, in the hopes of migrating the conversation to a safer subject. But the stealthy lass had already slipped away to converse privately with her mother.

"Go to the chapel, Isabel," Hallie bit out. "Perhaps you can ask God for forgiveness for prying into other people's affairs."

Isabel huffed out an offended breath. "Fine. But promise me one thing."

"What?"

The lass's gaze shifted from exasperation to concern. "Look after him. Look after Colban. During the battle. And after." Her eyes slowly filled. "Don't let him go."

Hallie had to admit Isabel's tears rattled her. The lass had always had an eerie sense of things. She might make a practice of sticking her nose where it didn't belong. But she was right most of the time.

"I have to let him go," she murmured. "He's not mine to keep. He belongs at Creagor. And I belong..."

She must have made an expression of distaste. Isabel immediately read her thoughts.

"To Archibald Scott?" Isabel's chin trembled. She looked like she might start shedding the tears in her eyes. And that would do no one any good.

Hallie sighed and made the only promise she could keep. "I can't disobey the king's orders. And I can't keep Colban from returning to Creagor. But I promise you, I'll die before I let the English harm him."

The air was still and pregnant, as thick with fog as the lair of Ian's make-believe dragon. Colban could barely see past the sixth line of Rivenloch soldiers as they marched toward Creagor. But they moved at such a courageously brisk pace that the mist curled out behind them and the bright Rivenloch banner fluttered at their fore.

Since Feiyan had brought word of the attack, she had the privilege of leading the charge. Hallie too had a place at the front of the lines. But since the intrepid lasses seemed intent on rushing to an untimely death, Colban maintained a position close to them.

It wasn't his first choice. What he really wanted to do was to send Hallie back to Rivenloch. To put her in the chapel with Isabel and the children, where she would be safe.

It wasn't that he doubted her prowess with a blade. He'd seen her spar with Brand and Gellir. He knew she was a warrior of superb skills.

But this was war. War. Where a slip on the grass or a twist of the wrist or blinking at the wrong time meant the difference between life and death.

He couldn't stop imagining Hallie sprawled on the sod, her body still, her eyes blank, her blood soaking the emerald green grass.

He steeled his jaw. He narrowed eyes as cold as stone. He clenched his fist around the haft of his claymore, its lethal blade riding on his shoulder as they marched in deadly silence toward Creagor.

After several miles, in the distance, he heard the faint sounds of battle. Disembodied shouts and the clash of steel on steel floated toward him like ghosts in the mist. Then a dull pounding shook the earth, as if a giant were stomping slowly across the glen.

He knew the sound. It was a battering ram.

In the next instant, the top of the towers of Creagor could be glimpsed through the fog.

Then, at Feiyan's command, the charge began.

With a mighty roar, the knights of Rivenloch unsheathed their blades and drove forward, rumbling across the sod like the deep roll of thunder.

As they funneled through the palisade gates, the destruction to the castle became apparent. The doors of Creagor were splintered and sagging on their hinges, damaged by the rabid beast of a battering ram. Mac Giric clansfolk stood atop the battlements in desperation, raining whatever heavy objects they could find down upon the enemy. The dust of battle from within the courtyard rose to meet the low-slung brow of gray cloud.

On the grassy slope, between the castle defenders and the Rivenloch knights, swarmed the enemy. Dozens of swordsmen. At the sound of the oncoming army, they dropped their battering ram and turned away from mac Giric to fight this new, deadlier foe.

Colban wasn't afraid. Hell, he'd singlehandedly fought the knights of Rivenloch in nothing but his braies. But his stomach churned at the idea of Englishmen coming after Hallie or Feiyan or any of the warrior maids.

How the Rivenloch men managed to keep cool heads and calm tempers as they watched their wives and daughters engage in mortal combat, he didn't know. He could hardly keep breathing.

As they closed the distance, he experienced a moment of terror when he lost sight of Hallie.

But it was nothing compared to the way his heart dropped when he found her again.

She'd engaged the enemy. Blocking a fierce sword blow with her shield, she lashed out with her blade to slash a second man's thigh.

Spinning, she hacked at the first man's arm, forcing the weapon from his grip.

But though Colban held his breath, waiting for her to be killed at any instant, he was soon reassured there was no cause for worry. Quiet, confident, deadly, and efficient, Hallie dispatched every attacker with ease and grace.

In that instant, he recognized what everyone in the Lowlands already knew. The Warrior Maids of Rivenloch were a force to be reckoned with.

His relief didn't last long.

In the next moment, two English knights came at him with raised blades, demanding his undivided attention.

The length of his claymore gave him an advantage. At first. His reach exceeded theirs, keeping them at a safe distance.

But it was a slow and heavy weapon. And when a third enemy soldier began to engage him, he was unable to recover quickly enough. He was clipped under the chin with the pommel of an English blade.

His head snapped back, and his helm tumbled off.

Simultaneously, the second man's blade grated along his chain mail sleeve, nearly stripping the gauntlet and claymore from his hand.

Then the first stepped in to give him a hard shove with his shield. Colban's heel caught on a stony prominence, and he fell backwards.

Thankfully, he had the presence of mind to keep his grip on the claymore. He braced his elbow on the ground and held the point aloft. As the knight lunged forward to give Colban a killing blow, the man's belly met the point of Colban's blade. Momentum drove the claymore deep under his ribs, killing him instantly.

Unfortunately, as the slain man fell, he took the claymore with him, leaving Colban to face the two remaining foes without a weapon.

Without a helm.

Without a hope.

CHAPTER 31

hallie sensed danger.

Like Isabel with her feelings about the future, she could tell when one of her own was in mortal peril in a skirmish. It was almost as if she had a falcon's eye view of the battle and could detect where her help was needed.

This time it was Feiyan.

Her agile cousin was leaping about with her usual skill, confounding the English with her strange weapons—a great fork that snapped swords in half, flying steel stars, and the slim, curved blade that looked frail, but was sharper and more lethal than any English longsword.

But though she'd managed to perplex three English knights who staggered about with damaged weapons and bodies, Feiyan didn't see the fourth man stealing up on her between two of his companions.

Hallie loped toward her cousin, clearing a path with a violent sweep of her sword. Just as Feiyan's eyes brightened in recognition, the man behind Feiyan lunged toward her.

Hallie wasted no time. She gave her cousin a hard sideways shove with her shield that widened Feiyan's eyes, but moved her out of peril. Then, using the back of her sword and the force of her shoulder, Hallie hacked at the attacker just below his knees, felling him like an ancient fir.

She didn't stay to see what happened next. Feiyan could handle what hazard remained.

Instead, her gaze was drawn again to the most immediate danger.

Colban.

He was downed. Blood trickled from his chin. He had no weapon. No helm. Just his shield. And that was quickly torn away by one of the two English knights brandishing swords over him.

If she'd had another instant to waste, dread would have kicked her in the stomach, stunning her to inaction.

But she didn't think.

She acted on impulse. Before she could be frozen by fear.

"To me!" she cried in savage demand.

She suddenly thought of Brand's hedgehog maneuver.

Against every instinct, she dropped her sword. In the few moments when Colban's attackers were distracted by her cry, she dove forward in mid-air with all the intensity of a hawk on the hunt.

At the last instant, she ducked her head, forming a tight ball and rolling once across the sod. Mid-plunge, she crossed her arms to pluck twin daggers from their sheaths at her waist.

When she rolled onto her feet again, she was too close to her foes for them to use their swords. Not that they would have had time to slash at her. She instantly thrust her daggers outward with killing force, plunging them into the enemies' shocked hearts.

As the two English soldiers fell backward, dying before they hit the ground, Hallie offered Colban a bloody hand.

His jaw was slack. His eyes were full of awe. But all she felt was relief that she'd been able to keep her word to Isabel. That she'd kept him unharmed.

"I owe ye my life," he marveled as he took her hand and let her help him to his feet.

The admiration and gratitude in his eyes tore at her heart. But when love softened his gaze, her soul melted, and her throat thickened with grief.

She'd killed for him and saved his life, aye, but for what? It was a hollow victory.

He would never be hers.

She'd only saved him for another woman.

He must have seen the truth in her eyes, for his face dimmed with sorrow and frustration. He opened his mouth to speak, but no words came out.

There was no time for regret. The battle still raged around them.

"Better claim your claymore ere someone else does," she choked out as she retrieved her daggers from her victims. She wiped the bloody blades on the grass and returned them to their sheaths.

Once Colban had wrenched his weapon free and reclaimed his helm and shield, Hallie swept up her longsword.

But there was little more to be done. Already the presence of Rivenloch reinforcements had given the mac Girics an advantage. They began pushing the English back through the sagging doors of Creagor.

Soon the English commander realized he was not only outnumbered. He was trapped between the mac Girics, who had the castle at their back, and the Rivenloch army, which blocked his escape.

"To Firthgate!" he cried. "Retreat!"

In the end, Rivenloch showed them mercy, allowing the English to flee through the palisade gates without pursuit. The English at Firthgate might be the enemy, but they were usually neighbors who could be trusted to keep to themselves. Their attempt to claim Creagor when it was most vulnerable was likely a feat they would not repeat. There was no need to encourage vengeance.

After the battle was over, everyone assembled within Creagor's walls. Formal introductions were made between the clans. The wounded were tended to. The dead were buried. The doors to the keep were repaired. A victory supper was prepared.

Hallie avoided Colban, fearful she might break down in tears if she had to look upon the man she'd loved and lost.

But while everyone else seemed suffused with victory, she languished in misery. And as she watched Jenefer's face light up with a triumphant glow, Hallie's melancholy turned to bitter resentment.

She hoped Creagor was worth it. She hoped her cousin appreciated the steep cost of her prize.

Laird Deirdre had expressly forbidden anyone to speak of the king's decision. She wished to deliver the news in her own time and manner. Sensitive negotiations were not to be rushed. And so she waited until supper to make the announcement.

Hallie supposed that was a wise choice. With Jenefer's bow and arrows put away and a full plate before her, it was less likely she would erupt in rage and do anything rash.

Her mother's careful diplomacy paid off. With cordial composure, she placed the sealed document on the table before Jenefer and announced the king's decision.

The mac Giric clan gasped in disbelief, cursing under their breath to learn the king had allowed Rivenloch to claim the castle they believed was their birthright.

But Laird Morgan quickly reined in their anger. He spoke of the mercy of the Rivenloch knights in their fight against the English. The king's will could not be argued, he said. Thus they owed Rivenloch the courtesy of returning to the Highlands as soon as possible.

"The sooner, the better!" Colban called out.

Hallie's heart splintered. She hadn't thought there was

anything left of her heart to damage. But now she realized—despite the king's decree, despite her impending marriage—she'd been clinging to the fact that Colban would at least remain nearby. She knew she might never be able to touch him, to kiss him again. But living close to him, she could look into his eyes, exchange a few words, share a secret smile, and remember what might have been.

With his declaration, she knew he had other plans. And his eagerness to return home bruised her spirit.

As the mac Giric clan began to absorb this news, making the best of things, Hallie stared stonily at her mother. When was she going to explain? When was she going to tell everyone about Jenefer's marriage? When was she going to divulge that the Highlanders were not being asked to leave?

Laird Deirdre looked ready to speak again when her sister Miriel clamped a hand on her forearm and leaned in to whisper something. Deirdre frowned, but after a few murmured exchanges, she nodded, and they both slid a sideways glance at Jenefer.

To Hallie's amazement, normally cocky Jenefer wasn't crowing about her win. And now that she looked closer, Hallie realized something about her cousin was...different. She seemed more grown up. Calmer. Kinder. More reflective.

Feiyan had told her much had happened at Creagor in the last few days. Perhaps being a hostage had doused some of the fire from hotheaded Jenefer.

But nothing could have prepared her for Jenefer's next words.

"Wait!" she said. "I don't want it. I don't want Creagor."

Silence fell over the hall.

After the shock subsided, a heated exchange erupted between Jenefer and her mother, who was understandably infuriated by Jenefer's dismissal of something she'd worked so hard to earn.

Hallie too was enraged by her cousin's callous and haphazard decision. What had caused her capricious change of heart? Did the selfish lass not even consider the sacrifices that had been made on her behalf?

But while Jenefer and her mother continued their war of words, Hallie started to wonder how Jenefer's decision would affect the rest of the negotiations. Was it possible Hallie wouldn't have to marry Archibald Scott after all?

Her gaze slid over to Colban. He must have been thinking the same thing. After a breathless glance of desperate hope, they averted their eyes. How the issue would resolve itself remained to be seen. There was no point—and great danger—in relying on fate and the whims of a king.

Hope had leaped up in Colban's chest like a spring lamb at Jenefer's rejection of Creagor. Not because Morgan might be able to hold on to his legacy. But because it might mean Hallie wouldn't be forced to wed someone else.

Still, he knew better. Spring lambs were foolish. While they frisked in oblivious delight, a conniving wolf could snatch away their hope—with the snap of its jaws in the blink of an eye.

It was unwise to hope.

Hope led to disappointment.

And no matter how much he cared for Hallie, he had to admit, when it came to kings and politics and arranged marriages, he was out of his depth.

He supposed he should have recognized that from the start. All Scots were pawns of the crown. But the closer one was to the king, the more critical the royal control of property and alliances and marriages became.

Creagor was a key border holding.

The warriors of Rivenloch were powerful weapons.

And Hallidis of Rivenloch was valuable currency.

Colban was trafficking with issues out of his realm of understanding.

And truthfully, when he thought about it, he realized he was actually freer than any of them.

No one dictated who a bastard took to wife. No one cared how many children an orphan sired. In a general sense, Colban might have to obey the king. But when it came to life choices, he answered to no one.

Instead of grieving his loss, he should be celebrating his freedom.

He didn't know how this argument would be resolved—whether Creagor would go to Morgan by default or Laird Deirdre would insist her niece follow the king's will to the letter.

But it didn't matter. And the sooner he accepted that, the better.

Either way, he intended to leave Creagor.

He'd stay long enough to stand up with Morgan if he was compelled to marry Jenefer. He'd defend Morgan, if need be, from her violent temper if she went unwillingly to the altar.

But he wasn't going to linger to endure the torture of watching Hallie exchange vows with a man she didn't love. It would kill him.

In the end, Laird Deirdre decreed that Jenefer could not refuse the gift of Creagor. But that didn't diminish the glacial fury that Hallie felt as she gazed upon her ungrateful cousin.

Much to her amazement, however, not a word was spoken of the price demanded by the king. Of Jenefer's betrothal. Or her own. Indeed, it wasn't until the clan was marching home that Hallie began to understand her mother's strategy.

Jenefer was a stubborn lass. She resisted commands

like a young ox resisting the yoke. The best way to manipulate her was to make her think an action was her own idea.

No one was allowed to reveal the fact that Jenefer had to wed Laird Morgan in order to win Creagor, because they knew she'd refuse on impulse.

Instead, her Aunt Miriel had slyly suggested that Morgan's people remain for a while to help Jenefer settle in. They no doubt imagined that familiarity would soften the blow of the betrothal.

As if she'd read Hallie's thoughts, Feiyan caught up with her as she was crossing over one of the silver ribbons of a burn that wound through the glen. She nudged Hallie with her elbow.

"She loves him, you know," she said.

"What?"

"Jenefer," Feiyan said. "She loves Morgan."

Hallie scoffed. "Impossible."

"I was as surprised as you are. But 'tis true."

"He's a Highlander. She hates Highlanders."

"Not any more. And she adores his wee babe."

"Jenefer? *Our* Jenefer?"

Jenefer had about as much use for babes as she did for a boar on a leash. She'd risked death, climbing to Creagor's nursery window to silence the squalling infant.

"Aye," Feiyan said, "and until that whole affair with his wife…"

"His what?" Hallie stopped in her tracks.

The knight behind her collided with her, muttered an apology, and continued on.

"'Tis a long tale," Feiyan said. "Suffice it to say it wouldn't surprise me if she *asked* to wed Morgan mac Giric within a sennight."

Hallie shook her head. "That's ridiculous."

"I told your mother. We're all wagering on it."

"You're wagering?"

Hallie's mother stole up beside them to chime in, "We're giving them a sennight. If they haven't settled their differences, confessed their love, and figured out that marriage is the best answer by then, we'll tell them about the betrothal."

Hallie had to admit the deception was a clever ploy. Flies were more easily lured with honey than vinegar.

Then she let out a silent sigh of self-pity. It was a shame her mother couldn't dream up a way to make her fall in love with Archibald Scott.

CHAPTER 32

Archibald Scott was inconsolable.

He should never have answered the knock on his bedchamber door. Normally, he let nothing interrupt his nocturnal entertainment. But the servant had said it was a missive from the king. And Archie had mistakenly assumed it was good news.

He couldn't have been more wrong.

Not only was King Malcolm forcing Archie to wed against his will. He was being required to marry a woman who carried a sword. Rumor said Hallidis Cameliard of Rivenloch was as tall as a Viking berserker, kept wolves as pets, and had a reputation as a callous, cruel, coldhearted bitch. Nothing like the sweet, pure, compliant lovers Archie preferred.

He chewed his thumbnail as he paced his bedchamber, past the comely young initiate Geoffrey had secured for them this evening.

Though at eleven years of age, the lad was a bit older than Archie liked, he was suitable for their purposes.

Pale. Blond. Naked and pure as the day he was born. Freshly bathed, then slathered in wool grease for Archie's pleasure, smelling like the innocent wee lamb he was.

The lad shivered despite the fire roaring on the hearth and stared at Archie with eyes as blue and wide as robin's eggs.

Normally, Archie relished a quiver of trepidation in the lads they deflowered. But this damned edict from the king had completely ruined his mood and chilled his libido.

Tonight the lad's terror was mildly annoying. After all, Archie's fears were far more real and debilitating.

The lad was lucky. At the end of the night, if he'd performed well and could be trusted to hold his tongue, he might return to service them again. If not, Geoffrey would be merciful and dispatch him with painless efficiency.

But for Archie, the torture would be ongoing. For the rest of his life, he'd be trapped in a household where no one understood his needs. Pressured to perform sexually with someone he despised and feared in order to continue the Rivenloch line and please the king.

He suddenly felt like he couldn't breathe. Rushing to the window, he cracked open the shutters to get a breath of fresh air. His vision blurred as he gazed in frustration at the stars taunting him from the black heavens.

He stamped a velvet-shod foot. "God's hooks, Geoffrey!" he snarled toward the night sky. "'Tisn't fair."

Geoffrey was the only one who understood him. Who shared his hunger. Who catered to his special requirements. What would he do without him?

Coming up behind him, Geoffrey massaged the tension from Archie's shoulders.

"We've always known this day might come," he murmured.

Archie didn't want to hear it. He wanted to believe that life would go on as it had for the last seven years. That his frequent explorations with Geoffrey, indulging their deepest, darkest fantasies together, would go on forever.

But the new king had destroyed those dreams. His royal parchment with its purple ribbon and blood-red seal, condemning Archie to a life of misery, seemed to smirk at him in mockery from the table beside the bed.

How he longed to cast the thing into the fire. To forget he'd ever read the horrifying words. To go on savoring this secret, fulfilling existence.

Archie's face crumpled as he turned to his friend. "Oh, Geoffrey, how will I ever live without you?" he despaired, picking at the ties of Geoffrey's brocade cotehardie. "Rivenloch is so far away."

"We'll find a way," Geoffrey promised, cupping his cheek. "I promise. Even if 'tis only once a year—"

Archie gasped. "Once a year? 'Tisn't nearly enough."

Geoffrey tipped his head forward till their brows touched. "'Twill have to be enough."

Archie managed to squeeze a tear from his eye. "I shall be miserable," he mourned.

"As will I." Then Geoffrey cleared his throat and lifted a brave chin. "But we shall make the most of it, be grateful for what we have."

Archie nodded. But he didn't feel grateful. Not at all.

The new whelp of a king who couldn't even grow a proper beard had condemned him to a loveless marriage with one of the most ferocious and feral warrior maids in Scotland.

Archie had met Hallidis of Rivenloch once before, though he didn't remember her well. She'd been a child then—pale, quiet, serious, cold. She and her cousins had snickered at him with the uncouth transparency of the young, mocking his reluctance to engage in what they termed sword *play* and what he perceived as dangerous bloodsport.

Now she was old enough to have earned a reputation for violence. And nothing could terrify him more than to be anchored to a woman with ice in her veins who wouldn't hesitate to lop off his head at the slightest provocation.

"Come now," Geoffrey urged, his eyes lowering to Archie's trembling lips, his tongue flicking out as if he longed to taste them. "We can't let a bit of bad news ruin our evening."

Archie was distracted by a movement behind Geoffrey's shoulder. The lad was stealing toward the door.

"Hey!"

Geoffrey turned his head to follow Archie's stare. "Hey!"

The lad squeaked, opening the door and wriggling through it as slickly as a trout escaping a net.

Geoffrey started to bolt after the lad, but Archie grabbed his arm to halt him.

"Shite, let him go," he said with a sigh. "He won't say a word. And I've lost my appetite. He was a bit too ripe for me anyway."

For an instant, rage simmered silently behind Geoffrey's eyes. Apparently, Geoffrey hadn't lost *his* appetite. And he'd probably gone to a great deal of trouble to secure the lad.

But he shuttered his anger and nodded his head. "As you wish."

Geoffrey straightened, sweeping up the royal decree from the table. Then he slipped it inside Archie's embroidered gambeson, beneath his leine.

"Be brave, Old Cock," he said, a pet name that always made Archie smile, since only two years separated them.

But this time Archie's smile was bleak as Geoffrey departed with a deep bow and an elegant flourish of farewell.

All the while, the king's decree rested against Archie's bare chest, burning an angry hole in his heart.

"You have to tell her today," Isabel insisted, as she'd been insisting every morn for the last seven days.

Hallie sighed as she shivered into a fresh leine. She wasn't about to tell anyone about her tryst with Colban.

Especially her mother. Her mother was so confident about Hallie's ability to put the clan before herself. How could Hallie disappoint her?

"Why would I do that, Isabel? 'Twould only upset everyone."

Isabel pursed her lips as she struggled into her own leine, which was beginning to grow tight around her blossoming chest. "'Tisn't just."

"Life isn't just."

"You deserve to be happy, Hallie."

Did she? Or was her happiness just the price of being the most powerful laird at the border?

"I will be," she lied, rifling through her garments to find a suitable kirtle.

"Nay, you won't."

"I'll learn to be, Isabel," she amended. "I'm not the first person to have an arranged marriage, you know."

"I know," Isabel pouted.

"Besides, I'll be in good company," she said, giving Isabel a teasing pinch at her waist. "Jenefer and I will be able to commiserate about our miserable husbands."

"Don't be so sure about that," Isabel said, drawing out a rose-colored kirtle for herself.

Hallie frowned, waiting for her to explain.

"I don't think Jenefer is miserable at all," Isabel said. "I think she's in love with Morgan mac Giric."

"You too?" Hallie scoffed. "'Tis what Feiyan said. In love with a Highlander? Jenefer? You *are* a dreamer."

Isabel pulled out Hallie's forest green kirtle, the one she said warmed up Hallie's eyes. "Wear this one."

Hallie shrugged. She didn't much care which one she wore. The ladies of Rivenloch were visiting Creagor today to deliver word of Jenefer's arranged marriage. Hallie should probably wear chain mail, in the event Jenefer reacted badly to the news.

"Let me plait your hair," Isabel offered. "I have a new braid I want to try."

Hallie frowned. Isabel's transparency was annoying. She knew who they'd see at Creagor today. Isable wanted to make Hallie look beautiful for Colban an Curaidh. The Champion. The One.

Rather than argue with Isabel, she shrugged. "Fine. But make haste. We're supposed to leave after we break our fast."

Hallie hated to admit it, but the thought of seeing Colban again made her heart flutter.

Part of her *longed* to see him. These last seven days had felt like an eternity. Visions of his sparkling eyes, his heart-melting grin, and his breathtaking body intruded upon her day and night, invading her thoughts and haunting her dreams.

Part of her *feared* to see him. Though it would be a blessing in some ways, she wondered if her absence had changed his feelings. Perhaps now that he'd returned to the bosom of his clan, he saw things more clearly. Perhaps his desire and affection for her had waned.

Not that any of it mattered. Her future was set on its course. Fate would not be waylaid.

Still, when they arrived at Creagor several hours later, fate had stationed Colban at the palisade gates. And one glance from him rocked the foundations of her world, making Hallie desperate to rearrange her stars and change her destiny.

Colban's reaction was well worth Isabel's special attention to her appearance. His jaw went slack. His nostrils flared. His gaze raced over her every contour, hesitating for an instant at her eyes.

The brief connection hit her like a bolt of lightning. Bright with energizing love. Hot with electric desire. Distance had increased the power of their attraction. Their love had not diminished. Not at all. It had grown to striking proportions. And proximity had made it erupt in a jolt of current.

Hallie caught her breath at the force of his gaze. She lowered her eyes before they could reveal the equally intense hunger burning there.

Isabel, however, had no compunctions about making her affections known.

"Colban!" the lass cried, breaking away at a run toward the gates and waving up at him. "How I've missed you!" Then she added cheekily, "How we've *all* missed you!"

If her mother thought it strange that Isabel would show affection toward the Highlander they'd held hostage, she didn't say a word. She was likely distracted by weightier matters ahead.

"May we enter?" Deirdre asked pointedly.

"Och!" Colban shook his head at his clumsy delay. "Aye."

He leaped down and opened the gates for them. As they filed past, Hallie focused her eyes on the path ahead. Still, she felt a heady thrill as she passed Colban, glimpsing his chest rise with a breath. She was suddenly glad she'd let Isabel dab her with vanilla and orange perfume.

"Your laird?" Deirdre prompted.

"O' course," Colban said, awkwardly closing the gates behind them. He beckoned a second guard patrolling the wall. "Stand watch, will ye?" Then he moved to the fore of the group. "This way, if ye please."

He led them across last week's battlefield, though little remained to mark the event. Rain had washed away the blood of war. The only scars left were muddy gouges in the grassy slope. The battering ram the English had abandoned was being butchered for wood near the castle wall. The doors to the courtyard had already been restored by carpenters.

Isabel skipped up beside Colban. "Well? Have they fallen in love?"

Hallie frowned. Isabel was badly in need of a bridle.

"Who?" he asked.

"Your laird and my cousin."

"Isabel!" Deirdre scolded. "Another word, and I'll leave you at the gates."

Isabel sighed and fell back beside Hallie, whispering, "I'll wager they have. I always know these things."

Hallie let her eyes drift down the length of the tall, handsome champion striding before her—remembering the feel of his broad shoulders, his scarred back, his firm arse. She wished Isabel were right about knowing things. She wished Colban an Curaidh could be The One.

When they entered the courtyard, a maidservant showed alarm at the unannounced arrival of such esteemed guests. She whispered something to Colban.

"It seems Morgan has not yet arisen," he said.

"What?" Helena burst out. "'Tis mid-morn. Is your laird a layabed? I won't have my daughter shackled to a—"

Miriel silenced her with an elbow to the ribs.

"Perfect," Deirdre intervened. "Don't wake him. We'd like to see the babe first."

"The babe?" Colban asked in surprise. "Ye mean Morgan's bairn?"

"Aye," she replied. "Take us to the nursery."

Puzzled at first, Hallie quickly recognized her mother's genius.

Assuring the match between Morgan and Jenefer required the approval and support of Jenefer's mother. Deirdre knew that once Helena held her future grandson in her arms, there would be no taking him away.

"Aye, let's see the babe," Helena agreed. Already she was eager to see her grandchild, even if his father was a layabed.

Along the way, Isabel chattered endlessly about Colban. Praising his patience with Ian, his kinship with Brand, and his tolerance for Gellir. Applauding his honorable chivalry towards her and her friends. Exclaiming over his prowess with the claymore as he singlehandedly fought the knights of Rivenloch to save Hallie.

By the time they reached the nursery, even her stoic mother had to raise an impressed brow at this paragon of virtue who had escorted them there. Colban, blushing to his ears, muttered an excuse and left them at the door. Hallie resisted the urge to throttle her little sister.

The babe seemed healthy and happy, for all the poor creature had endured in the last fortnight. The nurse, Bethac, said he was called Miles. Since the wet nurse had just fed him, she let the ladies pass him around. They cooed over the babe, who spent most of the time kicking his legs and sucking his fist.

When it was Hallie's turn, she hesitated. She'd never particularly cared for babes. But as soon as Miles snuggled in her arms and grinned up at her with toothless joy, her heart melted. Jenefer might not have fallen in love with the Highland laird as Isabel had predicted. But how could her cousin walk away from this adorable babe?

Sharp regret twisted her heart then as she felt Miles's tiny fist coil around her finger. She thought about the beautiful babes she and Colban might have made.

Gulping back painful hopes, she was handing the babe back to her mother when voices arose from the chamber next door.

They came from Morgan's bedchamber. And though the sound was muffled, those were definitely Jenefer's angry tones filtering through the wall. Without compunction, Isabel rushed to the window, throwing open the shutters.

Everyone was notably appalled at the idea of eavesdropping.

But nobody did anything about it.

In the end, Isabel's hunch proved correct. When the couple's quarrel resolved into a proposal of marriage, they all cheered and clapped at the resolution.

Hallie tried to be pleased about the outcome. At least one of them would be happily married, she reasoned. And yet she couldn't help but be bitter about the inequity of it.

Of course, she was pleased for her cousin. Jenefer had gotten the land she wanted. She'd won the husband she desired. And to watch her with Miles, she'd even gotten a babe she loved as her own. Life was going to have a happy ending for her.

And it wasn't as if Hallie didn't have something to gain. Her cousin's strategic alliance would strengthen their collective power along the border.

But watching Jenefer glow with affection over her adopted son, Hallie was bitten by a green demon of envy. Her heart ached as Morgan gazed down at Jenefer in awe and her cousin returned his stare with warmth and love and desire. Things Hallie would never have.

The rest of the day was long. Filled with wedding plans. And dreams for the future. Cooing over the babe's antics. Swapping stories with the servants. Discussing changes to the keep.

Hallie floated through it all with a cool, stiff smile that belied the torment in her heart.

Jenefer still didn't know about Hallie's role in the bargain, about her arranged marriage to Archibald Scott. She hadn't bothered to actually read the king's decree. And no one had bothered to tell her.

She'd find out eventually, of course. But Hallie wouldn't dampen her cousin's spirits on this special day by bringing up the cost she personally was paying for Jenefer's prize.

Colban made himself scarce the rest of the day, which was a blessing. Seeing him would have strained Hallie's efforts at appearing glad for the happy couple.

Indeed, she saw him only once more, as they departed through the palisade gates in the afternoon. He hopped down to open the gates, giving each woman a nod of farewell as they passed.

In front of her, impulsive Isabel stole a hug from him.

Startled, Colban awkwardly patted her back.

"Isabel!" Hallie hissed, wary of what their mother would think of her questionable behavior.

Isabel skipped off. Then it was just the two of them.

Their eyes met only briefly. But in that exchange, a universe of emotions orbited through her mind. Longing. Sorrow. Desire. Despair. Adoration. Melancholy. Love.

She loved him.

And she would never stop loving him.

A week apart had not diminished her feelings.

A month apart, a year apart, a lifetime apart would not make her love him less.

Her destiny was written. She would be wed to another. But her heart would always belong to Colban.

CHAPTER 33

Colban's possessions were packed. He stashed the heavy satchel at the foot of his bed, along with his claymore, his targe, his helm, and his chain mail.

Though he'd continued to serve as Morgan's right hand man at Creagor for the last five days—helping him make wedding preparations, hiring a priest and musicians, sourcing victuals for the feast—he didn't intend to stay a moment longer than was necessary.

He didn't even want to watch the ceremony, to be frank. But he'd promised to linger long enough to stand beside Morgan as he made Jenefer his bride.

After that, he was a free man.

Colban plucked a piece of lint from the gray velvet sleeve of the cotun he saved for special occasions. He'd be leaving these garments behind, changing into more road-worthy clothing of worn brown leather and wool. Where he was going, he had no need of silks and velvets.

Then he gave a rueful chuckle.

Where *was* he going anyway?

He didn't know. He only knew he wanted to get as far away from Rivenloch—and Hallie—as possible.

There was a knock on the door. "They're here!" sang Bethac through the closed door.

The Rivenloch clan had arrived. Companionable Rauve.

Serious Gellir. Lively Brand. Inquisitive Ian. Starry-eyed Isabel. Hallie's esteemed parents. The worthy knights and loyal servants. He greeted them all with a polite smile. But it was a smile that never quite reached his eyes. A smile he forced to his lips to hide his breaking heart.

And then he saw Hallie.

If she'd resembled a Valkyrie before, today she appeared to have materialized straight out of the misty realm of Valhalla. She wore a rich gown of midnight blue velvet, embroidered with white and silver vines. Her fair hair was caught in a silver circlet and partially fashioned into a knot of intricate braids that draped the tresses falling to her waist. Her pale skin lent her an ethereal appearance, furthering the impression that she was not of this world.

She should have been happy. Her cousin was getting married today. Rivenloch was gaining an ally. Peace had been forged.

Yet her face reflected all the bleak despair he felt.

In the midst of a sea of cheering and merriment, the two of them floated like deserted ships. Forgotten. Forsaken. Forlorn.

It was a day for Morgan and Jenefer, with all the festivity that entailed. There was a kiss to seal their union. Honey mead to ensure their fertility. A feast to feed the masses. Entertainment to maintain the cheer long into the night.

No one spoke of *Hallie's* impending nuptials.

Why would they?

But that fateful date—just ten days hence, by Ian's reckoning—was burned like a brand on Colban's heart.

He endured the celebration in the great hall with grace. But when the clans started calling for the bedding of the newly wedded couple, Colban made his escape. The last thing he needed to see was the newlyweds' bedchamber decked with candles and their marriage bed strewn with flowers. It would be easier to leave unnoticed while the crowd made their way upstairs, ostensibly to witness the consummation.

Of course, that tradition had been long ago abandoned. Now it was but a token nod to a primitive practice. Morgan's clansmen would feign to tear off the couple's clothes. Jenefer's maids would feign to protect her. And in the end, Morgan would defend his bride and chase them all out of the room.

Still, the rite provided good cover for Colban to slip away to the stairs on the opposite side of the hall.

He hadn't counted on being followed.

He'd ascended the winding steps and opened the door to his bedchamber when he heard someone close behind him in the corridor.

He turned. His eyes widened. "Hallie?"

"Colban."

She'd had too much to drink. That was immediately obvious. Her cheeks were flushed. Her eyelids sagged. Her circlet was askew. And she weaved on her feet like a wheat stalk teased by the wind.

"What are ye doin' here?" he asked gently.

"I wanted to see you."

That was unwise.

"Shouldn't ye be seein' your cousin to her marriage bed?"

She waved away his concern. "She's been there before."

Before he could stop her, she pushed past him into the room, then half sank, half collapsed to perch on the edge of his bed.

He gripped the edge of the door in indecision, not sure which would be worse. Leaving it open or closed.

She sighed. "I wanted to tell you how much I've missed you." She ran her fingers lovingly over the carved wooden post at the corner of the bed.

He wanted to tell her he missed her too. But he knew better. He *wasn't* half-drunk.

"I think ye should go," he decided. "The others will be lookin' for ye."

"Nah." She shook her head. "I told them I had to piss."

His mouth twitched. "Do ye?"

"Do I what?"

"Have to piss?"

She gave him a sloppy grin. "Nay."

Hell, even drunk off her arse and stumbling on her feet, Hallie had the power to tug at his heart. It grieved him to think of leaving her. But remaining would be even worse. And every moment of delay only increased his pain.

"Let's get ye back then," he beckoned. "I'll help ye."

She smiled and came to her feet. Too fast. She took a dizzy few steps toward him and staggered.

He caught her upper arms to steady her.

She placed her hands against his chest for balance.

"That honey mead is strong," she said, looking up at him with a sheepish grin.

He gulped. Her eyes were glazed with a dangerous combination of lust and liquor.

"Too strong," he agreed.

Then her gaze slipped sideways. She frowned in dismay as she saw his armor and satchel beside the bed. "What's this?"

He furrowed his brow. "I'm...goin'." This was exactly the kind of confrontation he'd hoped to avoid by stealing away.

"Going? Where?"

He shrugged. "Away."

"But you don't have to go now. Your clan is staying at Creagor."

"There's naught for me here," he said with a sniff. "Not now."

"I see." Though she tried to maintain her cool stoicism, the mead took a toll on her control. Her chin trembled. "When will you depart?"

"Tonight."

"So soon?"

"Why not?"

She lowered her gaze, as if she realized her next words were unworthy of her. "'Tis ten more days until my nuptials."

He pretended he didn't know what she meant by that. "Aye, 'tisn't much time to plan the weddin'."

When she looked up again, her eyes were filled with a desperate panic, as if life were pulling her under the sea and drowning her. "Kiss me."

His gaze was drawn to her lips. Lips he remembered were soft and warm. Lips that trembled with hope. Lips literally begging to be kissed.

And though it cost him every bit of cruel restraint, he muttered, "Nay, 'twould be a mista—"

She refused his refusal, crushing his velvet cotun in her fists and hauling him to her, planting her mead-sweet mouth on his with a fierce passion that took his breath away.

For a long, mindless moment, he let his emotions ride on a runaway steed. Felt the heady swirl of her affections as they wrapped around him. Returned her kisses with mad abandon.

But somewhere deep in his conscience the champion awakened. He knew the truth. Consummating their desire now would do nothing but sharpen their yearning and bring shame to the friendship they had.

It was a mistake to violate their honor. No matter how badly they both wanted this.

So using all his willpower, he broke off the kiss and set her at arm's length. "Nay, Hallie. We mustn't."

For one breathless moment, they stared at each other in a kind of shock. Astonished by the speed and fury of the fire they'd started.

"Take me with you," she blurted.

For the smallest instant, a tiny glimmer of possibility brightened his thoughts. In that split second of time, he saw a future where they fled Creagor together, companions in exile, living by their wits, stealing through the forest by day, making love by the fire at night.

It was a romantic notion.

And completely unthinkable.

"Ye know I cannot," he murmured. "And ye..."

She knew. He saw it in the dimming of her gaze. They both knew it. Hallie couldn't run from her responsibilities. And he couldn't be the one who'd deprived a man of his wife and a clan of their laird.

Despite her attempts to remain stoic, in her inebriated state, raw despair flooded Hallie's eyes. Extinguishing love's flames. Dampening her passion. Bruising his heart.

He reached up to caress her jaw.

"Och, my darlin' Hallie, do not despair," he said, brushing his thumb across her cheek to collect a stray tear. "Our clans are joined now. It may be a while. But we'll meet again." He wondered if that was true. "One day we'll look upon this time with fondness. Neither of us wants to tarnish this sweet memory with an unchivalrous and selfish act." If there was a harsh edge to what he said after that, it was no less bitter than what he felt in his soul at the cruelty of fate. "I'm not the kind o' man to make love to another man's wife," he said, lowering his hand from her face. "And in ten days, that's what ye'll be."

Hallie's throat clogged with tears.

She cursed the mead that had brought her emotions to

the surface. And she cursed the man before her who had dared to speak the ugly truth in such stark words.

But in the end, she knew he was right. At heart, they were people of honor, both of them.

It was better to deliver a *coup de grace* to their love than let it suffer a lingering death.

She had been foolish to think coming here would change anything.

"Where will you go?" she croaked.

He shrugged. "I'll let fate steer my course, I suppose."

Her brow creased. That sounded unwise. So far, fate had been a brutal navigator.

She reclaimed his hand in both of hers, hugging it to her breast.

"I'll yearn for you always," she said, her voice catching.

"And I'll ne'er forget ye, my beautiful Valkyrie."

Her eyes fogged. Before she could break down sobbing, Hallie fled the room. She didn't join the others, but instead made her way to the lowest levels of the keep, in a shadowy corner of a stairwell, to sorrow in peace. Like snow after a thaw, grief frozen for days escaped as hot tears, slipping between her lashes and rolling down her face.

She wept for lost innocence. For lost youth. For a love that might have been. For an unavoidable destiny. For her heart—shattered like glass and lying in bits on the ground.

When she was done with tears, when every drop of self-pity was wrung from the rags that remained of her life, Hallie felt a sort of inevitable peace.

She'd indulged in a flight of fantasy. That was all. What she thought she'd held within her grasp was but an illusion that had quickly turned to mist, like the night dissolving at dawn.

She had never been free to follow her heart. It was ludicrous to imagine she ever was.

Journeying home in the wee hours of the night with her

clan, she silently, soberly reminded herself of the facts.

In ten days, she would welcome her husband to Rivenloch. Denying that would only bring her pain. She had to accept the king's arrangements with as much composure and detachment as she would the acquisition of, for example, a cow.

Edinburgh. Why not? Perhaps Colban could lose himself in the bustling town. Hire on as a castle guard. Find fellowship among the royal soldiers. And companionship in the lavish brothels.

The thought should have cheered him as he waved farewell to the drowsy guard at the palisade gates, taking his leave of Creagor. He was free now. Free of responsibility. Free from judgment. Free to make his own decisions. To follow his heart.

Nay, he amended. Following his heart wasn't in his future. Following his heart would have made him turn round at once and return to Hallie.

Soon, he vowed. Soon he would be able to purge the beautiful Valkyrie from his thoughts. With each mile, the journey would become easier. Gradually her image would fade. Eventually he would have trouble recalling her face.

But at the moment, her snowy hair, honey skin, ice-blue eyes, and inviting lips were painted indelibly in his mind's eye. And neither the moon peering playfully through the shredded linen clouds nor the cold but gentle breeze nudging him onward in the quiet hours after midnight made him eager to seek his freedom.

At the hillock where the road branched to north and south, he cast one last look toward Creagor.

The warm glow of candlelight yet flickered from the windows of the great hall, where revelers reluctant to retire still sang and danced and drank.

From Morgan's window all was dark. His lifelong friend was doubtless celebrating his well-deserved triumph. A new castle. A new wife. A new life.

And somewhere deep in the castle, a warrior lass wept for lost love.

But she would recover.

In ten days, she'd pledge herself, body and soul, to another. Then Colban would become a brief, vague, pleasant memory.

It was that unsavory thought that made him turn back to the northern road, leaving his clan, his laird, and his love behind.

CHAPTER 34

Archie cracked open the garderobe shutters and gasped for air through the small gap, fanning himself with his embroidered kerchief. Sweat beaded his forehead and slicked his palms. His stomach roiled. His mouth watered. His head swam. For a moment, he thought he was going to be sick.

He prayed that wouldn't happen. Not today. Not while he was still wearing his finest burgundy brocade, a beautiful ensemble Geoffrey had helped him select for the occasion of his wedding. Geoffrey had said it showed off his form to a flattering degree, and the yellow-green trim matched the flecks in Archie's hazel eyes. At the moment, it likely matched the sallow color of his skin as well.

Thinking of his beloved Geoffrey only made Archie feel worse. His throat thickened, adding to his nausea.

But the feeling eventually passed, as it had every night since he'd arrived at Rivenloch six days ago.

He had yet to lose his supper.

At first, he'd wondered if he was being poisoned. It seemed likely, considering how hostile everyone was toward him.

He dabbed at his brow with the kerchief.

That wasn't quite accurate. Nobody was openly hostile. The Rivenloch clan were civil. Polite. Welcoming. Decent.

The laird and her husband had even afforded him special courtesies. His own bedchamber. An extra chest for his vast selection of garments. The daily hot baths he so enjoyed.

But he'd seen the clan folk whispering in the corners behind their hands. And he'd heard enough to know what they were saying.

In a clan full of warriors, Archie was as misfit as a duck in a dovecot. He had no interest in battle and no stomach for bloodshed. And no matter how Rauve, the captain of the guard, tried to encourage his skills, hoping to mold him into the protector everyone needed for their laird, Archie always ended up with a bruised and battered body and a face full of dust, feeling like a miserable failure.

He'd ultimately decided, despite their displeasure, no one was trying to poison him. What made him nauseous and dizzy was the anxiety of having to prove himself to these very demanding border clansmen...and women.

Disappointment was clear in everyone's eyes. His bride's father frequently frowned in concern. Her mother's cool smile was edged with pity. Hallidis's oldest siblings, Gellir and Brand, gave him glares of barely disguised contempt. Her sister, Isabel, regarded him with sorrow and despair, as if she wished he would vanish.

There were moments he wished he *could* vanish.

Only one person kept him from surrendering all hope and made Archie think there might be a chance at happiness in this household.

Ian.

Hallie's youngest brother.

He was blond. Frail. Young. Comely. Exactly the kind of lad suited to Archie's particular tastes.

A lad of intellect, he even seemed to bear some affection for Archie. He'd shown Archie his book of clever drawings and pretty letters. He'd demonstrated his designs for birds made of parchment that could actually fly. He'd even given Archie a pouch of what he said was dried mint and mugwort to help soothe his stomach, though at the time Archie had thrown it down the garderobe hole, fearing it might be poison.

The lad's one flaw was he was sometimes too forthright and forthcoming. Perilously prone to speaking freely and sharing information. He hadn't hesitated to explain to Archie that the reason everyone at Rivenloch hated him was because he wasn't a champion and he wasn't The One. Whatever that meant.

In any event, Archie had won Ian's trust, which was... fascinating.

Archie had never engaged a *willing* lover. Geoffrey always forced the lads they shared to do their bidding— with shame, threats, and on some occasions, violence.

The thought that Ian might come to Archie of his own free will was intriguing. Considering that, the lad might maintain Archie's interest for longer than usual, perhaps a few years, until he approached manhood. By then, Archie might have sons of his own, lads he could train specifically to his pleasure, another interesting prospect.

First, however, he would have to *make* those sons.

He'd survived the wedding. Despite the significance and weight of the ceremony, that wasn't what made Archie quiver and perspire with nervousness.

What troubled him was the bedding. And his history with women.

He'd never been able to perform with them. It wasn't for a lack of trying. Indeed, it was after several disastrous trips to the stews of Stirling that Geoffrey had pulled him aside, telling him he had something that might be more to his liking.

He'd been right. And that was the last night Archie had embarrassed himself with a woman. For the last seven years, he'd sought pleasure only with the young lads Geoffrey brought to his bed.

Tonight, however—on his wedding night—he had to succeed. He had to maintain an erection long enough to claim his bride's virginity and hopefully impregnate the lass. And he had to do it while her kin waited below for proof of his accomplishment.

"Are you all right?"

Archie cringed. Even the slightly impatient sound of his bride's voice from the adjoining chamber was intimidating. At least she'd foregone the traditional bedding ceremony. The only thing that could have made his situation worse was a room full of witnesses.

"F-fine," he replied, mopping his brow one last time. "Are you ready?"

It was a ludicrous question. She'd already been lying in their bed, completely naked and shameless—her breasts jutting out like a pair of pale targes from between the ropes of her hair, her impossibly long legs culminating in a strangely barren tangle of blonde curls—when he'd bolted for the garderobe in a panic.

"Aye," she said.

Steeling himself, he emerged from the garderobe, trying to focus on anything but the lass, who gazed at him in expectation.

"Isn't it rather bright in here?" he asked. Candles were lit all around.

"You prefer the dark?"

"Aye," he said in a relieved outpouring of breath.

He immediately circled the chamber, blowing out every candle he could find. The hearth still provided enough light to see the warrior lass, whose legs looked strong enough to strangle him. But there was nothing he could do about that.

"Why don't you get undressed?" she suggested.

While he appreciated her calm manner, it did nothing to minimize the terror her words struck in him. If he got undressed, she'd see...

Damn. He needed a drink. There was a stoppered clay vessel on the table beside the bed.

"Ah," he asked. "Mead?"

"Aye."

He crossed the room to the table, picked up the vessel, pulled the stopper, and quickly glugged down the entire contents.

She raised a brow, but said nothing.

The drink didn't fortify him at once, but it gave him the courage to at least take off his clothing. Taking his time, he draped his garments, one by one, neatly over the chest at the foot of the bed. By the time he got down to his undergarments, his head was buzzing with warm intoxication.

He closed his eyes and dropped his braies, trying to imagine he was standing, not before the stern and menacing warrior lass, but before her far more tempting little brother.

If Hallie hadn't been ogled and admired by men all her life, she would have felt completely humiliated by her new husband's behavior.

Fortunately, she'd never lacked self-confidence. She knew, being tall and imposing, she wasn't always to a man's liking. But she never failed to turn a man's head.

What was wrong with Archie, she didn't know. Perhaps he was shy. Or inexperienced. Or afraid.

But just as they'd been compelled to wed, regardless of their continuing lack of any common ground whatsoever, they were expected to consummate their marriage, to procreate and continue the Rivenloch line.

There didn't seem to be anything physically wrong with him. His body was clean. True, he had very little hair and a bit of softness around the edges. But he looked healthy enough, with no noticeable scars or deformities. She supposed she should be thankful for that.

When Archie dropped his braies, however, her gaze couldn't help but be drawn to the stunted member protruding from his curly brown thatch. And though she gave less credence to the size of a man's sword than the skill with which he wielded it, she wondered if such a short appendage could even breach her gates to give her a child.

With his eyes still shut, he floundered his way along the bed until he contacted her ankle. She shuddered at the clamminess of his palm. But as in warfare, she knew to give away nothing by her expression—neither fear nor revulsion.

He groped his clumsy way up her leg, still with squeezed eyes, as if he couldn't stand the sight of her.

For one sharply painful instant, she imagined how different this night would have been with Colban in her bed.

Then she forced herself to be present, in the moment, for her husband. It was the least she owed him.

He eventually clambered on top of her and fumbled between her legs, though the way his mouth was working with concentration, it must have been as difficult for him as hitting the quintain in the lists.

She took mercy on him and found his wrist, guiding his hand. "Here."

But he seemed to take sudden offense at this. "I've got it!" he snarled.

She released him. But already he was withering. In frustration, he mashed himself against her with all the grace of a walrus thrashing at a rival.

"Bloody hell!" he shrieked.

So sudden and violent was his outburst, she instinctively reached beneath her bolster, where her dagger resided, stopping just short of drawing it out.

"Now you've done it!" he continued, spitting the words like an epithet. "Why couldn't you just be silent?"

Anger stirred in her like a dark eel slithering beneath the still surface of a pond. But she wouldn't confront him now. Not on their wedding night.

One day soon she would explain respect to him. Respect. And honor. And duty.

Anyone else would have felt the point of her blade by now. She only held her tongue and her weapon out of courtesy—for him and for their guests who waited below for proof of their successful coupling.

He had failed. Humiliated himself. And blamed it on her.

But to admit that would shame them both. So it was up to Hallie to make things right.

Archie sat back on his haunches, clamping his shriveled member between his thighs. "We'll have to try again."

She didn't want to try again. Not when he'd been so unchivalrous. Besides, things would work out better this way.

Earlier, waiting for him to return from the garderobe, she'd worried he'd discover she wasn't a virgin. She'd planned to deceive him. Now there was no need.

"That won't be necessary."

She drew the dagger.

He tumbled back with an exaggerated gasp, his hands cupping his crotch. His reaction might have been comical if she weren't so utterly disappointed at the thought of being saddled with a simpering coward for the rest of her life.

Wincing only slightly, she pricked the tip of her middle finger with the point of the dagger, just enough to let a single drop of blood well from the wound. Then she smeared it across the linen.

His mouth went round in awe.

"No one has to know," she confided.

She gathered up the stained bedsheet, slipped from the bed, and left the bloodied linen in a pile outside the door as evidence of her claimed virginity.

When she returned to the bed, he was still gripping his crotch. He need not have worried. She had no interest in dealing with that part of him further this evening.

"'Tis been a long day," she said, forcing an encouraging smile to her lips. "We'll try again on the morrow."

As it turned out, the morrow was no better. Nor was the next day. Or the next.

Despite his best efforts—in various positions, in broad daylight, in complete darkness, warm from a bath, shivering in the cold, fully clothed, completely nude— nothing could keep him interested long enough to endure coupling with her.

A lesser woman would have deemed herself inadequate. Indeed, Archie would have had her believe it was her fault. Though he stopped short of accusing her outright, there was an edge to his muttered curses of frustration. Not once did he blame himself for his shortcomings.

But she knew better. Archie's incapacity stemmed from his overarching anxiety...about everything.

To his credit, over the span of the next several weeks, he overcame a few of his fears.

With Brand's guidance, he was able to develop some skill with a bow.

Gellir reluctantly taught him how to throw a dagger, and Archie hit the target about a quarter of the time.

Isabel convinced him to fish, although she had to tie the worm on the line for him, since he had an aversion to dirty, wriggling things.

He was never able to fight properly. His lunges and spins looked more like carole dancing than battle moves.

But Rauve at least showed him how to brandish a sword. Hallie supposed Archie could at least *look* fierce standing atop the castle wall.

He also developed an affinity for Ian, which somewhat softened her heart toward him. The fact that he could listen to her little brother's philosophies with patience and examine his inventions for hours on end did much to mollify her frustration with him.

Archie happily helped Ian with his experiments. He clapped with glee when one of Ian's parchment birds sailed successfully across the courtyard. He cooed over the geared pulley Ian fashioned by hand out of wood and rope. He nodded his approval of Ian's sketches, ruffling the lad's hair with almost fatherly pride.

If only he would do the one thing that would make him a *real* father, Hallie might be less aggravated by her situation.

Now, not only was she wed to a husband she didn't love.

She was stuck with a man who couldn't perform his one most critical task. Giving her children.

CHAPTER 35

Colban hadn't found what he was seeking in Edinburgh.

Neither did he find it in Linlithgow or Falkirk or Bannockburn.

Wandering once again, he trudged through the silent fog and the last muddy slush of winter, feeling as empty as the black-branched ash looming over the road. Without direction. Without a clan.

Nearly three months ago, he'd set out to find his place in the world. Instead, his heart kept getting pulled back, again and again, toward the clan that had taken him in. The man who was like a brother to him. And the lass whose image had never faded from his dreams, not even after weeks away.

What he was looking for he couldn't name. But perhaps he'd find it in Stirling.

Eventually, the mire beneath his feet hardened into well-traveled hardpack. The civilized smoke of peat fire mingled with the wild fog, filling the air with an acrid but welcoming stench. After three days on the road, he'd finally arrived at the town that served as the gateway to the Highlands. He felt like Stirling was his last chance to purge himself of a destiny he couldn't have and to look toward a fresh future.

He secured lodging on the high street and asked the innkeeper for the names of the town's best stews. He intended to plunge at once into freewheeling debauchery. Drink himself blind and forget Hallie between the thighs of a willing wench. Hell, a *dozen* willing wenches.

The first task he managed to accomplish. By the time he emptied his fourth cup of ale and staggered out of the inn, his head was spinning.

As for the stews, he didn't make it past the first doorway.

He was full of excuses. The glaring excuse being none of them were Hallie. This lass was too short. That one too ruddy. One reminded him of a nun he'd once met. Another was old enough to be his mother.

Then he realized any one of them could have been his mother. Struggling for survival. Trying to support herself and her bastard son. Painting on a smile that belied the horror of her existence. Subjecting herself to the tawdry whims of whatever brute pressed a coin into her palm.

Despite being steeped in ale, he instantly sobered.

Gazing around the room at young faces aged by abuse and rejection, he wished he had enough silver to free them all.

Discouraged, he returned to the inn, which by now was teeming with soused patrons.

"Ye're back quick," the innkeeper said with a chortle. "The lasses do right by ye?"

Colban shook his head and gestured for another drink.

"Nay?" As the innkeeper filled his cup, he leaned in close so no one else could hear. "Maybe ye're interested in somethin' out o' the ordinary?"

Colban frowned. "Out o' the ordinary?"

The innkeeper shrugged. "Somethin' of a...different... nature."

Colban's frown deepened. What the hell did that mean?

The innkeeper, sensing Colban's disapproval, raised his palms defensively. "'Tis up to ye. Just let me know if ye're in the market for, well..."

"Somethin' out o' the ordinary."

"Aye." He raised his brows toward the corner of the room. Alone at the table, a pale, black-haired nobleman with thin lips and a sharp nose sat with his beringed fingers wrapped around his ale, surveying the inn in quiet speculation. "If ye've got coin, the gentleman there can look after your...unusual requirements. I can make the introductions."

Colban studied the man. He looked like a lizard, waiting in coldblooded calculation, seeking his next fly.

The innkeeper confided, "'Tis said Sir Geoffrey procured *special entertainment* for the laird's son."

"The laird's son?"

"Aye, Archibald Scott himself, though he's gone now."

Colban furrowed his brows. Archibald Scott. That name sounded familiar. Wasn't it the name Isabel kept muttering at him at Morgan's wedding? The one he didn't want to hear? The name of Hallie's betrothed? Surely it couldn't be the same man.

"He's gone, ye say?"

"Aye," the innkeeper said, shaking his head. "Sent away by the new king. Wedded to a Lowland warrior bride as cold as ice." He shuddered.

Colban's world tipped on its edge.

Dread kicked him in the gut.

That had to be the same Archibald Scott.

But what "special entertainment" had Archibald Scott required? God's blood. What kind of twisted monster had the king sent to wed his Hallie?

He set down the ale. Done with drinking. He needed to speak with Sir Geoffrey. And for that he needed a clear head.

Hallie woke abruptly. The winter moon cast a thin sliver of light through the shutters. It was not enough to see by. But she didn't need her eyes to tell her what had made her stir. Her ears told her everything she needed to know.

Archie apparently thought she was sleeping. Otherwise, he wouldn't engage in such licentious activity. Wrinkling her nose at the pungent smell of wool grease, she heard the sounds of moist, rhythmic smacking and Archie snatching quivering breaths through his teeth, as if he were having a nightmare.

He was pleasuring himself.

She wasn't annoyed. Only mystified. He wasn't completely incapable of lust then. He was only anxious with her.

It was all ridiculous. No matter how fierce she was in battle, in bed she'd been as harmless as a kitten. She'd let him take the lead. She'd acquiesced with his preference for the dark, for silence, for complacency.

But now she had a reason for assertiveness, for urgency.

Sometimes in war, it was merciful to be quick. Rather than letting the enemy languish in unnecessary dread, it was best to dispatch things quickly.

Perhaps if she could waylay him while he was aroused...

Casting caution to the wind, she took swift action. While he was in the throes of passion, she tossed off the coverlet and flung a leg over his thighs.

He shrieked in surprise and threw up his hands.

"Here," she coaxed. "Let me help you."

Climbing atop him, she wrapped her fingers around his stiff, greasy stump, angling it toward her waiting womb.

But he shuddered beneath her, shriveling in her hand, letting out a mournful moan of defeat.

She silently cursed. She wasn't angry. Not really. Mostly she felt sorry for him. And for herself, she felt terribly frustrated.

They'd been wed for three months now, and this was the longest, most agonizing siege she'd endured. Despite letting down her guard and opening the palisade gates, he still hadn't managed to breach her walls and storm her castle.

"Sorry," he muttered. "But you mustn't frighten me like that."

Hallie sighed and rolled off of him. Of course, he blamed her.

But if he didn't take responsibility in the near future, consummate this marriage, and start exercising his marital duties, she feared a very ugly truth would come to light.

Hallie was with child.

She wasn't swollen enough yet for anyone to notice. But it wouldn't be long before her condition became apparent. And Archie would realize the babe wasn't his.

He only had to swive her once. Just once, and she could joyfully announce that they were expecting their first child. If it came a few months early, no one would blink. After all, babes came early all the time. As long as the child was whole and healthy, the clan would be delighted to greet the next Rivenloch heir.

"Good night," Archie groused as he turned his back, probably annoyed now that she'd interrupted his self-pleasure.

She couldn't get back to sleep, even when Archie began drawing in long, whining breaths of slumber.

She kept thinking about her babe. Would the child have Colban's soft brown eyes? His chiseled features? His golden hair?

She closed her eyes and dreamed. Of Colban an Curaidh in her bed. Of kissing his warm mouth and melting in his embrace. Of holding their precious babe in her arms.

Colban plopped a bag of coin on the table before the pale reptile of a man who sat in the corner of the inn.

The man opened the bag, peered in, then blinked slowly in approval. "Sit. Please."

He pulled up the bench before the table and sat across from Sir Geoffrey, purveyor of "special entertainments."

The man's lizard tongue flicked out as if tasting the air before he murmured, "The innkeeper says ye're interested in what I provided for the laird's son."

Beneath the table, Colban clenched his fists in his lap. It would do no good to express the urgent dread he felt about the devil who was now sharing a bed with Hallie.

Instead, he feigned nonchalance, fixing a bland smile on his face. "Aye."

"And are ye speakin' of age? Gender? Appearance?"

"Everythin'." He didn't want to think about what that meant. About what Archibald Scott's sexual perversions were. But the sooner he found out, the sooner he would know what kind of demon he was battling.

"Very well," Sir Geoffrey. "If ye come back on the morrow—"

"Nay!" At Sir Geoffrey's flinch, he softened his tone. "It has to be tonight." He felt like he was already three months too late.

"Tonight?" The man shook his head. "Ye must realize these things take plannin'. I can't just nab—"

"I'll double that," he said, nodding at the bag of coin, knowing full well he'd do no such thing. Since he didn't plan to actually avail himself of the man's services, he wouldn't pay another farthing.

Sir Geoffrey's eyes widened with greed. "I'll see what I can do."

"Come to my room in an hour," Colban told him.

He spent the first part of the hour packing, the second pacing like a caged wolf, imagining the worst. What secret perversions did Hallie's bridegroom enjoy? Was he rough? Cruel? Did he engage more than one lover at a time? Did he fornicate with animals?

He wished now he'd remained at Creagor. Perhaps then he'd be close enough to protect Hallie. Close enough to defend her against her villainous bridegroom.

At last, a knock came on the door.

Colban cracked it open a slit.

"Let me in," Geoffrey said. "We need to be discreet."

Though Colban had mostly recovered from his over-indulgence in ale, his stomach turned when he ushered Sir Geoffrey in with his guest.

The lad could not have been five years old. He was dressed in rags, pale and shivering, as filthy as a rat.

"This was the best I could do on such short notice," Sir Geoffrey explained. "But he'll clean up nicely. I've ordered a bath brought to your room, and his mother won't expect him home until morn."

Colban could barely suppress his increasing horror and rage.

"In the meantime," Sir Geoffrey continued, "why not get undressed, let the lad get familiar with ye?" He turned to the lad, who was biting his bottom lip. "Robbie, remember what I told ye," he sternly warned. "Ye must do as I say, or I'll have to hurt your ma."

The lad's lip quivered.

"That's a good lad." Sir Geoffrey smiled. "Do ye like toys, Robbie?"

The lad nodded.

"Why don't ye go on and see what the nice man has for ye to play with?"

Colban thought he would be sick, listening to this fiend

speaking in such dulcet tones about such sickening perversions.

Just then, a soft scratching at the door announced two maids, arriving with a small tub filled with steaming water.

But Colban had heard enough. When he glanced at wee, frightened Robbie, the sort of "special entertainment" Archibald Scott preferred, he made up his mind. He'd not let Geoffrey touch or threaten the lad again.

"Wait!" he shouted to the maids before they could leave. "Give the lad the bath he deserves. He's cold and miserable." He dug in his pouch of silver and pressed a coin into each of their hands. "Buy him a new set of clothes and send him home to his ma. Tell her she's never to speak to Sir Geoffrey again."

Geoffrey was gaping at him like a landed trout.

Colban should have left him like that. But his outrage, combined with the ale he'd consumed, compelled him to pay back the torment Sir Geoffrey had visited upon God knew how many innocent victims.

While the maids pulled Robbie to safety, one of them covering his eyes, Colban fought back for all the lads who couldn't fight for themselves.

Drawing back his fist, he plowed it into Geoffrey's aristocratic nose, which bloomed instantly with blood. He followed up with a punch to the man's scrawny belly, folding him in half. What he did after that, he only saw through a miasma of fury. But soon the fretful sobs of the maids shook Colban from his rage, and he realized the man wheezing on the floor with the ruined face and the battered body was no longer capable of fighting back.

"If ye e'er traffic in innocents again," Colban bit out, "I'll finish what I started."

He dragged the useless coward out of the room and left him gasping in the corridor.

"Take care o' the lad," he reminded the maids, taking one last pitying glance at Robbie, who reminded him far too much of Ian.

Then he swept up his satchel of belongings and his claymore, hurried down the stairs, and left the inn by the southbound road.

He wasn't worried about Hallie. She could handle herself.

What made his stomach knot with fear was the thought of her little brother in the company of such a monster. Sweet, naïve Ian could be so easily tricked. So easily misled. So easily persuaded.

He had to get to Rivenloch. He only hoped he wasn't too late.

CHAPTER 36

"I'm going to show Archie the old crannog," Ian announced as he leaned over the wattle fence enclosing the practice field.

Hallie was currently indisposed, straddling an upstart knight who was flat on his back, a cocky youth who had thought he could best her with a blade. Her palm was on his chest. His blade and shield were halfway across the field. And her dagger was at his throat.

She glanced up through the morning mist. Archie stood beside Ian, staring at her, aghast.

She sighed and let the knight up. Perhaps one day her husband would recognize that she was a real warrior maid with real warrior skills. It was her duty to keep those skills honed. She would have hoped, after three months of marriage, he would be accustomed to seeing her engaging in swordplay.

"The crannog?" she asked. "Why?"

A remnant from ancient times, the crannog had once been a home for her ancestors. A round wooden cottage on stilts, perched over the loch, it was half rotted away now and made a good place for fishing. Trout liked to shelter in the shadowy depths, among the sodden timbers.

"Archie said he wants to do an experiment," Ian said, an admission that made her husband blush.

"Aye," Archie rushed to explain, hefting up a fishing pole. "We're going to find out what kind of bait works best."

Hallie arched a brow. In winter? It wasn't the best time of year for fishing. Few trout would rise from the icy depths of the loch to snap at bait.

But she didn't want to discourage the only friendship Archie had forged within the clan. And Ian was enthused about showing Archie the crannog.

"Be wary in the mist," she warned, speaking mostly for Archie's benefit. "You don't want to fall in. The loch is nigh frozen. And those timbers aren't going to last forever." On the other hand, the crannog had been there for hundreds of years. It might well last for hundreds more.

"Don't worry about us," Archie said. "We'll be back by supper."

As she watched them disappear into the thick fog, hand in hand, she wished she could so easily cultivate the warmth Ian had for Archie. But then Ian was still a child. His affections were easily won by the slightest bit of attention.

The last man who'd given Ian such attention had disappeared without so much as a farewell. At least this one would stay.

Colban, driven by fear, fury, and the need to champion the helpless, traveled for two days without sleep to reach Rivenloch. The weather seemed determined to thwart him. Last night, heavy rains had drenched his wool cloak and caked his boots with mud. Today the world was robed in layers of fog as thick as a burial shroud, with branches of ashes and elms emerging from the mist like charred bones.

His feet were blistered. His shoulders were weary. His

lungs ached. But his sore and gritty eyes burned with the fire of valor and vengeance.

His arrival at Rivenloch castle naturally caused a stir. Isabel was the first to see him.

"I knew it!" she cried, tearing across the courtyard, while Gellir and Brand followed at more dignified pace. "I knew you'd come back!"

Overjoyed to see The One, despite his haggard appearance, she wanted to order him a hot bath and a soft bed at once.

"I'm not here to stay," he said gruffly. He had only one purpose in mind. Protecting them. And for that, there was only one solution.

He turned to the lads. "Where is Hallie's husband? Where is Archibald Scott?"

Gellir and Brand exchanged a silent, significant look of solidarity. It appeared there was no love lost between the brothers and their sister's new husband. And whatever grudge they might have held about Colban leaving them without a proper goodbye was gone now.

They detected the underlying threat in Colban's words. They knew his capacity for violence. And they wanted to be a part of it.

"He's gone to the crannog," Isabel volunteered. "The ruin on the loch."

"Alone?" he hoped.

"Nay, with Ian."

Colban's gut churned. He ground his teeth.

"I'll go with you," Brand said.

Colban glanced over at the lad. For an instant, his heart wrenched. How he'd missed the Rivenloch siblings. Only three months had passed, but it looked like Brand had grown another inch.

"I'm going as well," Gellir chimed in.

"Neither o' ye are comin'," Colban told them in no

uncertain terms. "'Tis somethin' I need to do on my own." He couldn't let these honorable young lads to see was the dishonorable death he intended to deliver to their sister's husband.

"I'll fetch Hallie," Isabel offered.

"Nay!" he roared, making the lass gasp and recoil in fright.

But that was good. She *should* be frightened. Hallie was the last person he wanted to see. The last person he wanted interfering in his plans for justice.

Colban might do unsavory things to the villain before he killed him. And he didn't want her witnessing that or, even worse, defending the monster.

Frustration made the siblings curse him as he took off alone.

Honor made them do his bidding.

He took his claymore and left his satchel behind in the courtyard. Inside it was the notebook he'd stolen from Ian. It seemed trivial now. For what he intended, he wanted no burdens, and he needed his arms free.

But he knew in his heart, if he achieved what he set out to do, he wouldn't be returning for his things. They'd belong to a different man. A man who would never slay a person in cold blood. A man worth of the title an Curaidh.

Nay, he wouldn't come back for his belongings. Not for a long while. Perhaps never.

He'd been to the crannog before. Isabel's friends had taken him there to catch trout on a clear fall afternoon. Today, with its broken timbers swathed in white fog, the ruin appeared to hover above the still water like a gray storm cloud. It seemed less like a congenial fishing spot and more like an ominous hiding place for dark and secret sins.

Mist blanketed the grassy slope and concealed the uneven ground, but it also softened the sound of Colban's progress as he stole toward the walkway of the crannog.

From the verge of the mossy bank, he crept carefully across the bridge of cracked planks, dodging the places where the wood had rotted through.

The door of the crannog was missing. He was able to peer into the entrance, through the mottled shadows where gaps in the walls occurred. At the far end, beneath part of the roof that was open to the sky, he could see the dark figure of a man close to Ian, set in sharp relief against the silvery loch beyond.

Stealing into the crannog, he heard the soft murmur of their voices bouncing off the misty water. Ian's young, inquisitive tones. The man's slick and patronizing responses.

The lad stood at the edge of the platform with a fishing pole, pointing down at something in the loch.

The man hadn't spotted Colban yet. But as he drew closer, from the dim interior of the crannog, Colban could see Archie clearly in the eerie overcast. His worst fears were realized.

The man stood behind Ian, to one side. His trews were unlaced. With one hand, he fondly rubbed the back of Ian's neck. With the other, he fondled his own lavishly greased prick.

Too sickened and enraged for words, Colban let out a snarl that startled both of them.

Archie jerked back, knocking over a clay vessel that splattered his boots and trews with the same kind of shiny yellow grease that coated his cods.

Ian dropped the fishing pole and spun around. He furrowed his brows, confused by both Colban's sudden appearance and Archie's curious condition.

Colban hesitated. Perhaps nothing had happened yet. Perhaps Ian didn't understand Archie's intentions. If so, he didn't want to destroy the lad's innocence. He didn't want to be the one to explain Archie's villainy to him.

In the next instant, he regretted that moment of hesitation.

Archie panicked.

He'd been caught with his trews down. Something that had never happened before. Not in Sir Geoffrey's sheltered world.

And this stranger clearly didn't approve. He was vexed. Worse, he looked as powerful and threatening as an angry ox.

Archie racked his alarmed brain to think of a reasonable excuse for his situation. A plausible reason for him to have exposed himself.

There was none. Words failed him. So in the end, he had to rely on the only leverage he had.

Ian.

Sweeping the lad up into his arms, he backed away toward the loch.

"I'll keep you safe," he murmured to the lad. "Don't worry."

But the visual message he sent to the intruder was altogether different. Narrowing his eyes, he skewered the man with a glare that reflected his dire warning.

If the stranger didn't back away and forget what he'd seen here, Archie would toss Ian in the loch. Considering the ice crusted along the edge of the shore, the lad wouldn't last long in the cold depths.

"Get back!" Archie screamed at him, eyeing the surface of the black water.

The man clearly got his message. He froze, lifting his palms in surrender.

"But Archie..." Ian protested, wriggling in his arms.

"Be still!" he hissed. "He's got a sword."

"But that's Colban. He's my friend. He wouldn't—"

"Hush!" he ordered.

So the little whelp knew his savior. That was unfortunate.

"Let the lad go," Colban said.

Archie wasn't about to yield his hostage. Especially now. He retreated with Ian another step, inches from the splintered edge of the wood planking, and bit out, "Back away."

His threat had some effect. The Colban fellow took a judicious step backward. But the man still had a claymore slung across his back. A huge blade that could cleave Archie in half from his shoulder to his ballocks, which were beginning to pucker in the chill air, despite a thick layer of wool grease.

"Take off your sword," Archie said.

The impatient lad began to struggle in his grip. Archie almost lost his balance on the wet wood.

"Nay, Ian!" Colban barked. "Don't fight him. Ye could slip and fall."

The lad went still, all but his incessant mouth.

"'Tisn't true, is it, Colban?" Ian said. "You don't mean to hurt anyone."

"Nay," Colban lied. "Not unless they deserve it."

But the silent rage burning in Colban's smoldering eyes told a different tale. The man knew exactly what Archie was up to, and he'd kill him for it.

For the moment, however, Archie held a valuable hostage. They both knew it. Without further prodding, Colban slowly unbuckled the swordbelt draped diagonally over his shoulder and let the weapon drop to the ground.

Archie was no fool. "Your dagger as well."

The twitch in Colban's eyes told Archie he'd guessed correctly. The man had hoped his surrender of the claymore would lull Archie into complacency. He was wrong.

As the man yielded his dagger with a scowl of frustration, Archie felt some of his self-assurance returning. Things were going to be all right now. He was regaining control. Recovering his wits.

He could sort things out. For Ian's benefit, he would say it was all a simple misunderstanding. He was only doing a bit of research. Ian would back him up. After all, he helped the lad with his research all the time. Surely, he could convince Ian he had his best interests at heart.

As for this meddling fellow, who would the clan believe? Hallie's husband and brother? Or a stranger who'd burst upon them?

Eventually, of course, he'd have to tie up the loose ends of his indiscretion, as Geoffrey was often obliged to do. He'd send someone to silence the interfering Colban forever.

Archie quirked up a corner of his mouth. Already, he felt himself becoming Geoffrey's Old Cock again.

Hallie might not have shared Colban's urgency as he fled the castle, but she had a long stride to match his. And the instant Isabel came running to her—wringing her hands at the knowledge she was breaking her word to Colban and praying he would forgive her, and then revealing that he'd set out after Archie with fire in his eyes and his claymore on his back—Hallie grabbed her sword and followed in his footsteps.

What she expected to find, why Colban was after Archie, she didn't know. But Archie was her husband and a member of the clan now. She owed him her protection.

She heard raised voices coming from the crannog before she even reached the walkway. She hurried forward, straining to hear their words.

In the past, her cousin Feiyan had remarked that

Hallie's one weakness was that she was more like hail than mist. Hallie preferred to meet challenges head on, striking hard, rather than using wiles and stealth.

Her cousin Jenefer thought Hallie's vulnerability came from her careful consideration of all outcomes before she took action. A fire might rage around her while she froze in indecision.

But the instant Hallie saw Archie dangling Ian over the icy loch, she proved them both wrong.

Drawing her dagger, she stole through the shadows of the crannog. When she was within striking distance, she saw three things that made up her mind instantly.

Archie's trews were open, his genitals on full display.

His jar of wool grease lay overturned on the floor.

And Ian was squirming in his arms.

Before she even finished fully calculating the significance of those ugly facts, Hallie pinched the dagger blade between her thumb and finger and fired it forward.

Time slowed as the dagger flipped through the air.

For a protracted instant, the only sound was the whistle of the blade before it sank into Archie's thigh, followed by his long, shocked gasp. Then his face paled, his eyes widened, rolling white, and he emitted a high-pitched thread of sound as the pain registered.

At a snail's pace, Colban swung his head toward her to find the source of the attack.

Hallie returned his fierce glare with a grim gaze of her own, before her attention was drawn again to Archie.

Archie took one staggering step, and his heel slid sideways on the grease-slickened floor. At that moment, he lost his balance. And his quarry.

Ian dropped onto his hands and knees at the edge of the planks. But before he could dodge away, Archie, trying to regain his footing, flung out his arm, knocking the lad off the end of the platform.

Hallie gaped in disbelief. She surged forward, battling her way toward Ian. But it felt like she was running through thick honey.

Despite her best efforts, she still didn't get there before Colban. By the time she fought her way past Archie to peer into the water, Colban was diving past her into the icy depths.

CHAPTER 37

Archie had never been stabbed before. He stared down at the leather-wrapped haft protruding from his leg in disbelief. Watched the blood oozing onto his fine velvet trews with dismay.

The pain was incredible. Moving was unthinkable.

And yet he knew he had to get away. Flee before either of the two emerged from the water.

He expected the lad would die, either from the cold or drowning. He was small and weak.

But his coldhearted wife likely thrived in icy water. And the claymore-toting warrior looked like the sort who would brave the frozen north to seek revenge.

There was nothing left for Archie here now. If either of them survived, Archie's sins would come to light. And he'd probably be strung up by his ballocks in the courtyard of Rivenloch.

He had to escape. Now.

He felt lightheaded, and his breathing was fast and shallow. He'd pass out soon if he didn't remove the dagger, which grated against the bone of his thigh every time he shifted his weight.

So when he heard the splash behind him of someone surfacing, he gritted his teeth and, using both hands, pulled the blade free of his leg.

Sobbing in anguish, he struggled to keep from fainting, dropped the dagger, and hobbled forward.

Each step was torture. Blood pulsed from the wound with every beat of his heart. But somehow he managed to limp through the crannog, across the walkway, and off into the safety of the woods.

Colban never felt the cold. Pumped full of fear, driven by desperation, he dove into the loch with only one thought. Saving Ian.

Thrice he came to the surface emptyhanded. Each time he lost a measure of hope. But the fourth time he emerged, he heard Ian's thin cry.

The clever lad had swum to one of the crannog supports and was clinging to the timber with blue fingers.

Colban lunged toward him. But as he neared, Ian screamed, "Hallie!"

Colban frowned.

"Where's Hallie?" Ian cried at him.

It was then Colban suddenly felt the ice in his veins.

He glanced up at the platform. Where *was* Hallie? Had Archie taken her? Had he hurt her? Or worse?

A soft splash sounded behind him, and he turned in the water to see the Valkyrie surfacing. The impetuous lass must have dived into the loch after him.

But as relieved as he was to locate her, he glimpsed a Hallie he'd never seen before. Her eyes were bleak with despair. Her hair hung in wet threads over a face as pale as snow. Her lips were blue and trembling. Never had he seen a face so lost and full of dread. Never had he longed so fiercely to remove her pain.

"Hallie," Colban breathed. "He's fine. Ian's fine."

"I'm here, Hallie!" the lad cried out.

She clapped a hand to her mouth in relief, and tears

spilled from her eyes. She didn't bother to hide them as she swam toward her little brother.

Colban helped lift them back onto the platform, first Ian, then Hallie. Finally, he pulled himself up. Only when they were all safe inside the shelter of the crannog did he notice the killing cold.

"Here," he said, handing them the wool cloaks Ian and Archie had brought. "If ye change out o' your wet clothing, these should keep ye warm for the journey home."

"What about you?" Hallie asked, shuddering violently.

"Wh-where's Archie?" Ian asked with a shiver, eyeing the cloak his friend had left behind. "Wh-wh-what did you d-do to him?"

The look Colban exchanged with Hallie was brief, but it spoke volumes.

Ian likely didn't understand what had happened. As far as he was concerned, his sister had thrown a dagger at Archie, who was only trying to protect him from Colban.

He prayed the lad had not been exposed to Archie's dark intentions. Prayed he'd been spared the monster's perversions.

But he could tell Hallie had recognized the nature of his sin. Her shaking might well be rage.

Their unspoken agreement then—the message Colban and Hallie exchanged in the course of a glance—was that they wouldn't reveal Archie's villainy to Ian. Not only was it too twisted for the innocent lad to comprehend. He wouldn't believe them. Wouldn't believe such evil could exist in a man, let alone the man he'd trusted and called his friend.

"I'll...go look for him," Colban said, surreptitiously tucking Hallie's bloodied dagger into his belt. There was no need to leave evidence behind.

"It should be me," Hallie countered, urgency in her eyes. "He's my husband."

That was exactly why it should *not* be Hallie. He couldn't expect her to kill her own husband.

"Nay," he said. "Ye're shiverin' like a lamb. I've got thick Highland blood. Ye just keep Ian warm, get him to safety."

He could see she wanted to argue, but she kept quiet for Ian's sake.

But when Colban swept up his claymore and buckled it on, the lad frowned in concern. "You w-won't hurt him, will you? He was only trying to k-keep me safe."

Meanwhile, Hallie's fierce and frigid gaze sent Colban an entirely different message. Not only did she want Colban to hurt him. She wanted him to hunt down the demon and send him back to hell.

Colban deflected Ian's question. "Don't worry, Ian. I'll find him. He was injured. He can't have gone far."

Though his words reassured Ian, for Hallie, they held the promise of retribution. He meant to keep that unspoken vow.

"Go on now," he said to Ian. "Get out o' your wet things before they... What was it? Crystallize." He winked at Ian.

Ian's eyes lit up at the fact that Colban remembered one of the scientific words he'd taught him.

But the moment of camaraderie was fleeting. After all, the last time Colban had seen Ian, he'd abandoned the lad without a word of farewell. Now he'd threatened the man Ian called friend. He hadn't exactly proved himself worthy of the lad's trust or affection.

Colban let his gaze linger on the two siblings for a moment. Long enough to preserve their faces in his heart.

Ian—safe and whole, with his innocence, God willing, preserved.

Hallie—grateful yet melancholy. As if she knew. As if she realized he was not coming back.

Then he set aside his regrets and turned his thoughts to vengeance as he followed the trail of blood into the forest.

Archie felt almost gleeful.

It might be delirium. But in spite of the throbbing in his thigh, in spite of the dreadful stains of blood and wool grease on his expensive trews that no amount of scrubbing was going to erase, he felt as happy as a lamb.

He'd escaped.

Never before had he attempted such a bold and daring act.

Geoffrey would be so impressed when Archie showed up at his door—the Old Cock, sporting a fresh pair of velvet trews, his newly won freedom, and a dashing scar on his thigh.

He lifted a trembling hand to wipe away the sweat that kept dripping into his eyes. He'd left his cloak behind, and the mist was thick among the trees. But he strangely didn't feel the cold. Not at all.

Perhaps it was the glow of success warming him.

Once, he tripped over a root on the path and fell hard onto his hands and knees. A sharp burst of pain shot through his thigh, and his vision grew foggy. He moaned, incapacitated, fighting the strong desire to surrender to a sudden weariness and agony. To lie down on the path and rest a while.

But a vision of his fierce, cold-eyed wife—whom he was convinced might miraculously rise from the loch in pursuit, tracking him to the ends of the earth—compelled him onward.

Ignoring the ache in his leg and the stinging in his palms, he limped along at a feverish pace and tried to focus on his next course of action.

Stirling was miles away. He'd have to use a false name. Find lodgings. Buy a new pair of trews. Possibly from a ragpicker, since he was in a hurry. He shuddered at the thought. Perhaps he could have trews fashioned while he rested for a few days to let his leg heal. Fortunately, he had enough coin on his person to hide for a while before he fled to safety.

He grinned in triumph, though the pain that began to permeate his good mood made it feel more like a grimace in his tight face.

He was going to be all right. Things were going to work out. Before long, he'd be sharing Geoffrey's bed again, enjoying sweet young lads to his heart's content.

Those were his happy thoughts when he glimpsed the first pair of yellow eyes, gleaming at him from the shadows beyond the mist.

Colban had no trouble tracking Archibald. The man hadn't taken the time to bind his wound. Drops of his blood marked the trail.

There was no reason to hurry. Wounded in the thigh like that, Archie wouldn't be able to go on much longer. If his torn muscles didn't give out, he'd faint from loss of blood. And things would work out better for Colban if the man was both unconscious and as far away from Rivenloch as possible.

Colban meant to finish him. It was what Hallie wanted. They both knew Archibald's vile secrets. The man was a rabid beast with an unspeakable disease. He needed to be put down.

To the rest of the clan, however, Archibald Scott was Hallie's husband, chosen by the king. Once his body was discovered, Colban would become the Highland bastard who'd murdered him.

As he stole through the gray mist of the woods, Colban's sodden clothing chilled him, and he shuddered with the cold. But his flesh was no colder than his blood as he envisioned what kind of death was fitting for a man who raped children.

A sudden piercing screech in the distance stopped him in his tracks. A shiver coursed up his spine.

Colban didn't believe in wicked spirits. But if they did exist, it would doubtless be in a place like this, where the mist curled along the forest floor and the dark pines loomed overhead like towering giants.

His heart pounded as the eerie sound faded.

After a moment, he cautiously continued.

The second and third shrieks were definitely human. The raw terror Colban heard in them made his bones quiver.

He unbuckled his sword belt and unsheathed his sword. He blew out a hard breath to expel his fear. Then, clenching his jaw, he held the claymore aloft in both hands, stealthily advancing toward the source of the sound.

The screams after that were bloodcurdling and full of agony, driving him to abandon caution and hurtle down the path.

What he saw made him skid to a horrified stop on the leaves. Lying on the path, several yards ahead of him, was Archibald Scott. Or what was left of him.

Surrounding him were five growling wolves. Their maws dripped with blood. Archie, barely alive, had been mauled by the beasts. His throat was bitten. His arms were shredded. His belly was slashed. His blood was everywhere.

On instinct, Colban immediately rushed forward, bellowing and swinging his claymore to frighten the beasts away.

The wolves snarled and snapped, but they slunk off into the trees.

As they disappeared into the mist, Colban looked down at the mewling villain and wondered if he should just let the wolves have the monster. After what he'd done,

Archibald Scott deserved a brutal and lingering death.

"Please," Archibald rasped out through his damaged throat, lifting one shaky hand. "Don't let them have me."

Colban might not let the wolves finish Archibald. But if the fool thought Colban would save him, he was mistaken. The man deserved to die. And considering the extent of his injuries, Archibald was beyond saving.

"I'll grant ye mercy on one condition." Colban hunkered down beside him. "Ye tell me the truth." He unsheathed Hallie's dagger. "Did ye touch Ian?"

"Nay," he said, coughing up blood. "Nay."

"Ye swear it? Not once?"

"Nay."

Colban nodded in relief. At least Ian had been spared. He hated to think of all the other lads who had suffered at this brute's hands.

Then Archibald's eyes got a glassy, faraway look, and his lip curved up in a smile that bared his bloody teeth. "But 'twould have been sweet, aye?"

Disgust and rage gave Colban the strength to finish the monster. One carefully placed thrust through Archibald's throat, and the villain's life gurgled out quickly on the path.

For his own safety, Colban had to begin counting the moments. He had blood on his hands. Everyone had witnessed his agitation when he'd arrived at Rivenloch, his insistence on finding Archibald. Hallie and Ian had seen his determination when he'd gone after the wounded man. All evidence proved Colban was the killer.

But he couldn't just leave the body to the wolves.

He didn't want Hallie to see her husband like this.

And he shuddered to think Ian might stumble upon Archibald's remains. It would be better if the lad thought Archibald had simply run away.

There was only one thing he must do, even if it took up precious time.

Half an hour later, sweat dripped onto his cheek as he wiped a grimy forearm across his brow. The wolves hadn't returned. And using his sheathed sword as a makeshift spade, he'd managed to gouge a hole in the forest floor, deep enough to bury Archie's remains. He covered the body with earth and leaves, disguising the grave. Then he rocked a small boulder over the remains to keep the wolves from digging them up.

He stabbed the dagger into the ground beside the boulder as a sign for Hallie, so she would know he'd kept his vow. Then he dusted off his hands and came to his feet.

He would leave now and never return. Colban an Curaidh would be no more. He'd change his name, go someplace far away. It wouldn't be the first time he'd started over, been given a second chance. This time, however, the new beginning wrenched bitterly at his heart.

If only things had worked out differently, Colban could have been the one wedded to Hallidis Cameliard of Rivenloch. He could have been the one playfully sparring with Brand and Gellir, marveling over Ian's inventions, charming Isabel. He could have been The One.

With a self-indulgent sigh, he began kicking dirt and leaves over the trail to cover the blood.

Then, in the distance, he heard a sound. Someone was coming.

Cursing his luck and snatching up his claymore, he fled down the path, leaving behind his name. His destiny. And the woman he would love forever.

Knowing what she knew now about Archibald Scott, Hallie didn't waste a moment. Once Ian was safely deposited beside a warm hearth at Rivenloch with plenty of maidservants to fuss over him, she slipped out in pursuit of the monster.

If Colban didn't find Archie, she'd scour the woods until she did. She wouldn't suffer the fiend to live.

Along the way, she tormented herself with self-doubt.

How could she have been so blind? So oblivious?

How could she have missed what was going on in her own household? Right under her nose?

And how would she ever manage to protect her clan if she couldn't even shield her little brother?

The signs of Archie's debauchery had been there in front of her all along. The way he preferred the dark. And silence. And pleasuring himself. The way he shriveled in revulsion when she touched him.

Then there was his curious affinity for Ian. He'd been spending more and more time with the lad. Alone.

Her stomach suddenly heaved. She stopped on the path, waiting for the nausea to pass. She wasn't sure what was making her more queasy. The sickening idea of what Archie might have done to Ian. Or the growing evidence, afflicting her more acutely each day, that she was with child.

She had to admit, having her husband dead would solve her problems where the babe was concerned. With no one alive to know otherwise, the clan would accept that the child was Archie's.

As she hung her head down, staring at her boots and waiting to recover, an improper thought slithered tantalizingly at the back of her brain.

Once Archie was gone, what was to stop Colban from marrying her?

For a brief, glimmering moment, the idea sent a thrill of hope through her. To be wed to the father of her babe felt like providence.

But she quickly locked that idea away. She dared not let false hope consume her. She'd done that before.

Besides, too much time had passed. Surely Colban had

found another lass by now. And Hallie had to at least *feign* to be stricken over Archie's death.

Meanwhile, she meant to make certain he *was* dead, to ensure the devil would never exercise his vices again.

Her stomach settled, and she continued down the path, wondering if Colban had found Archie or if she'd need to kill him herself. It wouldn't be a pleasant task, but after what he'd done to Ian, it wouldn't be difficult.

She focused on the leaf mulch, following the trail of blood droplets. They were growing closer together, indicating he had either slowed his pace or was losing blood at a faster rate. But when she entered the place where the path snaked through a stand of oaks, the blood trail suddenly disappeared.

She flinched in surprise, not by what she saw, but by what she *didn't* see. Where was he? Where was Archie?

She narrowed her eyes at something else leading off into the trees. Bloody tracks. The paw prints of wolves.

Hallie gulped. Had wolves attacked Archie?

It wasn't like them to come out in the middle of the day. But Archie had been bleeding. And he'd smeared himself with that disgusting wool grease. The hungry winter wolves could have mistaken him for a wounded sheep. They might have killed him in a blind frenzy.

She scanned the trees. No yellow eyes peered from the woods. The wolves had retreated. Yet there were no signs they had dragged the body away with them.

Then her eye caught on something familiar by the side of the path. Her dagger. It was thrust into a patch of freshly dug earth that had been hastily disguised by leaves and covered by a great rock.

Her breath caught. It was a fresh grave.

Hunkering down, she reclaimed her dagger, wiping the soil from the blade with her sleeve.

He'd done it. Colban had done it.

The truth sent a shiver of relief and gratitude through her. Colban had kept his word. The champion had saved her little brother from a monster. He'd rescued her from an unbearable marriage.

But at what cost?

Now Colban was a murderer.

He didn't dare return.

She choked back the hard lump in her throat and sheathed her dagger.

This was why she never clung to hope. No sooner did it take root in one's breast than savage fate showed up to pluck it out by those roots.

She decided to break the news quietly to Ian first. There would be time later, after Colban had an ample few hours to flee to safety, to tell the rest of the clan.

Upon her return to Rivenloch, she hunkered down beside him at the hearth, dismissing the maidservants to speak with him alone. Gently, while the fire softly crackled, she told him Archie was dead, that Colban had buried him in the forest.

She expected Ian to burst into tears or explode with rage.

He did neither. Instead, he nodded his head. "Where's Colban?"

"Gone."

"You have to find him."

"Listen, Ian." She had to explain everything to him quickly. Curb his appetite for vengeance before it had the chance to grow out of control. "We need to let him go. Colban shouldn't be punished for Archie's death. 'Twasn't his fault."

"I know."

"He was only trying to protect you."

"I know."

"If anyone is to blame, 'tis me," she reasoned. "I was the

one who wounded Archie. And I did it because I was concerned for your welfare."

"I know."

"What do you mean, you know?" she asked.

He shrugged. "'Tis the only rational explanation. I don't know what Archie did. But if Colban the champion and my sister the laird think he did something bad, then logic dictates he did something bad."

Hallie blinked. Ian might be young in age and innocent by nature, but he was wise beyond his years. "How can you be so sure?"

Ian screwed up his forehead, searching for a way to explain it. "'Tis like metals. Archie is...was...like quicksilver. His honor was always soft and changeable, and he clung to whatever those around him believed. But you and Colban? You're tempered steel. Your honor is strong and stable. You'd never hurt someone who didn't deserve it."

His words were simple, but touching. Her eyes watered, and for a moment she couldn't speak.

"So you'll go find him, aye?" Ian asked.

She wished it were that simple. "I can't. I have to let him go. *We* have to let him go. 'Tis for his own safety." She lowered her voice to a whisper. "You and I may know that Archie deserved what he got. But to the rest of the world, Colban is a murderer."

Ian's brow crumpled as he digested this information. Finally he asked, "Do you think he'll come back?"

She forced a smile of false hope to her lips. "Perhaps one day."

Ian nodded and returned to staring into the flames.

Hallie sighed. Ian was young and resilient. When one day turned into one week, then one month, then one year, and Colban never returned, Ian would eventually forget him.

She only wished *she* could forget him so easily.

Being with Colban once again at the crannog, even under such dire circumstances and for so brief a time, she'd felt her heart swell with yearning.

Instantly remembered the touch of his hands.

The taste of his lips.

The warmth of his love.

Lowering her hand, she caressed the haft of her dagger, the last thing he'd touched of hers, and a glistening tear fell onto the worn leather.

She would never know that kind of love again.

CHAPTER 38

Winter sent out one last snowstorm to blanket the Lowlands with white fleece that clung to the cold ground. Days turned into weeks as the earth slept. But the sun eventually returned, melting the frost and awakening the tender seedlings. The hills burst forth, first with snowdrop, then with cowslips and daffodils that dotted the green slopes with sunny yellow.

With white puffs of cloud blowing across a pale blue sky and a crisp breeze fluttering the festive pennants on display atop the castle battlements, the weather couldn't have been more perfect for Creagor's first spring tournament.

As he paused on the rise overlooking the castle, Colban couldn't help fearing he was making a mistake.

It was too soon to risk returning. Less than two months had passed since he'd buried Archibald Scott.

But his new identity as a knight-errant required that he earn what coin he could with his blade. In Dumfries, he'd traded his claymore for a Lowland sword, practiced until his hands were blistered and his arms ached. The blade was lighter and more agile, and he was pleasantly surprised to discover he had considerable skill with it. Indeed, The Sable Knight was beginning to make a name for himself on the tournament field.

So far, he'd been hired to challenge a brute who was terrorizing a local clan, defend a noblewoman whose honor was in question, and champion a merchant lass against her rivals. He'd spent most of his earnings on the trappings of nobility—a new shield, helm, and armor. Now he was down to his last shilling.

Nothing was more lucrative than a tournament. Particularly the one at Creagor, which had been hailed as a tournament to dwarf all others. There was no entry fee for contestants, so matches were based, not on bloodlines, but on merit. Thus the competition would feature the finest warriors in all of Scotland and beyond.

He couldn't afford *not* to go.

At least, that was his excuse.

But he definitely had an ulterior motive. One with crystal blue eyes, bright blonde hair, and enticing long legs.

For weeks, the beautiful Valkyrie had haunted him. Intruded upon his every waking thought. Danced through his dreams. Like a persistent angel, she followed him everywhere.

Every battle he fought, he fought in her honor.

Every challenge he accepted, he accepted in her name.

He lived and breathed and stayed alive for Hallie.

He ached to see her again. And he was certain Hallie wouldn't miss her cousin's tournament for the world.

He was well aware that only a fool would hope that anything could come of it. Lingering here only tempted fate and prolonged his pain. And for what?

He sighed. He truly must be a fool.

But just the prospect of glimpsing her again—even if it had to be at a distance, on the tournament field, through the visor of his helm—made his heart race.

For his own safety, he would fight anonymously as always—under a banner with no insignia, in a tabard with no crest.

Concealing one's identity was commonplace enough, especially for a knight-errant. In some parts of the country, it was the only way for a warrior who lacked the requisite nobility to compete.

Colban reviewed his plans.

The tournament would be two days long, with archery and entertainments on the first day, sword fighting and the melee on the second.

By day, he would wear a hooded cloak when he wasn't fighting in his helm. By night, he could sleep in one of the pavilions that had been erected for guests on the slopes of Creagor, far away from those flying the banner of Rivenloch.

As long as he was careful, he could be there and gone like mist, with no one the wiser.

Bracing himself with a deep breath that was half resignation and half anticipation, The Sable Knight descended the hill to refill his coffers and replenish his spirit.

Jenefer eyed the target at the far end of the range, pulling back the string of her bow. The crowd hushed. She held her breath.

Suddenly Isabel gasped beside her.

Rattled, Jenefer lowered her weapon in disgust and glared at the lass.

Hallie scowled at her as well.

"Sorry," Isabel said, blushing and hugging the quiver of Jenefer's arrows to her breast.

Jenefer would not normally be distracted by a gasp or a twitch or even a scream. But this was the first tournament she'd ever hosted. Archery was her event. And Hallie knew, more than anything, Jenefer wanted to win.

Hallie had shot well several moments earlier. But she

was currently in fifth place and nowhere near as talented as her cousin.

There were, however, a few archers from France proving quite competitive. Jenefer was vying with one of them for first place. She needed every advantage. What she did not need was Isabel the Quiver-Holder gasping just as she drew her bow.

Jenefer rolled her shoulders and took her stance again. The crowd silenced as she raised her bow once more, drew back the arrow, and took aim.

In the instant before Jenefer fired, Hallie was distracted by a hooded figure watching the contest from the far side of the archery range. He was clad all in black. His arms were crossed over his chest. His face was hidden in shadow. But he looked almost like...

She gasped.

"Shite!" Jenefer hissed, lowering her bow and turning to scowl fiercely at Hallie.

Hallie was mortified. "I am *so* sorry, cousin. I promise I'll..." She exchanged a look with Isabel. "We'll...be as silent as mice."

Jenefer grumbled, adjusted her stance, and resumed aiming her bow. When Hallie glanced across the range again, the hooded man had vanished.

To her consternation, her heart was pounding. But surely it hadn't been him. It was only a trick of the light. A figment of her imagination. Hundreds of knights and squires and merchants had gathered at Creagor for the grand tournament. There must be dozens of tall, broad-shouldered warriors she could have easily mistaken for Colban an Curaidh.

She kept her vow of silence to her cousin. So did Isabel. And Jenefer shot her third bull's-eye to win the competition.

When the crowd stopped cheering and Isabel finished

her quiver-carrying duties, she whispered to Hallie, "'Twas him, wasn't it?"

"What are you talking about?"

"That man in the hood. 'Twas him."

Apparently, Isabel had noted the resemblance as well. That couldn't be good. She feigned ignorance. "Who?"

Isabel elbowed her. "You know who. Colban."

Hallie tensed her jaw. "Don't be ridiculous. It only *looked* like him." She said it more to convince herself than her sister.

"I'm telling you, 'twas him, and I'm going to go find—"

"Nay!" Hallie said sharply. "Jenefer needs you to help set up the stage for Ian."

Isabel let out a peeved sigh. "Fine."

Isabel knew she had an important responsibility. Ian had created dozens of birds out of parchment, and he planned to make them fly. His spectacle would start an afternoon of entertainments—minstrels, players, dancers, and jugglers. It was Isabel's duty to usher the performers to and from the stage.

Besides, Hallie knew her little sister. If Isabel thought The One had returned, she'd blather it all over the castle within the hour and put Colban in mortal danger.

Then Hallie corrected herself. Colban couldn't be put in danger, because he wasn't actually at Creagor. It had only been someone who *looked* like Colban.

Still, the last thing she needed on this already chaotic day was for Isabel to stir up trouble. Even a reminder that her husband's murderer hadn't been caught yet could ruin the merry mood.

Colban cursed silently. Hallie had spotted him. He should have realized she might recognize him, even in a hooded cloak. He'd have to be more careful.

Still, as he slipped away through the crowd, he thought it had been worth the risk.

Hallie had been even more lovely than he remembered. Standing in the morning sunlight of the archery range like a goddess of the hunt, she'd fired off her three arrows with fierce concentration. Then she'd turned to her cousin Jenefer with a toss of her pale braid, a brilliant smile, and a friendly challenge in her bright eyes.

Colban's heart had flipped over at the sight. Until that moment, he hadn't fully realized how much he missed the enchanting Valkyrie. His last glimpse of her had been at the crannog, pale and shivering with frost and fear and rage. That had been the memory lodged in his brain.

Now it seemed the spring had thawed that memory. Like the snowdrops gracing the hills above Creagor, she took his breath away with her stunning beauty. Long blonde tresses as soft and sleek as silk. Rosy lips that he remembered tasted as sweet as they looked. A body that was strong and womanly at the same time.

But he'd flown too close to the sun. His gaze had lingered a moment too long. She'd caught him.

Perhaps he'd escaped soon enough. Perhaps she hadn't recognized him and had only been intrigued by the sight of a hooded stranger in the crowd.

He ducked into the shade of a curtain wall buttress. From this vantage point, he could safely survey most of the courtyard. Members of the mac Giric clan passed to and fro without spotting him. He recognized a few Rivenloch faces, as well as knights with whom he'd competed in recent tournaments.

Along the curtain wall, merchants hawked their wares, patrons counted out silver, and children played hide-and-seek.

Meanwhile, a wooden stage was being erected on the archery range. He wondered what sort of entertainments were planned. Certainly nothing to rival Isabel's play with the fire-breathing dragon.

Colban caught a passing youth and paid him to fetch an ale. Then he

settled into the shadows, leaning against the wall with his arms crossed to watch.

He smiled. From the middle of the field, Isabel directed a pair of burly lads in assembling the trestles, collected a few dozen colorfully dressed performers, and assigned her bevy of lasses to tend to their needs. She was in her element, calling out commands and herding people with the skill of a shepherd's dog.

When the spectators surrounded the stage, Colban saw Ian for the first time. As the lad mounted the steps, he seemed, impossibly, to look taller than Colban remembered. But then the last time he'd seen Ian, it was as a vulnerable victim in the hands of a monster.

He hoped the lad would one day forgive him for what he'd done. But at least Colban could be confident in the knowledge that the brutish Archibald Scott had never laid a hand on Ian. Nor would he ever.

Ian hefted a large basket onto the stage. Colban wasn't close enough to hear Ian's words, but the audience responded with cheers of enthusiasm.

Pulling the hood closer about his face, Colban pushed off the wall. Melting into the crowd, he made his way forward to get a better look.

The lad plucked a bright yellow object from the basket and held it high above his head. Then he gently pitched his arm forward, and the thing...flew.

The crowd gasped. Colban furrowed his brows. Was it a bird? It sailed smoothly over the heads of the assembly as they dodged aside to let it pass. Finally it drifted down to earth.

No sooner had it landed than Ian fired off another.

This one was vivid red and smaller, and he threw it with more force.

It shot out from his hand and made a loop in the air, then another, and another. Children shrieked as the mad bird swooped at them and finally stuttered to a stop on the grass.

The third craft, painted to match the sky, soared in a lazy circle before halting in mid-air and dropping straight down.

The fourth, decorated with black and yellow stripes like a bee, darted forward at great speed to sting an old woman on her wimple, sending her into gales of laughter.

Colban grinned. Clever Ian had made a whole flock of birds out of parchment. Birds that actually flew. He imagined the lad's notebook was now littered with dozens of illustrations and calculations he'd used to predict their flight.

Ian sent out a pair of white doves next, which sailed in wavering patterns, side by side. Then a brown owl that spiraled slowly to its demise. A black raven that shot like an arrow from the stage to the sward. Then a large, multicolored phoenix with a long tail that undulated through the air before the beast came crashing down at the feet of a squealing wee lass.

For his final performance, he rapidly unleashed a flock of six birds of different colors, one right after the other. Each made a single vertical loop in the sky, then descended at a gradual angle to the ground in the crowd's midst. But the last one stopped short when it struck Colban's chest.

Colban started to chuckle in delight. But the crowd around him had grown silent. He supposed, with his foreboding black garments and black hood, they expected him to have a black mood as well. And he supposed he should appease their expectations. After all, he needed to keep up his disguise. He should pick up the offending object and crumple it in his fist.

But when he retrieved the bright blue parchment and saw the beady black eyes painstakingly painted on its face, the feathers delineated in careful detail, he didn't have the heart to destroy Ian's handiwork.

Instead, he threw the thing back. It made half a loop, stalled in the air, and fluttered to the ground. He obviously didn't have Ian's flight skills.

The crowd remained silent, and he gazed toward Ian.

The lad had gone pale.

Colban frowned and turned on his heel. Ian couldn't possibly have recognized him. Not cloaked as he was. Yet he felt like the lad's eyes had somehow pierced his hood and looked into his murdering soul.

Colban shoved his way through the crowd, leaving before the lad could make his identity known. He made his way past the gates of the castle toward the safety of the pavilions as the soft strains of the next entertainment, a musical consort, floated over the courtyard.

So focused on escape was he, he didn't notice the pair of ice blue eyes observing him from atop the battlements.

CHAPTER 39

Watching the hooded man bolt across the field, his cloak flapping as he hastily ducked into one of the pavilions, Hallie knew it was Colban. It had to be. Who else had such a long and confident stride?

And yet there was enough of a sliver of doubt in her mind that she didn't climb down from the battlements at once to pursue and confront him. It could all be just her wishful imagination, after all.

Why would Colban return to the place where his own kinfolk might recognize him? Where he could be connected to Archie's murder? It made no sense. Such a risk would be foolhardy.

Even if she discovered it *was* Colban, what would she say to him? Go away? Perhaps it was best she didn't find out.

Hallie pressed at her temples. She had to concentrate on the tournament. She would be competing in the sword fights on the morrow. She needed to practice.

Though she'd told no one about her condition, and it was still indiscernible to all but the most observant eye, carrying extra weight in her belly was throwing off her balance. She needed to focus on her form and agility. The last thing she needed was worrying that Archie's killer was in danger of being discovered.

The stranger never returned to the courtyard. He didn't come to the feast in the great hall. He likely had a servant bring him supper in his pavilion, where he would sleep for the night.

But she knew she'd see him again on the morrow, for he no doubt intended to participate in the tournament.

All night long, Hallie fought combatants in her sleep. And lost. In her dreams, each time her conqueror removed his helm—whether he was short, tall, stout, thin, dressed in red or yellow or black—it was Colban. By morn, shaken by suffering so many imaginary losses, Hallie rose early, determined to regain her fighting confidence.

An hour on the practice field did her good. She sparred with Jenefer and Feiyan, who had risen at dawn. In no time, she'd found her center again. Renewed and laughing with her cousins, she looked forward to the contests ahead.

Gellir and Brand were still too young to compete in the matches. But rather than observing from the rows of stands constructed on the tournament field, they took up a position as close to the fighters as possible. They mingled with the knights at the perimeter of the field to study their weapons and watch their techniques. Ian joined them, making sketches of the various pieces of armor, inspecting greaves and poleyns and questioning the knights about the pieces' strengths and weaknesses.

Because there were so many contestants, the first few rounds of matches would occur simultaneously, with two challenges on the field at any given time.

Isabel had been awarded the honor of drawing the names of the competitors from a basket filled with slips of parchment. The winners of each contest would continue to the next match until the field was winnowed down to two combatants. The winner of that final match would be the tournament champion.

For the first match, Feiyan's name was drawn, along with that of Sir Renard de Bois. Because her fighting style was so unusual, full of clever acrobatics, she handily won the match.

Meanwhile, Sir Rauve triumphed by brute force over his opponent, The Blue Knight.

Over two dozen matches followed, featuring warriors from all over Scotland and beyond. Among the contestants were a Nubian fighter of great renown, a Bavarian knight who claimed to be descended from the Huns, and a warrior from the infamous de Ware family from France. One unidentified combatant was even rumored to be an English knight who had stolen across the Border to compete.

The fighting was thrilling, full of as much mercy as ferocity and as much good will as good skill.

The Rivenloch clan claimed some victories. Hallie's mother dispatched Jenefer's father. Laird Morgan defeated Hallie's father. Jenefer's mother easily conquered Sir Johannes of Bamberg. Feiyan's father sent Sir Morris of Stirling limping from the field. And Hallie left her Highland opponent, William of the mac Giric clan, in the dust.

Then Isabel announced the final two bouts of the first round—Sir Thomas of fighting Angus mac Ivey and Jenefer of Rivenloch fighting someone called The Sable Knight.

Hallie narrowed her eyes at her hotheaded cousin's competition. The Sable Knight was her mystery man.

No longer wearing his hooded cloak, he was dressed in full armor and a helm that concealed his face. Neither his black tabard nor his shield bore insignia of any kind. But his height and bearing still convinced her it might be Colban.

As soon as The Sable Knight began fighting, however, she changed her mind. She'd seen Colban fight. It was nothing like this. Colban was a Highlander, accustomed to delivering the slow, deliberate blows of a two-handed claymore.

This man fought as if he'd been born with a longsword in his hand.

Despite Jenefer's fierce attacks, The Sable Knight dodged them with a nimbleness uncommon for a man his size. He spun and thrust, countering her slashes with his shield, glancing them aside as if they were no more bothersome than Ian's parchment birds.

Still, there was something so familiar about him. The way he lunged. The way he powered forward with his shoulders. The way he hesitated in a gesture of chivalry to let his opponent brace for the next volley. If it wasn't Colban, it was someone with a hell of a lot of his mannerisms.

Jenefer eventually tired, and when, in angry exasperation, she overextended her blade, he rushed in close to disarm her. With the edge of his sword at her throat, she had no choice but to yield, spitting curses from inside her helm.

There was a brief respite for refreshments, and Hallie sipped at her watered ale, looking for the elusive Sable Knight. But he'd disappeared again.

The second round went more quickly. This time, Hallie was pitted against the Nubian warrior, Mashshouda. It was a tough battle. His technique was unusual, and he used his shield as a weapon just as much as his sword. But once she found his weakness—a lightness of foot that left him ungrounded—she swept him off his feet, winning the match and thanking him for a challenging skirmish.

The Sable Knight won again, this time against Sir Rauve. The stranger leveraged Sir Rauve's own power against him, sending him tripping over his own blade more than once. When he downed him for the last time, he planted his boot on Rauve's backside. The crowd found that more amusing than did Rauve, and Hallie longed to reward the Sable Knight's cocky gesture with a humiliation of her own if they were matched in the next round.

Before the third round of matches, Laird Morgan, who'd advanced to the next level, approached Hallie. He nodded toward The Sable Knight, who stood on the far side of the field, inspecting his blade.

"Does that knight look familiar to ye?" Morgan asked.

Hallie pretended nonchalance. "Which one?"

"The man all in black."

She pretended to study him. "Nay. Should he?"

Morgan shook his head. "He looks so much like—"

"Sir Dougal, aye?" Hallie quickly supplied, eager to distract Morgan. "The king's man. Is it him? Do you think he would travel all the way here from Edinburgh to take part in the tournament?"

"Nay. I mean—"

"How exciting! Sir Dougal. Jenefer must be so thrilled."

"Jenefer?" he asked with a frown. "She's grumblin'. She lost in the first round, ye know."

"Oh. Aye," Hallie replied, just glad to be changing the subject. "But there's still the melee. She loves the melee."

Morgan didn't reply, but narrowed his eyes once more at The Sable Knight. Then he shook his head.

Hallie breathed a sigh of relief when Isabel rang a bell to get everyone's attention for the third round of matches and Morgan bowed in farewell.

Sixteen contestants remained. Of the five of the Rivenloch clan—Hallie, Feiyan, Deirdre, Helena, and Rand—only three survived to proceed to the next level. Sir Rand, Feiyan's father, was defeated by a de Ware. And Feiyan fell victim to a small, quick fighter by the name of The Sparrow.

Hallie fought against Sir Thomas, scoring a narrow victory when she ducked under a particularly vicious blow and shoved him to the ground with her shield.

The last match was between Laird Morgan and The Sable Knight. Hallie held her breath as the two rivals faced each other. If that was Colban, Morgan would surely recognize him at once. They were practically brothers.

The Highlanders had not fared well in the tournament. Their claymores were a valuable weapon in warfare, where a single blow could lay a foe low. But in sparring, where killing was not the goal, they lacked the finesse and recovery to maintain ongoing combat.

Laird Morgan managed to land a hard first blow to the shield of The Sable Knight, one that made him stagger backwards. But while he prepared for a second attack, the knight swept in with his sword, doling out three blows of his own.

Again, Laird Morgan swung his claymore. This time, The Sable Knight ducked under the blade, and it swished through empty air, throwing Morgan off balance. Rather than let him recover, the knight planted his saboton in Morgan's hindquarters and shoved him farther. Morgan tripped and fell on one knee, but to his credit, he recovered and came up with his blade swinging.

Hallie narrowed her eyes at The Sable Knight. She got the distinct impression he was toying with Morgan. He could have dispatched him easily. But he preferred to prolong the match, which was quickly becoming more brawl than battle, as the two men used their elbows and knees to shove each other. Just like two brothers, Hallie realized.

No sooner did she have that thought than the match ended. The Sable Knight, apparently tiring of the match, snagged the hilt of Morgan's claymore with his sword, sending the heavy blade sailing in an almost graceful arc across the field. Then he used his shield to knock Morgan to the ground.

Unarmed, Morgan yielded. Hallie expected The Sable Knight to gloat then and perhaps plant his foot on Morgan's chest. Instead, he offered a hand to his fallen opponent, helping him to his feet. He even gave Morgan a humble nod, as if to say he'd been honored by the battle.

"That Sable Knight is quite good," Hallie's mother said as they broke for another respite.

Now only three Rivenloch fighters remained—Hallie, her mother, and her Aunt Helena. They discussed battle strategies as they sipped ale. By the chance of the draw, they might well be pitted against each other as opponents. But they all wanted *someone* from the Rivenloch clan to win the day.

"He might be good," Helena snorted. "But did you see what he did to poor Sir Rauve? I'd like to wipe that cocky smirk off the lout's face."

"What face?" Deirdre said. "He hasn't shown his face all day."

Hallie broke in, eager to steer the conversation to other fighters. "The Sparrow seems dangerous."

"Aye," Deirdre agreed. "I suspect 'tis a woman."

"Do you think?" Helena asked.

"Small, fast, clever," Deirdre said. "Took Feiyan completely by surprise."

Hallie nodded. It was hard to take Feiyan by surprise.

"And what about the Frenchman?" Helena asked.

"De Ware?" Hallie said. "I'd like to fight him." The de Wares had almost as much notoriety in France as the Rivenlochs had in Scotland. It would be satisfying to defeat him.

In the following rounds, however, it was Helena who was paired with Sir Evrard de Ware, who unfortunately sent both her sword and shield flying.

Deirdre defeated The Sparrow, making sure afterwards to praise the knight's great bravery and skill. There weren't many lasses with the courage to take up the sword, and this one was worthy of respect.

The Sable Knight trounced the Flemish Sir Guillaume, cutting short the man's flashy and flamboyant maneuvering with blunt force.

And with a distracting swipe of her shield and a strategic sweep of her sword, Hallie eliminated the last of the mac Giric warriors left in the tournament.

None of the finalists spoke during the next break. Now every warrior was truly on their own. No one could predict which of the four would be pitted against whom.

Hallie hoped she wouldn't have to fight her mother. Though Hallie was younger and stronger, her mother could read her like a seer and anticipate her every move.

But the first two names Isabel drew were Hallie of Rivenloch and Sir Evrard de Ware, which pleased Hallie greatly. She wouldn't mind putting the knight in his place after the drubbing he'd given her Aunt Helena.

It was easy to say. Not as easy to do. De Ware was strong and fast and clever. He made her defend herself at a breathtaking pace, hardly leaving room for attack.

Eventually, she managed to take the upper hand, mostly because she fought outside the bounds of polite French swordsmanship and relied on her wits, doing the unexpected. Her moment of victory came when she'd retreated, drawing his slashes far and wide, giving him the impression he was driving her against the fence, and then rolled forward suddenly in the dust to come up at his throat.

He took his defeat with good-natured grace, chuckling in amusement at her trickery and bowing deeply in her honor.

Then the contest between her mother and The Sable Knight began.

Their battle was intriguing, more like a contest of wills and wiles than a physical fight. Rather than coming at her with a forceful attack, he held back, as if testing her mettle. Laird Deirdre too withheld her fiercest blows, forcing him to take the lead. This went on for several moments as they circled, their blades making only occasional contact.

The crowd began to lose patience, calling out for the fighting to begin.

Finally, Deirdre unleashed a barrage of blows.

To Hallie's amazement, he easily deflected them all.

But her mother, aware now that the knight was capable of mounting a good defense, understood she'd have to fight with more brains than brawn.

They battled back and forth, like cats playing with mice, each waiting for the other to make a deadly mistake.

He almost got her once, and the gasps from the crowd were evidence of how close the sword that whistled past her head had come.

While she was recovering, he followed up with an onslaught of aggressive attacks that she caught on her shield. Finally, one hard strike from his sword cracked her shield in two, rendering it useless.

She tossed the thing aside, intending to continue fighting.

But The Sable Knight lowered his weapon and backed away, offering her the opportunity to fetch a new shield.

If it had been Hallie, her first instinct would have been to seize that opportunity.

Her second instinct—and what her mother did—was to yield.

Laird Deirdre lowered her sword, announcing that The Sable Knight had won the match fairly.

The crowd cheered her act of chivalry—and his—and she waved at them in thanks and recognition. Hallie realized at that moment that, for a laird, winning the clan's respect was far more important than winning the match.

She was still considering her mother's wisdom when the two combatants exited the field and she heard Laird Deirdre murmuring to The Sable Knight.

"You know, if you have no affiliations, if you're truly a knight-errant, the forces of Rivenloch would be glad to have you among our ranks."

He gave her a nod of thanks, but didn't reply. And once more, Hallie was struck by his strong resemblance to Colban. What it was, she didn't know. His scent? His mannerisms? The shape of his body? The sensation persisted, no matter how unlikely and irrational it seemed.

Giving her head a mental shake, she strode away to splash water on her face, half to wash away the grime of the field and half to sober herself from distracting thoughts. She had to prepare for the championship match. After all, how could she gaze at her opponent as they exchanged mortal blows, wondering all the while if he was the father of her child?

CHAPTER 40

When Hallie returned to the field, it was with new determination. She tossed her braid over her shoulder and settled her helm down over her head, loosened her shoulders and blew out a hard breath.

This was it. No matter if she fought Colban an Curaidh or the Devil himself, Hallie planned to defeat The Sable Knight and claim the title of champion for Rivenloch.

As he'd done with her mother, the knight began by goading her with gentle taps that were easy to block, drawing her gradually into the fight. For one horrifying, distracting moment, the manner of his fighting seemed all too much like the Highlander's seduction. The way he lured her in. Tempted her. Made her desperate to engage him…

Hallie slammed the portcullis on that thought before it could lay siege to her concentration.

The Sable Knight was an opponent, nothing more.

Hallie adjusted her shield. Her gift was her patience and perseverance. If he insisted on taking tentative, non-lethal jabs at her, all she had to do was wait for him to tire of the game.

When he finally changed the rhythm of his advances and lunged forward, she was ready for him. She cast off his sword and surged forward with her own, pummeling him in the ribs.

He recovered quickly, but she could see her swift counterattack had rattled him. Much like her eager response to Colban's kisses had thrown him off-balance.

Mortified once again by the direction of her musings, Hallie retreated, slicing through the air as if mentally murdering her thoughts.

Meanwhile, he circled her cautiously, looking for an opening.

She gave him one. But it was a deceptive advantage. When he attacked in the gap she intentionally left between her sword and shield, she spun, scissoring her arms to catch and deflect his blade.

Sometimes that trick could disarm an opponent. Not this one. The knight clung to his sword with an iron grip.

They battled back and forth in a straightforward manner for several exchanges, lunging and hacking, thrusting and blocking.

Then he made a unique move. One she should have anticipated, since she'd seen it before.

He swept his blade over her head, missing it by only a few inches. Then he flung his shield at her, releasing it toward her right shoulder. While she was distracted, dodging the flying shield, he finished his spin, bringing his blade low to sweep her off her feet.

He almost succeeded. At the last instant, recognizing the maneuver, she leaped over the blade.

It *had* to be Colban. That was the ploy he'd shown Brand and Gellir.

On the other hand, she supposed anyone could learn a trick like that.

She had to finish the fight and find out for certain the identity of The Sable Knight.

He had surrendered his shield, wagering his tactic would end the match. Hallie could have easily won by taking advantage of his vulnerability.

But her mother had taught her a valuable lesson. Chivalry was more important than victory. So she retreated, picked up his shield, and tossed it back to him.

The crowd cheered. The knight inclined his head in thanks, and she swore she could imagine Colban's crooked smile beaming out at her from inside that helm.

As a warrior, Hallie was renown for remaining cool, even in the heat of battle. And although The Sable Knight was challenging her composure, she knew she had to rely on that gift if she wanted to win this skirmish.

Rather than wielding blows that would finish him off, she began pestering him with small, quick attacks. Her sword became a swarm of bees, stinging in the gaps of his chain mail and thumping against his helm.

Forced to defend against each minor offense, he became annoyed. Once he was annoyed, his return attacks became careless. Fueled by his temper and sheer frustration, he grew negligent.

Finally, as every foe did when confronted by a horde of bothersome pests, he lashed out with a wild and reckless slash, as if he could wipe them out in a single blow.

Almost without fail, when a warrior's sword slashed right and his shield went wide to the left, he left himself open to attack. Hallie took advantage of that moment to lunge forward, bowling him over with her sword, her shield, and all of her strength.

He fell backwards into the dirt, taking her with him. She ended up astride his body with her blade at his throat.

She'd won the tournament. But there would be time to celebrate later. Right now, she wanted to know just one thing.

While the crowd cheered, she leaned forward and whispered, "Tell me your name." Her heart pounded as she waited for his reply.

Rather than answer her, the lout slipped his shield

under her blade, pushing it away from his throat, threw her off of him, and fell heavily on top of her with *his* sword at *her* throat.

Her gasp was echoed by the crowd. How had he done that? How had turned the tables on her so quickly and stolen her victory?

She struggled beneath him. But it was to no avail. She still had her sword in her grip, but the wrist of her sword arm was anchored to the ground in his steel gauntlet. She was well and truly conquered.

"Fine," she bit out in disappointment. "I yield."

The knave cocked his head as if he hadn't heard her.

"I yield," she snarled.

He let her up, but she coldly refused his hand when he offered it. She was vexed. The lout had usurped her triumph and snatched glory from Rivenloch. Worse, he'd refused to give her his name.

Colban supposed a gentleman might have let the lady win. But she didn't need the purse that came with the championship. He did. And her hastily whispered question had caught him off-guard. Fearing exposure of his identity, he did what came naturally in a sword fight, overthrowing his opponent by any means possible.

If it were left to him, he would have remained atop the magnificent Valkyrie, tossed aside their swords and helms, and continued his assault, drinking in her beauty, touching her face, kissing her lips.

But he had been lucky enough already, earning the privilege of fighting with her. He had hoped to catch a glimpse of Hallie from afar. But even in his wildest dreams, he hadn't imagined the two of them would engage in close combat.

She was just as amazing as they said. Competent. Calm.

Deadly. The match could have easily gone her way. He wanted to tell her so. But speaking would have revealed his identity. Besides, she might have perceived his praise as condescending.

He lingered just long enough to receive the applause of the crowd and the satchel of silver for his efforts from Laird Morgan and Jenefer.

Then he repaired to his pavilion to prepare for the final event, the melee.

He paid a servant to fetch supper from the castle—pork pies, ruayn cheese on brown bread, apple tarts, and ale—for him and the three French knights sharing the pavilion.

They were halfway through the meal when an unexpected guest arrived.

"I knew it!"

"Shite," Colban breathed.

It was Morgan. With an angry slap of the pavilion flap behind him, he strode to where Colban was and gave him a hard shove that almost knocked him off the trunk where he was sitting.

"Hey!" Colban complained, trying not to spill his ale.

"Where the devil have ye been?"

Colban scowled. "I thought ye'd be a wee bit glad to see me."

"Well, ye thought wrong. I've been worried sick about ye for weeks."

The three French knights began to murmur in speculation among themselves.

Colban sniffed. "Ye know I can take care o' myself."

"Is that so? Well, in case ye didn't realize it, ye're a wanted mur-..." Morgan glanced at the others and lowered his voice. "Tell me the truth. Did ye kill Archibald Scott?"

"Aye," Colban said stiffly.

"What?" Morgan's eyes widened.

"But I had my reasons."

Morgan hissed, "Would one o' those reasons be lustin' after the man's wife?"

Insulted, Colban stood up and gave Morgan a hard shove into the pavilion wall. "Ye know me better than that."

Morgan's eyes smoldered into his. Then he pushed away from the pavilion wall, brushing off the sleeve of his cotun. "Why did ye return?"

"*I* didn't," Colban told him. "The Sable Knight returned." He shrugged and grumbled, "He needed the coin."

"Ah. So ye won't be stayin'?" Morgan's tone was cool and lordly. But Colban knew that his friend—his brother—was hurt.

"Ye know I cannot," he said, "not after what I've done."

Morgan compressed his lips. He *did* know. "Isn't there some way—"

"There you are!"

Isabel burst into the pavilion so suddenly she startled a squeak out of one of the French knights who was changing out of his leine. The lass—sweaty, out of breath, disheveled—paid the knight no mind.

"What the devil?" Colban seized her upper arm and steered her away from the others.

This was not good. Not at all. Morgan would have kept Colban's secret. But if Isabel had recognized him, news of his arrival would be all over Creagor in a matter of hours. Hell, she may have spread the gossip already.

"What are ye doin' here?" he demanded.

"I've been looking for you."

"How? By peekin' in all the pavilions?"

"Aye." She shrugged. "How else was I to find you? I mean, after you *ran* away from the tournament field..."

"I didn't..." He scowled, glancing at the other knights to be sure they weren't listening. "I didn't run away," he whispered. "I came here to prepare for the melee."

"You did?" Her skepticism slowly evaporated. "So you're not leaving yet?"

"Nay."

She gasped. "I know what you're doing." She clasped her hands as if in hopeful prayer. "At the end of the melee, you're going to stage a dramatic reveal. You'll pull off your helm, announce who you are, and ask for my sister's hand in marriage."

"What?" Colban exploded.

"What?" Morgan echoed.

The French knights began talking furiously again.

"You know you love her," Isabel insisted. "You always have. And she loves you."

Colban wanted to deny it. He couldn't. And hearing that Hallie loved him made his heart go soft and his tongue go silent.

"Is that true?" Morgan asked him.

Colban frowned. "That's not why I..." He didn't want Morgan to believe he'd killed Archie to win Hallie. But he also couldn't discuss his real reason while Isabel was here. She wouldn't understand. And she'd tell everyone.

"Besides," Isabel said, turning very pink and biting her lip, "I know something about Hallie you don't. Something almost nobody else knows."

Colban waited for her to elaborate.

"'Tis a secret," she said.

Colban waited.

"You musn't tell anyone," she said.

Colban waited.

"Because if anyone finds out—"

"Are ye goin' to tell me or nay?" Colban growled.

"Aye. Aye." She took a deep breath. "Hallie is..." Isabel lowered her voice to a tiny whisper. "She's with child."

"What?"

"She's going to have a babe."

Colban suddenly felt sick. Not because Hallie was secretly carrying a bairn. Such a thing might be expected, since she'd been wed for three months. Nay, what made him feel ill was the fact he'd just trounced the hell out of a pregnant woman in the tournament.

"Ye're certain?" Morgan's tone was skeptical.

"I swear," Isabel said. "She doesn't know I know. But I'm her sister. And after Gwendolyn, Hallie's maidservant, told her sister Alyce, who told Bonnie the kitchen wench, who shared it with her cousin Margaret, 'twas only a matter of time before Margaret told me."

Morgan looked dizzied by her explanation. Clearly, half the servants already knew Hallie's secret.

"Anyway," she continued, "I thought you should know, since it might be..."

"Might be what?" Colban asked, still feeling faint.

Isabel blushed and lowered her head. "It could be yours, aye?"

Colban froze.

"What!" Morgan said, cuffing Colban's shoulder.

"'Tis highly unlikely," Colban said. "We only..." He glanced at Isabel, far too inquisitive and worldly for her years.

"Isabel!" Outside the pavilion, someone was calling her. It sounded like Jenefer. "Isabel!"

Isabel sucked in a quick breath. Before she rushed out, she turned to him, her brow furrowed with worry. "Don't tell her I told you." Then she was gone in a flurry.

Morgan turned to him. "Ye got her with child?"

"'Tis possible." He arched a brow. "But don't be castin' stones at me when ye know very well ye're not without sin."

Morgan rubbed a hand across his jaw. "What will ye do?"

Colban sighed and straightened. "The right thing."

"But ye said it yourself. Ye don't know if the bairn is yours."

"It probably isn't. We only had one night together."

"One night?" Morgan released a breath of relief. "Well, then, 'tisn't yours. She was with Archie for weeks."

Colban knew that. "Her child needs a name. And a father."

"'Tisn't like that bairn is not goin' to be abandoned like ye were, Colban. Ye know that, aye?"

On some level, he did know that. The Rivenloch clan would ensure the child had all the love and care it needed, even if it was born a bastard.

But if there was the slightest possibility the bairn was his, he couldn't walk away and leave Hallie alone to raise the child. Hell, he realized, even if the child *wasn't* his, he didn't want her to have to bear the burden of being both a laird and a widowed mother.

"'Tis far too dangerous," Morgan warned. "The Rivenloch clan has every right to string ye up for Archie's murder."

"'Tis a risk I have to take."

Morgan shook his head. "Ye should never have come back, brother." Then he gave Colban a rueful smile. "Though I'm glad ye did. There's no one I'd rather have steal my silver in the tournament."

Colban lifted a corner of his lip. "'Twas my pleasure."

Then a great horn sounded, calling the combatants to return to the field for the melee.

Colban would wait until after the battle to find Hallie. After all, she might well refuse his offer. And if she did, it would be better if he didn't reveal himself to her clan. He would quietly slip away, avoiding execution and continuing his existence as The Sable Knight.

In the excitement of preparing for the melee, Hallie's disappointment at losing the sword battle was completely forgotten.

Jenefer had prepared something quite special. Melees had always been a risky event. Brutal and chaotic, they were little different from an actual battle. Casualties piled up on all sides. Rather than training knights for war, melees served to cripple fit warriors and diminish one's forces. Indeed, for a time, melees had even been outlawed in England.

But for this event, Jenefer had specified that weapons were to be blunted. She'd even had her armorer forge dulled swords for those who didn't bring their own. Best of all, Gellir, Brand, and other younger lads who were usually excluded from tournaments could safely participate. It was a genius idea, exposing them to the dynamics of a real battle with none of the dangers.

That was the intent.

And at first it went remarkably well. Over a hundred warriors took the field when the fighting began. Rather than the savage curses and groans of pain that usually accompanied a melee, the air was filled with laughter, grunts, and good-natured ribbing.

Gellir, of course, took it all very seriously. Before long, he was leaping into the fray against Sir Rauve and their father and even Laird Morgan, as if he were suddenly their equal.

Hallie fought close to Brand. While he was in no peril of being slashed or stabbed, his wild antics could get him trampled or cost him an eye.

All was going well, and Jenefer jested that, at this rate, they would all tire before anyone triumphed.

Then the first scream floated across the battlefield.

CHAPTER 41

olban was not happy. True, with blunted weapons,
the melee was more like a rough game than a
mock battle. But Hallie was in the thick of it,
putting herself and her babe at risk.

He could see why no one had noticed Hallie's condition.
The lass might look slightly thicker around the middle, but
her cotun and chain mail hid it well.

He shuddered. The blades might be blunted. But some
of the combatants dealt out rib-bruising, bone-breaking
blows. And since only Isabel and a handful of maidservants
knew Hallie's secret, none of the Rivenloch clan were
exercising extra caution. Someone needed to protect her.

Maneuvering close, he made it his duty to watch over
her. In turn, she seemed to be watching over Brand.

To Colban's pride and chagrin, Brand used Colban's
shield trick to knock the de Ware knight off his feet.
Meanwhile, Hallie held off the Nubian knight long enough
so Brand could retrieve his shield. Colban in turn protected
Hallie from a fierce attack by the Hun descendant.

So intent was Colban on both defending himself and
looking out for Hallie that he didn't at first notice the
strange commotion at the far end of the field.

The sound started as a series of startled shrieks and
then quickly rolled across the field like thunder as the

fighters began bellowing in outrage and confusion. Peering over the heads of the other knights, Colban saw warriors surging rapidly outward in retreat, as if a wild boar had been dropped in their midst.

He turned to locate Hallie. But she'd disappeared.

Scanning the crowd, he spotted her. Rather than fleeing with the others, the intrepid lass was heading straight toward the danger.

"Bloody hell."

Narrowing his eyes above the oncoming wave of warriors, Colban glimpsed the flash of a claymore. Not a blunted sword meant for a friendly melee. But a killing weapon sharpened to dole out death. Already, its silver edge dripped with blood.

Colban didn't think. He reacted.

Fighting his way through the retreating knights, he cursed as he saw the claymore rise and fall, over and over, hacking out destruction. A handful of fighters were trying to stop the murderous man wielding the weapon. But their blunted blades were useless against him.

As Colban struggled forward, he saw fallen and injured knights. Sir Rauve. Hallie's father. Several of the mac Giric clan.

The man was swinging his claymore in an arc like a reaper, heedless of where it landed. Most knights leaped out of the way. A few brave souls tried to engage him. But they were repelled by the wounding blows of his great weapon.

Then, just as the claymore lifted high in the air again, young Gellir rushed in to attack the rogue warrior.

"Nay!"

Colban hurtled forward. But time dragged at his heels. His sabotons tore up chunks of sod. His armor clanged as he shouldered knights out of the way. But already the deadly claymore was reversing direction, plunging toward Gellir.

He'd never arrive in time to save the lad.

Laird Deirdre would.

With seasoned grace and speed, she thrust her shield between her son and the claymore an instant before the blade would have split his skull. Still the power of the heavy sword pummeled the shield hard enough to knock Gellir to the ground and throw Laird Deirdre off-balance. She staggered to one knee.

The warrior withdrew his blade, preparing for a second blow, this one meant to hack the laird's head from her shoulders.

With a savage roar, Colban leaped forward, blocking the claymore with his blade. The impact to the blunted weapon rattled his teeth and shuddered through his bones. But he managed to deflect it enough to save Laird Deirdre.

Then he faced the wild Highlander alone.

The man was tall and broad of shoulder, though not as big as Colban. He was clad in weathered leather and chain mail stained with blood. The sounds issuing from the shadows of his helm were like the groans and growls and snarls of a feral beast.

Colban didn't wait. He lunged forward with his weapon, hoping to pierce the man's heart by force before he came round with the claymore. But the warrior threw off Colban's blade with as much ease as tossing off a cloak.

Recovering, Colban swiftly attacked again, this time with a powerful strike at the man's sword arm, trying to disarm him and keep the others safe.

Any other man would have dropped his weapon instantly. He'd hit the rogue with enough force to numb his arm, if not break it.

But something was wrong with the savage. Like a Viking berserker, feeling no pain, either drunk or enraged or suicidal, he continued with his aggression, wildly swinging his blade at everything in his path.

Colban fell back for only a moment to summon his strength again. But in that splinter of time, disaster struck.

Brand had followed in Colban's wake. Eager to prove his worth, the lad took advantage of Colban's instant of retreat and charged the warrior on his own.

Hallie was on his heels.

Brand had cast aside his shield to grasp his sword in both hands. He thrust directly forward with every ounce of his strength, aiming for the vulnerable spot just under the edge of the man's helm.

He never made it. The edge of the claymore caught his blade, showering sparks as it slid down the length toward Brand's hands.

Before Colban could move toward him, Hallie intervened.

Lunging forward, she used both hands to crack her blade down on top of the claymore, diverting it just enough so it slipped away from Brand's weapon—and his wrists.

Colban immediately grabbed the foolhardy lad by the scruff of his chain mail and yanked him back out of the claymore's path.

Then he turned his attention to Hallie. She was still finishing her downward chop when the madman bent his elbow and struck her in the head with the heavy pommel of his claymore.

Colban's heart plunged as Hallie fell backwards. He watched helplessly as her helm, dented by the blow, flew off her head and tumbled through the air. His breath caught as her beautiful blonde head hit the ground with a horrific thud. Her eyes shut. Her mouth fell open. Her body stilled.

So shocked was he, he let down his guard.

He hardly felt the kiss of the claymore as it sliced through the chain mail, cotun, and flesh below his ribs. He only felt a slight concern that blood was leaking from his side.

That concern was dwarfed by the fear that Hallie was dead. And by the stunned silence on the field, that fear was shared by all.

Even the crazed warrior.

The man staggered, dropping the bloody claymore from his trembling gauntlets.

With an awful sob of horror, he stumbled back and then tore away from the field. Most of the Rivenloch clan chased after him. But he leaped onto an enormous warhorse and rode away at neck-breaking speed.

Colban fell to his knees beside Hallie. His heart pounded against his ribs.

She couldn't be gone. He refused to believe she was gone.

Yet she lay as still as death.

Even when he brushed her hair back from her face with his gloved hand, she didn't move. Didn't speak. Didn't breathe.

He clapped her lightly on her cheek. Tried to revive her. There was no response.

"Hallie," he croaked, pressing her hand between his own, praying silently while the crowd whispered in speculation.

"Is she…?" It was Laird Deirdre. She had gone white. Her pale lips trembled.

Beside her, Brand looked on in worry, probably blaming himself. And beyond Brand stood Gellir, as rigid as stone.

Colban shook his head, refusing to consider the possibility. He grasped Hallie's shoulder and gave it a hard shake. Then another. Then a third. To no avail.

Forgetting his secret identity, he tore off his helm and bent closer. He ignored the gasps of recognition from the crowd, lowering his ear to listen for her breath.

No air issued forth.

He pulled off his gauntlets. In desperation, he wrenched

up her shirt of chain mail and tore open the buckles of her cotun. Placing his palms atop her leine in the middle of her chest, he pressed down repeatedly, trying to force her lungs to work.

He paused. There was no response.

"Wake up, Hallie!" he demanded, resuming his pumping.

He paused again. Still no response.

"Damn ye, wake up!"

He applied pressure again and was almost ready to give up when a curious image popped into his head. An illustration he'd seen in Ian's notebook. Instructions on making a ball out of a sheep's bladder.

The sketch showed a lad blowing air into the flat bladder to inflate it.

Could such a thing be done with lungs?

He acted on instinct, ignoring the crowd's murmurs of shock and disapproval. Bending close, he covered her mouth with his in a kiss of desperation and blew lightly between her lips.

Nothing happened.

Maybe it required more. He took a deep breath and blew with greater force. This time he felt her chest rise as her lungs filled.

The air came rushing back out.

He tried again.

The air rushed out once more.

With the third breath, he began to feel lightheaded. But he didn't dare stop.

This time, as the air flowed out, she coughed awake, and her eyes fluttered open.

The last thing Colban heard was a great gasp of awe from the clan.

The last thing he saw was Hallie's confused face.

The world went black, and he toppled over, unconscious before he even hit the ground.

"Is he going to be all right?" Hallie knotted her fingers.

Colban was awake, but exhausted from his ordeal, stretched out atop Morgan and Jenefer's bed. Morgan, staring down at his right hand man, shared Hallie's worry. Jenefer too looked on with fierce concern.

The healer, Bethac, an old woman with a cheery face, patted Hallie on the arm and gave her a wink. "Och, aye. He's lost a good bit o' blood. But the cut is clean and shallow."

A linen bandage encircled Colban's waist now. But Hallie had seen the nasty gash that cut across several inches of his abdomen. She'd let him squeeze her hand while he endured every agonizing stab of Bethac's needle as she stitched the wound shut. She'd stared into his eyes, lending him her strength as sweat beaded his face and he clenched his jaw against the torment.

Bethac packed her herbs and tools into her satchel. "Colban always *was* a fast healer. Weren't ye, lad?" She gave him a fond pat on the cheek. "Ye'll be good as new in no time."

After the healer left, Jenefer bit out, "I only wish we'd caught the bloody villain who did this."

Morgan sighed. "I'm just grateful no one else was seriously injured."

Colban murmured, "I'm glad no one was killed."

Jenefer and Morgan's eyes locked pointedly on Hallie.

She squirmed uncomfortably. She'd already heard the tale numerous times from her siblings. How she'd looked like she was dead. How Colban had performed a miracle, breathing life back into her. But now she wanted to focus on Colban. And she'd just as soon forget how close she'd come to dying.

Colban, sharing her discomfort, murmured, "Hallie wasn't killed. Not exactly."

"The hell she wasn't!" Jenefer said. "I saw it, Hallie. You weren't breathing. 'Twas miraculous. If 'tweren't for Colban, we'd be digging a grave for you right now."

"'Twasn't a miracle," Colban protested. "'Twas science."

Morgan smacked Colban's shoulder with the back of his hand.

"For God's sake, don't argue the point, ye dunderhead," he chided. "'Tis your savin' Hallie and her ma that's put ye back in good graces with the Rivenlochs."

"It has?" Colban asked.

Jenefer crossed her arms. "Well, 'tis put you back in *my* good graces, and if anyone wants to challenge me on that..."

Colban frowned. "But what about Archibald?"

"He deserved to die," Hallie said.

She'd never uttered those words before, and they shocked Jenefer and Morgan.

Morgan narrowed his eyes. "What did he do?"

When Hallie refused to say, Morgan looked to Colban, who also sealed his lips.

Jenefer defended her. "If Hallie says he deserved to die, then he deserved to die."

"That's what Ian said as well," Hallie told Colban. "He said if Colban the Champion thinks Archie did something bad, then logic dictates he did something bad."

"Ian said that?" Colban breathed.

"Aye."

He looked as if a yoke had been lifted off his back. "I'm truly forgiven?"

She nodded.

Colban let out a relieved breath. "Then there's somethin' I'd like to ask ye."

"Aye?"

Morgan cleared his throat. "Would ye like us to—"

"Nay," Colban said. "Stay. Ye can bear witness."

Hallie stiffened. Bear witness? What was he going to say?

"Hallidis Cameliard o' Rivenloch," he said, "if 'tis your will, 'twould be my great honor to be a husband to ye...and a father to your bairn."

His confession, at first so sweet and adoring, twisted quickly into a mortifying revelation of her secret. Bloody hell. How had he found out she was with child?

"Wait," Jenefer burst out. "You have a bairn, and you didn't tell me?"

Hallie blushed in answer, clasping a defensive hand across her belly. But her heart was breaking. Was that the only reason Colban was asking her to wed him? Out of honor?

"How did you know?" she mumbled.

"Isabel may have said something," Colban admitted.

"And how did *she* know?"

Morgan tried to explain. "'Twas through a tangled web o' gossip. But the point is Colban knows, and he wants to do the honorable thing."

Jenefer smacked her husband on the shoulder. "The honorable thing? A marriage is based on more than honor."

"How can ye say that?" Morgan asked. "After all, Hallie's *first* marriage was based on honor. She honored the king's bidding."

Jenefer scowled. "And you see how that ended up."

"And what about us?" Morgan said. "Our marriage was ordained by the king as well."

"But we didn't *know* that."

"Still, 'tisn't a bad way to start a marriage, with honor."

"Pah!" Jenefer spat. "Hallie and Morgan? They've spent a lifetime doing the honorable thing. Don't they deserve something more?"

While Morgan and Jenefer continued their skirmish, Hallie let her gaze slide to the man lying on the bed, who was looking at her with bemused adoration.

"I love ye," he silently mouthed.

She bit her lip. This wasn't going to be a marriage of honor or convenience or duty. This would be a union based on respect and generosity. Honesty and patience. Forgiveness and devotion.

Reaching across the bed, she took his hand. He lifted it to his lips and kissed the back of her hand with genuine affection.

"I love you too," she mouthed back.

epilogue

t was time. The wedding feast was over. Hallie had gone upstairs.

Even if this was the bride's second marriage, Colban knew Morgan wasn't about to spare his right hand man the indignities of the wedding night ritual.

A mob of rowdy mac Giric men hefted Colban up on their shoulders and bore him up to her bedchamber, threatening to remain to witness the consummation. Colban feigned to be mortified that they would wish to gaze upon his wife as she lay in their bed.

But when he opened the door to the gleeful shrieks of the Rivenloch ladies guarding his bride, one glance at Hallie made him glad his clansmen could feast their eyes on the prize he'd won. And then it made him want to get rid of them as soon as possible.

"That's enough, ye greedy sots," he chided, winking at Hallie. "Out with ye."

They crowded around the door to steal a glimpse, cursing in mock complaint when Colban pushed them back.

Hallie dismissed her ladies with a grin, and after they all dutifully filed out, Colban closed the door.

Then he took a moment to look at his stunning bride.

He still couldn't believe she was his. That the stars had aligned and everything had worked out right.

The clans had agreed it was wolves that had killed Archibald Scott.

The king, made aware of Hallie's condition, had granted her request to wed Colban.

Now Colban was going to be Morgan's neighbor. He was getting a second clan. Brothers and a sister. And the most beautiful woman in all of Scotland as his wife.

He would be her helpmate, her right hand man, her champion. No longer would she have to shoulder the burden of leadership alone. No longer would she have to face the prospect of raising a fatherless child. No longer would she be forced to wed a man she didn't love.

He intended to cherish his wife for the rest of their years. Starting tonight.

Hallie's shining hair, crowned by a silver circlet, fell like pale satin over her lovely shoulders. Her lips, full and ripe, curved up in the slightest hint of a smile. Her eyes beckoned him with sultry blue promise.

"Are you going to stand there all night, Highlander," she murmured, raking his body with her gaze, "or do you want to show me what you can do with your trusty blade?"

Giving her a smoky grin, he pushed off the door, unbuckling his belt.

Hallie shivered with anticipation. Though it had been months, her body remembered well the thrill of coupling with him.

This time, however, it was different. More thoughtful. More tender. There was more than wild passion in their lovemaking.

Together they crested the rise of their desire with their eyes locked, their hands clasped, their souls entwined. A deeper bond secured them, promising an infinite well of joy and love in the years ahead.

As their bodies glided together in the pursuit of pleasure, the pressure growing inside them was more than physical. It was the blossoming of something more. A union as powerful and everlasting as metals forged into steel.

They ascended together, soaring above the earth. Timeless. Weightless. When they could remain aloft no longer, they gasped in ecstasy, bursting into a thousand fragments and falling softly to the ground like flakes of snow.

Hallie lay back on the bed. Satiated. Drained. Exhausted. A warm and welcome carelessness settled over her in the afterglow of love. For those few moments, she felt no responsibility. She felt only utter bliss.

Summoning up the strength to turn her head toward Colban, it appeared he shared her carefree euphoria. A soft sparkle of delight lingered in his shining brown eyes. But the rest of him lay as limp and spent as a landed salmon.

For several long moments Hallie reveled in this haven, far from the outside world. Here there was no responsibility. No conflict. No challenges to face. No problems to solve. There was only peace and contentment.

Eventually, the elixir of love soothing her mind wore off, and her sense of honor and obligation returned. After all, she couldn't dwell in a lofty paradise forever. But it was enough to know this place existed. And she intended to return to it as often as possible.

She smiled at her husband, who never ceased to amaze her with his gentle humor, his fierce devotion, his honest heart, his unflagging courage.

But duty called. She had a precious gift for him. One she'd managed to conceal until this moment. One she couldn't give to anyone but him.

Before she could speak, Colban's eyes lit up. "I have a wee gift for ye."

She supposed hers could wait. "Is it the wee gift you keep in your braies?" she teased.

He clucked his tongue at her. "Wicked wench."

He threw back the linens and hopped up from the bed. She rose on one elbow, savoring the sight of his sculpted shoulders, his broad chest, his narrow hips. Then he crouched down to fetch something from under the bed.

When he rose again, what he showed her took her breath away.

She scrambled upright. "Is that..."

He grinned. "Your own claymore."

Her fingers trembled as she clasped the haft in both hands.

It was magnificent. A long blade of flawless polished steel. A hefty crossguard. A leather grip, soft and yielding. Heavy, but well-balanced.

"Do ye like it?"

"Oh, aye," she breathed. It was the best wedding gift ever.

"I did that bit on the pommel myself," he mumbled.

She turned the sword to look. He'd carved her name.

"You did this?"

He nodded, coloring.

"'Tis perfect," she sighed.

Her heart melted. This man, born under the most unfortunate circumstances, had pulled himself up from his humble beginnings and become a champion. He'd shrugged off his past. He'd mastered the sword. He'd embraced chivalry. And now, never turning down a challenge, he'd learned to write her name.

She smiled through tears that came as often as spring storms lately, and she vowed she'd never tell him the Ls were backwards.

Colban was noble, inspiring, generous, kind, strong, principled, everything a woman could want in a husband... and a father.

"I have a gift for you as well," she said, placing the claymore carefully atop the coverlet.

She took him by the hand, pulling him down to sit beside her on the bed. Then she placed his palm over her swollen belly.

"The babe growing here," she murmured. "'Tis yours, Colban."

He stiffened. "What?"

She gave him a gentle smile. "'Tis true. You're the only man I've ever loved."

"But Archie…"

She shook her head. "Was never capable."

It took an instant for him to understand and digest this news. When he finally accepted it, he nodded in wonder.

"The babe is ours," she assured him.

Awestruck, he gazed at her rounded abdomen. "Ours," he echoed.

She lifted her face, and he rewarded her with kisses. Grateful kisses that began innocently enough, but became more and more fervent and passion-filled. Desire rose in her again, demanding satisfaction.

Once more, they journeyed skyward, sailing above the clouds to steal a glimpse of Valhalla, and then returned to earth, careful to dodge the lethal edge of the claymore sharing the bed with them.

The candles burned low as Colban's breathing slowed and grew deeper. Hallie, lulled by the sound, closed her eyes and snuggled into the crook of his arm.

"So much has happened in the last year," she marveled.

"Mm," he agreed. "Scotland has crowned a new king."

"My cousin has wed a Highland laird and has a castle of her own."

"Morgan's gained a dotin' mother for his son."

"You've become a master of the longsword," she said, "and Grand Champion of the first Creagor tournament."

She could see her praise pleased him. But he replied, "And what about ye? Ye've been wed and widowed and wed again."

"Ours was a beautiful wedding," she mused.

"Especially the butterflies."

Naturally that would be what Colban liked most. Unbeknownst to their parents, Ian had rolled his model trebuchet atop the wall walk and loaded it with pieces of colorful parchment. After they'd recited their vows on the steps of the chapel, he'd fired it over the crowd, where it released dozens of parchment butterflies that twirled and fluttered down above their heads.

Hallie sighed. "I wish Feiyan could have been there."

"Where do ye suppose she's gone?"

Hallie shook her head. "No one's seen her since the tournament, since she slipped away after that warrior."

"I can't believe she went off alone."

"No one could have followed her. She has a habit of... vanishing."

"I hope she's all right. That savage wasn't right in the head."

"She'll be fine," Hallie assured him, though she couldn't be certain about that. Feiyan was clever, sly, and elusive. But she was on her own, facing a foe twice her size and as full of murderous rage as a bull.

"Well," Colban said, "I suppose she *is* a warrior daughter of Rivenloch."

At that moment, the babe inside her kicked, and Hallie gasped. She seized Colban's hand and placed it over her belly.

Colban grinned. "It seems we may have our own warrior daughter."

Hallie smiled back. She wouldn't know for several weeks whether the babe was a lad or a lass. But one thing she knew for certain. As she gazed at the man who had once been her Highland hostage, the man who was now her beloved husband, watching his soft brown eyes twinkle with fatherly pride, the Rivenloch rallying cry had never seemed so true or so fitting.

Amor vincit omnia.

Love conquers all.

THE END

THANK YOU FOR READING MY BOOK!

Did you enjoy it? If so, I hope you'll post a review to let others know! There's no greater gift you can give an author than spreading your love of her books.

It's truly a pleasure and a privilege to be able to share my stories with you. Knowing that my words have made you laugh, sigh, or touched a secret place in your heart is what keeps the wind beneath my wings. I hope you enjoyed our brief journey together, and may ALL of your adventures have happy endings!

If you'd like to keep in touch, feel free to sign up for my monthly e-newsletter at www.glynnis.net, and you'll be the first to find out about my new releases, special discounts, prizes, promotions, and more!

If you want to keep up with my daily escapades:
Friend me at facebook.com/GlynnisCampbell
Like my Page at bit.ly/GlynnisCampbellFBPage
Follow me on Twitter @GlynnisCampbell
Follow me on Instagram @glynniscampbell
Follow me on Goodreads @glynnis_campbell
Follow me on Bookbub @glynnis-campbell
And if you're a super fan, join
facebook.com/GCReadersClan

ABOUT THE AUTHOR

I'm a *USA Today* bestselling author of swashbuckling action-adventure historical romances, mostly set in Scotland, with more than 20 award-winning books published in six languages.

But before my role as a medieval matchmaker, I sang in *The Pinups,* an all-girl band on CBS Records, and provided voices for the MTV animated series *The Maxx,* Blizzard's *Diablo* and *Starcraft* video games, and *Star Wars* audiobooks.

I'm the wife of a rock star (if you want to know which one, contact me) and the mother of two young adults. I do my best writing on cruise ships, in Scottish castles, on my husband's tour bus, and at home in my sunny southern California garden.

I love transporting readers to a place where the bold heroes have endearing flaws, the women are stronger than they look, the land is lush and untamed, and chivalry is alive and well!

I'm always delighted to hear from my readers, so please feel free to email me at glynnis@glynnis.net. And if you're a super-fan who would like to join my inner circle, sign up at http://www.facebook.com/GCReadersClan, where you'll get glimpses behind the scenes, sneak peeks of works-in-progress, and extra special surprises.

* 9 7 8 1 6 3 4 8 0 0 9 6 9 *